BY THE ORCHID AND THE OWL

THE ESHOLIAN INSTITUTE BOOK ONE

MARIAH MONTOYA

Cover Design by Beautiful Book Covers by Ivy

Editing by Shannon Pring

Map by Freelance Cartography

For anyone who's ever had to hide

a vital part of themselves

in order to belong.

This one's for you.

THE
UNINHABITABLE
ZONE

EELER

BI

BASCITE
MOUNTAIN

SICKIMORE

ALDERWICK

WYNDRIP

MERKWELL

GRAYCOTT

VARCHMOUTH

THE ISLAND OF
ESHOL

GILDENLEAF

HALLOW'S
PERCH

ST

YELLOWSEEK

WASTEON

BELLIVIEW

CARDINA

THE
ESHOLIAN INSTITUTE

CHAPTER

1

The clock on my nightstand had ticked close to midnight when I finally abandoned my sheets and hefted open my rickety window pane.

There weren't many times I'd snuck out—especially on nights where I damn well knew I needed as much sleep as I could get—but these rarities always involved my best friend, Quinn. Whenever she left a little painted rock on my windowsill, it meant *meet me at the House ASAP.*

The green-painted stone that squatted outside my window now had appeared there nearly an hour ago, but Fabian's and Don's creaking footsteps outside my door had only just faded into their own room.

My fathers wouldn't punish me for sneaking out, not like Quinn's strict, Mind Manipulating mother would. But I still had no desire to watch their faces sink into disappointment if they caught me dropping into our flower garden the night before my world changed forever.

Like I was doing now.

Lifting myself from my crouch, I brushed soil from my bare knees and eased my window shut behind me before creeping through the begonias and onto the street gilded with flakes of moonlight.

My nightgown swished around my legs as I hurried down the street, but it wasn't the only sound. Frogs yelped to each other beneath water-logged storefront porches. Bats swooped and clicked. A constant torrent of crickets reverberated off the canopies rising on either side of Alderwick's line of houses, and distant thunder nearly always moaned from some corner of the island.

No lights were on, though, and I was confident nobody would see me as I stuck to the shadows, taking a sharp corner right after I passed the town square to sneak behind the apothecary and to a certain tree a few steps into the jungle.

I could smell Quinn's smoke before I could even make out her sil-houette, and I grinned despite myself as I climbed the rungs we'd nailed into the trunk when we were ten. The House, as we called it, was noth-ing more than some floorboards and a twining bamboo wall cradled within our favorite tree, and there were always a few too many scarabs scuttling along the bark. But we were still fond of the hideout even after all these years.

"What, no Lander?" I asked, plopping down beside her and curling my arms around my knees.

Besides Quinn and me, Lander Spade was the only other eighteen-year-old in the village of Alderwick. The three of us had been fast friends since the day we could play pentaball in the streets, but Quinn and Lander had been... well, sucking each other's faces off, to put it bluntly, for the last two years.

Quinn angled her face toward me, her curtain of ruby-red hair part-ing around her faint smile. As always when she snuck out, one of her mother's hand-rolled cigarettes (stolen, of course) dangled between her fingers, and she exhaled smoke in a perfect oval. She'd asked me if I'd wanted to try enough times for her to know I'd pass, so she didn't hold the cigarette out to me as she said, "Nah. He's sleeping like a big, dumb baby anyway. I knew you'd be the only one still awake."

She'd gotten that right, at least. Tomorrow morning, a stranger would whisk us away to an institute that hulked by the edge of the sea, where every eighteen-year-old on the island would be gathered like a herd of sheep for the Branding. The Good Council would grant each of us one of the five sanctioned magics, and then we'd have five years of training to master our gift. To hone it. To prove our worth as citizens of the island of Eshol.

Only those who could pass a benchmark got to come home. The rest...

Quinn cut me off from those forbidden thoughts with a smirk as she said, "Did you say goodbye to Wilder?"

Wilder was my not-so-official kind-of crush who happened to be a year younger than us, and therefore wouldn't be coming to the Institute until next year. Wilder and I had never let ourselves get serious, knowing that our age would inevitably break us apart come my Branding time. But we'd shared a kiss. Or five.

"If a quick fondle in his uncle's barn can count as a goodbye," I murmured, swiping at a flying insect near my face to hide the blush climbing up my neck.

"Rayna Drey, you naughty thing!"

Quinn smacked my arm, but when she took another drag from her mother's cigarette, I could see the expression on her face tighten amid the smoke, and I knew she was about to divulge the real reason she'd summoned me to our little treehouse for the last time.

"I heard my mom talking while she was making me do her puppet work."

Right. Mrs. Balkersaff used her Mind Manipulating gift both as a counselor for troubled villagers and as a way to make her children

3

behave. It was always an uncomfortable visit at their house when Quinn was finishing up chores with a washed-out expression, her mother having cleaved through her mind to will her into doing them.

"Just because Mom forces me to quit talking doesn't mean I can't hear," Quinn said now, rolling her eyes. "And God of the Cosmos, did I *hear* today, Ray. You know Mrs. Pixton, the one always burning pies at the bakery?"

I nodded. In Alderwick, even if everyone didn't exactly know each other, we knew *of* each other. I could picture Mrs. Pixton's skinny legs and stout upper body, and I knew exactly why she'd be in the company of the village counselor.

"Her son didn't pass his test, did he?"

The Final Test at the end of those five years of training. The pass or fail that would dictate our futures.

"He was exiled," I went on when Quinn didn't answer right away.

Because that's what happened to those who *didn't* pass—to those who couldn't demonstrate enough control of their gifted magic. Banishment. And considering the fact that bloodthirsty pirates circled our island's domed shield of protection like vultures, waiting for each year's offering of outcasts...

Well, I'd heard enough whispers about what those pirates did to the outcasts to know I didn't want to join them.

Quinn blew out another cloud of smoke. "Actually, Mrs. Pixton is convinced her son is still on the island, locked up somewhere and waiting for her to rescue him. She's in denial that he was exiled and wants to confront the Good Council about it."

"Wait, what?"

Thunder splintered the air, closer than before. I felt the vibrations of it on my very tongue, and a monkey overhead shrieked in answer.

"Well, you know how those Final Tests go..." Quinn started.

4

Yes, I did, but only because of Quinn's snooping. Fabian and Don didn't talk about the Final Test or anything related to the Esholian Institute, because the Good Council had forbidden anyone from doing so. To avoid giving certain inductees the advantage of foresight, apparently. But when had Quinn Balkersaff ever let something like a silly little rule stop her from doing what she wanted?

"The Good Council will put everyone in a life-threatening situation," she continued, "and the ones who can save themselves quickly and efficiently with their given magic get to stay on the island. With Mrs. Pixton's son, apparently, they locked him in a trunk and threw him to the bottom of a lake." I tried not to cringe at the casual way she'd said that. "Reports say he was exiled after failing to save himself within a certain time frame, but Mrs. Pixton... she was insisting he's still locked in that trunk, using his powers to keep from drowning but never able to break free." Quinn's eyes cut to mine. "She became so escalated that my mom had to sedate her."

I frowned, chewing over those words.

"Do you think she's right?" I didn't know why I was asking such a thing; the Good Council wouldn't just abandon someone at the bottom of a lake—the whole reason they exiled those who failed their tests was to... well, cleanse Eshol of inferior magic. Mrs. Pixton had probably just gone crazy with the grief that she'd never see her child again and was inventing reasons her son might still be on the island. To maintain hope.

Quinn held out her cigarette like she was examining her fingernails. "I think the Good Council should pull those little sticks out of their assholes and stop tossing away their unwanted citizens like pieces of literal garbage. But that's just me."

Of course Quinn would think the one thing that would get her into the most trouble if anyone else heard. She'd always been a furious blaze

5

of a person, and I couldn't help but think that she'd do well with the ability to control fire itself.

But the Branding activation was completely random, with each inductee having an equal chance of acquiring any of the five magics once the Good Council pressed that faerie metal to our skin. I listed them silently in my head. Mind Manipulating. Element Wielding. Shape Shifting. Wild Whispering. And Object Summoning, the gift both my fathers carried and used in their little blacksmith shop across the street from the church.

"I've got to go," I whispered, mostly because the thought of the Branding made the nerves in my stomach rise up to my throat, but also because... sleep. We both needed sleep. Tomorrow morning, we'd leave Alderwick for five years—and maybe for the rest of our lives if we didn't keep our wits about us. I'd known this was coming my whole life, and this... this *thing* Quinn had told me about Mrs. Pixton's paranoia wasn't going to do anything to help me pass my own Final Test in five years.

"See you bright and early, Ray." Quinn waved her cigarette dismissively.

I waved back before shimmying down the ladder and hurrying my way back home. A light drizzle tapped uneven beats onto my head, and I folded my arms tighter across my chest. Not because I was cold, though. The mugginess of the air was making it hard to breathe, or maybe that was fear itself, clogging up my windpipe as if that would somehow save my life in the face of danger.

Bed, I told myself. *Just get back to bed, and then mull over what Quinn said.*

But when I made it to my house with its thatched roof and line of mud-caked boots by the front door, I saw the jittery light of a candle through the window.

A candle that had definitely not been lit when I'd snuck out.

Shit. So much for avoiding my fathers' disappointed faces.

Sighing, I sidled inside—through the front door they'd unlocked for me. There was no use trying to sneak back through my window when they had obviously already checked my room and witnessed my empty bed.

"Where did you go?" Fabian asked quietly from his favorite armchair once I'd clicked the door shut behind me, cutting off the constant growl of nighttime.

"The House. With Quinn."

There was no use lying to him, either. We'd always been close, so close I'd been calling him by his first name since I could talk—definitely not something Quinn or Lander Spade could relate to. Unlike their parents, Fabian had never so much as glared at me for too long, evident even now. Even with his slender legs crossed and delicate arms folded in the shuddering candlelight, his features were already softening like warm butter.

Beside him, Don, who had stomped into our lives when I was three and become every bit a father to me as Fabian, was doing slightly better at pretending to be mad: he'd pushed out a more exasperated, beady stare framed by his ruddy face.

Before either of them could say anything, I blurted, "What if I don't want a magic?" Because without the Branding, without a power, I wouldn't have to take the Final Test and risk exile in the first place. "What if I just refuse to go tomorrow?"

I knew even as I said it, though, that I didn't have a choice. Everyone on the island of Eshol was branded whether they liked it or not.

"You know what they say." Fabian laced his fingers together. "The magic woven into Eshol is the only thing that keeps us safe from the monsters beyond our shield. We must each bear a thread of that magic to keep our fortifications tight."

7

He didn't have to add the last part of the pledge we'd all learned in the village schools: *when a thread snaps, when a person can't bear their magic, they jeopardize the safety of everyone else on the island.*

I just couldn't see how Mrs. Pixton's son would have been that big of a liability.

"I'm flattered you want to stay with us, kid," Don said, his forehead scrunches easing, "but I know *I'm* getting grumpier and uglier by the year. There's no reason a bright soul like you should stay with two crotchety old men like us when your whole potential waits for you at that institute. Right, Fabian?"

Fabian didn't answer. His jade-green eyes were tracking my face, and when Don nudged him with his shoe, he sucked a whistle of air through his nose.

"I should have given this to you a long time ago, Rayna."

Without lifting a finger, without blinking or so much as glancing in the hallway's direction, Fabian used his Summoning magic. I could feel it in the slight stirring of the air, in the way the dust motes picked up around us, in the way my skin prickled.

A faint rattling sound later and something came swooping toward us from the hallway closet, flying past all the shelves with their cinnamon and clove candles to land neatly in Fabian's outstretched hands.

He lifted it up and offered it to me.

A knife that rested in his palms like a metal corpse.

CHAPTER

2

"What is that?" I breathed, eyeing the weapon but not touching it.

Of course, that was about the stupidest question I could ask. It was a knife, obviously, but...why had it been in Fabian's closet? And why was he offering it to me now?

"It was your mother's," Fabian said gently, still holding it out to me. "It's all I ever kept from her. And not that I think you'll need it," he added with a sharp note of warning in his voice, though the flash in his pupils told me that might not be quite true, "but maybe it'll remind you that you are not powerless, Rayna. You do have a bit of your mother's... fight."

God of the Cosmos. This was by far the most Fabian had ever talked about my mother, a topic he usually avoided at all costs. The only reminder that I'd even *had* one—that I wasn't some female clone of Fabian himself, down to the heavy tangle of blonde curls, the upturned jade-green eyes, and the dusting of freckles on our noses—was my complexion: a few shades darker than Fabian's delicate cream-colored skin.

I finally reached out to take the knife's handle, rubbing my fingers along the ridges engraved there.

Bone. It had to be made of bone. And the sheath...

Some kind of leather I couldn't place.

As if my hands were acting of their own accord, I slipped off the sheath and took in the blade beneath it. It wasn't quite rusted, but tarnished with gray, and curved in the shape of a sharp and cruel quarter-moon.

As much as I appreciated the gesture to give me something of my mother's, revulsion settled heavily on my skin. I couldn't imagine using this on anything, not even to gut a fish. But the blade sang of... of something far worse than defense.

Who had my mother *been*? I only knew of a few villagers with knives like this, and they were all used for hunting. Red brocket deer and crocodiles and the occasional boar.

The question hesitated on my lips, but Fabian abruptly said, "I'll put it in an inside-pocket of your bag."

Instantly, the leather sheath flew back over the blade and the knife soared across the room, nestling itself deep into one of my three bags that rested on the sofa. I'd been packing all day: clothes and toiletries and all the little coppers I'd been saving for the Esholian Institute. Now the knife would join my possessions.

I could only hope I'd never have to use it.

"You're gonna do great, kid," Don grunted heavily. "No matter which magic you get, you'll smash your test and get to come back so I can bug you for the rest of my life."

I swung my head back toward my fathers, wanting so badly to ask them what their Final Tests had been like. But I knew they wouldn't tell me. I'd asked a hundred times, and they'd never yielded, although sometimes Don's mustache would twitch as if he was about to. *The Good*

10

Council forbids us from talking about it for a reason, Fabian would always tell me.

Well, if their Final Tests had been anything like what Mrs. Pixton's son had endured—locked in a trunk and thrown to the bottom of a lake—I couldn't blame them for *not* wanting to relive that.

"Can you play for me?" I whispered instead, sinking into the sofa between all my bags.

Don and Fabian exchanged looks. Then nodded.

Their twin lyres picked themselves up from against the wall by the front door and rose in the air, hovering overhead. I stared at them—not the lyres, but my fathers. My best friends. Their nightgowns hid the brands mottling their left shoulders, but I knew those marks better than the lines of my own palm by now: circles of scarred flesh filled with the imprint of the Esholian crest, a bulbed, five-pointed star. That same brand would mark my own shoulder in two nights. It would infuse my blood with magic that I didn't want, had never asked for.

And then my five years of training would begin.

I will *pass the test*, I told myself. *I have to pass.*

Leaning my head back against the sofa, I let my eyes close as the lyres began strumming themselves in midair. My fathers' harmonies ebbed and flowed over each other like two twining streams, and soon I felt the magic scoop me up and carry me gently to my own bed for the last time.

"Eat something," Fabian ordered me the next morning, when pink-tinged sunlight gushed through the shutters. My assigned Good Council elite would arrive any minute to take me away.

"Not hungry," I chimed, but the platter of wobbling pancakes clattered in front of me at the kitchen table anyway.

"How about some syrup?" Don sent the glistening bottle of syrup toward my pancakes and tipped it so that a drizzle cascaded down. "And a sprinkle of cinnamon, of course," he added, nodding at our cinnamon shaker, which lifted itself up with a jolt and tilted sideways over my pancakes.

"Okay, okay, thank you." I whisked up a fork and shoveled a few bites in my mouth, then took a swig from my mug of coffee. "I'm going to go check my hair one more time."

I raced to my room, where a mirror leaned lopsidedly against the wall opposite my bed. I smoothed out the creases in my tunic and tried to pat down the flyaways in my ponytail. I'd meant to braid it into a swirling crown for today, but I'd slept in—typical for me to do so on such an important morning. Raking a comb through it now would just puff up all my curls like a hornet swarm.

Maybe if the Branding gives me Shape Shifting, I'll be able to change my hair a little bit. Make it straighter and glossier, like Quinn's.

The knock on our front door made me flinch.

I made it back to the living room just as Fabian opened the door.

The man in our threshold, probably in his forties and with neat sideburns, wore a cloak clipped together with silver buttons, though a single circle of sheer fabric allowed me to see the brand on his left shoulder: the same as Fabian's and Don's, but with a red dot of ink in the center to indicate that he worked for the Good Council.

I blinked at it as I stepped between Fabian and Don to face him. How strange, that this man flaunted his burnt skin when it was usually so frowned upon to do so in public. Even magic itself was limited to the home or council-sanctioned jobs, never anything casually performed on the streets for fun.

Apparently, members of the Good Council could show off their power rather than keep it restricted like they demanded of the other islanders.

"Greetings." The man had pulled a script from an inner pocket of his cloak and now stepped forward, filling the doorway. "Are you Ms. Rayna Drey?"

"That's me." I tried to hold my chin up high.

"And you are" —The man cocked an eyebrow at my hair— "ready to go?"

"I..." I turned to face my fathers one last time. They would follow me out to the square and watch our departure, of course, but this was the last moment I'd get to share with them in this cottage, where we'd cooked and danced and bickered together for the last eighteen years. I blew out a deep breath and stepped forward to let them both gather me into a final hug.

"We'll see you in five years, Rayna," Fabian murmured.

"Don't eat any funny mushrooms, kid," Don sniffed, and I knew that was his way of telling me he loved me.

"I love you, too," I told him. "Both of you."

Before they could say anything else to make that knot in my throat grow even bigger, I ripped myself away and hurried to gather my bags on the sofa.

The Good Council elite nodded once, pivoted on a heel, and led the way outside. I stumbled after him. Neighbors lifted their heads from their gardens as we trooped past, Fabian and Don following closely behind. The elderly Mr. Toko poked his face out his front door to wave with a gnarled hand. Village kids pressed their noses against their windows to gawk, and from the shadows of an alley, I saw Wilder watch me pass, his mouth clenched.

13

How many times had I done the same? Peeked through shutters to watch the eligible inductees of the year march off with these strangers from Bascite Mountain? And now I was the one being marched off.

When we finally reached the village square, where Quinn and Lander were already waiting with their own bags and a second Good Council elite, I stopped to rake my stare over the carriage sitting primly in the center of it all. Topped with diamond-tipped spires, it sat on wheels with spokes that glittered gold in the sun.

Quinn swiveled toward me, her well-oiled hair flying over her shoulder.

"There you are! I'm glad you made it in time. I thought you might have died."

"Good morning to you, too, Quinn. Hey, Lander."

Lander, in a white tunic that contrasted strikingly with his ebony skin, passed a gentle glance my way, smiling in that quiet way of his.

"Hey, Rayna. How are you feeling?"

I glanced at the Good Council elite as he took my bags from me. "Great."

A lie, but he knew that, and so did Quinn. As Fabian and Don caught up, she drawled, "I think we're all going to get the same magic. I really do."

Another lie, to keep the ground steady beneath our feet. Because as much as I hated to leave Fabian and Don behind, I really, really hated the idea of being separated from Quinn and Lander at the Institute. If only she was right, and our Branding activated the same magic in each of us so that we could stick together....

"Okay, all loaded," the second Good Council elite called, hooking a silver belt around his waist and clipping it to the reins of the carriage. After the one who'd fetched me did the same, they both pressed assessing stares onto Quinn, Lander, and me.

"In you three get!" they called. "It's time."

Oh. The Good Council elites were our coachmen, too. I wondered if they would use Summoning magic like my fathers' to propel our carriage upward, or if they were Element Wielders who could control the wind.

Turning, we spared a last glance at our families hovering on the edge of the square. Fabian and Don smiled at me, holding hands. Quinn's mother nodded once, and her little brother hopped up and down with a frantic wave. Lander's grandma mouthed goodbye. There was no Wilder among the small crowd, but that was to be expected; only family members were allowed to see us off. I'd always wondered why, but after what Quinn had said last night?

Well, I could see why the Good Council wouldn't want people like Mrs. Pixton to show up. Anyone who had already lost sons or daughters to the Esholian Institute and the Final Test and the pirates beyond our dome might cause a scene.

I swallowed.

And stepped into the carriage.

Just as we were settling into the cushioned leather seats—Quinn and Lander squished together on one side and me on the other—odd, bubbling movement snagged my eyes through the vacant driver's box window.

The two coachmen, reined like horses, were shrinking... but also lengthening.

I watched, clutching Quinn's hand across the seat, as beaks ripped through the skin of their faces. Their arms melted inward, forming the broad plane of feathered wings, and talons shot through the leather of their shoes. Their skulls rounded. The one who'd fetched me grew two bright red plumes on either side of his head.

Shape Shifters.

15

"That's hot," Quinn said, and Lander shot her a bewildered look. "What? Maybe you should try Shape Shifting, Land. Then we can role-play when—"

"Ew, ew, ew." I threw Quinn's hand away from mine. "That's as bad as hearing Fabian and Don through the wall." But I knew what she was doing: distracting us as the coachmen spread their giant wings and the carriage lurched forward and—

I still screamed when the world tipped back, when Quinn and Lander fell forward and my head slammed against the leather seat behind me as we rose.

Up, up, up.

The beat of their wings rushed through my ears, and our village fell away as the carriage jolted higher and higher. I closed my eyes until I felt the coachmen level out, until we were soaring. Away.

Only when my heartbeat had steadied did I peer out the window to see if I could catch one last glimpse of Fabian and Don.

Nothing. My fathers were already lost among a cluster of thatched houses, and soon the jungle swallowed even that.

But Quinn was pointing at something else out the window. "Look."

I followed the line of her finger to see the mists of the Uninhabitable Zone—a place we'd only heard stories about from villagers who'd ventured near—eddying and swirling on the western horizon, as thick and milky as the rumors claimed. Nobody who'd plunged into those mists ever came back out.

The irrational side of me thought it looked like shadows stirred from within, watching our carriage fly high and away.

CHAPTER

3

According to Lander's wristwatch gifted to him by his grandma, it took us little more than an hour to fly to the edge of the island, where the Institute campus hulked by the sea.

During that hour, I braved more and more glances downward, watching the terrain of Eshol rise and fall in heaps of hills and jungle, sometimes speckled with villages three times bigger than our own. Soon, we were passing Bascite Mountain, the largest peak on the island where the majority of the Good Council lived. Even from Alderwick, I'd been able to spot its snow-dusted peak during rare moments when the clouds dissipated.

Now, as our carriage whizzed by, it still towered over us, and I felt the unnatural cold radiating from it, frosting the windowpanes. Roads and structures and lights made little glittering trails that spiraled up and around like it was a jagged horn poking through the top of the world.

"Don't think I'd fancy living there," Lander murmured, shivering.

"Are you kidding?" Quinn popped her eyes out at him. "Imagine living without all the gnats and other insects, above everyone else. And to see *snow!*"

As much as I agreed with Lander, I had to admit that Quinn had a point about the snow—I'd never seen the stuff up close. But even that sight was nothing compared to the water that soon sparkled on the horizon.

The sea. They called Eshol an island, but just like the Uninhabitable Zone, I'd never actually *seen* that vast expanse of waves and whitecaps supposedly surrounding us before this moment. Now, though, as the carriage began its descent, I couldn't rip my attention away from it.

A different world. It was a completely different world out past that shore, where stray glimmers in the air betrayed the presence of the famous dome shielding us from... I squinted at the clusters of dots along the horizon.

"Pirates," I breathed. Pirate ships.

"Forget them," said Quinn. "Look at the Institute, Ray."

I forced my attention toward where she pointed.

There, blooming larger and larger as we angled further downward, lay a sprawl of twisting streets and buildings ranging from ramshackle, squatting ones to polished ones that gleamed and towered. Trees cluttered the gaps between buildings, remnants of the jungle spilling from the closest mountainside. And people, so many people, scurried to and fro like swarms of beetles.

But as I looked closer, the seemingly chaotic sprawl actually seemed to take shape. A circle of five wedged sections surrounded an enormous cobbled courtyard with a fountain dotting the center, headed by a golden domed structure that had to be at least three stories high.

I shifted my attention to the right of the campus, where a single estuary, like a winding silver snake, led out to the cliffs towering over the shoreline and separated the sprawl of classrooms from a neat line of houses on the other side.

The most massive houses I'd ever seen. More like castles than the cottage I'd lived in all my life.

"Oh, I am going to *love* living here for the next five years," Quinn said, eyeing those mansions hungrily.

Free. That's what Quinn was now that she didn't have a mother to invade her mind and force her into doing things she didn't want to do. I couldn't blame her for her excitement, even though my own stomach clenched.

Our carriage nearly skimmed the various rooftops as the coachmen beelined for that courtyard, where a throng of young adults lined its circular edge to watch our landing. Their faces became more detailed as we drew near, some gaping up in awe, others watching with sculptures of boredom, and still others utterly distracted, chatting with friends as if they'd seen a dozen carriages land before this.

Which, I reminded myself, they probably had.

I wondered if we were the last to arrive, or if there would be others after us.

Just as I felt bile rise in my throat, our coachmen swung their giant wings upward and brought us to a rocky touchdown next to the fountain.

The carriage jostled, then slowed to a screeching stop. I looked Quinn and Lander in the eyes as the crowd pressed in on us, as the coachmen morphed back into their human shapes.

"We'll stick together until Branding, okay?" I grabbed their hands, and they clutched me back. "Don't let go, no matter what."

Before either of them could reply, however, the carriage doors were wrenched open. Dozens of strangers swooped in to pull us out, and Quinn's and Lander's hands slipped from mine.

"*Welcome,*" a chipper voice called out instantly, though I couldn't pinpoint the source, "to the Esholian Institute for Magical Allocation and Refinement, where worthy citizens are made!"

Face after face smiled or stared at me. Hand after hand dragged me deeper into the crowd or pushed me away. It was chaos unleashed, louder and wilder than anything I'd ever experienced back at home.

I twisted, trying to find Lander's ebony mop of hair or Quinn's red-headed figure, but even the carriage had gone, pulled off to who-knew-where.

"Don't worry about your stuff," said a boy beside me. I blinked down at his hand on my elbow as he led me to the outer rim of the courtyard. "The coachmen keep hold of it until after the Branding."

"Are you a teacher?" I asked him, and it wasn't until he threw back his head with laughter that I narrowed my focus to get a good look at him: lanky, lean, slicked blonde hair, and extremely boyish. Smooth cheeks and narrow shoulders. Definitely no older than me.

"Do I look like a teacher? I mean, don't get me wrong, darling, I could probably teach you a thing or two." He winked at me, and I recoiled. "But no, I got here only a few hours ago. You just looked a little stunned back there, and I didn't want the next carriage to run you over."

"Next carriage?"

The boy pointed, and I watched, letting my mouth fall open, as a vessel even bigger than ours barreled toward the courtyard—this time pulled by a flock of hundreds of toucans that barked and brayed as they landed.

"The coachmen must be Wild Whisperers?" I guessed aloud as the carriage landed... right where I'd been standing seconds before.

"Could be," the boy said beside me. "Or, who knows? Maybe they're Mind Manipulators, forcing the toucans to obey from within the carriage."

There were fine lines, I realized in that moment, between the different types of magic. They could all do similar things, just through unique methods.

I also knew in that moment that I'd rather befriend a bird than control one.

When I turned to tell the boy this, though, he had already pushed back into the crowd to welcome the other newcomers. And I hadn't even found out his name.

I sucked in the words I had been going to say, suddenly feeling even more lonely despite this flock of loud, sweaty strangers around me.

Too many. I'd seen too many people my age in the last thirty seconds alone, and when I raised myself up on my tiptoes, the sea of bobbing heads only seemed to expand.

"Quinn? Lander?" I called weakly.

Nobody answered. Nobody even glanced my way as a young woman shot up through the crowd, standing proudly on... nothing. A pedestal of air alone.

The hubbub trickled to a quiet. One by one, nine other young men and women rose above our heads through various forms of magic. Lengthening their legs or levitating themselves or—in one man's case— pushing himself up on a swarm of bees.

When only the swarm's buzzing and a hundred different breaths rang through the courtyard, the first young woman called out in that same chipper voice I'd heard upon stepping out of the carriage.

"Now that you're all here, we'd like to give instructions and your tour of campus. But first thing's first, a little lesson."

She gestured at her shoulder, where her brand flared against her skin. I lifted my gaze from that pedestal of air to take in her outfit, and held back a gape. Nothing but a band of fabric around her midsection and thin straps for sleeves.

My own tunic suddenly felt... much too stifling in this condensed body heat.

I scratched at my stiff, too-high neckline as the woman continued.

"We—" She gestured at the other nine "—are your class royals of each sector. Every year, the newest fifth-years are chosen for the title: a prince and a princess for Element Wielding, a prince and a princess for Object Summoning, and so on. Our job is to help you." She paused, a smile carving its way into her cheeks. "But also to make sure you behave."

All around me, my peers shifted their stances, glancing at each other uncertainly. My own heart stammered, especially as I thought about the knife in my bag... and the idea that a weapon might not be allowed. The woman laughed at our fidgeting, but it was one of the so-called princes beside her, standing on some kind of solid, invisible rock, who cleared his throat next.

"Don't worry too much about that."

My gaze snapped up at the sound of his voice, deep and serious, but... with a smirk pulling at the corner of his mouth. As if he enjoyed watching us squirm even more than the woman did. Despite all that, I couldn't deny how stupidly handsome he was, with deep brown locks of hair that curled above his ears, tan skin, and wide shoulders that marked him as a man rather than a boy.

The moment I thought that, his attention flicked toward me, and I collided with eyes of smoky quartz that narrowed slightly before he began speaking to the whole crowd again.

Dammit. Had he been reading my mind? Surely, he wasn't a Mind Manipulator, since he was standing on nothing but solid air. He had to be an Element Wielder.

"Here at the Esholian Institute," the prince continued, "it's not too difficult to behave. You are free to do whatever you want—" He gestured at the first woman's scantily-clad outfit, as if to say, *see*? "—save for messing with the island's shield, running away, or..." A pause as his eyes skimmed over the crowd. "Killing each other."

A chill nipped at my spine as the prince's smirk returned with even deeper menace.

"Now, on behalf of the Good Council, we'd like to demonstrate what will happen to you if you *do* try to run away, mess with the island's shield, or kill another student. And to give you a hint, it's the same thing that happens to those who fail their Final Tests. Enjoy."

I stiffened as the courtyard cobblestone fractured beneath my feet. All around me, screams shot into the air. Someone's fingernails dug into my arm before tearing away again as the world tilted.

I didn't even have time to look for Quinn or Lander again before the entire ground sucked me down and swallowed me whole.

CHAPTER

4

My body hit a surface that speared me with frigid teeth from every direction.

I couldn't help the gasp that filled my lungs with salt and death. Couldn't help but kick and scream against the punches of the sea until a line of rope flashed before my eyes and I plunged a hand out to grab it.

The rope reeled me in, and I clung to it with my teeth chattering.

Was this real? It couldn't be. It had to be a Mind Manipulating trick, or an earth and water stunt pulled by the Element Wielders. And as the rope dragged me straight into a ladder rising up the side of a ship and sun-crisped faces leered down at me, I told myself that the pirates were just Shape Shifters who had sprouted hooks and tattoos and wooden limbs as surely as the coachmen had sprouted feathers.

This isn't real, this isn't real. It's just a demonstration.

But damn, did the princes and princesses of the Esholian Institute make their demonstrations *feel* real. Because as a rough pair of hands— one with a missing finger—yanked me onboard, my clothes hung drenched and heavy and *cold*.

The woman with the missing finger grabbed me by the chin and wrenched my face this way and that, clucking her tongue impatiently.

"What kind of magic do you have, girl?"

"W-what?" I couldn't believe they were taking this so far. Was I actually expected to speak right now? "I don't have one yet. My Branding isn't until tomorrow."

Her four-fingered hand came flying so fast, I didn't even register the sting of the slap until after my face was angled sideways.

"*Lies*," the woman hissed. "Everyone tossed from that damned island has a magic, and *magic*, my dear, is worth its weight in gold around here. Now tell me which one you have so I know how much I can sell you for."

"Not that you'll be able to sell her for much," someone behind her snickered, followed by general chuckles of agreement. "The island only throws away their scraps. This one won't make us more than a pound or two."

Clearly, I was expected to engage. Throwing my fiercest glare at the so-called pirates, I said, "I get it. I won't run away or mess with the island's shield or... or kill anyone." *And I* will *pass the test. I'm not anybody's scraps.*

Instantly, a tugging sensation sucked me back up into a world of solid ground. I blinked against the happy stroke of sunlight on my face as the crowd around me muttered and rubbed their heads.

"*That*," called the brown-haired prince, still standing on his pedestal of solid air, "is what awaits you if you can't prove your worth. This island doesn't tolerate the weak or the out-of-control, but the pirates out there?" Something shifted in his voice. "They would love to tolerate you."

The first woman smiled in that plastered way and called out with her chipper voice, "Now at this time, we would like you to please follow your nearest prince or princess so we can give you a tour and lead you to the Branding arena, where you will all be staying tonight in preparation for the ceremony."

Within the span of a blink, she and the others sunk back into the crowd.

Chaos exploded again, elbows and shoulders pushing against me as everyone surged toward their nearest guide. As if we *hadn't* just sunk into the island itself and hallucinated a possible future as a collective unit.

I let myself get swept away by the current. My nearest guide wasn't the cocky, smirking prince, but a different, higher-pitched one with a buzzcut. I focused on every word he said as we swept from the courtyard to a small, red-bricked road branching off of it.

The golden domed building was the Testing Center, where we would perform quarterly practice tests before the final one. The wedged section of buildings behind us was the learning sector for Object Summoners—I felt a pang of longing for Fabian and Don at that—and the section over to the left, full of cages and miniature stadiums, was for Shape Shifters. When we meandered through the section for Wild Whisperers, monkeys perched on the rooftops, watching us pass, and butterflies spiraled around our faces.

Then we came to the largest road that ran from the courtyard to the estuary I'd seen flying in. Bascite Boulevard, our guide said it was called. From where we stood, the Element Wielder section lay on one side, crowned in what looked like a perpetual layer of brewing clouds. On the other side, the Mind Manipulator section sported neat rows of all-white, impassive-looking classrooms that gave me chills.

"Looks like they torture people in there," a girl next to me murmured.

I tried to catch her eye, to think of a joke related to torture (was it even possible to make a joke about torture?), anything to make a friend here... but she had already plunged forward with everyone else, and soon there were too many bodies between us for me to even reach her.

My arms seemed to hang too awkwardly at my side.

Like a tide squeezing through a ravine, we crossed an arched metal bridge over the estuary and came to the row of those gigantic houses lining the other end of Bascite Boulevard—five on each side.

"These here are the Shape Shifter houses," our guide said now, and I realized I was closer to him than ever before. I could see the sweat darkening the back of his shirt and the amber buzzcut frosting his head. He was the one who'd been sitting on the swarm of bees. "Boys' house on the left, girls' house on the right."

The Shape Shifter mansions sat across from each other like mirror images of one another. They were made of brick with shingled rooftops and sweeping staircases leading to their front doors. Dark, but cozy. A few older kids lounged on those steps, smoking and watching us pass. One of them had horns protruding from either side of his head.

As I watched, a buddy nearby smacked the guy's arm, and his horns melted back into his skull. Yep, I could definitely imagine them imitating pirates for fun.

"Now, these are the Element Wielder houses," the buzzcut prince was saying, pointing to the next pair of mansions.

These ones were made of what looked like black alabaster, with widespread windows and people milling about on the flat, gated rooftop, as if to be closer to the sky. As we passed, a young woman from the girls' side lobbed a snowball at us. She looked vaguely familiar, and I realized with a double take that she was from Alderwick. Her name was Julie or Joyce or something like that. It had been three years since she'd left, and I'd never interacted with her beyond a polite nod or hello.

27

The woman didn't notice me, anyway. Her snowball hit a boy next to me, exploding on his head, and she and her friends doubled over with laughter.

"Are you okay?" I asked the boy, but he didn't seem to hear me. He'd stopped in the middle of the tide to yell at her... wanting to fight or flirt, I couldn't tell.

Feeling sicker and lonelier by the moment, I moved on as our guide called out information about the third pair of mansions.

"These are the Object Summoners'. Friendly lot, as you can probably tell."

Indeed, the Object Summoners lived in quaint wooden houses with gingerbread-style turrets and wraparound porches lined in green trim. The lump in my throat rose and fell with each of my breaths as I thought of Fabian and Don once living in the left one.

If only they were here. If only I could run into that house and find them sitting in their favorite armchairs and give them one last hug and—

A single tear slipped out. Shit, no. I could not be crying right now.

I batted it away, raised my chin, and just barely caught the buzzcut prince's next words.

"—my sector, the Wild Whisperer houses."

The fourth pair of mansions looked the most... normal to me, minus the sheer size of them: made of chiseled stone with huge, street-facing balconies and tangled ivy climbing up the sides. A few older kids waved from the balconies, various birds squatting on their shoulders.

I blinked again with dry eyes. Good. I would not cry, and I *would* make friends. After, of course, I had found Quinn and Lander and asked them what the hell they'd thought about that little demonstration in the courtyard.

"Finally," the buzzcut prince said, "the Mind Manipulator houses. A rule to live by." He stopped abruptly, causing a few inductees behind

28

him to run into his sweat-drenched back. "Do *not* mess with the Mind Manipulators. And if you end up being one of them..." he gave a nervous chuckle. "Please be nice to the rest of us."

I couldn't disagree with his assessment. The Mind Manipulator houses, the last pair on Bascite Boulevard, were made of that same impassive-looking marble as the classrooms back by the courtyard, with looming pillars and hundreds of little windows framed by black shutters.

Like eyes peering into your soul, I thought.

I could only hope that I wouldn't have to live in there for the next five years.

"Now this..." Buzzcut spread his arms as we approached the end of the boulevard, which opened to a field capped by a curved stone stadium. "Is the arena where we hold assemblies, play pentaball, and— tomorrow—host the Branding."

Through the gaps between bodies, I could see the field. Perhaps usually carpeted with clean-cut grass, it was now thoroughly trampled as the hundreds of newcomers began leaking onto it, formulating clusters of cliques. Dozens and dozens of tents, canvas and bamboo, from the looks of them, lined the field, and just as many carts of food were being pushed around by second- or third-years.

"For tonight," Buzzcut said, "you may eat dinner and find a tent to stay the night in. Every tent will be supplied with nightclothes, sleeping bags, and generic toiletries. Your belongings will be returned to you when your magic is activated and you join a sector."

A voice within our group shouted out, "Which ones are the girl tents?"

Buzzcut raised a ginger eyebrow. "The tents are not separated into girls' ones or boys' ones tonight. Tonight, you may do whatever you wish. Besides, of course, killing anyone, messing with the shield, or running away, as Coen Steeler said."

Coen Steeler. The man with the annoying smirk. I remembered how he'd said it wasn't difficult to behave, and I felt my heart flop away from me like a damned fish. Were they really allowing us to just...sleep together? In tents on the Branding ceremony field? I'd kissed Wilder, of course, but anything further than our touching and groping... I wasn't prepared for tonight. Not at all.

Quinn and Lander. I had to find them right now.

As soon as Buzzcut released us, I marched forward, narrowing my eyes into calculating slits that only took in general colors and shapes. I'd known Quinn and Lander my whole life, so why was it so hard to pick them out now?

Left and right, in and out, I zigzagged between tents and groups of shrieking, laughing boys and girls, ignoring the smells of food that wafted out from those carts and made my stomach absolutely ache with its emptiness.

No, I would not eat until I'd found them. Until I'd—

There. A sheet of silky red hair.

Manners aside, I pushed through a mass of limbs and sweat-sparkling skin to reach her, where she was chatting amiably with a group of other girls.

"Quinn!"

"Rayna, *there* you are." Quinn pulled me into a lazy hug with one arm. Her other hand held some kind of sandwich with sprouts hanging out, which she deftly snuck into mine. "Here, do you want the rest of this? I've had my fill. Rayna, this is Jenia... what did you say your surname was, Jenia?"

"Leake," the nearest girl said, and her eyes, sultry and gray, scanned my whole body. She had permanently pouting lips and hair a brighter blonde than mine, except hers was glossy like Quinn's. I forced myself not to touch the stray strands of my own mess of curls. "And you are...?" she asked me.

"Rayna." I attempted a smile.

"Well, obviously. I heard her say your name. I meant how do you know her?"

I blinked. The possessiveness in the tone, the pure lack of warmth... I couldn't see how Quinn wasn't downright scowling at her as she cut in with, "She's my best friend from home. I'm glad you found us, Ray. We were just talking about these hot-as-shit Shape Shifters over near the stadiums who are actually turning into lions right in front of the first-years."

"Oh. Wait, what?" Hot-as-shit Shape Shifters? Where was Lander? I took a bite of the sandwich and was about to ask when another girl barged toward us.

"Guys, they're letting people pet them now. C'mon, you have to try it."

And she pulled Quinn and Jenia with her, toward the Shifters, away from me.

For some reason, I stood rooted to the grass, and Quinn didn't even look back.

CHAPTER

5

I stared after her, suddenly feeling not so hungry anymore.

After all that effort to find her, she was just... gone. I could trail after her, try to locate the lions and their makeshift petting zoo, but the steel-gray look in Jenia Leake's eyes kept me rooted to the spot. And the way Quinn hadn't even *glanced* back to see if I was following or not... the stupid lump in my throat was back.

Throwing my last bite of sandwich in a nearby bin, I hauled in a deep breath.

Lander, I thought. Quinn might be overcome with this... this *frenzy* for the first few days until after the Branding, when things settled down, but Lander would understand this pit in my stomach and help me through it. And he might need support, too, always having been the shyest of our trio.

Resolve hardening, I licked the stickiness off my fingers and began my search. Again.

But as the sky overhead dampened with clouds and the fat plops of rain that usually accompanied nighttime began to fall, too many people were wafting into tents with their newfound friends. Thankfully, the tents were so big, there didn't seem to be any couples able to sneak into one on their own, so there was no moaning or any other kind of sex noise as I wove through them. But I did hear more tittering, more whispers like they were sharing secrets—sounds that made my shroud of loneliness tighten around me.

When only a few stragglers and the class royals patrolling the area were left wandering outside, desperation kicked in. I'd have to find a tent to sleep in, anyway. If anyone welcomed me.

I poked my head through the flap in the nearest tent and said, "Lander?"

Seven pairs of eyes. A few head shakes. I withdrew and tried another tent.

And another. And another.

Finally, when I was just beginning to think I'd never find a familiar face again, I peeked in the ninth or tenth tent and—

"Hey!" His boyish face lit up. "It's the girl who thinks I'm a teacher. What are you doing? Get your ass in here, darling!"

I only hesitated for a moment. The boy was sitting in a circle with four others, surrounded by pillows and blankets and little bags of toothbrushes and combs. Closing the flap of the tent behind me, I sat next to him.

"I do *not* think you're a teacher. I just didn't get a good look at your lack of facial hair before I spoke."

I felt a little bad, but the others snickered and the boy grinned.

"I'll take that insult." He stroked his smooth chin. "You see, my old man didn't grow a beard until he was thirty-five, so I'm kind of waiting for my *stud* to kick in."

"You're going to have to wait a long time, then," another kid laughed, and turned to me. "What's your name, by the way?"

"Rayna," I said again, but this time I didn't feel like I was... admitting something shameful like I had in front of Quinn. "What about you guys?"

They spouted off their names, which I promptly forgot, until—

"Rodhi," the smooth-faced boy said. I could remember that one. Even if he thought *way* too highly of himself, he was sort of sweet. He was the first one to show me an ounce of kindness, anyway, so when he peeked over his shoulder, as if someone might see us through the canvas of the tent, and brought out a silver, curved flask from his boot, I inhaled but... kept quiet.

"Whoa, you didn't tell us you snuck in some goodies!" one of the others exclaimed.

"Well, I was waiting for the right moment." Rodhi shook the flask, and I heard the sloshing of liquid. "I think there's enough in here for us all to take a nice gulp."

"What is it?" I asked, trying not to sound nervous.

Rodhi mimed throwing a lock of hair over his shoulder like a princess. "Just the most Grade-A bascale you'll ever taste in your *life*, darling."

The others rubbed their palms together eagerly, but I blinked. The most potent alcohol I'd ever had was some acai wine with Fabian and Don in front of the fireplace.

Rodhi noticed my hesitation. His smile slipped.

"You've never had bascale?"

"Uh.... My home village is pretty small." A lame exclamation, but a true one.

Rodhi stared at me incredulously, then shook his head.

"Okay, I'm going to pretend you were literally raised in a decrepit barn, then, and explain. You know how it's the metal bascite that activates our permanent powers when it merges with our skin and sinks into our bloodstream?"

I nodded.

"Well," he continued, "all that metal, native to the island, of course, is sitting at the top of the highest mountain of Eshol, just *waiting* to be stolen, you know? And sometimes, certain *connected* people who may or may not have grown up in Belliview, you might say, are able to nab some ale infused with bits of that stolen metal."

I stared at Rodhi, noting the features that did indeed mark him as someone who'd grown up in Belliview, the capital of Eshol that sat in the shadow of Bascite Mountain: the combed hair, the loose way he talked, even the crispness of his clothes.

"To be clear," I said, nodding at the flask, "there's actual *faerie* metal in there?"

Not that I knew much about bascite, the substance that would be burned into all of our shoulders tomorrow night. But I knew enough to blink at his flask as if it might catch on fire at any moment.

Rodhi nodded eagerly. "Essence of it, yeah. Drinking it doesn't give you any permanent magic, but as long as it's in your system, you'll get little wisps of power."

"So..." I shook my head, astounded that Fabian and Don and the other villagers had hidden this phenomenon from me. Or were we so far removed from the rest of Eshol that they'd truly never heard of it either? "You can know what sector you'll be in *before* Branding?"

Excitement flared in my chest at the thought. To just *know* what kind of power the brand would trigger in me would alleviate so much anxiety.

The girl on the other side of me, however, shook her head. "It's not like that."

"What?"

Rodhi shrugged. "It's like our powers don't know what shape they want to take until the actual Branding. Before then, drinking this stuff..." He smiled down at his flask like a mother might gaze at her newborn. "Totally random every time."

So it would be like rolling dice, then. A drinking game and nothing more. That didn't sound like it would undo the knot of worry in my stomach, but... I shook away my misgivings and said, "I'm in."

Anything, anything at all, to maintain the new, delicate friendship I'd formed with the people in this tent.

Rodhi clapped me on the back, unscrewed the cap, and said, "Bottom's up, bitches." Then he swallowed.

At first, nothing happened. Rodhi smacked his lips, set down the flask, and burped. I glanced around at everyone else's eyes, pinned on his face as if waiting for some kind of monster to claw its way out of his sockets.

"Might not be strong enough..." one of the boys started to suggest—and then he smacked himself in the face. "Hey, what the hell?"

"Ha! Do it again, but this time a little lighter." Rodhi stretched his arms up in the air, perfectly at leisure. "Wouldn't want to give you a bruise before Branding."

As commanded, the boy smacked himself in the face, gentler this time.

"You're Mind Manipulating right now?" I almost yelped.

Rodhi turned toward me. "Yeah! It's not super clear, but I'm getting a hazy outline of your thoughts. You're thinking about quills? Or is it quicksand? No, it's a quickie! Get your mind out of the mud, Rayna!"

Quinn. I was thinking about Quinn. He'd simply snagged the first sound.

I tossed aside the thought of her and forced my lips into the shape of a coy smile. "You can never judge a book by its cover."

Fabian had taught me that. Don, in response, had always told me that covers were the critical first impression that could make or break whether someone even gave a book a chance.

I brushed away thoughts of my fathers as Rodhi held the flask out to me.

"Your turn, my scandalous friend."

My stomach churned. "Um, someone else can go before me."

Rodhi only paused to take in the faltering smile on my face for a second. Next second, he shrugged and passed his flask off to the girl beside him. She drank.

The tent dropped into frigid cold, our breaths puffing out in front of us, frost icing the tips of our hair. The girl clapped her hands to warm it back up.

Around the flask went. With the next gulp, a single hibiscus popped up from the floor of the tent, right in front of the boy who'd hit himself in the face. He laughed, plucked it, and passed the flask. After the next kid took a swig, our pillows jiggled in place all around us, as if he were tugging at them using invisible strings.

His Summoning magic hit me with nostalgia, but I shook it off, once again, as the girl beside me shivered when her hair turned a startling shade of violet.

My turn, now. I grabbed the flask from her and brought it to my lips.

Only one drink, I told myself. It wasn't like I was going to get drunk on it.

I tipped my head back and drained the rest.

A cough snagged in my throat. The drink was *sour*, but also tinted with something undeniably sharp and metallic. Almost like blood.

I cleared the cough from my throat and handed the empty flask back to Rodhi, who cocked his head at me, waiting.

"Anything?" he asked.

I was about to shake my head, disappointment flooding me, when I felt it.

Something in my bones shivered awake.

Whispers wafted out from my newfound friends around me. Such little whispers that they felt like tickles crawling over my skin, and I quivered, but... then I could suddenly hear the grass shrieking below the weight of the tent, and my skin twitched all along my body, as if begging to shift into something else, and electricity crackled between the gaps in my fingers, and I felt an invisible hand reach out from me as if to pick up any loose objects and drop them in my lap.

I crawled backward, my back brushing the wall of the tent.

"Rayna, are you alright?" Rodhi reached a hand out toward me.

No. No, I wasn't. I...

I exploded with it.

Something—something I couldn't define. Not a wall of wind, but pure, malleable energy that burst outward and knocked my friends on their backs.

They screamed. Outside the tent, voices faltered, but I couldn't stop whatever it was from extending further and further outward, lifting the flap of the tent, pushing against the canvas walls as if eager for a way out. A sob cracked in my throat.

Pounding footsteps outside. A snarl at others to go away. I cradled my head as pain began to build there, shrieking for release, shrieking for me to explode again.

Someone stuck their head through the flap in the tent.

And I met his eyes—deep, gold-flecked brown like smoky quartz—through the haze of my pain.

The sector prince named Coen Steeler did not wear a single hint of a smirk this time.

His eyes scanned the inside of the tent, my friends picking themselves up and me huddled in the corner, rocking and cradling my head and *shaking*...

Before I knew it, he had bent toward me, picked me up, and thrown me over his shoulder before carrying me out of the tent, into the star-kissed night, and away.

CHAPTER

6

"Breathe. Deeply. Right now."

Pure, primal command laced his every word. He'd hauled me through the campsite and into a narrow alley between two of those mansions on Bascite Boulevard, and set me on the ground with my back against the wall.

I grappled at my throat, choking on it. The power and the pain.

"In and out," he commanded again, sinking onto his knees before me. "With every inhale, you are going to suck that power back in. With every exhale, you are going to feel the pain leave your body. Okay?"

"I can't," I gasped. "It wants *out.*"

Indeed, it was tearing at me from the inside-out, roaring for more and more and more. But I didn't want to explode again. Didn't want to hurt anyone else.

"I know," Coen said, still aggressive, but... with a hint of gentleness now. "But you have to contain it, so you will. In and out, like I said. Do it with me."

And he mimicked breathing for me, such a simple task I'd taken for granted before now.

Still gasping, I copied him, pretending he was my mirror image, pushing out the pain and reeling the power back in. In and out. In and out.

After a few minutes—or maybe it was an eternity—the nameless terror faded. Like a monster dissolving back into my blood.

I leaned my head back against the wall of the mansion behind me.

"What was that?" I asked weakly.

Coen didn't answer. He only stood and crossed his arms, and even in my exhausted state, my eyes caught on those muscles folded over such a broad chest. This man could snap my neck in half a second, if he wanted to. He was a fifth-year, meaning he had to be around twenty-three years old, and here I was, barely eighteen and ready to puke on his shoes at any moment.

Yet he'd helped me through it. Had seemed to know what *it* was. So I clenched my teeth to keep them from chattering and repeated, "What *was* that?"

Coen clucked his tongue. In the dim light cast by the dusting of stars overhead, I could see a vague smirk returning to his tan face. "Well, well, well, aren't *you* demanding, for someone who owes me her life?"

"My life?" I repeated, trembling to a stand, if only so I didn't feel so much smaller than him. My knees quaked, but I locked them in place.

"Yes, your *life*." Coen narrowed his eyes at me, as if unsure whether to take me seriously or not. "That right there was raw power, without shape or form or container, triggered by the bascite in that stupid ale you drank. And it could have blasted you to bits that *I* would have had to clean up if you hadn't gotten hold of it like you did."

"That's why you saved me, then? So that you didn't have to clean up bits of my literal flesh?"

I don't know where my anger was sprouting from, but that little half-smile tugging at the edge of his mouth, the way he continued to stand there with his arms folded as if I were a naughty child... it heated me.

He only fed that heat when he said, all trace of gentleness gone, "More or less. Now." He rummaged in his pants pocket and brought out a pearl-sized pill pinched between his forefinger and thumb. "Luckily for you, I had this on me tonight. Take it."

"I don't need a pain reliever," I said, even though an ache still touched the back of my neck. "My head is—"

"This isn't a pain reliever."

I stared at him. *Don't eat any funny mushrooms,* Don had told me jokingly before I'd left. This wasn't a mushroom, but it might as well have derived from one, for all I knew. What the hell was happening to me right now? I just... wanted to go to sleep, not face... this.

Coen sighed at my silence.

"It's a power inhibitor. It'll prevent that—" he swirled his free finger in my direction "—from happening tomorrow when they brand you. Because when they brand you," he pushed on before I could retort, "that same bascite that triggered your innate power tonight? It will be permanently infused in your blood, and in a higher dose. So you won't just have one of the sanctioned magics in your system. You'll have that monster, too. Constantly triggered. Constantly raging."

That monster. I blew out a puff of shaky air.

"Maybe I should find an instructor. Tell them what happened. Maybe someone can help me harness it, or get it to go away, or—"

"No. Listen to me." Coen dropped his folded arms. "What's your name?"

My voice was a jumbled murmur as I said, "Rayna Drey," for the third time tonight, suddenly so, so weary.

Coen pinched his brow together. "Rainy Days?"

"No." My voice rose now. "*Rayna Drey.*"

42

"I see. Rainy Days doesn't make much sense anyway, does it? You're not a soft little drizzle." His lips tilted up. "You're more like a raging hurricane."

"No, I'm not." I didn't want to be a hurricane. I didn't want to be destructive.

Coen ignored me. "What village are you from... Rayna?"

"Alderwick." I kept my eyes on the pill still between his finger and thumb.

"Pretty repressed village? Full of frightened, branded adults who conceal their magic unless it's for a Good Council-sanctioned job?"

My eyes snapped from the pill to his face.

"Thought so."

Coen leaned closer to me, and it took every shriveled piece of my remaining willpower to keep my stance rigid, to not let him push me back against the wall.

"There is a reason, Rayna Drey, that every single place on this island besides here at the Institute is so heavily stifled. Here, we can do whatever we want, go wherever we want, bed whomever we want, because they have eyes on us *everywhere.*"

They. The Good Council, I knew, and goosebumps scuttled along my arms.

"But out in the villages," Coen continued, "they have to rely on sheer fear. All it takes is one person breaking the law, one person using magic on the streets in an inappropriate manner, one execution in every village, for people to obey. To stay small and quiet and never expand the limits of their power that they found here at the Institute."

I couldn't escape the weight of his daggered gaze as his words sunk in.

"The Good Council," I began slowly, tasting the words as I said them, "wouldn't take kindly to power they didn't grant me. Power they can't control."

A nod. I stroked my throat, the inside of it gritty from my haggard breathing.

"They would exile me? Before the test?" I paused. "Right on the spot?" That demonstration earlier today had seemed like an unnecessary threat with my Final Test lurking so far in the future. I couldn't imagine facing that woman with the missing finger *now*. *Tomorrow*.

Coen didn't nod this time. He didn't have to. I let my hands drop.

"Well, shit." A thought struck me. "But how can I even keep this a secret? All those inductees in the tent saw it happen." It didn't feel right to call them friends anymore, as if I'd betrayed their trust somehow.

Coen swiped his free hand through his hair. "Yeah, about that. I erased their memories for you... just short-term," he added as my mouth dropped open in horror. "No big deal. They won't remember a thing after entering their tent for the night. And don't worry about all those people I hauled you past." A smug smile as his eyes raked down my body, as if remembering what it felt like slung over his shoulder. "I made them feel *very* interested in looking away."

I stared at him.

"You're a Mind Manipulator."

He didn't even deign to answer that; it was obvious.

"But..." I swallowed. "I saw you standing on nothing but solid air this morning. I thought you were an Element Wielder. Or maybe even an Object Summoner, levitating yourself."

"Oh, so you were checking me out?" His lips curled. "But very astute, I'll give you that. I was actually standing on the fountain in the middle of the courtyard. I simply changed everyone's perception of what they saw. Wanted to look as cool as everyone else, you see."

44

I almost gasped. Almost, but didn't want to give him the satisfaction. To think that he was such a powerful Mind Manipulator that he could manipulate *everyone* in that crowd at the same time...

To think that he'd already been in my mind, manipulating *me*, that he'd probably been the main caster of that pirate ship illusion...

"Stay out of my head," I snapped suddenly. "Don't enter it again without my permission."

His eyes flared for a second—in shock—before narrowing with that sly smile.

"Of course. Now, are you going to take this or not?" He held out the pill again.

I folded my arms, a perfect, dominating replica of him earlier.

"Why do you have it?"

"I can't answer that."

"Where did you get it?"

"I can't answer that either."

I scoffed. "Bet you're fun at parties." It was a lame insult, but the only one my jumbled brain could think of.

I wasn't expecting it when he leaned even closer, so that I could smell the rich, earthy scent of him, something that reminded me of the grove of black bamboo outside the eastern side of Alderwick. When he whispered against my hair, his breath tickled my neck.

"I am the *king* of parties here at the Esholian Institute." His hands—rough, wide, and strong—were in mine suddenly, placing the pill in my palm and folding my fingers over it. "I appreciate your dilemma, little hurricane. Under normal circumstances, I would tell you to never accept a drug that some random man offered you in an alley, so it's up to you whether you take this or not. But if you don't..." He withdrew slightly, frowning down at me. "You'd better figure out how to

45

contain that power, because the Branding will make it ten times stronger."

He turned without another word and strolled away, down the alley and onto Bascite Boulevard, leaving me standing in an alley with a pill and a pumping heart.

CHAPTER

7

I couldn't go back to the tent.

Not only would Rodhi and the others no longer remember me, but based on the heavy silence of the arena, vibrating with the hum of crickets and the plopping of raindrops on tents, it sounded like everyone was asleep at last.

Plus, I couldn't risk anyone's life again. The thrum of power within me had faded, but what if it regenerated once I fell asleep? What if I exploded again?

When I stepped out onto the vacant Bascite Boulevard, therefore, I began walking in the opposite direction. Away from everyone else, over the bridge, to the courtyard.

Here, that fountain Coen had supposedly been standing on tinkled peacefully, blending in with the sound of the heavy drizzle. I surveyed the sections of buildings in every direction and aimed for the one with the most trees. The treehouse I'd built with Quinn when we were ten wasn't the only tree I'd ever climbed. We used to dare each other to go higher and higher, until we were in the canopies with the monkeys and sloths.

Those memories left me feeling oh so very heavy right now.

Trying to focus purely on my present situation, I found the perfect tree nestled between two stone buildings, its canopy of leaves spread wide over the massive fork of its limbs.

A jump and a grunt later, I had swung my legs over its lowest branches and nestled myself in the crook of its arms. Lonely. I was lonelier than I'd ever been in my life, but there were no tears to clog my throat now. Only dry, aching hollowness.

In the starlight, I brought the pill in front of my face and examined it.

"What are you?" I breathed—to the pill itself or to the power it was supposed to repress, I didn't know. Coen had saved my life, so I doubted he'd try to ruin it by feeding me a harmful drug, but still... all that he'd said about the Good Council...

I closed my eyes, processing it.

Tomorrow was the Branding. If the bascite they would force in my blood made me burst with something ten times more powerful than what I'd just experienced, if I hurt anyone in that crowd, could I even blame the Good Council for hauling me away right then and there and tossing me to the pirates? My blood was wrong, somehow, twisted and monstrous, like a disease swimming through my veins, ready to bite.

But this pill would negate it, according to Coen. Suppress the monster and let the Good Council-sanctioned magic rise to the surface. Or—had he said that last part? What if the pill suppressed *all* magic, and nothing happened when they Branded me?

Sleep on it, Fabian would tell me. Perhaps that was all I could do for now.

So I slipped the pill in my front tunic pocket and let my dreams pull me under.

"Hey, stop it. You're tickling me."

For a moment, I forgot everything. I was back in my bed at home, the birds were whistling, and Don was poking me awake.

Then I sat bolt upright.

And almost fell from the tree.

Three separate monkeys scurried away, chittering to each other in the soft, orange light of dawn and a salt-stained breeze wafting in from the ocean.

"What, were there bugs in my hair?" I muttered, patting my head... and stopped. Whereas last night my curls had taken on a truly unruly shape after the bascale incident, now it flowed down my back in two tight, intricate braids.

My hands shifted down to the front pocket of my tunic in a panic.

A lump. The pill was still there, but that thrum in my chest... it was completely gone. That horrible, clawing power and the bascite that had triggered it must have left my system. For now.

I loosed a sigh and peered up at the three pairs of monkey eyes blinking at me through the tree's canopy.

"Thank you?" One of the Wild Whisperers must have taught them how to braid hair. Did that mean they could understand human language, even if I couldn't understand them? I cleared my throat and said, more earnestly, "Thank you. Really. I was beginning to look like I might have some troll ancestors."

The joke fell flat, of course. *Monkeys don't laugh*, I reminded myself, and shook my head. Last night had really tangled up every thought in my brain.

A brain that a Mind Manipulator had already infiltrated once. Even if it was just to make me believe the fountain in the courtyard was invisible, even if he *hadn't* been solely responsible for the pirate hallucination, that thought left a sour tinge on my tongue. And everything Coen had said flooded back...

"Rayna?"

I jumped and looked down, blinking.

"*Lander?*"

"What are you, uh, doing up in a tree?"

His face came into view, neck craned to look up at me. At the same moment, a fourth monkey skittered up the trunk and swung past me to join the others, but even that didn't faze me. Lander was here.

Biting back a sob, I jumped down, landed in front of him on my hands and knees, and rose up to throw my arms around his neck.

"You found me. Oh, where have you been? I spent all night searching for you."

"I spent all night searching for *you*," he said, slowly hugging me back. "You and Quinn. Have you seen her, by the way? I can't believe we got separated so quickly."

"I..." My breath stumbled. How could I tell him that Quinn had abandoned me, hadn't even asked about him, and surely wasn't searching for us? No, it would be better to let him see her once everything had settled and she came to herself. "I haven't seen her, no," I finished, wincing internally at the lie all the same.

"Oh, no. I was really hoping you had. I hope she's doing okay." Lander withdrew and raked a startled gaze over my braids. "Are *you* okay?"

"Fine," I said, waving a hand. If I couldn't tell him about Quinn, I sure as hell couldn't tell him about the bascale and Coen Steeler and the pill. Not yet. For now, I was content to let the familiarity and joy at his presence inflate in my heart. I hooked arms with him, and said, "How did you find me?"

We began walking, arm and arm, back toward the courtyard.

"Those class royals woke everyone up and told us we had free rein of the entire Institute until Branding tonight. The others began to wander off to explore, but I... I didn't know anyone, so I just kind of stood there." Lander's ebony cheeks flushed. "But then one of those monkeys came up to me and started pulling on my sleeve, and it led me straight to you."

"Huh." I almost stopped. "Maybe you're going to be a Wild Whisperer, Lander."

We came to the courtyard, now bustling with people. Not just inductees, from the looks of it, but older students, too, who were showing off their various powers. This was a mingling, then, a get-to-know-you free-for-all before we were separated into sectors. Yet there seemed to be a wall already, an invisible one, with all that flirting and giggling and posing on one side and Lander and me on the other.

As we hovered on the edge of the courtyard, a group of rowdy boys ran past us, throwing rocks at the monkeys that had followed us along the rooftops.

"Hey!" I started, whirling, but Lander placed his other hand on my shoulder.

"Don't, Rayna. Don't make enemies before Branding. You never know who'll end up in your sector."

"Spoken like a true diplomat," I muttered through my teeth. Lander's entire line of family had been the mayors of Alderwick for generations—a small leadership role given the size of our village, but a political one nonetheless—and Lander himself was expected to take on the mantle once he returned home from the Institute. No one had ever seemed to doubt he'd pass his Final Test.

Lander sighed. "I don't want to think about politics. Let's go explore like everyone else, and maybe we'll see Quinn somewhere along the way."

51

I kept my mouth shut and went along with him.

We meandered through the jumble of roads and alleys and buildings, taking closer looks at every part of campus and passing jaunty groups of other inductees. The whole time, I kept half an eye out for Coen, though I didn't know why, and Lander kept swinging his neck around for any hints of Quinn.

No sign of either of them, until we had ambled to the Shape Shifter section.

There, Lander was just telling me, "It would be awesome to be able to—" when he stopped dead. I followed his gaze and felt him shrink beside me.

Quinn was there, with Jenia and... a lot of older Shifters. All men. All strikingly handsome, though I couldn't see how you'd ever know what a Shifter truly looked like, if they could manipulate any part of their appearance.

Quinn didn't seem to mind, however, and before I could pull Lander back around the corner, she'd reached out to stroke one of their chests, laughing, running her nails down his skin.

"Do it again," we heard her say. It was Quinn's voice, but... higher-pitched than usual. Sultry, somehow, and I still couldn't move to drag Lander away as the Shifter grew, his muscles bulging out far past the scope of normalcy, and she shrieked and dragged her fingers over every dip and curve again. Beside her, Jenia clapped.

"Quinn?" Lander whispered.

She didn't hear, and I finally found my muscles again.

I yanked him away until we were in the shadows of an adjacent building, where I gripped his shoulders.

"Lander, don't read too much into it. It's her first time being around anyone her age besides you and me. She just needs time to adjust..."

He ripped himself away from my grip, hurt crunching his features.

"This is the first time *I've* been around anyone else our age, too, and you don't see me going around, pawing at every hot girl I see. This is..."

"Talk to her, then," I said, switching tactics, desperate to wipe that pain off his face. "Next time you get a chance, talk to her and tell her that there needs to be some new boundaries moving forward if you're going to stay in a relationship together."

Lander rubbed the bridge of his nose, as if willing himself not to sniff.

"I don't know, Rayna. That sounds an awful lot like the start of a breakup."

It did, but I didn't want to confirm that out loud. I only slung an arm around his shoulder and squeezed tight. "C'mon. Let's go find one of those carts of food, eat some lunch, and bask in the sunshine until Branding. Clear our minds."

He nodded, his gaze dropping low, and I felt it for the first time in my life.

A spark of anger toward Quinn.

The Good Council arrived just as the stars were ebbing into view between clouds.

The arena had been utterly transformed. Instead of tents, there was now a stage set up right where Bascite Boulevard opened up to the field, a neat row of chairs for the Good Council members before it, and hundreds of smaller, more rickety chairs behind them, where all us inductees would sit until our names were called.

As we filtered onto the field and claimed our seats—the placement didn't matter, one of the class royals declared as she directed us, since everyone's name would be pulled out of a hat—I didn't know where to look first: the arch of flickering flame above our heads, courtesy of older Element Wielders, the rest of the Institute's students filling the stadiums surrounding us, or the Good Council members themselves.

Five of them had come to witness the Branding. Two men, two women, and one... I didn't even know *what* to call her. A goddess, maybe, because her skin glowed brighter than starlight, her icy-blue eyes framed by razor-sharp bangs and a thick flow of the blackest hair I'd ever seen. She sat in the middle of them all, front and center, far more regal than any of the so-called princes or princesses here.

As Lander and I settled into our seats, I observed the too-slender back of her neck over all the inductee heads in front of me, and a shiver nipped my own.

Shape Shifter. She had to be. Nobody else could achieve that level of beauty.

"I think she's a crone," Lander breathed, having followed my stare. "A crone trapped in a young woman's body. It just... it doesn't look right."

He'd been in a strange mood since the Quinn thing and seemed to be saying the most ominous things possible in response to everything, but I couldn't disagree.

That. That was who'd stare me down when the stamp of bascite met my shoulder, when it sunk through my skin to mingle with the blood in my veins and trigger... whatever monstrous magic had exploded from me last night.

If Coen was right and the Branding activated more raw, uncontrollable power in me, *that* was who'd feel the surge of it first. And from the way she sat, rod-straight, in her chair, I knew she'd be pissed if I so much as knocked her over.

The pill felt as heavy as a marble in my front pocket.

I had to decide, and soon.

"Young ladies and gentlemen!"

A middle-aged man with a jovial face hopped onstage. His cheeks were tight and shiny, and his rounded spectacles winked in the firelight. The crowd—from the soon-to-be branded to the onlookers in the stadium to the Good Council—fell quiet.

"I am your president, Mr. Gleekle, and I want to personally welcome you all to this crucial stage in your cultivation as worthy citizens of Eshol!"

His voice... it seemed closer than it should be, as if an unnatural wind had picked up each word and sent it streamlining straight to my ears. I was willing to bet everyone else was experiencing the same thing, and that the unnatural wind actually split off into thousands of different directions to amplify his speech.

"You see," Mr. Gleekle continued, smiling wider despite the drop in his tone, "the world outside of Eshol is bursting with more than just pirates hungering for the magic that will soon be granted to you. It is full of slavers and murderers and thieves and monsters, dangers beyond our comprehension. This island is safe, but only if we make sure each and every citizen is able to control their magic and use it for the greater good of our society."

Deep, pounding silence followed those words, as if even the beating of thunder in the distance had paused like the beating of our hearts. My mind churned with images of that four-fingered pirate and other vague, shadowy figures behind her. Slavers and murderers. Thieves and monsters. Perhaps the Good Council wasn't so intimidating compared to *them*.

Mr. Gleekle clapped his hands, and the spell broke. "Now, each of you are going to join us on stage when we call your name. Mrs. Wildenberg?" He motioned someone toward him with a fat finger. "If you could please bring the hat out."

An older, ashy-skinned woman hobbled onto the stage, hoisting up an upside-down sunflower hat that had to have been enlarged by Shifter magic.

"Thanks, Joanne," Mr. Gleekle told her, and then turned back to us. His eyes, I noticed through the glint of his glasses, stayed firmly away from the Good Council in the front row. "Mrs. Wildenberg will pull each of your names from the hat, completely at random, of course, and then I myself will brand you on behalf of the Good Council itself. You might feel a little pinch as your magic takes shape, but do not panic. Once it is clear which form your magic has taken, please join the rest of your new sector in the stadium until the end of Branding."

Shifting movement as everyone twisted left and right to try to make out which sector was sitting where in the stadium. For once, though, none of the older students were showing off their magic. Each sector seemed to bleed together.

I wondered, ever so briefly, if Coen was thinking about me, or if he'd already forgotten our little conversation in the alley last night. The way he'd sauntered off, the portrait of nonchalance, seemed to suggest the latter.

If I just knew *where* he'd gotten this pill from... or why... or how...

That bubble of bliss that Lander had brought with him seemed to pop inside me. Now. Now was the moment I had to decide. Trust Coen, a Mind Manipulating man I'd just met, or trust that the Good Council wouldn't toss me away before the test?

Because deep down, I knew that whatever had happened last night would happen again on a much larger scale when that faerie metal became a permanent part of my system.

What would my fathers tell me right now, if they were here?

Don would tell me to be wary of funny mushrooms, of course, but Fabian would tell me to trust my instincts. And then Don would go, *well, yeah, but never trust your instincts when it comes to mushrooms, my Auntie Greta did that once and she...* and Fabian would say *this is different than your Auntie Greta who thought she saw the God of the Cosmos tap-dancing on a frozen lake, Don,* and then they would bicker the whole night through.

What would *I* tell myself to do, if I was giving my own self advice?

My answer came when that Good Council *thing* in the beautiful female body turned to assess the crowd behind her, and I saw the purely predatory hatred ripple in her ice-blue eyes.

No, I might not fully trust Coen, but I didn't fear him like I feared *her.*

As two other instructors brought out a cart of hundreds of metal rods capped with circular bascite stamps, I fished the pill from my pocket.

And popped it in my mouth.

Then swallowed it dry.

Nobody saw, not even Lander, whose eyes were focused on the stage now, but...

Something quieted within me as the pill settled in my stomach, like a faint whine in my ears that I hadn't even realized was there just... dropping away.

Onstage, Mr. Gleekle spread his arms and boomed, "Let the Branding begin!"

57

CHAPTER

8

Mrs. Wildenberg dipped a withered hand in the upside-down sunflower hat. When she brought out the first scrap of paper, even the flickering firelight arched over our heads seemed to pause, waiting.

"Archie van Grouse!" her warbled voice rang out.

A boy two rows in front of me trembled to a stand and walked to the stage, hands in his pockets as if he wanted to paint a portrait of casual indifference.

It didn't work. When he had climbed the two steps up to the raised platform and stood in front of Mr. Gleekle and Mrs. Wildenberg, facing the crowd of thousands, I could see his hands shaking in his pockets.

One of the instructors at the cart brought up a single poker with the bascite stamp on the end, and the other instructor hovered his hands over the brand. Instantly, fire poured from the instructor's fingers onto the bascite, heating it up to a flaming white circle of light, like a miniature moon on a stick.

Mr. Gleekle took the brand delicately and faced Archie.

"Only a pinch," he repeated with a jolly smile, and pressed the brand to the boy's shoulder.

Archie flinched, but no sooner had he done so than the orange imprint of the circle on his skin faded, and he gasped.

I felt a tug at my front pocket, right where the pill had been.

All around me, everyone else gasped, too, as their pockets emptied and hundreds of different items zipped toward the stage, landing in a clinking pile at the boy's feet: wristwatches, necklaces, rings, even a flew flasks like Rodhi had tried to hide, and rubbers that made several people around me shriek with mirth.

Mr. Gleekle beamed, spreading his arms wide.

"Object Summoner! Well done, boy, well done."

The group of older students directly behind us began to cheer and reel the boy toward them with their magic. Archie flew off the stage, down the aisle, and toward the stadium on his tiptoes, as if being pulled in by rope.

Mrs. Wildenberg was already pulling out another name.

"Chasity Lingerium!"

They brought out a brand-new poker for this girl, whose shoulders were hunched inward as if she'd rather shrivel up and die. When Mr. Gleekle pressed the new brand against her shoulder and she winced, Lander leaned in close to me.

"At least they're being hygienic about it, giving us our own brands and such."

"Mmm-hmm."

There had to be a *lot* of metal on the top of Bascite Mountain if they could afford to give everyone their own imprint. Although, come to think of it, the bascite on each stamp would have to sink into every person's skin to work, leaving nothing left for the next inductee.

A moment later, Chasity clutched her head, sank to her knees, and screamed.

"Mind Manipulator," Mr. Gleekle said, rather somber for once, but the group of older students to the left of us cheered. I stared at the girl, Chasity, who must be... reading hundreds of different minds right now, judging from the sound of her screaming. Was this how Coen Steeler had reacted when he'd been branded?

Was he in the crowd right now, cheering as she jerked and writhed?

Just as I thought this, the girl snapped upward, her arms at her side, and lumbered toward the Manipulator audience like a dead corpse walking. Someone in her new sector, I had no doubt, had just ordered her to shut up and join them.

On and on it went, and the randomness of the name calling was its own special kind of torture. Every time Mrs. Wildenberg's hand dipped inside the sunflower hat, my breath caught in my throat. But my name was not called.

A short, curvy brown-haired girl became the first Wild Whisperer when a literal tree behind the stage reached for her with its branches and hoisted her high in the air. Another girl became the first Element Wielder when the ground shuddered beneath our chairs at her branding. One of the boys who'd tried to throw rocks at my hair-braiding monkeys became the first Shape Shifter when fangs shot from his mouth and a tail ripped from the back of his trousers.

Everyone—save for the Good Council, who sat stick-straight in their chairs and never reacted to a single branding—laughed at that, a ripple of mirth at the expense of someone else, but I kept my lips clamped shut and clutched my stomach.

If the pill suppressed *all* my magic rather than just the raw, shapeless one, I would be worse off than the boy with a hole in his trousers. I didn't even want to imagine what the Good Council would do if nothing happened at my brand's touch. Send me back to Alderwick? Investigate me? Toss me to the pirates anyway?

Just then, Mrs. Wildenberg called Quinn's name.

There she was, merely five columns to our left, her hair shining like liquid ruby as she stood and strode to the stage, her chin high and determination set on her face.

A face I'd known so well until yesterday.

Beside me, Lander balled his hands into fists, watching her climb onstage with a tight, clenched expression. I placed a hand on his arm.

Quinn lifted her sleeve, and Mr. Gleekle brought the brand to her bare shoulder. She barely twitched at the hiss of molten fire against her skin, and then—

Quinn's hair exploded into flame.

Hot, living flame, dancing on her head like a turban. Thick, gray smoke billowed out from her head, more potent than all the cigarette smoke she'd ever breathed out.

The crowd of onlookers to our right burst with cheers and pulled her toward them with a lasso of wind.

As she passed us, I saw only feverish joy lighting up her face, like fire sparked in her pores as well. Part of me—the part of me that would love her no matter what and hoped she came to her senses soon—sagged in relief for her, that she didn't have to follow in her mother's footsteps and learn the ways of Mind Manipulating.

Beside me, tension seemed to leak from Lander's posture as well.

The rest of the Branding seemed to speed up, names and faces and magics blurring together—until Lander himself was called up.

He rose on surprisingly steady legs, gave me a calm nod, and joined Mr. Gleekle onstage. *Please let him be in Element Wielding, too,* I prayed. Maybe if Lander and Quinn were in the same sector, they wouldn't fall apart.

Lander sucked in a breath as Mr. Gleekle pushed the brand against his skin.

And fur sprouted from every inch of his body.

His form shrank and hunched, his nose lengthening and arching. Within two blinks, a humanoid anteater was standing where he had just been, and the crowd between Summoners and Wielders screamed out their approval.

Then they all morphed into identical anteater-like figures to welcome him, and I watched as Lander shrank back into himself and sheepishly joined his new sector. The Shape Shifters.

Maybe Quinn would notice him again, now that he could grow unnatural muscles, I thought. Or turn into a lion that she could pet.

Slowly, but surely, the chairs around me emptied. I took note when Quinn's friend, Jenia, became swarmed with vibrant butterflies circling her head like a halo, but after that I quit focusing as nausea, thick and sour, churned in my gut.

What would be worse: if the pill didn't work like it was supposed to and I exploded with that raw, shapeless power? Or if the pill worked a little *too* well and I exploded with... nothing? The crowd of thousands would stare at me, the island's first dud, the first—

"Rayna Drey!" Mrs. Wildenberg called.

After hours of Branding, everyone in the crowd was beginning to lose interest as they whispered among themselves and their new recruits.

Thank the God of the Cosmos for that. Only the remaining inductees watched me push myself forward, toward that stage.

I climbed the steps, saw the shininess of Mr. Gleekle's cheeks up close, and turned to face them. The Good Council.

The middle one—she was the only one who mattered—pinned me with her ice-blue eyes. A fathomless void eddied in there, like a sea of... of death, frozen over.

I couldn't maintain it, the eye contact. I looked away as the instructor with the fire power heated up my brand, and Mr. Gleekle turned to face me.

"Are you ready?" he asked cheerfully. Only to me.

No. No. No.

"Yes," I said.

"Jolly good. Just a pinch, then."

I lifted my sleeve, and he pressed the brand against my shoulder.

A half-second of scorching pain that seemed to sink through all my layers of skin and meld with my blood, and then—

Nothing.

Nothing in my bones shifted.

No whispers, no shrieking grass, no electricity crackling between my fingers.

The Good Council leaned forward as one.

The rumbling of low conversation in the crowd died down to watch, and I cursed Coen, the prince of the Manipulators, hated him, wanted to scream at wherever he was, for doing this to me. Had he really given me a pill to erase every hint of power within me?

"Just relax," Mr. Gleekle murmured, his smile rooted in place. "Let it come out."

I clenched my teeth, willing myself to change shape or sprout with flame or summon anything, anything at all, from the mass of breathing, hushed bodies before me.

That hush only seemed to ripple toward me. Soon, people were craning their necks as if looking for my power somewhere in the aisles.

My vision narrowed. I could feel the Good Council's eyes on me, but I couldn't make myself meet their stares—*her* stare—and they were going to exile me, they were going to toss me away like a piece of garbage, and I would never see Fabian or Don again, I would never get to master my potential, and I...

Something slunk up the middle aisle, slow and deliberate.

I blinked. Rubbed my eyes. Peered at the thing people were craning their necks for a good look at. And I heard it now, the gasps snaking up the rows of seats.

The Good Council twisted to watch, slivers of shock finally breaking the masks of their faces, just as some vital part of me cracked open, brimming with awe.

As a tiger, snow-white and striped with deepest black, padded up to the stage and settled on its haunches before me.

CHAPTER

9

"*Pet me.*"

"W-what?"

I'd heard the growl vibrate in the tiger's throat, but my mind—it had translated the sound automatically into words. Human words.

"*Pet me,*" the tiger repeated. "*I haven't been petted in ages. I usually eat anyone who gets too close to me, you see, but I'm dying for a good scratch.*"

He didn't have to ask me a third time. My hand shot out to stroke the massive, silky arch between his flicking ears, and the crowd seemed to suck in a gasp.

Beside us, Mr. Gleekle shifted uncomfortably, leaning away.

"Wonderful, wonderful. We have another Wild Whisperer!"

But the cheers that came from my new sector's section in the stadium sounded more wary than exuberant, the applause hesitant. I'd heard of the rare tiger on Eshol, but never a *white* one. And I'd never, ever heard of one venturing near humans. Even Wild Whispering humans.

"Who are you?" I breathed down at the creature.

"*My name is Jagaros.*" The tiger closed his eyes, purring.

"I'm Rayna," I said, swallowing. "Rayna Drey. It's—it's nice to meet you."

Truly, it was. Relief flooded my entire body, washing out all that dread and self-disgust, as I threaded my fingers deeper into his fur. Coen's pill had worked, suppressing the forbidden power but letting a lawful, normal one creep through.

A Wild Whisperer. I could handle that. I *liked* that.

"How can you understand me?" I asked him. "I'm not growling, am I?"

It *sounded* like I was speaking normal human language, but I couldn't be sure.

"*Unlike mortals, animals can understand the strange yapping of your kind even when they can't usually mimic it to talk back,*" Jagaros said. "*So no, you are not growling, but I am. The magic acts as a translator for you.*"

"Amazing," I breathed.

Jagaros sighed, the sound a casual snarl in the back of his throat.

"*Okay, they're staring a little too much for my liking. Place your hand on my back and I'll walk you to your new sector. And Rayna?*"

"Yes?" I answered, doing as he instructed and letting him lead me offstage. Everyone indeed stared, their eyes following our movement to the stadium—leaning away, like Mr. Gleekle had, to keep their distance.

"*Do not,*" Jagaros said, his shoulders shifting to and fro as he prowled forward, "*trust a man with a fake smile or a woman who is not a woman at all.*"

"Noted."

I hadn't even dared to glance at those ice-blue eyes after my Branding. I didn't dare now, either, but I could feel the sting of her attention on the back of my neck, like two pricks of frigid ice picks.

66

The fact that a beast as graceful and terrible as Jagaros could also sense her otherworldly presence did nothing to warm me.

And the man with a fake smile—that must be Mr. Gleekle himself.

When we'd finally made it to the stadium and I could see the mass of faces gaping at us in shock up close, the tiger's skin rippled under my touch.

"Have a good time, then, Rayna Drey. I shall see you again."

He began slinking away, but I called after him, "Wait! When will that be?"

"Whenever I need more pets," Jagaros said over his snow-white shoulder. *"Which will not be often."* He paused, then, his eyes narrowing at a young man sitting on the first ledge of the stadium. *"What are you looking at?"*

"N-nothing," the man stammered, and it was then that I realized this whole section of the crowd could understand Jagaros as well. A blush creeped up my neck.

Our conversation hadn't been private, not from everyone.

Jagaros hissed out a curse once, the Wild Whisperers around me flinched, and I watched as the white tiger bounded off into the night.

I couldn't even hear the results of the rest of Branding, what with how many Wild Whisperers—my new peers, I realized with a pleasant jolt—reached their hands out to congratulate me with thumps on my back, or hissed excited questions in my ear as soon as I had squeezed in between them all.

"What did the tiger say up onstage?"

"Have you ever *seen* it before?"

"You're so lucky! He was beautiful."

I answered everyone to the best of my ability in a hushed voice. Before I knew it, Mrs. Wildenberg was hobbling away with the emptied sunflower hat, the other two instructors were hauling off the cart of used brands, and Mr. Gleekle was spreading his arms wide again.

"Now that you've all joined a sector," his wind-carried voice cried, "you may go see your houses for the first time and meet the members of your new Institute family. And remember, classes start tomorrow at sunrise, so don't stay up too late!"

His chuckle was lost in the rumble of the crowd as everyone sprang upward.

And began running.

I followed, forcing my legs into a jog as my sector streamed around the stage and onto Bascite Boulevard. I didn't know *why* we were running, but I wasn't going to disrupt this newfound sense of belonging to ask stupid questions.

After a thousand stomping footsteps and a hundred cheers that sprang into the night, my sector split off into two different directions: the girls to the stone mansion on the left, and the boys to its twin mansion on the right. Behind and before us, other sectors were doing the same, rushing into their designated houses like forks in a river.

I hurried up the steps to my new home for the next five years, passing beneath that giant balcony overhead and crossing through the white-trimmed doorway. The foyer, as massive as my entire *cottage* back at home, split into two different staircases in the back. One spiraled upward while the other dropped down. Between them, a giant cuckoo clock seemed to watch the whole room.

No sooner had I made it into this foyer when someone slammed the double doors shut behind me, and I was pushed toward a lump of girls in the center of it.

The rest of the female Wild Whisperers, young women ranging from nineteen to twenty-three years old, surrounded us with clasped hands, forming a ring of connected bodies that drew us closer and closer together.

"What—?" someone beside me began.

The women around us sucked in a unified breath and began to chant:

> We, the whisperers of the island
> Welcome all who've heard
> Any part of this great, big wild
> From boundless bud to rarest bird

I jumped when something spiraled up my ankle. A vine, snaking from everywhere and nowhere at once, winding tighter and tighter around me and then spilling toward the girls on either side of me. Lacing us together. As the chant continued, more and more vines stitched us even closer, until we were nothing but a tangled knot. Until I couldn't exhale.

> Each plant sings a song of old
> Each animal has a tale
> Each creeping, crawling little thing
> Speaks to us as well.
> So we listen to each warble,
> Each hiss and howl and growl,
> We protect and care, this we swear,
> By the orchid and the owl.

When they broke apart, cheering again, the vines holding us together snapped away. Several girls stumbled forward with hands on their chests, and I unleashed my stiffened breath.

"Welcome, new Whisperers, to the house of the wild!"

The princess of our house, a small-framed, sharp-chinned brunette I'd seen patrolling the arena last night, was standing in front of that cuckoo clock between staircases. Her hands flew together behind her back, and a beady-eyed parakeet shifted from talon to talon on her bony shoulder.

"We are happy to take you under our wing, both literally and met-aphorically," she said, "but please note that anyone older than you here at the Institute is your superior. We have a better grasp on our magic, and we won't hesitate to use it to put you in your place."

It was more or less the same warning the princes and princesses had given yesterday—a threat none of the older villagers in Alderwick had ever dangled over our heads back at home. I briefly wondered about that, but the Whisperer princess was already continuing on as if she *hadn't* just implied we belonged in her parakeet's bill.

"Your bags are already upstairs on the topmost floor, where you'll find the first-year bunkroom and three dozen vacant bunkbeds to claim. You'll all share the single bathing chamber beside it, but don't worry." Finally, a smug smile cracked her mouth open, just a bit. "Next year, you'll only have to share with three others. And by the time you're a fifth-year like *me*, you'll get a room and bathing chamber all to your-self."

It was hard to believe that a single house could fit so many rooms, but I supposed it was as deep as it was tall. I wanted to go explore it, but the sharp-chinned brunette clapped her hands twice. Her parakeet soared off her shoulder, and the older girls began pressing drinks into our hands—not bascale, thankfully, but what looked like sparkling acai wine—and introducing themselves with expressions ranging from bored to eager.

Kaya. Wren. Sorcha. Bailey. Lilith.

I learned too many names to count. It wasn't until I was on my second drink and introducing myself for the tenth or eleventh time when I noticed her.

Jenia Leake. Shit. I'd forgotten that she'd joined the Wild Whisperers when those butterflies had swirled around her head.

She was deep in conversation with a beautiful fellow first-year, a girl with rich, bronze skin who had curtly introduced herself to me as Dazmine earlier. As I watched, another girl—the short, curvy one who'd been the first to join the sector when that tree had hoisted her high with its branches—sidled up to them and said something with a smile.

Jenia turned to Dazmine. So loudly I could hear from halfway across the foyer, she said, "It's a wonder that tree was able to lift something so heavy. Poor thing."

My blood froze. The girl's face drained of all color. She had heard, of course. Everyone on this side of the foyer had.

She started to turn away.

I lurched forward, catching her by the arm.

"I thought your Branding was cool," I said quietly.

Her eyes widened as she recognized me. The girl with the tiger.

"Thanks. Yours was, too! Did it..." She paused to tuck a strand of brown hair behind her ear "...scare you, to touch him?"

Jenia was regarding us from the corner of her eye, so I turned my back on her, blocking her view of the girl. "Not really. He was kind of cute, actually."

Of course, Jagaros would probably rip my face off if he heard me say that, but still, I was glad to see a trembling smile lift up the girl's mouth.

"I'm Emelle," she said.

"Rayna." I had spoken my name so many times by now that the syllables were becoming more and more foreign on my tongue each

71

time. Before I could overthink it, I asked, "Do you want to go claim a bunk with me?"

Relief softened Emelle's face.

"Yes, I really would. This is..." She gazed around at all the people and the parakeet zipping around the room, her eyes flicking briefly toward Jenia. "A bit overwhelming."

"Agreed," I said. "Let's go."

Jenia watched us pass her by, the gray of her eyes reduced to slits.

CHAPTER

10

The next morning at dawn, Emelle and I wandered to the dining hall together.

We'd claimed the same bunk, her on bottom and me on top, and after we'd located our luggage in a pile of other bags in the corner of the bunkroom, we'd ventured to the bathing chamber together with fresh nightgowns from home.

The bath had been bliss, even though it had felt... less private than my tub back home, that was for sure. A dozen clawed bathtubs lined the wall of the chamber, each with a half-moon rack and skimpy curtains half-heartedly shrouding each space. Emelle and I had bathed side by side, talking through our curtains, then retired to bed earlier than anyone else.

I couldn't even remember the others coming to bed, I'd slept so deeply.

Now, the birds out our bunkroom windows were chirping at everyone to wake up. It was strange, to hear those chirps but also hear the translation in my head: *"Wake up, the sun's out, wake up!"* I spared them a last glance as Emelle and I trailed downstairs after the others, both of us already dressed in new outfits for our first day of classes.

"I overheard someone saying *our* downstairs connects with the guys' downstairs," Emelle said as we reached the bottom of the steps and faced a rounded corridor with three separate doors.

The women in front of us pushed open the middle one, and we followed them, coming out into a massive hall filled with circular tables.

Emelle was right. Both boys and girls of the Whisperer sector mingled, which meant... I glanced up at the ceiling. Boulevard Bascite must be right above our heads.

We made our way to the queue trailing from an open, widespread kitchen window, where a kindly-looking cook was handing out platters of mouth-watering breakfast. Steaming eggs, golden toast, and a medley of berries, from the looks of it.

"I'm starving," I moaned. When Emelle gave me a cockeyed look, I added, "I've been pretty nervous up until this point, so I haven't eaten much for the past few days."

True, of course. But Emelle couldn't know that my nerves had skyrocketed beyond the normal scope of inductee butterflies. She couldn't know, either, that I'd fallen asleep with my mind churning with images of Coen and Jagaros.

The Mind Manipulator and the tiger.

Both of whom had saved me in different ways.

After we'd finally accepted our platters of breakfast from the house cook, we were just scanning the room for an empty table when a familiar voice yelled out, "Hey! It's the girl who thinks I'm a teacher!"

I jumped, almost dumping my food, and found Rodhi grinning at me at a nearby table, surrounded by a group of friends.

"What are you doing just standing there? Get your ass over here, darling!"

74

Right. He had no idea who I was beyond our initial meeting in the courtyard, since Coen had erased his most recent memory of me.

Leading Emelle over to him, I said, "I don't think you're a teacher *now*. I just didn't get a good look at your lack of facial hair before."

Rodhi laughed like before, stroking his smooth chin. "My old man didn't grow a beard until he was thirty-five, so I'm waiting for—"

"—your *stud* to kick in?" *Stupid*, I chided myself when his face fell a bit. *Why did I have to go and ruin his joke just because I knew what he was going to say?*

But then Rodhi's boyish face split into his widest grin yet.

"Oh, I'm going to like you, I think. What's your name, by the way? And yours?" he asked Emelle.

Once we'd introduced ourselves—again—Rodhi burst into the story of his own Branding, how he'd been the very last one to be called up (which explained why I didn't remember him during the ceremony), and how a flock of toucans had bombarded him with bugs and slugs as a welcome gift.

"Fascinating," Emelle whispered after he'd jumped up to go hail another group of his friends strolling into the dining hall. "I've never seen someone so... lively."

I opened my mouth to respond when a sultry voice pierced the din of the hall.

"I'm just so glad we were granted the same magic, sis." It was Jenia, once again with the bronze-skinned beauty named Dazmine. But this time, both of them were talking to the princess of our house, that sharp-chinned brunette with the parakeet on her shoulder. I could have sworn they had strayed near our table on purpose. And...

Sis. I tried not to let my head swing back and forth between Jenia and the house princess. They didn't look alike upon first glance, but when both pairs of gray-slitted eyes glanced my way, I caught the resemblance in their expressions.

Sisters. Great.

Jenia's older sister shrugged. "The Whisperer magic must really like our blood."

Emelle and I stayed silent, pretending to be unengaged, until the trio moved away toward the kitchen window to grab their own breakfasts.

One of the young women at the table with us spoke up. "Don't worry about *Princess* Kimber. She's way more interested in the mirror than the orchid and the owl."

"But she's a class royal," I said around a mouthful of scrambled egg. "Wasn't she picked based on... I don't know... expertise or something? Passion?"

"You would think, but Kimber's more like the royal of bitches, if anything."

Emelle and I clapped our hands to our mouths, but the others at the table were engaged in their own conversations, so no one besides us had heard. Still...

The young woman, a second-year named Wren, if I remembered correctly, had a black bob, strikingly slanted eyebrows, a ring glittering on one side of her nose... and exactly the kind of expression that made oh-so high and mighty people hesitate.

Before we could respond, she pushed back her plate and hoisted herself up.

"C'mon. I'll take you guys to your first class so you're not late. First-years always get History first thing on Mondays. I like to think of it as a special kind of torture, considering how drab Mr. Fenway is."

Emelle and I exchanged bemused glances. Our sector's class schedule had been posted in the foyer the night before, so we already knew

76

that our first class was A History of the Esholian Biome in Classroom 3A, but this was the first we were hearing about the instructor. And it *would* be hard to find the right building without a guide.

"We'd really like that," I told her.

Wren pressed her lips together to smother a smile.

Five minutes later, Emelle and I were following her back through the dining hall, up the stairs, and out onto Bascite Boulevard, illuminated in pools of gold from the sunrise and streaming with students walking toward campus.

As we joined the flow, birds chirped at us from overhead.

"*New friends, new friends, hi, new friends!*"

"Hello," I said.

"Hi, there!" Emelle called upward, positively beaming.

"Pesky buggers," Wren said, though not without a hint of affection.

The monkeys, too, were waiting for us on campus, squatting on rooftops and lounging in the tree I'd slept in the night before Branding. I recognized the ones who'd braided my hair—something about the specific spots of fur on their tails—and waved.

This time, when they chippered back at me, I heard, "*Glad to see you're looking freshened up. We were beginning to think you had some troll blood in you.*"

They shrieked with laughter, clutching each other in the tree, and I scowled. That was *my* joke, although... at least they'd actually found it funny.

"What was that about?" Wren asked, cocking an eyebrow as we passed.

I didn't want to explain my past sleeping arrangements, so I shrugged. "Just some silly monkeys, I suppose. Is this it, then?"

77

She'd stopped us right in front of a crumbling stone facility with a slanted roof, where a few steps led down to a door situated halfway underground.

"This is it," Wren sighed. "Good old Mr. Fenway likes his must and mold, that's for sure. Good luck, you two."

"Thank you," I said. I wouldn't have wanted to be late on our first day.

Beside me, Emelle nodded earnestly, and Wren raised two fingers in farewell.

Mr. Fenway did indeed seem to like must and mold.

He wasn't just an old man, but an old man with bags under his eyes and a hunch to his back, plus a severely receding hairline. When the rest of the class had finally trickled in and filled the fifty or so seats in the classroom, he coughed.

"Hello, children. I..." He coughed again, then thumped his chest. "I am pleased to see so many of you join the sector of Wild Whisperers."

"*Children,*" Jenia scoffed to her friend—Dazmine—from two rows back. "Well, to a man on his deathbed, I guess we are."

Mr. Fenway didn't appear to hear, or maybe he just chose not to acknowledge her. He twined his hands together behind his back and began a monotone ramble that I was sure he'd repeated dozens and dozens of times before now.

"One thousand years ago, faeries ruled this island, their powers tending to the land in every way. Conjuring rain to water the vegetation, encouraging trees to reach their fullest height..." A cough "...and helping balance out the delicate nature between life and death among the Esholian animals."

78

Like the persistent whine of insects, Jenia was whispering to Dazmine over Mr. Fenway's speech, no doubt ridiculing him or the idea of faeries. One seat ahead of her, a guy I'd never noticed before was lounging back in his chair, chuckling at her every insult and mockery.

I didn't like the looks of him: greasy hair that curled near the nape of his neck, hooded eyes, a too-casual swagger about him—nothing like Coen's playful smirk or Rodhi's inherent confidence. This was just pure contempt for everyone else around him, besides perhaps Jenia herself.

"Then," Mr. Fenway continued, raising his wispy voice slightly to drown out Jenia's whispers, "the faeries began to die out."

A young man with a broad build in the very front row gasped softly.

"Why?" he asked, his tone low—and perhaps a bit slow.

"What is your name, boy?" Mr. Fenway asked, squinting at him.

"Gileon, sir." The young man drew out every syllable, and the greasy-haired boy huffed out a scoff of amusement, which made Jenia grin.

"Well, Gileon," Mr. Fenway began, "faeries lived for eons, but it was difficult for them to reproduce, and soon, their offspring became more and more rare. So they died out about five hundred years ago, the last of them laying themselves to rest at the top of what is now known as Bas-cite Mountain."

He nodded somberly as Gileon gasped again.

"Yes, yes, yes, it was very sad—so say the birds who pass their stories down from generation to generation. And even sadder..." Another cough "...was that the island, without its protectors, began to die, too."

On the opposite end of the classroom, Rodhi was clinging on to every word, his knee jittering as if the lack of talking was literally going to kill him. But it made me respect him all the more, that while Jenia whispered and tittered, he kept quiet.

"Plants shriveled up," Mr. Fenway persisted over the drone of her lowered voice, "predators overhunted and starved themselves out. The birds, I have heard, quit singing. Yet before the island could collapse completely, not long after the last of the faeries died, *she* came. The head and founder of our Good Council. Dyonisia Reeve, whom you all saw witness your Branding last night."

Ice-blue eyes, star-bright skin, razor-sharp bangs and flowing black hair. I couldn't shake the image of her out of my mind as Mr. Fenway went on.

"Dyonisia sailed in from the outside world and beheld the decay of the island all around her. She is the one who discovered bascite at the top of the mountain. For, you see, every other part of the last faeries had disintegrated like everything else ... except for the magic metal in their blood. That metal, bascite, remained."

Magic metal in their blood? I'd always known that bascite came from the ancient faeries, somehow, but I'd never known it came from their *blood*. How many faeries, exactly, had to have died to leave heaps and heaps of their remains atop Bascite Mountain—enough for generations of inductees, year after year? Enough for people to steal and dissolve into ale?

Mr. Fenway broke into a coughing fit, then wiped his mouth. "Excuse me. As I was saying, Dyonisia formed this remaining metal into brands, that when stamped on a human's skin, as you know, joins our own blood and grants us vague remnants of the faeries' old powers. Once Dyonisia garnered enough branded people to revive the island, humans wishing to escape the terrors of the outside world sailed in in droves, repopulating what had once almost died. And now we, thanks to Dyonisia's discovery and invention, care for the plants and animals of our dear home as the faeries once did."

The classroom burst into murmurs at that. Across the room, Rodhi couldn't contain himself any longer and cried, "Bascite came from *blood*? Wicked!"

But I stayed silent. I couldn't get those ice-blue eyes out of my head.

Dyonisia Reeve. The founder and head of the Good Council. At least I now had a name to put to that cruel, beautiful face. And another thing:

If the last faeries had died about five hundred years ago and Dyonisia had discovered the island not long after, then...

Through Shape Shifting, I was sure, regenerating her organs and bones and skin time and time again, the leader of our island had to be hundreds of years old.

A crone in a young woman's body, indeed.

CHAPTER

11

After History, Emelle and I returned to the house for a quick lunch before doubling back to campus, where our next two classes would take place in Building 3C—a double block of Befriending Predators & Prey with an instructor named Mr. Conine.

Mr. Conine didn't even let us enter the classroom, however, a steepled, two-story structure slightly less shabby than Mr. Fenway's. Instead, he greeted us outside the front door and then, when all fifty of us had gathered around him, said, "Follow me, everyone!"

We traipsed through the Whisperer sector, toward the jungle that grew thicker and thicker the longer we walked. Monkeys swung through the treetops, hurling jokes down at us, which Rodhi never failed to reciprocate.

"Oh yeah?" he called upward as we passed the last of the buildings and slapped through the beginning of a marsh, the ground spongy beneath our feet. "Well, *your* mama's so dumb, she threw away the banana and ate the peel!"

I cringed. "Rodhi, this class is called *befriending* predators, not antagonizing them."

"They started it," he muttered. "Nobody gets to talk about my ma like that."

Emelle gazed upward, awe-struck. "I think they actually like it, the banter. Listen. They thought it was funny."

She was right. I never thought I'd hear so many monkeys snickering in a tree before, but here we were, traipsing beneath a whole *layer* of snickering, chortling shrieks. Even Mr. Conine glanced upward to shake his head at them, amused.

He stopped us right before the ground became too mushy to hold our weight. Before us, a swamp swathed the ground between crooked, moss-cloaked trees, several films of algae patching it with murky green.

Mr. Conine turned to address us, the tan, leathery skin of his face and graying circle beard completely at ease.

"Your first task, ladies and gentlemen, will be to wade through this marsh without getting eaten alive."

A couple people chuckled nervously. Mr. Conine raised a bushy eyebrow.

"You think I'm joking? Well, perhaps you will think differently when the crocodiles emerge. They are always hungry, and to them it doesn't matter if their food can talk back or not."

Even Jenia snapped her mouth shut at this. For some reason, I had assumed that befriending predators would require little more than saying hi. Apparently, my instant connection with Jagaros had been a rare case.

I should have suspected so when he'd hissed so viciously at the others.

"Lesson number one, then," Mr. Conine said. "Crocodiles love praise." Without further ado, he began wading out into the swamp, and when everyone stood rooted to the spongy ground, he called over his shoulder, "Now, please!"

We jolted forward after him.

The algae-caked water rose to my knees, then my waist. Rodhi mumbled something about unsanitary conditions, which I had to agree with, and Emelle... poor Emelle had the marsh clear up to her chest. She took quick, shuddering gasps, her arms roving in circles to propel herself forward.

To our right, someone screamed.

And then I felt it, a rush of muck swirling around my ankles and a great swooping pressure as a scaled, grayish-green snout broke the surface before me, followed by a pair of piercing yellow eyes with slitted pupils.

Around me, I could sense other crocodiles rising on either side of Rodhi and Emelle as well, but I kept my eyes firmly locked on the one in front of me.

"*A midday snack?*" the crocodile grunted, gliding nearer.

"Oh," I said, "you deserve much better than me."

The words came out as near-squeaks, but the crocodile paused.

"*Why do you say that, Wild Whisperer?*"

So he was aware of the nature of what I was—what we *all* were—and had still ascended to snack on me. I blocked out the pleading of those around me and said, "Surely, someone as handsome as yourself would want something tastier than *me.*" I dropped my voice as if telling a secret. "I'm afraid I had turnips for breakfast."

God, I hoped crocs couldn't pick up on lies.

"*Handsome?*" the crocodile asked, cocking his head.

"So handsome," I repeated, nodding, "what with your scales and your... your teeth. You've got to have the biggest teeth in this entire marsh!"

"*I do,*" the crocodile said importantly.

"And," I pressed on, "you could probably protect me from all the other crocodiles here. If any one of them so much as snapped at me, *you*, my friend, could tear them apart in an instant. That's how strong you are."

"*Well, of course.*"

"Let us stroll together, then, and talk about better snacks for you than myself."

My heart pounding in my throat, I began wading forward again, this time with the crocodile gliding alongside me. All around us, several other classmates were plunging forward, too, while others still gave desperate compliments in a standstill.

Halfway there, I chanced a glance behind me and held in my sigh of relief at the sight of Emelle and Rodhi among those pushing forward. Ahead of us, Mr. Conine was already clambering up a slippery slope.

By the time my crocodile and I got to the other side, we had agreed that a nice, fresh crab from the seaside would suffice... which I promised to bring him within the next week.

I scrambled up the slope, and my crocodile sunk back beneath the algae.

Mr. Conine cocked a bushy brow at me.

"Clever to offer him something in your stead, but make sure to follow through with that promise. Otherwise, you'll never be able to return to this swamp again without him ripping you to shreds on sight for what he'd consider a betrayal."

I nodded.

"Yes, sir. Thank you."

Great. Now I'd have to figure out how to catch a crab who could talk back. The thought of a little crustacean snapping its claws at me, begging me to let it go while I hauled it to a crocodile marsh... it made me sick to my stomach.

Later. I'd dwell on it later. For now, I watched the rest of the class slowly but surely make it to the bank, soggy and reeking of rotten eggs, until only one was left: the greasy-haired boy who had scoffed at Gileon in History.

"C'mon, Fergus, you've got it!" Jenia cried.

Emelle, huddling close to Rodhi and me as she shivered from head to toe, passed me the faintest of smirks—probably at the sight of Jenia's perfect figure drenched in just as much filth as the rest of us.

In the swamp, Fergus was saying, "No, I don't want to pick moss out of your teeth, you ugly brute."

Within half a second, the crocodile was surging forward with an open jaw.

Within the next half second, tree roots shot from the ground at Mr. Conine's feet and wrapped the crocodile from snout to tail, holding it back, before—*snap*.

The crocodile tore from the makeshift ropes and lunged for Fergus...

Who was already clawing his way up the bank, cursing.

"What kind of a teacher do you think you *are*," he seethed, raising himself to a stand before Mr. Conine, "sending us into that nightmare on our first day?"

Mr. Conine just observed him calmly.

"I'd hardly say calling it an ugly brute is anyone's idea of praise. That was a female, so she took particular offense to that."

"I never wanted this," Fergus said, clenching his fists, and even Jenia held back to bite her lip. "I never asked to be a stupid crocodile whisperer. I would have picked any other sector besides this one." And he stomped off.

Rodhi whistled. "Too bad for him we have to go back through the swamp to get home."

86

"No." Mr. Conine tracked Fergus's trek deeper into the jungle. "Even *I* wouldn't want to mess with the crocodiles twice in one day. We'll go around. And remember." His eyes skipped over each of us. "*Our blood* does not choose what form our magic takes. None of you had any talent like crocodile whispering lurking in your veins before Branding. Rather, the magic itself decided, the moment it merged with your blood, to make you a Wild Whisperer."

He paused, and the creak of the jungle, the thickness of the humidity, the chit-chatting monkeys and high-pitched birds high up in the treetops, pressed in on us.

"Do not," Mr. Conine said, "disappoint the magic that chose its shape within you."

Befriending Prey was a *lot* easier than Befriending Predators.

Once we'd returned to the classroom and made our way inside, Mr. Conine had an Element Wielder colleague come by to magically swipe the water and grime off our clothes and bodies.

I still felt an invisible layer of filth on me anyhow, but I couldn't complain. Not when we all spent the next hour of class sprawled on the floor, playing with capybaras.

At dinner that night, we told Wren about Fergus's meltdown.

"Ahh, I've seen guys like him before," she said, digging into her coconut bowl filled with fruit and seeds. "He doesn't just think he's better than everyone else. He expects everyone else to think it, too. I mean —" She swallowed thickly "—take me, for example. *I* think I'm better than everyone else, but do you see *me* going around demanding everyone to bow to me? No. That, my friends, is for guys like him."

"You know," Emelle said, "I'd love to have your self-esteem, Wren. I really would."

At that moment, Rodhi returned from wherever he'd been (I was learning not to question it when he scurried off, since he seemed to have friends in every corner of campus) and thumped his hand down on our table.

"Guess what, all you pretty little darlings? Including you, goth girl," he said to Wren, who scowled at him. "You can go ahead and thank me right now, because *I* just got our whole sector into the coolest party on campus tonight. *We* are going to the Manipulator house."

I paused mid-chew. Swallowed.

"The Mind Manipulators? How... how did you manage that?"

Not that I knew the rules or etiquette for inviting other sectors over, but... if there was a party at Coen's own mansion, surely I'd see him there? I hadn't caught a single sight of him since that night in the alleyway, and a small, doubtful part of me was beginning to fear I'd made him up.

Rodhi beamed. "I just made out with one of their third-years beneath the stadium, and she invited us all afterward. I know, I know, selling my body for the sake of your popularity, how sad. Anyway, see you all there!"

He practically skipped away, leaving even Wren gawking.

"What a *weirdo*," she said finally, her voice brimming with admiration.

Two hours later, Emelle and I were powdering our cheeks and swiping oil on each other's eyelashes in the bathing chamber, preparing for the party.

The powder was Emelle's, but the oil came from my garden back at home, squeezed from one of our castor plants and mixed with a bit of charcoal powder for color. I had retrieved it from an inner pocket of my bag and paused when my hand came in contact with my mother's knife.

Even just looking at that weapon felt... wrong. Especially now that I was a Wild Whisperer. The handle was made of *bone*. The sheath of *leather*. And whatever profession the Good Council assigned me to after my Final Test (if I passed, of course), they wouldn't make me go hunting down the same animals I could talk to.

I'd snatched the vial of black castor oil and hurried after Emelle without touching the knife again.

Just as we were finishing up, a fourth-year peeked in.

"Rayna? There's some Shifter outside asking to see you. I think his name's Lander? Should we let him in? We never allow members of other sectors to come inside unless they've been given express permission by someone they—"

"Yes," I said immediately, setting my vial down. "Hold on. I'm coming."

Glancing at Emelle, I hurried after the fourth-year to the front doors, where I threw them open and found Lander standing on our steps with his hands in his pockets.

I'd never seen him cry. Not once. But that was definitely silver emotion lining his eyes.

"I went to talk to her," he said. "I went to talk to her thinking that maybe she'd find me cooler now that I'm a Shape Shifter, but I found her... kissing. Someone else. I broke it off right then and there before I could even *think*, and she just... she just watched me go, Rayna. She didn't even try to stop me."

My heart plummeted.

Quinn... how could she *do* that to him? How could she do that to *us*, the three childhood best friends, the perfect trio?

89

That trio, or perhaps the illusion it had been, was shattered now. I knew that as I took in Lander's face, mere seconds from crumpling. I'd assumed Quinn would revert back to her old self after a few days, not casually throw away their relationship like it meant nothing.

"Oh, Lander." I held the door open wider. "I'm so sorry."

A few fellow Whisperers jostled past me just then, cocooned in a haze of perfume as they headed to the Manipulator house, with its thumping music and strobing lights—where Emelle and I were supposed to meet Rodhi and Wren, and where maybe, just maybe, I would see Coen again.

But then Lander's breath hitched, and I made a decision.

Reaching out, I pulled him into the foyer, where Emelle stood with her hands clasped in front of her, trying to hide her curiosity behind a pleasantly concerned expression.

"Hey," I told her, "you go ahead without me. I'm going to hang out with my friend from back home tonight."

But Emelle shook her head.

"I'm not going to some Manipulator flirt-fest without you. Can I stay?"

I nodded, so the two of us led Lander upstairs to the empty bunk-room, letting the music and lights of the neighboring party flood through the window.

As Lander hooked his arms around me and finally broke into sobs.

CHAPTER

12

Lander stayed with us deep into the night, until the rest of our sector finally trickled back into the bunkroom after the music from next door had died down.

In the end, it was Emelle who got him to break out of his sobbing fit—not by attempting to cheer him up, as I did, but by telling him softly of her own breakup the year before, and how much her heart still lay in pieces over it.

You'd think such a thing would have made him cry harder.

I was still pondering it the following morning, when we reached our first class of the day, The Language of Plants 101, taught by none other than the same instructor who'd pulled our names out of that sunflower hat. Mrs. Wildenberg.

Like Mr. Conine, Mrs. Wildenberg met us outside Building 3E. After we'd all gathered, she led us to the arboretum situated between the back buildings and the rising slope of the mountainside.

Here, rather than a jungle floor tangled with ferns and thorns and roots, the ground rippled with soft grasses and rows of flowers between the trees. A sanctuary of sorts, courtesy of Mrs. Wildenberg's guiding magic.

"Now, I want you all to lay down on your backs," she told us in that warbling voice, slowly bending to meet the grass on her hands and knees. Once she was firmly on the ground, she eased her frail body backward to sprawl out. "Close your eyes and listen to what you hear. We will discuss it during our next class period, but for now, just take note of each different sound."

We did as she said, Rodhi whispering that this certainly beat wading through the crocodile marsh.

I closed my eyes and let the warmth of the dry season sweep over me.

Like the night before Branding, when all the five magics had teased me before that shapeless power burst out, I could hear the grass shrieking beneath my weight. But the more I listened, shifting from side to side as if to alleviate its pain, the more I realized the sound was actually a high-pitched whistle. A calling, of sorts, to the heavens. Even the blades that weren't smashed under someone's body let out that whistle, faint but shrill and piercing all the same.

I shifted my attention to the trees on either side of me.

The roots... I could hear them sucking up water from the soil, a crinkling, slurping wet sound. And the leaves themselves were—I squeezed my eyes tighter, straining to listen—humming. Yes, that was humming, low and pulsing, like a mother shushing her baby to sleep. Tuneless, but calming.

Apparently, the Branding hadn't just made me understand animals. It had sharpened my hearing, too, letting me in on nature's song if only I concentrated hard enough.

A song that was disrupted, once again, by the hissing laugh of Jenia.

"I wish," Rodhi whispered to Emelle and me, "that girl could just be exiled right now. That would give me a nice night of sleep, I think."

"Don't joke about that," I breathed back. "Please."

The thought of banishment and pirates still left my gut in knots, because that would have been me without the pill Coen had given me.

"Sorry," Rodhi muttered. "No more 'mean girl gets exiled and relieves us all of our pounding headaches' humor. Got it."

I elbowed him. Rodhi snorted.

When Jenia's laugh had faded again and nature's song flooded back into my ears, I focused on the flowers. Each one, it seemed, crooned a different tune.

The lilacs sang out distinctly feminine songs, twirly and bright. Their voices made me think painfully of Quinn and all the times we'd climbed trees together, slept under the stars together, braided each other's hair.

I shifted my concentration again before a lump could form in my throat.

The violets' tune was rather sexy and somehow... breathy, like they were constantly ramping up their verses with increasing vigor and passion. Their voices made my stomach curl and flutter. A face flitted in my mind against my will before I could swipe it away, so I shifted my concentration once again to avoid thinking of Coen.

The orchids—the orchids sang with such clarity it brought tears to my eyes. Charming and pure, their voices made me think of home and friendship and love.

On and on, I listened to each flower's tune, then brought myself back to the wider range of song. The blend of sounds washed over me, until something seemed to tug at my heart: a tether of sorts, flowing out from me to connect with it all.

Why do I have this dangerous, shapeless power inside me? I asked the lilacs. *Where did it come from?*

Does Coen have it, too? I asked the violets. *Is that why he knows so much about what happened to me and how to keep it locked away?*

What am I supposed to do with it? I asked the orchids. *Keep it a secret forever, and never let it build or grow, never strive to understand it?*

I heard their answers, heard the subtle changing pitch of their songs in response. But unlike tigers and monkeys and crocodiles, I couldn't instinctively understand them. It was like a foreign language, my understanding fluttering just out of reach.

As if they didn't want me to know.

Our fifth and final class on the schedule was Worms, Spiders & Insects.

The instructor, we soon found out after filing into Building 3B and settling into desks, had permanent, calculating slits for eyes that seemed to cut into everything they landed on. Her arched eyebrows and chestnut hair tucked primly behind her ears only added to that sharpness.

Jenia began whispering to Dazmine, "This is going to be my favorite class, I think, since the butterflies chose me during Branding. Did you see how they—?"

"Butterflies," the instructor interrupted, shutting the classroom door with a snap, "are among the dumbest insects and therefore feel most comfortable around humans of a similar nature. Now, this is not an open-discussion class, Ms. Leake, so I would appreciate it if you merely listened unless your name is called."

A chilling silence. The back of Jenia's neck flushed. I sank deeper into my seat, hoping the instructor wouldn't notice me. Although the fact that she already knew all our names without ever having met us... I doubted shriveling up would prevent her attention if she wanted to call on me.

On either side of me, Emelle bit her lip and Rodhi absolutely beamed.

"My name," the instructor began, "is Ms. Pincette. I am the island's leading researcher on the nature of insects and the connection they pose to us who are gifted with Wild Whispering powers. Much like plants, you will find that worms, spiders, and insects are significantly harder to understand than animals, even with your magic, so this first year of class will focus on dissecting their various values first."

Ms. Pincette whirled toward her blackboard stretching from one end of the classroom to the other and plucked up an unused stick of chalk.

"Let's start with spiders. Can anyone tell me why spiders would be useful to us? I trust you will think beyond their spot in the cycle of life."

Rodhi's hand flung upward.

"Yes, Mr. Lockett?"

"My pa says they bring good luck," he said eagerly.

Ms. Pincette waved a hand. "Purely superstition. Anyone else?"

Rodhi's smile sagged. Nobody said anything. Nobody dared even *blink*.

"Very well, then." Ms. Pincette turned to scribble something on the board, her wrist jerking with harsh, sharp strokes. When she was done, the class gasped.

One hour ago, Mitzi Hodges and Norman Pollard confessed their undying love for each other behind the hibiscus bushes in the arboretum.

In the back of the classroom, Mitzi Hodges and Norman Pollard blushed.

"How could I have known this?" Ms. Pincette said.

This time, Rodhi raised his hand more hesitantly.

"Yes, Mr. Lockett?"

"You used the spiders as spies?"

A slight smile crept onto Ms. Pincette's face. "Exactly. I used my spiders to spy on every single one of you the hour before this class. Most of you were doing just as Mrs. Wildenberg said and listening to the plants, but *two* of you snuck away to use that time for confessions... among other things." Her lips twitched. "Your task before the end of this class, then, is to find a single spider hiding in this classroom. There are fifty of them listening in on us now, so once you find one you may leave. But I warn you... it might be harder than it looks. They are notoriously silent, so you must gather all your wits to catch the sound of their creeping. Begin."

It took a moment for the screeching of chairs to fill the classroom as everyone began, dazed, to get out of their seats... and hunt.

Jenia, Dazmine, and Fergus headed straight for the baseboards and cornices. In the back, Mitzi Hodges and Norman Pollard rifled through their own pockets, as if to catch the spider who'd sold them out. Rodhi wandered over to Ms. Pincette's desk, where she had sat to observe us. I watched him bend low to inspect the cracks around the polished wooden legs, whistling a jaunty tune that had Ms. Pincette raising her eyebrows at him.

Emelle and I aimed for the shelves lining the far classroom wall and began picking out book after book. To no avail. I coughed, waving the dust away, and—

An idea hit me.

"Emelle," I said out of the corner of my mouth, "tell me a secret."

"What?"

"Tell me something you've never told anyone else."

Understanding sparked in her eye as she slid a book back in place.

"My breakup last year... it didn't hurt because I actually loved him. It hurt because our parents had sworn us to be married and I wanted so badly to please mine. But we... weren't compatible in our ideas of how to have a good time."

Emelle's ears flared with a sudden pink hue. She lowered her voice even more.

"He liked to spank and choke and... a lot of other things that I didn't enjoy."

"By the orchid and the owl," I muttered, the phrase slipping out after only a few days of hearing the older women say it all the time. "I'm so sorry, Emelle."

She shrugged. "My parents will just have to get over it. I'm happy to be free of him, and after seeing your friend Lander go through so much grief over losing someone he *actually* loved... it changed my perspective a bit. Your turn, now."

I paused. I couldn't risk telling her about what had happened the night before Branding, not when certain listening ears might report it to the Good Council.

What was a secret I'd never told anyone? Something, perhaps, I hadn't even admitted to myself?

It spilled from me before I could rethink it.

"There's a fifth-year who I think is... really attractive." God, that sounded so lame, but Emelle's eyes widened all the same. "Like," I forced myself to continue, "I've never been super into anyone back at home." Indeed, I hadn't even thought of Wilder since I'd left Alderwick, and I was sure he hadn't thought of me. "I've kissed exactly one boy, and that was more because I was curious about what it would feel like than anything else. And I did enjoy it, but not as much as I imagine I'd enjoy kissing *him*." I was rambling now, trying to scramble through the realization.

"*Who?*" Emelle whispered.

"I—do you hear that?"

We both paused.

Like the subtlest of fingernail taps against glass came a *click, click, click:* multiple spider legs scuttling closer to hear what we were saying.

Emelle mouthed something to me. I nodded, and stooped down low. She hooked one leg around my neck and mounted herself up on my shoulders.

I raised her up on trembling legs, letting her peer over the upper ledge of the bookshelf.

"Got them!" she exclaimed. "Let me down."

I lowered her to the floor as a few fellow classmates glanced in our direction, looking puzzled and frustrated. Emelle opened her hands to reveal two long-legged orb weavers hulking in her palm.

"Very good, ladies," Ms. Pincette said from across the room.

We decided to wait for Rodhi before heading back to the house, which took... a while, surprisingly.

By the time he emerged from Building 3B, grinning so widely I thought his face would crack open, the rest of our class had already filtered past us. I could hear the clamoring sounds of other sectors heading home for the day, too.

"What the hell...?" I began.

"I'm going to marry her," Rodhi declared, catching up with us.

"Who?"

"Ms. Pincette, of course. Have you ever seen a woman so fine?"

Emelle giggled into her hands. I gaped at him in horror.

"She's an instructor!"

"So? I'm technically an adult, aren't I? And even *you* thought I could pass as a teacher myself. Sometimes you think so small, darling."

He began marching in the direction of the courtyard, not a single doubt slumping his narrow shoulders. Exchanging raised eyebrows, Emelle and I followed.

We rounded the corner of a building. And stopped.

There in front of us, four people squatted behind one of the pillars on either side of a stairwell that snaked back to the courtyard: Jenia, Dazmine, Fergus, and a boy I'd never seen before—from another sector, then.

With their backs to us, they didn't notice us rooted in place behind them, watching as they snickered down at the young, burly man twirling in circles in the entrance to the courtyard. Gileon. And...

I squinted, horror blooming in my chest.

A stick, as if moving all on its own, was jabbing him in the back over and over, flying out of his reach whenever Gileon turned to try to grab it. Gileon tripped over his feet, landed on his knees, and groaned when the stick whacked him across the back of the head.

"That," said Fergus smoothly, nudging the stranger next to him, "is what I call a real power. I don't know why I got stuck with this stupid tree shit."

An Object Summoner, I realized with a bolt of shock. The stranger squatting next to them was a Summoner, controlling the stick for Fergus, Jenia, and Dazmine's entertainment. Hurting Gileon for fun.

For the first time in—well, ever—pure, undissolved rage flared within my veins.

"Stop it!" I sprang forward, seizing the Summoner's raised hand. Immediately, the stick down below dropped, but I didn't dare let my gaze stray downward to make sure Gileon was okay. "That's sick."

Fergus's eyes narrowed on me as his friend yanked himself out of my grip.

Jenia rose to a stand.

"Look who it is. The girl with the self-righteous stick up her ass. Her friend Quinn told me all about her," she added, turning to the others. "Said she's never stepped a toe out of line and looks down on anyone who does."

"I do not," I seethed—only pausing when Emelle touched me briefly on the back of my arm. *Do not engage.*

"Look," Rodhi said, stepping up beside me, "what you're all doing is a really shit way to have fun. If none of you can think of another way to entertain yourselves besides poking at a fellow classmate like chimps, you're even stupider than you look."

Rodhi made to push past them, but Fergus grabbed him by the collar.

"Look, you twig. I don't care how many friends you have or how smart you think your mouth is. I could snap your bony frame in half, if I wanted."

"Why don't you try, then?" Rodhi bit out.

I groaned, and Emelle shouted, "No!" but too late—

Fergus had nodded at his Summoner friend, who lifted a hand again.

And I felt something like an invisible hook drag me to the ground. Rodhi and Emelle, too, crumpled beside me, until all three of us were flat on our stomachs, our chins grinding into the cobblestone pathway, while Jenia shrieked with glee.

CHAPTER

13

"Let us go," I spat out against the dirt.

How? How could an Object Summoner *choose* to use their power like this? In all my years living with Fabian and Don, I *never* could have imagined them directing their whimsical, witty magic in such a cruel and spiteful way.

"You know, I'm not so sure I want to," Fergus said from above me. "I don't particularly like being called stupid. Or being scolded like I'm a toddler."

"Please," Emelle cried, her neck cranked sideways. "Why are you doing this?"

That newfound rage crawling through my veins... it made me agree with Fergus on one thing: our powers, so far, seemed useless. Because all I wanted to do in that moment was throw a vine around all their throats until they let us go. But I had no idea how to call out for one or ask it for help or direct it in any capacity.

Fergus droned on above us. I focused my vision on the shallow cracks between cobblestones, where a single fire ant was scurrying past my nose.

"Help us," I whispered to it, my breath rough and raw. "Please."

The ant paused and turned to look at me, antennas raised. This close, I could make out the hairs on its head and its mandible flexing in and out.

"Please," I whispered again, just as Fergus gave Rodhi a single kick.

Rodhi grunted. The ant scurried away.

For the next several seconds, I lay pressed against the ground, wincing as Fergus kicked Rodhi again and again. How had it come to this? Why did they—

Fergus's scream cut my thoughts short.

Followed by the screams of Jenia, Dazmine, and the Summoner, too.

As an entire colony of fire ants burst from every crack near the stairwell and surged up each of their legs.

I scrambled to my feet. Emelle helped up Rodhi, who groaned. For a moment, the three of us were frozen in space, watching the chaos unfold before us.

They twisted and hopped and scratched at themselves, shrieking and, for all intents and purposes, looking like four sped-up versions of Gileon's earlier dance. I felt no pity, though, as hives sprouted along every inch of their skin.

Until the Object Summoner seemed to get ahold of himself, and sent the ants flying away—from himself and from the others.

I barely had time to blink. Barely had time to even take a breath before Fergus barreled at me with his hands spread wide.

"You bitch! I know it was you!"

He pounded me into the wall behind me, anchoring my neck to the stone.

My heels jerked up, leaving me on scrambling tiptoes. Blood rushed up my head, and my throat wanted to gag but couldn't.

"Don't you dare," a drawling voice said suddenly.

Fergus released me immediately, his hands flying to his own throat. He gasped, then fell to the ground, flopping about like a fish on sun-baked land.

"Go," the newcomer told Jenia, Dazmine, and the Summoner.

They sprinted off, scratching at their arms and legs, without a backward glance.

I lifted myself from the wall, panting and taking Coen Steeler in.

Real. He was real, not some twisted figment of my imagination. And he was glaring down at the jerking boy at his feet, such fury radiating from him that I almost couldn't speak.

Almost. Chancing a glance at Emelle and Rodhi, who were watching with shock-wide eyes, I asked, "What are you doing to him?"

"Making him think he's drowning," Coen said without looking at me.

I stared, horrified, at Fergus's writhing figure. "Stop it. Now."

"He hurt you." Such a hard, unyielding tone... but Coen wrenched his glare away from Fergus to meet my gaze, and Fergus fell still between our feet, raking in gasp after gasp. "Are you okay?"

I touched my neck, right where a bruise, no doubt, was already purpling.

"I'm fine."

"Hmm." Coen's hand twitched as if he wanted to touch my neck, too. But he clenched it into a fist instead and returned his glare to Fergus. "Don't touch her or her friends ever again, okay? I'm not allowed to kill you, but I *am* allowed to make you wish you were dead."

Fergus nodded, hatred boiling in his eyes, and hoisted himself up.

We all watched him limp away until he was gone.

"So." Coen leaned against the stone wall I'd been pushed against, folding his arms and ignoring Rodhi and Emelle completely. "I missed you at my party last night. I would have thought you'd want to take a tour of my room. I have my own private one, you know, as the Manipulator prince."

Rodhi's eyebrows shot through his hairline before a grin formed on his face. Emelle pressed her lips together.

I, however, stared at Coen, straining to make sense of his words.

A coded message, that's what this was, I was sure—about the pills, maybe? Did I have to take it more than once? Suddenly, I hated myself for telling him to stay out of my head. He'd be able to drop private thoughts into my mind right now if I hadn't.

I cleared my throat, well aware of Rodhi and Emelle clinging on to each word.

"I thought that was a one-time thing?"

Coen studied me carefully. "Some people like it weekly."

Rodhi actually gasped in delight at that. I glared at him, but Coen just pushed himself away from the wall and started down the stairwell. "I'm having another party this Friday," he threw over his shoulder. "I expect to see you there."

Rodhi whipped toward me once Coen had disappeared from view. "What. Was. That?"

"Nothing," I said a little too quickly.

Rodhi scoffed. "He saved you from Mr. Greaseball, told you about his *room*, and said he likes it weekly. You, my darling, are straight up lying right now."

"He said *some* people like it weekly," I muttered, avoiding even Emelle's gaze. From the crooked twist of her mouth, I knew she was thinking about that secret I'd told her in Ms. Pincette's classroom and putting the pieces together.

I bent low to the ground before either of them could say anything else and found a single stray fire ant wandering along a line between cobblestone. "Thank you," I told it, hoping it would relay the message to the rest of its colony—wherever they were, now that the Summoner had blown them away.

Then I started down the stairs, toward the courtyard, without another word.

I had a lot to ponder tonight. How had Coen known I was in trouble? Why hadn't he told me to begin with that I'd need a suppressant pill once a week?

And what was I supposed to do about the damned flutter in my throat at the thought of his gaze on mine?

We found Gileon in the dining hall, sitting alone and sniffling into his plate.

Emelle—timid, shy Emelle—was the one who marched over to him and nodded at our table, where Rodhi and I had just collapsed on either side of Wren to tell her about the day's events. I smiled at the sight of her raised chin, and smiled even wider at the sight of Gileon heaving himself up to follow her to our table.

He sat down. "Hi."

"Hi," we echoed.

"How are you doing?" I asked.

Gileon massaged the back of his neck. "I'm okay. I think there's a ghost in the courtyard, though. It was attacking me after Ms. Pincette's class, and I'm scared it's gonna follow me around forever."

"Oh, don't worry about that," Rodhi said. "Rayna got rid of that ghost."

Gileon turned massive, moon-round eyes on me. "You did?"

"Um... sort of. But not without help." I laid a hand on top of his. "The point is, nobody's ever going to haunt you again, okay?"

I hadn't meant to sound so assertive, because really, how could I prevent someone else from picking on him? But I felt sure that Fergus and the others wouldn't anytime soon, at least, not with the threat of Coen and his Manipulating torture lurking around every corner. None of them had shown up for dinner tonight and I felt smug pleasure at the thought that they were probably getting all their ant burns treated right now.

Gileon leaned his head against the back of his chair. "That is such a relief to hear. I thought I was doomed."

Wren, who'd paused with her fork halfway to her mouth, gave me a look.

A look that clearly said, *you better protect him with everything you've got.*

I nodded. We all nodded. Now that we'd seen what kind of damage the power of others could do, it seemed there was nothing else *to* do besides defend those who couldn't defend themselves. Even if it put a target on our backs.

Because as much as I felt, deep down, that Fergus wouldn't bother messing with Gileon in the near future, I had no doubt he—and Jenia, too—would find ways to mess with Rodhi, Emelle, and me... for interfering, for the fire ants, and for Coen.

Ways that didn't require physical touch. Ways that would hurt even worse.

The rest of that first week passed by in a blur. We learned about the effects of farming in History, helped estuary otters line their dens with leaves in Predators & Prey, laid in the arboretum some more while Mrs. Wildenberg rambled about the meaning of different tunes, and tried to direct worms through mud mazes using different vibrations in our throats while Ms. Pincette frowned at us.

Jenia, Dazmine, and Fergus never looked our way a single time during any of those classes. Apparently, we heard through rippling whispers, they'd been spending each night in the sick bay next to the dining hall, where night medics tended to their ant bites—a relief for me, to not have to sleep five bunks down from Jenia.

An irrational part of me feared I'd wake up to her slitting my throat with my own knife still tucked firmly away under my bunk. The fire ants, after all, had marked her perfect face with oozing red bumps.

Despite the constant, loitering suspicion that I now needed to watch my back at all times, though, I felt a sense of... normalcy sink in. I ate every meal with Wren, Emelle, and Gileon. Rodhi mentioned Ms. Pincette's stunning womanhood about once a day. And Lander stopped by every night to say hi.

A routine. That's what I'd needed to feel at home, and that's what was slowly developing now. Even if it had only been a week since I'd slept in a tree.

Finally, Friday night rolled around, which meant Coen's next party. Lander said that he was going to play a game of pentaball with some of his friends, Wren was downstairs teaching Gileon how to swing a punch (we didn't even ask), and Rodhi was off doing Rodhi things, so Emelle and I found ourselves alone together, contemplating which outfits to wear.

"I think I'm going for a skirt tonight," Emelle said, pulling out a swath of black gauze. "Or should I wear a dress?"

"Hmm. I like the skirt."

I laid out my own outfits from home, biting my lip at the stiffness of each of them. All I had were tunics and pants with collars and buttons and no flare. It had never bothered me until I'd arrived here and seen everyone else wearing so much... less.

Just for one night, I wanted to feel free in my own body.

Emelle glanced at my face.

"Do you want to wear my dress, then? It's a little long for me anyway, but I think it would fit you perfectly. And I can help you refashion some of your own clothes this weekend." I glanced back at her, surprised. "My mom is a seamstress," she clarified. "A Shifter, if you can believe it or not. She grows or shrinks her fingers depending on what size she needs them to be in the moment. I used to help her all the time, even though I was slower at it."

"I would... really like that, Emelle." I smiled. "Thank you."

Five minutes later, I stood in front of the bunkroom wall mirrors, discovering what I looked like in a dress for the first time.

My hair was tamer than usual, thanks to some curling gel Emelle had let me borrow and a fancy clip the shape of a heliconia that she had used to pin the top half of it back. Rather than wild, it merely looked... thick, with rippling waves flowing down to the small of my back. My eyes were outlined in smoky black, and my body—

I felt pleased and terrified at the same time, looking at my body.

Emelle's dress hugged the swell of my breasts and the curve of my hips, flowing outward at my upper thighs. The neckline itself spilled halfway down my cleavage, where each side joined in a row of tiny, descending black pearls.

Pearls that reminded me of the pill I had swallowed five days ago.

"Are you sure you're okay with me wearing this?" I asked Emelle, gulping.

"I'm *more* than okay with it." She cast me a sly look that I knew had everything to do with Coen's cryptic words the other day. I'd refused to answer any of her questions about him, but she knew I was nervous about this party for a very particular reason. "You look beautiful."

I turned to her, surveying her tight, form-fitting top and slitted skirt. "So do you. Okay, let's go, I guess."

We made our way downstairs, out onto Bascite Boulevard, and toward the Mind Manipulator mansion. There, lights flashed from all those little windows, and music, once again, pulsed against the gathering darkness. Up ahead, I could hear the shouts of Lander and his new Shifter friends as they played pentaball. Behind us, the shrieks and laughter of other parties joined the cacophony.

The birds, for once, were silent.

Reeling in a slow breath, I stepped up to the Mind Manipulator entrance, nodded at Emelle, and knocked.

CHAPTER

14

A woman opened the door partway, breathless and stumbling.

"Sector?" she asked with a hiccup, only half her face visible through the crack.

"Whisperer," I said.

"Okay." She slammed the door shut.

"Um," Emelle said, but the next second, we heard the clicking of many locks and the door swung open wide. The woman gestured, and we stepped inside.

It was like stepping into a sky of throbbing stars.

Lights blared and whirled from every corner of the foyer, which was cramped with glittering, sweaty bodies that swayed to the pulse of music. A few people even grinded against each other, and more than a handful of couples were draped over each other on pristine white couches that bordered the room.

"Rayna! Melle!"

Rodhi appeared through the throng, spreading his arms wide. He slung one around each of our shoulders and kissed us both on the foreheads.

"So glad you were able to make it this time!" From the waft of his breath, I could tell he was already drunk. "Come here, I want to show you something."

Grabbing our hands, he tugged us through clumps of bodies, to a counter near a twin staircase in the back, where an upperclassman was pouring drinks into dozens of tiny glass vessels. Rodhi grabbed two and pressed one into each of our hands.

I winced, trying not to let the memories freeze me up. Never, ever again would I drink this stuff. "I'm not a huge fan of bascale, Rodhi."

But Rodhi laughed. "It's not *bascale*. Why would you need *that* stuff when you already have powers? No, this is just pure, uncontaminated ale, my darling."

He was gone again before I could reply, charging at a Mind Manipulator in our year. Emelle giggled, brought her drink to her lips, and swallowed it in two chugs.

I shrugged and was about to taste mine when it was plucked out of my hand.

"Rule number one," drawled a soft, dangerous voice that made the back of my neck prickle, "don't drink random shit at a party when you don't know what might trigger your condition."

Emelle mouthed, "What?" but I shook my head as I turned—and yanked my gaze up to find smoky quartz eyes already rested casually on my face. As if the party bored him, and the flush I could feel climbing up my cheekbones was the only thing interesting enough to look at.

"There are people around," I said in as normal of a voice as I could muster. I wasn't too worried about Emelle—although I'd done my best to keep my secret from even her—but someone else might have heard.

"So?" Coen Steeler passed my vessel of ale off to the nearest random person, who took it without asking a single question. "I'm talking about your liver disease." The crook of his damned mouth kicked up. "Obviously."

"Right." I nodded and glanced at Emelle, who'd never looked more confused.

A moment later, she shook her head as if to clear it and slapped a hand on my arm, her eyes already glazing over. "I'm going to go find Rodhi, okay?"

"Okay."

I watched her wander off and felt a sliver of proud satisfaction at all the heads already turning in her direction, following the sway of her hips.

When she was gone, though, and no one could hear us, I rounded on Coen.

"Liver disease? Really?"

He shrugged, his lips crooking. "You told me to stay out of your head, so I've had to get creative when it comes to getting secret messages across to you."

"Privacy," I bit out. "I'd like some privacy with you. Right now."

I was tired of asking the orchids questions that they refused to answer clearly.

Coen didn't even try to hide his smirk. "At least let me take you on a date first." When I hardened my glare up at him, he sighed. "Okay. Come on. But if anyone asks what I'm doing bringing a first-year into my personal room, I *will* have to say some vulgar things about you that you might not like to hear."

His scrutiny zeroed in on my dress, raking the downward path of the black pearls, as if taking note of exactly what he would say.

I tried to twist my face into a smirk that matched his own. "I can handle that."

Besides, I already had plenty of vulgar things to say about *him*, starting with his broad shoulders and muscled chest. I just wasn't going to say that out loud.

"Very well."

He put one of those hands, gentle yet sturdy, on the small of my back now, guiding me downstairs and through one of the doors opposite the Mind Manipulator dining hall. A few people glanced our way, curiosity raising their eyebrows, but no one stopped to talk to us or ask what we were doing.

That, even though their assumptions were wrong, seemed obvious.

When Coen closed his bedroom door behind us, the thumping music faded.

"Where does that music even come from, anyway?" I asked, trying not to stare too obviously at the details of his room: a king-sized bed layered with dozens of fluffy, white pillows, a vast marble dresser in one corner, and an open archway to a private bathroom in the other—all lit by a single flaming lantern hanging from a hook on the ceiling. The glow of it made the room shimmer with shadows.

Coen folded his arms. His signature stance, it seemed.

"You burst with unexplained power, take a pill from a stranger, join the Wild Whisperers by attracting a magnificent white tiger to your side, get shoved against a wall by the greasiest bully I've ever seen in my life, and demand privacy with a dangerous Mind Manipulator all in your first week at the Institute, and *that's* the first thing you ask? Where the music is coming from?"

I stared at him, waiting—though a small part of me whimpered at what he'd just said: *dangerous* Mind Manipulator. He didn't seem dangerous to me, but then again, I'd just watched him torture Fergus on dry land without lifting a finger.

"The music," Coen said when it became clear I wouldn't retract my question, "is part of a very complex Manipulating charm placed around this house. Anyone who comes near here—near the foyer upstairs, to be exact—will hear it. But it is not real. It's all part of the imagination of the caster, who makes you *think* it's real."

"You said you'd stay out of my head!"

"*I'm* not in your head. My buddy Garvis is. He's the one who cast the charm." Coen stepped toward me, and when I stumbled back, my ass hit the edge of his bed. "Next question. I know you have plenty. I can see them all brewing in your eyes."

I refused to shudder at the thought that he was deciphering—correctly, too—the moods of my eyes.

"Do you have the same power?" I asked, deciding to skip the topic of the pills for now. "Do you have to suppress it, too?"

Coen bowed his head.

Now I *did* shudder. For an entirely different reason.

"Are you and I the only ones?"

Coen grimaced. "No. But if you think I'm going to give you names and jeopardize anyone else's safety, you can—"

"I don't need names," I said quickly. "That's not what this is about. I'm just trying to figure out... how this happened. Where it *came* from."

"So am I," Coen said. When my eyes flared, he added, "I know where *my* power came from, as well as the others'. I don't know where yours came from, though. Which is exactly why I have a couple questions to ask *you* now, little hurricane."

The way he said that nickname, soft but with the edge of that growl I'd heard the night before Branding, made my knees hollow. I sat deeper into the edge of his bed to steady myself.

"I'm not a hurricane."

"Oh, but you *would* be, without the pills."

114

I only pursed my lips at him. "What do you need to know about me?"

"Well, you said you're from a village named Alderwick, right? The one kind of near the Uninhabitable Zone? I looked into it, and it seems Alderwick's about as far as you can get from the coast, save for Belliview and Bascite Mountain itself. So—who the hell are your parents?"

I blinked at him. *I looked into it...* as if he'd been researching me.

"Rayna?" Coen prodded.

"Fabian and Don," I got out. "My parents are Fabian and Don."

He sat down next to me, the bed sagging under our combined weight. I stiffened at the warmth of his body, afraid that if I let myself relax, I'd melt into him.

"Both men, then?" he asked.

"Yes." I raised my chin, unable to keep out a note of defiance.

"And your mother? You don't know anything about her? Who she is?"

The answer was no, but I hesitated. Images of that tarnished knife flipped through my mind. But beyond that singular weapon, which I still didn't know anything about, Fabian hadn't given any real details about my mother beyond the barest basics. I'd asked him plenty of times, and he'd always provided the same clipped response.

I fell in love with a visitor from a coastal village, she fell pregnant, she stayed long enough to give me you, and then she left.

I'd never questioned that Fabian was my biological father, what with all our shared features, but...

"Are you saying you think my mother was a—?"

I couldn't even say the word out loud. Couldn't even stomach it.

Coen dipped his head.

"Are *you* a...?"

115

Pirate's son, I couldn't say... and then all the implications of it rushed out at once.

"But how'd they get through the shield? And I thought they're after our magic, to sell it or use it for themselves? That's why they're always circling the island, right? Why would they even *need* bascite if they already have this... this..." I looked down at my chest, as if I could see the raw power slumbering there. "This *thing*?"

"Well," Coen began slowly, his eyes flicking up to the ceiling as something thumped above us, "first thing's first, that *thing* in both of us can kill if not contained properly, as evidenced by your first experience with it last week. And a weapon is only as good as the wielder, so if you can't even wield it... it would make sense if the pirates are searching for a way to shape their power. To harness it."

"With bascite?"

It didn't make sense. The *pill* was the thing that contained my raw power, not the bascite. The bascite itself had simply given me magic that was already shaped, already harnessed. Right?

Once again, Coen seemed to trace the shifting mood in my eyes, but this time he didn't offer me any answers. He simply turned his gaze to the lines of his hands.

"When we were children, some... others and I were dropped onto one of the coastal villages—Hallow's Perch—about twelve years ago. I don't know how the pirates got us through the shield, but it was supposed to serve as a sort of... distraction. While the other villagers were gawking at us, the pirates tried to cleave through the shield themselves."

"And?" I asked when he fell silent for a moment.

"And their attempt failed." Coen shrugged. "The villagers took pity on us, though. Knowing the Good Council would execute us if they knew where we'd come from, they adopted all of us. Different families, of course, but we continued to grow up together, and it was only when we tried some bascale when we were teenagers that we all just... exploded with that power. And realized our mistake in thinking we'd never be found out when one of us..." His throat bobbed. "I considered him a brother, and he died from it. And I knew I had to find a way to save the rest of us."

"Hence the pills," I said, sensing, somehow, that he didn't want me to acknowledge the brother thing now or anytime soon

"Hence the pills," Coen repeated, relief softening his jaw.

Silence for a beat. In the quiet, the many footsteps thumping overhead seemed to bloom louder. I went rigid, realizing that I'd been angling toward him.

"How often do we have to take the pills?" I asked after a moment.

"Once a week. After a week, if you don't take another one, you'll feel it stir."

As I expected.

"And you... have enough for me? To take every week?"

For some reason, the question cracked something open inside me, leaving a vulnerable, fragile hole. If he *didn't* have enough, there was no way he'd choose me over his lifelong friends.

But Coen said, "Of course I do, Rayna. In fact..." He got up from the bed long enough to rummage through the top drawer of his dresser, then returned with another one. "Just in case I don't see you before Sunday. Take it then."

I accepted the pill from him, daring to turn, to face him fully. So many questions tipped the edge of my tongue. How did the children of pirates break through the shield when the pirates themselves couldn't? Was Coen content to never talk to his parents again, never know what had happened to them? And another thing—*I knew I had to find a way to save the rest of us...* that implied he himself had made the pills, somehow, right?

117

But maybe I could read his moods, too, because I knew from the way his speckled brown eyes had hardened, like molten quartz solidifying, that he didn't trust me enough to tell me those things. Yet.

So I just said, "I give you permission from now on." When he arched a brow, I amended, "Only to talk to me mind-to-mind. Not to change my perception or erase my memories or... whatever you did to Fergus the other day."

And that quickly, his eyes became molten again, churning with liquid rage.

"I would *never* do that to you. Never—"

The door burst open, and suddenly Coen was on top of me.

Kissing me.

His mouth fused with mine. His tongue swept away every retort on my lips, the taste of him filling me with something exotic and dark—like the space between stars.

"Oh. Am I interrupting?"

Coen rolled off me lazily and sat up, swiping a few fingers through his mussed-up hair. I sat up, too, panting, dizzy, confused, and... perked. Wanting.

But there, in Coen's doorway, stood Kimber with that parakeet on her shoulder. The princess of my house, and Jenia's older sister.

Her eyes narrowed on me before rounding on Coen.

"I didn't realize you'd... expanded your tastes."

Ugly. Vile. That's what I was under Kimber's gaze. Nothing but a slug we'd study in Ms. Pincette's class. I crossed my arms over my chest, near tears.

"Did you barge in here to criticize my choice in women, Kimber, or is there something else you need to tell me? Because I'd really like to get back to—"

"There's a fight upstairs," Kimber said through gritted teeth. "You're needed."

Indeed, a series of smashing and banging echoed over our heads, rattling the lantern on its hook and flinging that flickering light in every direction.

Coen sighed at the ceiling. "I see. Fine." Turning toward me, he placed a finger under my chin, lifted it, and drawled, "Until next time, little hurricane."

Then he strolled after Kimber, who threw me a look of deepest disgust over her shoulder just as her parakeet squawked a single word at me. "*Slut!*"

Leaving me sitting on his bed, the pill still in my hand and my breath a tousled mess in my lungs.

CHAPTER

15

I'm sorry about that.

His voice was in my head by the time I climbed into my top bunk that night, Emelle already snoring beneath me. But how was I supposed to talk back to him?

Just like you're doing now.

Even in the confines of my mind, that damned voice was a gentle, growl-tipped caress, and... it chuckled as I thought that.

Okay, maybe I don't *want you to talk to me mind-to-mind,* I thought, trying to block out every mental image of him on top of me, of the feel of his—shit. No. I couldn't be remembering this while he lounged in my mind, couldn't let him know that the taste of his tongue still filled my mouth, that dark and exotic...

Don't worry, came his unhurried voice. *Every woman at the Institute wants to have a good tumble with me.*

I scoffed against my pillow. *I think you're too big for your own britches.*

Oh, much too big, he agreed. *I was ready to bust out of my pants with the feel of you squirming beneath me.* A quick laugh at the blush that oozed into my mind, but then his voice sobered. *I'm only sorry that you didn't choose it for yourself. I couldn't let anyone think we were doing more than —*

I know, I thought back, rather quietly for being in my own mind.

Because while Kimber's disgust was painful, her suspicion might have been detrimental—for me and the mysterious others that Coen was protecting.

Did you... I rolled over in bed as some other girls tiptoed into the bunkroom, whispering loudly. *Did you ever date her? Kimber? She seemed sort of angry.*

Thankfully, Kimber had her own private bedroom, too, as a fifth-year and our house's princess. Unlike Jenia, who was due to return to the bunkroom any night now, I'd never have to worry about Kimber hovering over me while I slept.

Silence in my head, though I still felt his presence: a mass of sly strength.

Coen?

I like it when you say my name, he finally chuckled. *And yes, we did. For three years. But I don't want to dwell on it any more than I have already.*

Three years? Any hope that I might be something special to him deflated like a popped tire. Compared to three years, I was a speck of nothing and no one.

You are not nothing.

Right. I'm a pirate's daughter. A pirate who abandoned me as soon as she—wait. My thoughts stuttered as the realization hit me. *If my mother was a pirate, then she got through the shield undetected. And stayed for nine whole months without anyone ever suspecting her of being an outsider.*

Yes, said Coen.

It had already occurred to him, of course... although he'd had a week to mull it over whereas I'd only had a few hours. The implications of a pirate successfully breaching our dome...

Do you think she's still on the island, I asked after a breath, *or do you think she made it back through the shield?*

Coen's presence seemed to hesitate. Beneath me, Emelle gave a violent snore.

I think, he started slowly, *there's no way of knowing for sure unless your father can give you more information about your birth. Perhaps you could send him a letter, asking him?*

I blinked against the darkness. A letter. Why hadn't I thought of that already? No messengers traveled between the Institute and other villages, but surely, I could befriend a bird who would deliver it for me?

Perhaps my gift had its merits, after all.

I will first thing tomorrow. And... and I'll let you know what he says.

I couldn't see a reason to distrust Coen. He'd saved me more than once, let me in on his secret, and led me to understand my own. We were from the same people, and in equal danger if the Good Council ever found out about what loitered beneath our skin.

Great, Coen said, as if he hadn't heard every rationalization I'd just waded through. *Then I'd better leave you be so you can get your beauty's rest.*

I pushed it way, way down—the desire to ask him to stay.

Goodnight, I said, all confidence and ease.

Goodnight. And Rayna? Coen's voice sharpened to a lethal quiet. *I can't get the taste of you out of my mouth either.*

The next morning, when the birds chirped at us to wake up as they did every morning, the other women shushed them before rolling over and sinking back into soft, even breathing. No classes today meant sleeping in for most of them.

Not me, though.

I slipped out of bed and shook Emelle by the shoulder.

"Hey, Melle, I'm going for a walk, okay? I should be back around noon."

She waved a sloppy hand, still reeking of ale. After leaving Coen's room last night, I'd found her dancing within a swarm of guys, swaying much too violently for my liking, so I'd brought her home and put her to bed.

"You do you, Rayna," she said now, her words merging with another snore before she'd even lowered her hand.

I got dressed as quietly as possible, then slipped downstairs. Just as I reached the landing to the foyer, a braided, black head appeared at the top of the staircase leading downward. Dazmine. I almost stopped in my tracks, but decided to round the corner without saying anything. To pretend I hadn't seen her.

"Watch your step," came Dazmine's voice, softer than I had expected.

I paused, glancing downward for some kind of obstacle on the floor. There was nothing. I whirled back toward her, where she, too, had paused on the landing.

"Was that a threat, Dazmine?"

Her eyes bore into mine. Behind her, the cuckoo clock gave a mechanic chirp, signaling that it was eight in the morning. For a second, I thought Dazmine wouldn't answer. Then...

"A warning," she whispered, and hurried upstairs.

I was still thinking about that as I settled into one of the polished wooden chairs in the study chamber, which was tucked away at the end of a hallway leading from the foyer.

Here, dozens of desks sat against the walls, stocked with papers and fountain pens. I grabbed one of each and stared at the blank piece of paper.

What to write him? How to word it so that no one besides Fabian — and Don—could understand what I was asking if it happened to get intercepted?

As I was tapping the pen against my chin, a small voice squeaked, *"What are you doing up so early?"*

I followed the voice to the windowsill, where a mouse perched on the ledge.

"Writing a letter," I said, too surprised to think of anything but the truth. Why was I surprised, though? This was my new normal, wasn't it?

"I wish I could write letters," the mouse said, rather mournfully for such a squeaky little thing.

"Really?" I couldn't help but let myself get wrapped up in this conversation. "Do you have friends or family far away? Perhaps I can send a message for you."

"No," said the mouse, *"all my friends and family live in the walls with me. But if I had hands to write a letter, I'd have hands to grab all the cheese in the cupboards."*

"Oh." That wasn't what I'd been expecting. I returned to contemplating my letter, until the mouse scrambled closer, stopping at the head of my paper.

"I could help you word your letter if you get me some cheese from the kitchen."

I blinked at it. "Thank you... so much. But this is rather a private letter..."

The mouse blinked back at me. "*Private? I can't imagine why you're doing it so early in the morning, but aren't you writing to your father Fabian to find out more about your heritage? Or am I mistaken?*"

My mouth fell wide open. I dropped my pen.

"How did you know that?"

The mouse cheeped its equivalent of a scoff.

"*We mice hear everything that goes on between every house's walls. We just don't sell that information like those horrible eight-legged beasts do.*" It shuddered. "*But it's a good thing you told Coen Steeler to communicate with you via mind from now on, because my friends and family can't be there every time to kill the spiders listening in on your secrets.*"

When I continued to gawk at the mouse, its tail twitched.

"*We killed them for you,*" it said slowly, as if it thought I might be stupid, "*three bold jumpers, one woodlouse, and a crab spider. That monster from the Good Council sent them to spy on Mr. Steeler, but they usually never catch anything of importance because he's always spoken to his other friends mind-to-mind about important matters. Last night was the first night they learned anything of substance. But we killed them before they could scuttle away and report anything.*"

Still, I gawked, even as the horrifying realization swelled inside me.

Dyonisia Reeve suspected Coen... of what, though? Did she know he and his friends had come from beyond the island's shield? Or did she simply suspect him of hiding a deeper magic than his bascite-granted Mind Manipulating one?

And another thing—I'd thought Dyonisia was a Shape Shifter, not a Wild Whisperer. Unless... maybe she had such a tight grip on the other

Good Council elites that she'd asked one of them to send spider spies for her and translate their findings.

"What's your name?" I asked the mouse finally.

"*Willa*," it replied promptly. A female, then.

"Well, Willa, I will give you cheese every day of your life if you help me with this letter—and alert me to any suspicious spiders creeping in for a closer listen. You don't have to kill them. Just tell me if they're there."

Willa didn't even pause to consider.

"*Deal. Now, here's what I want you to write.*"

Half an hour later, after finishing the letter to Fabian and sneaking into the kitchen for some cheese, I finally started outside for my morning walk—to the Element Wielder house down the street.

I had exactly three tasks left for today: find a bird to send the letter for me, see if I could talk to Quinn, and catch a crab for my crocodile friend in the swamp (calling him a friend helped with the nerves.)

Three tasks. If I did it right, I didn't see why I couldn't merge them into one.

So on my way to Quinn's house, I threw my head skyward, where gray clouds were stirring. "Hey, you!" I cried to some neon green honeycreepers chasing each other above the rooftops. "Can one of you come down here for a second? I have a question."

Three of them flitted down and zipped around my head as I walked.

"*Yes?*"

"*Yes?*"

"*Yes?*"

"Do you think one of you could send this letter for me? To my father in Alderwick?" I held out the sealed envelope... which looked much too big for a honeycreeper.

"*Oh, no, we're not strong enough for that,*" one of them chirped. "*But hold on! Let me get one of the crows. They're too bored and grumpy for their own good anyways. They need something to do.*"

All three of them whizzed away.

I stopped, waiting in the middle of Bascite Boulevard, until one of the honeycreepers returned with a large-billed crow, who flapped itself to my feet.

"*What do you want?*" the crow squawked.

"To ask if you would send a letter for me."

Willa had told me back in the study chamber that though birds of all species were social creatures, they didn't affiliate with any one side of a human conflict and therefore could be trusted to deliver a message—but only if they felt like it. I was not to goad any of them too much.

The crow cocked its head. "*Say please.*"

Okay, then. If that was what he wanted...

"Please, oh mighty crow, would you brave the rough and stormy skies to send a letter for me? I would be eternally grateful."

I'd meant to dramatize it, but even as I said it, a raindrop plopped on my head.

The crow's beak seemed to smile. "*I don't need that much pizazz, but since you asked nicely... sure. Name and address?*"

After I had given him instructions and he'd clamped the letter in his talons, I added, "If you happen to see the tiger Jagaros on your journey, tell him I say hi!"

"*Absolutely not.*" The crow ruffled his feathers. "*We aerial creatures do not dare speak to the king of Eshol. He would tear our beaks off just for sport.*"

And the crow flew away, up into the drizzling sky.

I stood there, staring after him as rain peppered my face. King of Eshol? Neither Mr. Fenway nor Mr. Conine had ever mentioned a monarchy among the animals of the island, and Jagaros himself had certainly never mentioned being king... although I supposed there hadn't been much time for him to give me much backstory, what with the crowds of thousands staring at us.

I made a mental note to ask my instructors about it on Monday— or maybe I'd just ask Willa once I made it back to the house—and turned toward Quinn's again.

Only to find her already standing there in the street, facing me.

CHAPTER

16

"Quinn?"

I stepped toward her, wiping a string of wet hair from my face.

Something was off about her appearance. She still wore party clothes, and though her ruby-red hair was slightly more ruffled than usual, it was... dry, I realized. Quinn was dry.

She let me approach and, when I'd stopped before her, said, "Rayna. How nice to see you." The words didn't match her tone, though, as if a wary mask shielded her true feelings. "I was going back to my house when I saw you...?"

The silence stretched, and I realized she was asking for an explanation.

"A crow," I said rather lamely. "I was talking to a crow."

"Oh. Right. Wild Whisperer now, and all that."

"Yes."

This was not at all how I'd imagined our reunion would go. Even after what had happened with Lander, I hadn't expected her to go from obliviously carefree with me the night before Branding to... whatever this was.

I gestured at her dry hair, desperate to return a sense of normalcy to our conversation.

"It looks like you've got good control of the rain already. That's so cool!"

"What?" Quinn looked down at herself. "Oh, yeah. I can make the water sort of... skirt around me, leave me alone. I'm not advanced enough to make an umbrella for you, too, though, I'm afraid."

"It's okay." I waved a hand. Breathed.

She said, "Well, I'd better—"

"Will you go hunt a crab with me?" I cut in.

Quinn's mask didn't reveal a flicker of surprise, but she said, "What?"

Briefly, I explained the deal I'd made with the crocodile.

To my relief—and terror, as if part of me had been hoping she'd say no—Quinn shrugged. "Sure, I guess. I've been meaning to visit the beach anyway."

Silently, we began walking side by side toward the Testing Center. Behind it, I'd heard, there would be a stone staircase leading down to the shore. Although we weren't allowed to mess with the shield, we were allowed to dip our toes in the sea.

I spent the entire ten-minute walk there trying to come up with a way to broach the subject of Lander, constantly wiping the rain from my eyes. But even that subject dropped from my mind when we finally rounded the enormous Testing Center and came to the top of that staircase sandwiched between wrought-iron lampposts.

"Wow," was all I could say.

I'd known there was a drop down to the ocean, but I must not have gotten a good enough look from that carriage in the sky. I saw it now, though. Stared down at it and felt a swoop of dizzying fear. Because the

Esholian Institute campus was truly perched on the edge of a cliff that went down and down and down.

Even the staircase had to zigzag as it descended, hugging the cliff's edge with little more than a flimsy wooden handrail. And down below... Quinn and I had always mused about the white, sandy beaches we'd get to lounge on at the Institute, but down below was the furthest thing from white and sandy you could get.

Rocks, sharp and spiky, cluttered the ground. Only a narrow strip of gritty sand, dark gray in the rain, separated those rocks from the clash of the sea.

Beyond it, of course, the air shimmered with the domed shield, and even from here I could see the pirate ships dotting the waves past it. Was my mother out there with them, wondering what had ever happened to her lover and daughter? Or was she still somewhere on Eshol, avoiding me on purpose, keeping her identity hidden?

A streak of lightning in the distance made me blink. Made me remember myself and who I was with and what I had to do.

"Element Wielders first?" I said, in an attempt to get Quinn to smile.

She didn't. She just began the march downward, and I followed.

When we were near enough to the bottom that I could breathe again, I finally said, "So who'd you spend the night with?"

Not that it was my business, but... we had once told each other everything. And maybe it would be a good way to segway to Lander.

Quinn shrugged.

"Some Object Summoner, I think. I woke up in the Summoner house, at least." She stepped down from the last ledge of the staircase and nodded out at the shimmering dome. "Someone from my house tried to mess with it last night. The shield. He shot a spear of ice at it to see what it would do. It only rippled for a moment, but the princess of my house electrocuted him twelve times as punishment. In front of everyone."

"Oh. Wow. That's horrible." I stepped down after her, wondering why she'd told me *that*, of all things. We began picking our way through the rocks, toward the ebbing tide. Down here, a thick mist clung to even Quinn's clothes, and the rain came down harder than ever.

"Why..." I cleared away the accusation in my voice. "Why didn't you at least break up with Lander before moving on?"

Without looking at me, Quinn said, "I couldn't find him. The three of us stepped out of that carriage and got separated immediately, remember?"

Now the accusation crept back up my throat, because what kind of an excuse was that?

"You didn't even try," I said quietly.

She stopped. Turned to me. A single bead of rain broke through her own personal shield and rolled down her forehead.

"Don't you dare," she said, "try to tell me what I did or didn't do, Rayna. Just because *you* couldn't fathom making a single new friend didn't mean *I* was going to whine and whimper until I'd found you two."

Heat rushed up my chest at that. From the corner of my eye, I saw yellowish-brown crabs lifting their tiny shelled heads from the sand to observe us and talk to each other in quick, clicking whispers.

"*Look!*"

"*A faerie?*"

"*No. One of those invasive humans from the school!*"

Ignoring them, I shook my head at Quinn.

"What happened to you?"

She tipped her head back in a laugh.

"You wouldn't understand, Rayna. You've always been content to stay small."

Even the crabs hushed.

"Excuse me?" I breathed.

Quinn wrinkled her nose. "I said what I said. You never wanted to come here to the Institute. You always planned to return to Alderwick and live the rest of your life alongside your fathers. You never wanted any friends beyond me and Lander. But *I* did." Something foreign lit in her eyes. "I wanted out. I wanted more."

I shut down the heat, the mortification, the anger. Let the pounding of the rain wash warm fury over me instead

"I didn't realize we were using human beings as stepping stones to make ourselves feel bigger, Quinn. Loving my fathers, wanting to stay friends with you and Lander... those things don't mean I'm small. It just means my love for you all is big." I paused to collect my breath. "Humans aren't just objects to discard when you grow bored of them."

A dry laugh. "They are if they hold you back."

In the distance, another bolt of lightning cracked through the clouds, and Quinn pressed on before I could respond.

"You *knew*, Rayna. You knew how my mom treated me. You knew the hell I went through with her back at home. Having her constantly in my mind, controlling everything I did... it erased my sense of self, and you *knew* that. Yet you know where I saw you heading to last night when I came to see you?"

I didn't say anything, but understanding flashed through me.

"The Mind Manipulator house," Quinn said grimly. "A Mind Manipulator abused your best friend for years, but you're choosing to fraternize with them now."

"Quinn—"

"I also," she persisted, "heard what you did to Jenia and the others. Were you jealous of my friendship with her? Is that why you made the ants attack?"

"I didn't." I shook my head to clear it. "I did, but they were harassing a—"

"Oh, spare me your self-righteous bullshit, Rayna. You. Hurt. Them. And there is no excuse for hurting people."

Faster than my heart could even stop, Quinn struck out with her hand.

I flinched, but the fire that erupted from her palm sped toward one of those crabs instead.

The rest of the creatures burrowed back into the sand, but that single unlucky one... it lay blackened and motionless among the rocks now.

"There you go," Quinn said. "A crab for your crocodile. Glad I could help." She turned back toward the zigzagging stone staircase. "See you around, Rayna."

I watched her go, thoroughly drenched now, only relaxing my shoulders once she'd disappeared over the cliff's edge high above me.

Then I sat on a rock by the dead crab and watched the waves crash onto the gritty land before me and the lightning splinter through the clouds. I gazed at the pirate ships where my mother might or might not be staring back in my direction.

It was only when the other crabs rose again, this time to observe the scorched one of their kind at my feet, that I cried.

And cried.

And cried.

CHAPTER

17

On Sunday, the sky was still damp and draped in clouds.

I took my pill. I hauled the dead crab—which our house cook had let me keep in the kitchen ice box overnight—to the crocodile swamps and threw it in. I snuck Willa some more cheese and asked her if she knew anything about Jagaros being king, to which she merely squeaked and scurried away.

I shrugged. It was hard to care, with Quinn's words hanging so heavily over my shoulders. I hadn't slept with those words scooping out my insides all night.

A Mind Manipulator abused your best friend for years, but you're choosing to fraternize with them now.

You have always been content to stay small.

You. Hurt. Them.

"Rayna?"

It was Emelle, followed by Lander. I turned from where I'd been leaning against our bunkroom's balcony railing, watching the lazy Sunday afternoon strolls of people down below, to force a smile at them.

"Are you okay?" she asked.

I almost said yes. Almost said I was fine. Then a stray tear skidded down my cheek, and I said, "I don't know. I..." I hesitated, feeling the weight of Lander's eyes. I didn't want to dig deeper into his wounds by telling him what Quinn had said about us, but I also... needed to know if she was right about all the other things.

Emelle leaned against the balcony beside me, and Lander drifted to my other side.

"Tell us," she said softly. "You've been off all weekend. Did something happen with...?"

She widened her eyes a bit, and I realized she meant Coen. That was the last time she'd seen me acting normally before my conversation with Quinn, after all—at the party, talking to Coen. The few minutes I'd spent hunting her down and taking her to bed didn't count, since she'd been too drunk to walk straight.

"No, Coen's fine. It's just... was I out of line, with Jenia and the others? Was I... evil for turning the ants on them and hurting them like that?"

Emelle passed a worried glance to Lander over my head.

"As kindly as possible, Rayna, what the hell are you talking about? Of course you weren't out of line! They had us pinned to the ground. You saved us."

"They didn't *all* have us pinned to the ground," I countered. "That Object Summoner did. Maybe I should have told the ants to bite *only* him until he let us go."

"Out with it, Rayna," Lander said, a hint of exasperation breaking through his gentle demeanor. "What's got you troubled about this?" He'd heard, of course, what had happened with the ants. Everyone on campus had heard, though I was sure the story had inflated with exaggeration the more it was passed from ear to ear.

Something broke free in my chest when he placed a steady hand on my upper back. Emelle, too, grabbed my arm, and I just... let it out. Every detail and word of what had happened on that rocky shore.

When I was done, Emelle was visibly cringing, and the blood had drained from Lander's face.

"She really said you and I were holding her back?" he asked.

"Not exactly. She just said that people should be discarded if they hold you back. And she's sort of discarded us, so I just assumed... *have* we been holding her back, Lander?" I pressed a desperate stare onto him. "Can you think of a time back in Alderwick where she—I don't know—said she wanted to go do something and we told her no, or wouldn't do it with her, or made her feel unimportant?"

"No..." Lander said slowly. "She always told me she wanted to relocate to Belliview after our Final Test if the Good Council would allow it, take some painting classes from the city's finest artists, and I said... I said I'd go with her."

When shadows seemed to claw at his eyes, I knew what a sacrifice that had been for him, to tell Quinn that, especially since everyone expected him to take over as mayor one day. And like me, he wasn't good with change.

"I think," Emelle spoke up, "that you both deserve better anyway."

She didn't balk or flinch when Lander and I jerked our heads her way. In fact, she raised her chin and... was that a clenched jaw? Tightening *Emelle's* face?

"You two are the kindest, most thoughtful people I've met in a long time," Emelle plunged on, "and if she doesn't think you're worth your weight in gold, then you both deserve someone who does. I agree with you, Rayna, that people shouldn't just be abandoned on a whim... but they *should* be let go if they're choosing to fill your soul with poison."

That hardened face, I knew suddenly, came from her experience with her ex-boyfriend. The way he'd treated her—it would have fossilized something crucially soft in her, if she hadn't got away.

And perhaps that was what Quinn's words would do to me, if I kept trying to get her back. If I kept ruminating on what I'd done wrong and what I could have changed in the past and how we'd gotten to this rotting, wretched point.

It was Lander who said, "Thank you, Emelle." I opened my mouth to say it, too, when Coen's voice brushed against the inside of my mind.

What's wrong?

Nothing's wrong, I managed to think through my surprise. And I *was* feeling the tiniest shade better.

You feel sad. Or relieved? I can't tell.

Are you always perusing people's minds to spy on their feelings?

No, he chuckled. *But your mind happens to be unnaturally interesting.*

I didn't know what to say to that as warmth coiled around my body. Thankfully, Coen continued without waiting for a response.

And I was going to invite you to play pentaball against some friends of mine and me, but if you're going to take that tone...

Pentaball sounds great, I thought immediately. A distraction — that's what I needed right now. Against *you, though? Not* with *you?*

Nah, I think I'll enjoy making you flush with some nice, cathartic anger when I beat you. Besides, he added, *I have my team already. You get yours and meet me on the field in five minutes.*

And just like that, his smug presence left my head. Oh, how I'd love to wipe away that smile that was surely crooking his mouth right now.

I turned to Emelle and Lander.

"Feel up for a little game?"

After we'd rounded up Rodhi, Wren, and Gileon, the six of us made it to the field arena just as Coen showed up with four others.

"We're playing against *them*?" one of his teammates said incredulously, examining all of us from head to toe and stroking his mustache. He had a narrow face, and his hair was tied back in a ponytail.

Wren scoffed at the assessment and marched over to the nearest section of the stadium, where she said she'd be content watching us mutilate each other. Each team technically only needed five players anyway; members beyond the basic five were considered backups.

Because pentaball, even without magic, got ugly. Quinn, Lander, and I had gotten our fair share of scratches and bruises playing in the streets back at home. I shuddered to think what the game would be like now with all our powers.

I didn't shudder, however, at the idea of what Quinn might think if she saw me playing it with Coen and the others. Surely, she had to know that not *all* Mind Manipulators used their powers like her mother had.

Still, I felt a tremor of guilt at the thought that I hadn't helped her more. Hadn't told Fabian and Don more about her troubles at home. Maybe something could have been done. Maybe Quinn's mother would have stopped.

Coen's voice grazed my mind.

Come back to me, little hurricane.

Quit eavesdropping on my internal dialogues.

There you are. I could have sworn his voice was *smiling*. I almost smiled back, when I remembered—

Did you know the Good Council has been spying on you? I made a mouse friend who said she killed some spiders in your room.

Apparently, they were going to report back to Dyonisia Reeve about our entire conversation.

I felt Coen's shock flit across my mind, but it was gone in another instant.

I'm not surprised. My breakup with Kimber last dry season got pretty ugly and sort of... put us both on their radar. It probably has nothing to do with the pills and everything to do with the fact that Dyonisia Reeve likes to spy on anyone who demonstrates a tad too much power—even lawful power.

What... I tried not to let my own shock ripple through my mind. *What was so ugly about your breakup that it caught the entire Good Council's attention?*

Another time, maybe. I don't want to think about it right now.

As if we hadn't just had a private conversation, Coen flicked a thumb at his narrow-faced friend. "This is Garvis, a Mind Manipulator like me."

Okay, then. Another time was fine by me, and it was really none of my business anyway. Still, though, I felt a little queasy at the thought that social drama could trigger Dyonisia's attention.

Coen nodded at the two identical women behind him, who had high-angled cheekbones and skin darker than Lander's. "These are Sasha and Sylvie, both Object Summoners. Twins, of course. And this is Terrin, my favorite Element Wielding maniac." He gestured at a man with a ruddy beard, grizzled hair past his shoulders, and an overall unkempt look, who grinned at us and rubbed his hands together.

I couldn't help but raise an eyebrow, surprised that they weren't all in the same sector. Were these the other nameless pirate children who'd grown up with him?

You're a little too astute for your own good, Coen scolded me in my head.

140

Ignoring that, I pointed at each of my own friends.

"This is Melle, Lander, Gileon, and... Rodhi?" I turned. Rodhi had taken a few steps toward the twins and was now... circling them.

"Which one of you did I make out with under the stadiums that first night? I didn't know there were two of you!"

Sylvie—no, Coen had said that one was Sasha—raised a finger. "That was me."

Rodhi's face slackened with incredulousness.

"But you told me you were a third-year Mind Manipulator! I thought that's the only reason our sector was invited to all the Mind Manipulator parties, because you're part of the house!"

Sasha shrugged. "I lied."

Coen cut off Rodhi's next inhale, rushing through his next words. "Everyone knows how to play pentaball, I'm assuming?" He nodded at Terrin, who unslung a mesh bag from his shoulder and dumped twelve items on the grass: ten balls—each ranging from smooth-surfaced and pale yellow to bumpy and bright turquoise—and two half-moon discs on metal plates.

Emelle had told me back at the house that she'd never played before, but it was Gileon who said, in his slow, low-pitched voice, "Four balls for each team, right?"

"Five," Coen corrected without blinking, although Garvis furrowed his brows at the obvious misstep in simple addition. "Each team gets one disc and five balls. Every ball has to make it through the disc on your opponents' side of the field."

"Whichever team gets all five balls in their opponents' disc first," Terrin said with a savage grin, "wins."

Emelle scratched at her arm nervously. "Does it matter how we get it in? Kicking or throwing?"

Lander spoke up before the others could, turning toward her. "There are no rules in that regard, but..." He angled closer to her, lowering his voice, "most people choose to fling it in underhand. More accuracy that way."

She nodded, just as Coen said, "The only true rule is you can't use magic on the ball. It has to go through the disc by means of your actual hand or foot... or whatever body part you want to use." At this, Coen's smirk actually seemed to brush up and down my body, as if reminding me of the various body parts I could use in other ways. I stuck out my tongue, and he continued with a smile nipping at his mouth, "So Sasha and Sylvie can't guide a ball through with their invisible Summoning hands, and Terrin can't send it in on a gust of wind."

Rodhi finally tugged his awe-struck gaze from the twins.

"I think we should add a new rule just for this particular match." He leveled a stare at Coen—a significant feat considering that Coen was two heads taller and packed with three times more muscle. "Everyone is only allowed to use first-year magic."

"Deal," Coen said immediately, to my surprise.

And to the others' surprise as well, apparently, because Terrin cursed as he stomped off to go set up the discs, the twins traded grimaces, and Garvis stopped stroking his mustache.

Rodhi, Lander, and Emelle, however, looked significantly more cheered as they each picked up a ball. I grabbed an orange, dully spiked one and handed the last one—warty and toad green—to Gileon, who was scratching at a spot on his head as if still dissecting the rules.

Coen's team grabbed their own balls and lined up to face us.

I glanced to the sidelines, where Wren gave us all a mocking thumbs-up. I could tell from her twisted expression that she thought us all the vilest of creatures for wanting to play with balls in a muddy field.

Perhaps we were.

142

"Ready?" Coen said, shifting himself into a predatory stance.

I can't wait to see what kind of magic baby Coen could do once upon a time, I crooned, knowing he was in my head and wanting to catch him off guard.

He didn't even blink. *I can't wait to show you.*

"Set," he said aloud, and everyone crouched, poised. "Go!"

I lunged into my first running step.

Coen didn't target me first, but went straight for Emelle, who hadn't yet moved. I flew past him, pounding the grass with a lengthening stride, eyes set on the disc at the other end of the field...

The ground bucked beneath my feet.

I pitched forward, falling on my knees.

"Sorry!" came Terrin's gruff, gleeful voice from behind me—which meant he'd decided to steal my ball before making a run for our disc.

Good.

I sent a quick, three-note whistle to the grass before I rolled and scrambled into a run again. Mrs. Wildenberg hadn't yet taught us how to communicate with plants, only what their songs meant, but I had to try, didn't I? And I remembered how she'd said three short whistles in a row encouraged them to grow *very* quickly.

A curse and a thump behind me, and I knew it had worked. The grass had shot up around Terrin and wrapped around his ankles.

His ball went flying to my left, and after half a second's thought, I veered toward it, scooping it up with my free arm.

Only to feel a tug, like an anchor rooting itself deep into my core. Ten paces away, Sasha flashed me a wicked grin and held out her hands expectantly.

I felt it, then, the pull that neither Fabian nor Don had ever deigned to use on me: Summoning magic wrapping its tendrils around every

143

part of my body and urging me to follow its wafting path, right into Sasha's extended hands.

But just then, Lander barreled past on four furry legs, still clutching his ball with an unchanged human hand—to abide by the rules, I was willing to bet, so that he could roll his ball into the disc with a non-magically altered body part.

"Lander!" I chucked one of my balls at him, unable to resist Sasha's pull.

Lander caught it with his free hand mid-leap, made it to the enemy disc, and flung both his and mine through.

By the time I stumbled to Sasha against my will, she only had one ball to steal.

And so the dance continued.

Rodhi was circling Sylvie. Gileon, still hugging his original toad green ball to his chest, was swinging his heavy arms at Garvis, who frowned at him as he tried to snatch the ball away. Emelle was circling the middle of the field, unsure of where to go, and Coen... Coen was at our disc, flinging his third ball through.

"SHIT ALL OVER THEM!" came Rodhi's sudden roar.

The kingfishers twirling over the match obliged with laughs that sounded a lot like *tee, hee, hee!*

Fat white clumps rained down, hitting each of our opponents on the top of their heads.

I took my chance. Catching up to Sasha, I reclaimed my ball while she was busy wiping filth from her eyes, and swiveled around—

To come face to face with Coen, who must have looped around to block me.

"Not so fast." He clicked his tongue, but I couldn't take him seriously with the crown of shit splattered over his head and oozing down

144

his shoulders. I laughed, and he turned toward the nearest twin. "Hey, Sasha, can you transfer all this bird poop onto Rayna's head instead?"

"No!" I cried.

In a flash, Sasha's magic had siphoned all the filth from his hair and body—but mercifully, she'd flung it all to the ground rather than on to me like Coen had asked.

I back-pedaled.

Coen followed casually, a predator hunting prey. There were only two balls left on the field now, my team's right here in my arms and his team's in Sylvie's, so I knew he was playing defense... but right now it was *me* who felt defensive.

"As you should," he said aloud, all haughtiness and ease from having heard my thoughts. "It's a good thing you have a Shape Shifter on your team, or we would've smoked you within minutes."

"I don't know," I called, still back-pedaling—toward *his* disc, dammit. I'd need to find a way to get around him. "I thought the birds came in handy."

He was grinning now. "So does the fact that we're all holding back, I'm sure."

I stopped, right before my heels hit his disc.

"You're toying with me."

"Absolutely," he agreed, and... were his hands actually sliding in his pockets right now? As if he hadn't a care in the world and felt so confident he could catch me that he wanted to savor the moment?

Behind him, Sylvie had come sprinting toward us with her ball, but Rodhi chased her right into Gileon's waiting arms, who carefully took the ball and held it out to Lander, who began to leap away with it on shifted hind legs... only to slam into a pillar of solid ice from Terrin.

145

Coen, meanwhile, wasn't even making a move to steal my ball from me. He simply cocked his head, observing me like you'd look at a menu in a village diner.

"You know, this isn't a good strategy, whatever you're doing," I seethed.

"Isn't it?" He was past a smirk now, his grin widening into full-blown glee. "You seem so disarmed right now that you're not even trying to make a run for it. Which means I've got you trapped here, across the field, which means your team can't win."

Shit. He was right.

But for some reason, my feet didn't want to move when I knew he'd pounce as soon as I so much as twitched.

"How about this, little hurricane?" He leaned toward me, so that I had to crane my neck to look up. "I'll give you a ten second head start. I'm curious to see how fast you can run, anyway."

Dare I call him a bastard? I threw up my best glare. "Fine."

"Run," Coen whispered.

CHAPTER

18

I shoved past him and ran.

This time, Terrin was too busy to trip me up with a sudden swell of ground, and the twins were thoroughly distracted by a whooping, weaving Rodhi to tug me toward them. I made it halfway to our disc without anyone noticing me when Coen's voice filled the empty spaces in my mind, and I knew he'd begun his chase.

You're faster than I thought you'd be, I'll give you that.

I get it from my mother, I shot back without forethought—not because I knew that for certain, but because Fabian had never been the athletic type. And even if he'd been my biological father, Don sure as hell didn't have a body built for speed.

It was a mistake to think about my mother right now, though. As soon as I did, something heavy seemed to slam into my chest. Not a person, but the weight of Quinn's words again.

A Mind Manipulator abused your best friend for years, but you're choosing to fraternize with them now. I couldn't picture my own mother—beyond, perhaps, a slender, dark hand holding the handle of that crescent knife—but I *could* picture Quinn's mother. Quinn's red-haired controlling, Manipulating mother who'd torn my best friend to pieces right in front of me.

Coen's next words hurled right through all those thoughts, scattering them.

I'm sure your wonderful ass has something to do with it, too.

I almost tripped from the shock of that. Was he trying to distract me? From my guilt and anger? If so, it was working. Knowing his eyes were on my backside as he chased me—it made the ache in my chest drain straight to my toes.

I brought my arm back to fling the ball through my team's disc...

Just as Coen's own arms wrapped around me from behind, immobilizing me.

"I'll take that," he whispered in my ear, plucking the ball from my hand.

I whirled, feeling a Jagaros-worthy hiss rise in my chest, but he was already gone, sprinting toward the other side of the field, where...

Garvis dodged Lander and hurled his team's ball through their disk.

"Game!" Coen called.

Rodhi kicked angrily at nothing, Lander morphed back into his regular self, and Emelle turned to locate me, standing alone on our side of the field.

Slowly, I made the walk of shame back to where they had congregated,

"That was cheating," I whispered to Coen as he tossed my ball from hand to lazy hand. "I would have made it if you hadn't said... that."

"And here I was thinking you liked hearing the truth," he muttered with a half-grin, which just made my stupid heart flutter in my throat. Great. A guy had called my ass wonderful, and I'd become so thoroughly distracted that I'd quit thinking about Quinn *and* lost the game for my team. And that put me somewhere between grateful and pissed.

148

Emelle sagged. "I sucked at that game. If you'd had Wren instead of me..."

We all glanced toward Wren on the sidelines, who had rested her head in her palms, closed her eyes, and now appeared to be taking a nap.

"Nah." Rodhi pretended to really contemplate it. "I think you're just a *tad* more into it, darling."

"I can teach you," Lander jumped in. "If you want to practice with me, Emelle, I can teach you the basics, and we can find ways to utilize your magic."

I tried not to stare too openly at the blush that patched Emelle's face.

Garvis, meanwhile, was staring at Gileon, stroking his mustache.

"You know you're pretty hard to read, buddy. I could barely hear your thoughts, let alone get my own voice inside your head."

Gileon shrugged. "Thick-skulled, my ma always said."

"Mmmm." Garvis frowned. "Perhaps."

Rodhi turned to Sasha.

"Why did you lie to me about being a Mind Manipulator? I would have enjoyed our little make-out session just as much if you'd summoned my—"

"Breakfast!" Coen called suddenly. "Come have breakfast with us in our kitchen—to celebrate your epic loss. Wake your friend up and invite her, too."

He strode off to collect all the balls and discs before I could get a good look at the grin slipping from his face.

But I knew. I knew from the way he kept interrupting Rodhi that *he* was behind Sasha's lie. He must have sent her to go figure out an inconspicuous way to invite my entire house to his party that first night— to keep tabs on me. And she must have chosen the kiss and lie route, pretending to be a Mind Manipulator so infatuated with Rodhi that

149

she'd extended the invitation to his entire sector. It would have worked, too, if Lander hadn't needed me that night.

But Coen hadn't known that, so he'd tracked me down the next day—had found Fergus pinning me to a wall... and erupted.

Which meant—I steadied myself, watching his distant, well-sculpted figure bend to throw all the stray balls in the mesh bag—it meant that Coen Steeler, the prince of the Mind Manipulators, had been watching me, tracking me, and guarding me since day one. Since the moment he'd carried me from that tent.

And *that* put me somewhere between awe-struck and terrified.

Luckily for my often too-active brain, I didn't have a whole lot of time to overanalyze the concept as the next month of classes rolled by and all of our instructors decided to send us home with practice work that kept us up late into the night.

Mr. Fenway assigned us essays. Mr. Conine told us we had to make friends with at least three different tapirs over the course of the next several weeks. Mrs. Wildenberg sent us home with potted bamboos to tend to, and Ms. Pincette...

She was the worst of them all. We were supposed to catch a spider eavesdropping on us. Every. Single. Day. We weren't to kill the spiders, only to tell them the password of the week, silly made-up things ranging from "humblebugger" to "megaslime" and watch the creatures scuttle back to report our success. The only one who didn't complain about that assignment was Rodhi, who would probably go to his grave defending every chestnut hair on Ms. Pincette's head.

What with all the work piling up, though, I lost track of time and almost choked on my coffee when Wren mentioned the first quarterly test.

The three of us—Wren, Emelle, and I—were curled up on a sofa in the foyer, sipping from our mugs while we worked on those essays for Mr. Fenway. The room was filled with soft voices as other groups of Wild Whispering women did the same. From across the room, Jenia was muttering to Dazmine, occasionally shooting scathing glances my way. She'd returned to the bunkroom completely healed about a week ago, but hadn't said a word to me despite her constant prattling to others.

Although, I had to admit, I wasn't getting much work done right now, either—not with Coen making snide, playful remarks about my brainstorming process in my head.

The way you think is fascinating. I swear, I've never known someone who could have so many thoughts at once. It's like putting my head through a beehive.

Maybe the way you think is just slow and I'm the normal one, I retorted, raising my mug to my lips. Our house cook had brewed the coffee with tons of spices—cinnamon, nutmeg, and clove—so I could taste the heat that reminded me of home before even taking a sip.

Maybe our minds balance each other out, came Coen's reply.

That's when Wren said... something, and I shushed him, spluttering.

"What did you just say?" I asked her.

Wren looked up from the pile of papers on her lap.

"I said it's bullshit how female Wild Whisperers are always assigned the least cool jobs after the Final Test. Like..." She lifted her notes. "Two hundred and fifty-two years ago, we tended to mangos and tomatoes, and now we... hmmm... *still* tend to mangos and tomatoes. Meanwhile, the men get to go off and deal with plagues and famines."

I knew better than to interrupt Wren in the middle of a tirade, but as soon as she'd closed her mouth with a scowl, I said, "No, what did you say before... all that?"

151

"Oh, about the first quarterly test?"

She looked vaguely disappointed that I hadn't responded to her rant with equal gusto. I made a mental note to bring the subject back up later.

"Y-yeah."

"I said I can't believe it's already next week."

"The first quarterly test is next week," I repeated.

I caught Emelle's eye, and saw my own nerves printed all over her face. The instructors hadn't talked much about the quarterly tests, but I knew they were mere *tastes* of what was to come at the end of our fifth year. And they would be held in the Testing Center rather than out in the wilderness of Eshol.

Still, the thought that my first one was next week...

Did you pass your first quarterly test? I shot into the buzz of my own mind.

I was pleasantly surprised to find that Coen was still there.

Of course.

So humble. I paused. *Is it easy to pass? They're not dangerous like the Final Test is, right?*

His laugh in my head was a little too nervous for my liking.

No, they're not dangerous. Just very, very uncomfortable.

Great. That makes me feel so much better. I inhaled the spices in my coffee, telling myself to breathe as I felt Coen's voice break into a chuckle.

Always here to help.

CHAPTER

19

The day before the test, I was straining to hear Mrs. Wildenberg in the arboretum when I caught a pair of fierce yellow eyes glowering down at me in the umbrella tree spread above us.

Startled, I looked to my right. Emelle was meditating. To my left, Rodhi was dozing. Gileon was listening way too intently to Mrs. Wildenberg, his eyes round and his fingers digging into the ground, for me to want to disturb him.

I blinked at the eyes. Ever so slowly, they blinked back.

And a striped white tail twitched through the leaves.

Jagaros.

I eased myself to a stand, careful not to rustle the ferns behind me. Nobody glanced my way, not even Jenia, who was whispering, as always, to Dazmine and Fergus.

"To further clarify," Mrs. Wildenberg was saying, her eyes closed, "a faster tempo usually means a positive reaction, so if you're going to ask a question..."

I snuck through the jumble of vines and trees and ferns, away from her warbling lesson, before she could finish that sentence.

Jagaros was already sitting on his haunches in a clearing surrounded by irises.

"*Rayna Drey. You look just as anxious as the last time I saw you.*"

I moved forward to run a hand through his fur, and he closed his eyes, sighing.

"The anxiety faded for a bit," I explained, "but it's back now that the first test is tomorrow."

"*Ahh, the test.*" Jagaros leaned into my touch. "*But not the real one, right?*"

"No," I sighed. "The real one's in five years. But this one will be a good indicator of how I'm doing so far, so I really don't want to mess it up."

Jagaros flopped down, crossing his giant paws. I sat down next to him to continue my strokes, this time along the rippling ridge of his spine.

I opened my mouth to ask him where he'd been, but he interrupted with, "*Tell me of your training.*"

Training. The word alone sounded laughably absurd in reference to my sector. Just in the last few days, I'd glimpsed Element Wielders learning how to throw fireballs combat-style and Shape Shifters hurtling themselves into one another in different animalistic forms, yet here we were among the flowers. Meditating.

I pushed down my snort. Recollected my thoughts.

"Well, I know the basic preferences of every animal within a ten-mile radius of the Institute, so I know how to get on their good sides. I've befriended some monkeys, a crocodile, a mouse, a handful of capybaras, and maybe-sort-of a tapir who literally quakes in his hooves when I so much as say hello. But I can't talk to insects or plants very well."

Indeed, the only time I'd gotten either one to do as I asked was that one time with the fire ants and when I'd had the grass trip up Terrin during pentaball.

The orchids and the other flowers still wouldn't answer my questions about my power. Or Coen's, Garvis's, Terrin's, or the twins' power. I'd asked about all of us. To no avail.

"*I see,*" Jagaros said over the buildup of his deep, rumbling purr. "*Perhaps,*" he added as if he'd read my mind, "*you should ask them different questions.*"

I gnawed on my lips and sucked in a quick breath through my nose.

"A crow told me you were king of Eshol, but he wouldn't elaborate." I purposely didn't mention the letter that particular crow had taken off with; Fabian still hadn't written back, or maybe he was unable to. "And my friend Willa—"

"*Willa?*"

"The mouse," I said. "And my *friend,* like I said, so don't you dare even fantasize about eating her."

"*Wouldn't dream of it,*" Jagaros said, licking his maw.

"I'd hope not, because she's the sweetest, most loyal little thing you'll ever meet. Not that I want you to meet her," I added, and he huffed. "But anyway, she refuses to talk about you. Just scurries off whenever I mention your name."

Jagaros said nothing.

"And," I pressed, "Mr. Conine said there's no known monarchy among the animals of Eshol, no hierarchy that would suggest such a thing as kings or queens."

Still, Jagaros said nothing, but his purring hesitated.

"So I guess I'm asking you what the hell that crow was talking about?" I couldn't help the questioning tone that crept into my voice. "Sorry, is it rude to ask a tiger about his royalty status?"

155

"Yes," Jagaros answered. "*Yes, it is, but I will oblige because I happen to like you more than most humans.*" He flicked his tail once. "*I am a king, yes, but of a long-forgotten past, when faeries still ruled this island. Most of the animals have forgotten, but the birds have an annoying propensity to pass stories down from generation to generation.*"

I paused with my fingers woven deep in his fur.

"The faeries ruled a thousand years ago, though."

Jagaros dipped his head.

"You're a *thousand* years old? What *are* you?" Definitely not a typical tiger, with that lifespan. My next whisper cracked through me. "Are you a faerie?"

Jagaros lifted his head to face me, so close that I could smell his breath—a waft of sky and earth and blood. "*Not anymore.*"

A bite of fear bolted through me, but then Jagaros had closed his eyes again and settled his massive head in my lap. I resumed my pets, my heart scampering.

"Why you?" I was still whispering. "Why did you answer my Branding instead of—well, any other animal?" Not that I could call him an animal anymore, but still.

Jagaros took some time to answer... so long, in fact, that I could hear Mrs. Wildenberg releasing our class through the thickness of the foliage. I'd have to go soon, before Emelle or the others realized I was missing and started to worry.

"*They were afraid,*" he said finally. "*Afraid of that deeper power they sensed imprisoned within you, scrabbling for a way out. But I was not, and so I came to you. I am still not, and so I will come to you again and again, no matter how much your power shifts and grows and tries to break free.*" He opened a single eye to peer up at me. "*Your power does not scare me, Rayna Drey.*"

156

I swallowed the swell of tears in my throat.

"It scares *me*, Jagaros. I don't understand it. I don't know where my mother and the other pirates got it from. Surely, they had to have sailed in from somewhere—another island, maybe, or another continent. Surely, they didn't just drop from the sky? If I could just learn more about *them*, maybe I could understand myself and where that part of my ancestry came from."

None of the schools back in Alderwick had ever taught us much about the world beyond Eshol except that it was full of monsters, and Mr. Fenway, too, kept his history lessons contained within the island.

A small, skeptical part of me had begun to wonder if that domed shield existed to keep us in just as much as it existed to keep those monsters out.

Jagaros arched his back in a sudden, lazy stretch.

"*I think,*" he said, "*your best bet would be to start with a map.*"

The next day, all of us first-years lined up outside the Testing Center, waiting for the last of the second-years to finish trickling from the building so we could go in.

After hours and hours of waiting, my toes were curling in my shoes at the anticipation, until Coen's voice flitted in my head.

I can feel your stress from the other side of campus, little hurricane.

I know you breezed through your test this morning, I thought back, *but that doesn't give you the right to judge others for some nice, proper nerves.*

He chuckled darkly. *You just don't want me to leave next year.*

I'd been trying not to think of it actually, but—

"Is he in your head again?" Emelle asked.

"Unfortunately," I said, hoping he'd hear.

157

He did, sent me an image of his middle finger, and slipped from my mind.

Rodhi sighed, bouncing on his tiptoes to see over the jumbled mass of first-years between us and the front swivel doors of the Testing Center.

"If you two would just get a room already and spare us this grotesque amount of flirting, I think I'd get my appetite back sometime within the next month."

"Oh, please." Emelle ripped her wandering eyes from the crowd around us—to find Lander, a sly part of me suspected—and rounded her attention on Rodhi instead. "As if you don't flirt with every human being with boobs. And sometimes ones without boobs, too."

Rodhi flexed his knuckles. "I've got to practice for Ms. Pincette. By the time I make a move on her, I'll be so good at it that she'll be physically incapable of resisting me."

Gileon, who'd been watching the Testing Center without tracking our conversation in the slightest, suddenly said, "Hey, Wren, over here! Right here!"

I couldn't see over all the heads like Gileon could, but sure enough, Wren had barged through all the bodies and found us moments later. Her usually black clothes were dusted with lively yellow pollen, and some kind of mucus coated her hair in a slippery sheen.

"How did it go?" I dared ask.

"I passed, but barely." She raked off a handful of mucus from her hair and lobbed it to the cobblestone. "It was Ms. Pincette's test that did me in. That was probably worse than the fourth quarterly test last year, where I had to sit in a private testing room with Mr. Fenway and pretend I didn't smell his digestive issues."

"You got stung?"

158

Gileon nodded slowly at one of her arms mottled with burns. Out of all of us, Wren was definitely his favorite, what with her dedication to teaching him new combat techniques every night—to ensure he never got picked on again, she'd told me in private.

"Oh, it's nothing I can't handle, I guess. Got into a bit of an argument with a bee, that's all. Political differences," she added at Emelle's arched eyebrow.

"What? No fair!" Rodhi exclaimed. "*I* want to have a nice little debate with a bee! *Do you or do you not believe that honeycombs should be taxable?* Oh, look! I think we're going in."

Indeed, everyone around us shifted on their feet, and the next second, the crowd was shuffling toward the doors.

"Good luck," Wren muttered to all of us.

By the battered expression on her face, it looked like I might need it.

CHAPTER

20

The inside of the Testing Center spread into a lobby with multiple archways leading to different floors.

Mr. Gleekle stood in the center of it all, greeting everyone with jovial waves and quick bounces on the balls of his feet. I hadn't seen him since the Branding, and the sight of his shiny pink cheeks stretched in a smile that Jagaros had warned me not to trust... it only made the tangled nerves in my stomach tighten. But as president, the man was bound to show up now and again, and besides—the lobby was in way too much disarray for him to make true eye contact with anyone, let alone me.

Everyone pushed and shoved each other toward their sector's archway, where spindly engravings marked the gold semi-circles above each of them—not, to my surprise, labeled with the type of magic, but rather the phrase each sector swore by:

BY THE ORCHID AND THE OWL
BY THE MOONBEAM AND THE MIST
BY THE LOCKPICK AND THE LYRE
BY THE FEATHER AND THE FANG
BY THE TEMPEST AND THE TIDE

I fought my way toward my sector's archway, already having lost Emelle, Rodhi, and Gileon, and came face-to-face with a narrow staircase shooting upward into darkness.

Dragging in a deep breath, I started up... and thankfully only had to suffer the ink-dense shadows for a minute of labored breathing, because cheery sunlight flooded over my shoes when I came to the top.

Here, a row of windows surrounding a vast waiting room and half our year's sector already sat in plush gray seats.

I found the others, sat beside them, and waited. The room bloomed with whispers until a door on the far end opened and Mr. Fenway said, "If you could follow me, class, you will be taking your History portion as one."

We jumped up and followed his hobbling figure through the door, where a testing room much cleaner than his usual classroom sat in perfect condition, each desk already sporting packets of paper and skinny fountain pens.

I chose a desk and plopped down. Around me, everyone else did the same. Mr. Fenway sat in a bloodred velvet armchair at the head and rasped, "No talking, please. No looking at your neighbor's answers. No distracting your neighbors by fidgeting." His aged blue eyes strayed toward Rodhi at that. "Begin."

The first question had my heart calming down immediately: *In 329 AF, a hurricane ravaged the island and left Esholian crops in ruins before Element Wielders could temper it. How did Wild Whisperers of the time react?*

Easy. Much too easy. We'd learned this in the first few days of class. The Wild Whisperers in each village had coaxed the seedlings out of hiding and prompted them to grow faster by singing them special lullabies day in and day out. They'd had to take shifts with each other, to continue that rapid rate of growth, but had managed to replace all the crops within a week.

Smiling down at the paper, I began to write.

An hour later, we were all back in the waiting room. A few people were asking each other about their answers on the test, but Emelle, Gileon, Rodhi, and I chose to pass the time by bouncing a rubber ball back and forth between each of us. Leave it to Rodhi to pull a random rubber ball out of his pocket when we most needed it.

As much as I felt confident about the History portion, I didn't want to push my nerve's luck by talking about it, and the others seemed to think the same.

It wasn't long, anyway, before Mr. Conine emerged from the same doorway and read a name off a scroll flowing from his grip.

"Pierson Kadder. You're first, bud."

The Predators & Prey portion of the test would be a one-on-one examination, then. I tried to shake away the tremors in my arms.

"I wonder what he'll ask us to do."

Emelle tracked Pierson Kadder's trek to the door, where he followed Mr. Conine through and shut it behind him.

Rodhi bounced the ball to Gileon across from him, who just barely caught it.

"I'm kind of hoping for some more crocodiles so grease-face over there gets a nice fat fail." Rodhi nodded toward the other end of the waiting room, where Fergus had an arm draped around Jenia's shoulders while she said something to Dazmine that made the girl laugh. Only... I wasn't sure I believed that laugh was real, not after the warning she'd given me between staircases that one day.

I continued to study her bronze-tinted face as the minutes leaked by. Was she happy? What was going on behind that firm, rather tense guise of hilarity?

"Dazmine Temperton."

I jumped, as if the universe had caught me thinking about something I wasn't supposed to and was manifesting those thoughts now for everyone to hear.

But it was just Mr. Conine again, poking his head into the waiting room to call on the next person.

I sagged in my chair again, then noticed Pierson Kadder hadn't returned.

There had been another door in that classroom. Had Pierson been told to go through it to whatever lay on the other side? Maybe for another test?

"It's your turn, Dazmine," Mr. Conine repeated.

Dazmine hopped up and followed him into the classroom.

And didn't return.

Slowly, the room emptied.

Mr. Conine called name after name, until I was the only one left among my group of friends. Just like during the Branding, the name calling seemed completely random, so I had no idea when I'd be summoned.

No one returned, and my nerves began clenching extra hard when, suddenly, the only four left in the room were me, Norman Pollard, Fergus, and Jenia.

Norman, bless him, sat between me and the other two, blissfully ignorant of how his very presence acted as a blockade between two mutually hateful parties.

I hadn't found myself alone with either Jenia or Fergus since the incident, and I sure as hell didn't want to be caught alone with both of

163

them in the Testing Center, so when Mr. Conine stuck his head out for the fourth-to-last name, I prayed—

"Norman Pollard," he called. "Come on, Norman, let's see what you've got."

Shit, shit, no.

I hunched into myself, crossing my legs and arms as if I could protect my core from the awkwardness that was surely about to dawn between us.

The door to the testing room slammed shut behind Norman and Mr. Conine.

Silence for a beat.

Fergus lifted his head with a savage half-grin, his arm still slung around Jenia's shoulder.

"Hey, Drey. It's been a while. How are you doing?"

The words—they were casual. So, so casual, I might have missed the ire squeezed between each syllable.

"Fine," I answered, and did not ask how he was. The shorter this conversation was, the better for all of us.

"Learned any upper-division magic lately?" Fergus asked. "I mean, like, beyond the ant thing?" He gestured at his own body to remind me of the damage I had inflicted. Jenia, still tucked beneath his arm, twisted her perpetual pout into a leer.

"No," I said.

"Cool, cool. I have. See, after that little incident, I decided I wanted to make sure that would never happen again, so I've been hanging out with some older guys in my house who're teaching me how to *actually* use this Whispering shit."

He withdrew his arm from around Jenia and leaned forward. Eager.

"Do you want to see, Drey?"

164

No, no I didn't, but I kept my limbs crossed and my teeth clamped. If only Mr. Conine would reappear and call my name, get me out of here...

"Show her, babe," Jenia said, sticking her nails into Fergus's arm.

At first, nothing happened, and I couldn't understand the way both their lips curled in obvious excitement.

But then—then—

I jerked my head down, where something black and fuzzy was blooming at my feet, as if rising from the carpeted floor.

Mold.

Mold that boiled up toward me, licking my ankles, spreading in every direction.

Yelping, I withdrew my legs from the floor, hugging them to my chest, but even that position wasn't going to save me. The mold was festering at such an alarming rate that I jumped up and scrambled over the arm of the chair to the next seat over. And the next seat, and the next, and still that mold bubbled into being everywhere I turned, save for where Fergus and Jenia sat.

Where they watched with nothing but hate and cold amusement.

I leaped over the arm of the last chair and shot for the stairwell. To hell with the Testing Center, if staying here would bury me alive in this toxic, black revenge.

Yet my mind raced at the idea that Fergus could wield this much power. Had he even *said* anything to the mold, or was he and the mold internally connected at such a deep level that he didn't need to? Mrs. Wildenberg hadn't even approached the topic of fungus yet, and I wasn't sure she ever would.

Just as I hurtled down the first step of the staircase, the testing door flew open.

And just as quickly, Fergus's mold shrunk back to nothing, like a worm retracting back into the soil.

"Fergus Bilderas." Mr. Conine rubbed his eyes with heavy fists, as if he thought he'd seen something a moment before. Then he turned to me, where I stood stock-still at the top of the staircase. "Rayna... what are you doing? You weren't going to bail on me, were you?" He chuckled.

My very bones rattled within me, but I shook my head, refusing to look at Fergus and Jenia in their little corner.

"No. No, I was just..."

I didn't know what kept me from telling him about Fergus's little prank, except for the thought that maybe this was it. Maybe now that he'd taken his revenge and scared the piss out of me, we were even, and this would be the end of it.

Slowly, I wafted back into the room and sat back down, trying not to stare at the ground where I swore a ghost of mold had stained the carpet.

"Fergus," Mr. Conine repeated. "Come with me, please."

Wary. He'd been wary of Fergus since Fergus's first temper-tantrum in that swamp. Even now I could see the stress lines digging into his forehead as Fergus kissed Jenia's brow and bounced onto his feet to follow.

A moment later, the door closed, and Jenia and I sat staring at each other.

Jenia dropped her gaze from mine to inspect her cuticles. My heart couldn't quit pounding against the inside of my skin like a drum straining to erupt.

"Kimber had a plan to get him back, you know," Jenia said.

My vow to stay silent melted through my teeth. "What?"

"Coen Steeler, of course." Jenia looked up. "My sister, Kimber— our house princess, in case you forgot—she was really torn up about their breakup last dry season and was trying to make him see reason. But then you came along and had to weasel your way between them before she could."

So many different responses rattled around in my brain, but the one that came out, soft as a whisper of leaves in the arboretum, was "Why do you hate me?"

Jenia tilted her head.

"I don't hate you, Rayna. You just tried to hoard your best friend from everyone else, set ants on me because you knew you couldn't compete with my looks, and slept your way to the top of the social chain in a matter of weeks." She paused to examine her cuticles again. "Why would I hate you for that?"

"I have not," I said through shaking lips, "slept my way to anything."

No, all that teasing with Coen had amounted to exactly nothing. Nothing besides a tormenting build of desire in me that I'd never experienced with anyone else. To think that I'd been using him for some stupid social ladder? It was absurd.

Jenia feigned a curious tone. "Why're you holed up in his room every weekend, then, if not to sleep your way to the top?"

Getting medicine to prevent my power from bursting through my skin and cutting you up into tiny, fleshy pieces right now.

"That's what I thought," Jenia said, her eyes blazing with triumph. "Listen."

She leaned forward, as if to tell me a secret even though we were a room apart.

"You might feel good about yourself right now, but once Coen and his friends pass—or *fail*—their Final Tests next year, who are you left with? All your friends are either fat, weird, or stupid, and you're nothing but a dirty little whore pretending to be an angel."

167

The testing door sprung open. Mr. Conine appeared once again.

I stared and stared at Jenia, who in turn stared at her cuticles.

"Rayna Drey," Mr. Conine said. "Thanks for your patience, Rayna."

"Good luck!" Jenia called brightly. "Lovely chatting with you, dear!"

Dear. Everything—from my blood to my bones to my brutally twisted heart—had frozen inside my skin. I had to force myself to up-root my ass from the chair. Had to force each step toward Mr. Conine, blinking and blinking as I tried to get rid of Jenia's words, to toss them away like they were nothing.

"Are you alright, Rayna?" Mr. Conine asked quietly when I'd neared him.

"Fine," I mumbled.

"You'll be okay." He clapped a comforting hand on my shoulder and motioned me to follow him. "It's nothing more than what we've done in class."

Right. The test. Perhaps Fergus and Jenia had meant to dismantle me piece by piece so that I'd fail it. And while this one didn't officially count, it would make or break my first impression to the Good Council, so I really, really needed to do well.

After all, I couldn't have Dyonisia Reeve picking my name out from a list of general passes and investigating me further all because I'd let a little mold and name-calling get into my head. I couldn't allow her to notice me.

"I'm fine," I said again, raking in a deep breath.

Letting my insides melt back into place.

And following Mr. Conine into the testing room without looking back.

CHAPTER

21

The room had completely transformed since our History test mere hours ago.

Rather than desks and papers, it now overflowed with various animal prisons situated throughout the room in meandering patterns, like a snake's lair. And there *were* snakes in here, writhing together in a tank to my left, eyeing the young capybaras in the cage next to them. There were terrariums of buzzing crickets, wire cages of frantic mice, aquariums of fish and frogs and snails. There was even an entire coop of plumed peahens nesting in straw.

On a perch above this conglomeration, watching everything, sat a spectacled owl.

I blinked at it. The owl didn't blink back. Even though my entire sector was named after it, I had only seen two or three of its kind my entire life. They were as rare as white tigers and usually kept to themselves even at night.

"Um." I looked up at Mr. Conine, who'd settled himself into that bloodred velvet armchair at the head of the room—perhaps the only unchanged thing about this place. I could barely hear my own voice over the din of all the animals, though.

"*It looks so good,*" rasped a snake.

"*Don't make eye contact,*" said a capybara to another.

"*Where are you, oh glorious moon?*" sang a cricket.

"*Let us out! Let us out!*" cried the mice, reminding me painfully of Willa, while the fish and frogs and snails rambled meaninglessly.

The peahens, on the other hand, were gossiping amongst themselves, something about a peacock who'd cheated on one of them with a heron.

"Your first Predators & Prey test," Mr. Conine said over this jumble of conversation, "is to find out what our owl friend here would like for dinner. If you can unleash the appropriate quarry for him to feast on, you pass."

"What?" I said, sounding dumb to even my own ears.

Calmly, Mr. Conine reworded himself.

"A huge part of being a Wild Whisperer is the ability to correctly interpret animal desires based on their unique form of communication. This owl," he said with an upward nod, "is hungry, and wishes for a specific meal. Your task is to figure out which meal, out of all the ones before you, he would like you to release so he can hunt."

My stomach actually flopped at the thought of that—of lifting any of these lids or opening any of these cage doors, just to watch the owl dive and tear through whatever animal I had just forced out into danger. It was cruel, but brilliant.

Because owls, Mr. Conine had taught us, never spoke in a straightforward manner. With any other animal, I could simply ask which of these scurrying or slithering options they wanted, but owls only spoke in riddles and timeless wisdom. I'd have to navigate metaphors and life lessons to get to the root of his desires.

"Begin," Mr. Conine said.

I looked up at the owl, trying to drown out the cacophony of all the other animals. "Hello!"

The owl's head quirked toward mine. "*Pleasantries are on the horizon,*" it hooted, "*but so is danger.*"

"Right." I swept a hand toward the hubbub of the room. "Would you like me to get you something to eat?"

"*I wouldn't be a fool to say yes.*"

"Okay." I paused, sorting out that phrase and flipping it around. Yes, he wanted me to get him something to eat. "What would you like?" I was reminding myself of a waitress, but... this was it. The first real test that didn't involve paper and pen.

The owl fluffed its wings. "*I'm craving something crunchy, but without bones.*"

Crunchy, but without bones? My eyes strayed around the room, until they landed on the aquarium of snails. Snails didn't have bones, did they? Just those swirling shells? And I wouldn't feel too guilty about feeding a snail to an owl, to be honest.

Not like how I'd feel if I opened that mouse cage.

I started toward the aquarium, but the owl added, "*Something that would one day become something else if left unharmed. Perhaps a flying beauty.*"

My footsteps faltered. A flying beauty? Obviously, snails didn't fly, so I'd have to scratch that option out.

Transformation had to be the key. The first thought that came to mind regarding *that* was a caterpillar, but... I stooped low to examine a single jar of the squirming creatures on a spindly table.

They wouldn't be crunchy. A *cocoon* might have fit the bill for both requests, but nothing like a cocoon hung among the makeshift branches and leaves in the jar.

The owl's neck snapped this way and that before his orange-sharp eyes landed on me again. *"It's something that needs eternal warmth, but lives in darkness."*

Just like that, Fergus's black mold bloomed in my mind's eye again: a creeping toxicity that savored warmth and moisture and dark things like Fergus's own heart.

I shook my head. No. Owls didn't eat mold. I had to push what Fergus had done far away again, focus on my task at hand.

Warmth and darkness. That sounded like the perfect habitat for worms, which definitely didn't have bones but also couldn't fly or give the owl a nice crunch.

God, I was going to fail my first Predators & Prey test. *Why* couldn't it just give me a straight answer or point or something, the lousy bird? Maybe if I followed his eye contact…

No, the owl was staring at *me* unblinkingly, not any of the cages.

Think, Rayna, think.

I circled the mass of prisons again, hunting for any hints or signs I'd missed the first time.

Something crunchy, but without bones. Something that would one day become something else—perhaps a flying beauty—if left un-harmed. Something that needs eternal warmth, but lives in darkness. They all seemed to contradict each other.

"Any more qualifications?" I threw up at the owl weakly.

" The answer lies beneath."

I couldn't look Mr. Conine in the eye. Had it been this hard for everyone else, too? Should I just open a cage at random and hope it happened to be right?

In that moment, my ears perked up at the peahens' gossiping conversation.

"—he wouldn't even fertilize it, the bastard."

172

"No! That's just immature, honestly, even if he's mad at you."

"Well, he did later, but only after we'd made up."

The answer lay beneath: beneath the peahens who were... nesting.

My eyes flew wide as I realized what the owl wanted.

Eggs. Crunchy, warm eggs living in the darkness beneath their mothers' breasts. If they were early enough in the fertilization process, there wouldn't be any spindly bones in the yolks yet, but if they *were* fertilized, they'd turn into flying beauties—as long as the owl left them alone. Left them untouched.

Which he wouldn't.

"Do I really have to do this?" I asked Mr. Conine.

Mr. Conine's eyes seemed to gutter.

"The test is the test, and the cycle is the cycle. Part of being a Wild Whisperer is bearing the pain of that cycle, of balancing the love and suffering of predators and prey alike."

I nodded, even as my heart cracked in as many pieces as those eggs would.

Feeling it, embracing it, hating it anyway, I walked forward and unlatched the wired door of the coop.

The mother hens, realizing what was about to happen, began to scream.

The owl swooped down.

The next test was indeed through the other door—which I rushed through as soon as Mr. Conine gave me a pass, if only to get away from the screaming.

Mrs. Wildenberg sat in this room, in an identical bloodred velvet sofa, but this time with a pleasant rustic table before her. An array of potted plants spread across this table, along with some steaming cups of what smelled like hibiscus tea.

"Rayna, right? Rayna Grey?" Mrs. Wildenberg squinted at me through the steam of her tea.

"Oh, it's actually Drey."

"Right, right." She nodded and gestured weakly. "Please sit down."

I sat opposite her, in a wooden chair that clashed rigidly against my spine.

"Okay, Ms. Grey. Here are some—oh, I forgot. Would you like some tea?"

I almost said yes, because the smell of it made my mouth water and surely it was dinnertime. But I remembered what Coen had said: *don't drink random shit at a party when you don't know what might trigger your condition.* Perhaps the same applied to a testing room. And since I didn't know which instructors would report to the Good Council if they witnessed any slice of superfluous power...

"No, thanks," I said, folding my hands neatly over the desk.

"Okay, okay, no problem." Mrs. Wildenberg's ash-white hands shook as they picked up a pile of cards before her and handed them over to me. "Here are some questions that I would like you to ask the hibiscus and passion flowers and poinsettias. Listen well, and tell me what you think they are saying back to you. You should be looking for simple yes or no answers for now, dear, nothing more."

"Got it," I said, looking down at the first card.

It read: *Do you know who I am?*

I repeated the question to the hibiscus plant in its purple-painted ceramic pot, and closed my eyes to listen.

The hibiscus usually murmured its song with a steady tempo, like the monotonous ticking of a clock marching forward in time. But now

174

it sped up like an excited heartbeat, a positive affirmation rather than an uncertain pause.

"Yes," I told Mrs. Wildenberg, who was listening in to make sure I got the right answer. "The hibiscus knows who I am."

Saying that out loud sent shivers twining around my bones. The hibiscus, its petals, its stems and leaves and roots and even the soil it grew in—it knew me. And since Mrs. Wildenberg had taught us that all the flora was connected, stemming from the heart of Eshol itself... that meant the island itself knew me, even though I knew very, very little about the island.

Jagaros's words came back to me then: *Perhaps you should ask them different questions.* Why had I been so obsessed with asking the flowers and trees about my *own* power when I should have been asking them about... well, themselves? Of course they hadn't wanted to tell me anything when I hadn't yet befriended them.

Sucking air through my teeth, I read aloud from the next card, directing this question to the passion flowers in their metal garden beds.

"Will you allow me to get to know you?"

The passion flowers usually sang a soft yet chaotic melody, like a million fluttering butterfly wings. As soon as the last sound of my question left my lips, however, that chaos split into absolute pandemonium, loud and fast and off-key.

"Yes," I told Mrs. Wildenberg. "The passion flowers will allow me to get to know them." I paused, then, listening to the screech of their song. "They are... *desperate* for me to get to know them," I dared add, even though I was only supposed to discern yes or no questions.

But I felt it in the very marrow of my still-shivering bones: that the plants before me wanted to tell me a secret, but couldn't do so until I understood their essence on a deeper level than I did now.

175

"Very good," Mrs. Wildenberg said, her eyes fluttering as if only halfway paying attention. I was, after all, her second-to-last test subject of what I was sure had been a very long and strenuous day for such an aging mind.

When her chin finally slumped down against the middle of her collarbone and I was sure she'd nodded off completely, I set the stack of cards down and leaned in close to the poinsettias—such vibrant, spirited things, who sang swaying tunes of success and cheer.

My lips nearly brushed their bright red leaves as I whispered, "Are the faeries truly extinct?"

Jagaros had said he wasn't a faerie, not anymore, but I wanted to know what Eshol itself thought of that. If it truly considered him pure tiger and nothing more. Perhaps it was an invasion of his privacy, but... *he* was the one who had told me to ask different questions, so I tucked away a whisper of guilt and listened closely.

The poinsettia's swaying tune slowed, like a ship thudding against a shore.

No. The faeries are not yet extinct. Not all of them.

My blood dropped, but I asked, "There are more faeries out there? Besides Jagaros himself?"

At this, the poinsettias and passion flowers and hibiscus plants all swept into a song that, for the life of me, I couldn't understand.

Mrs. Wildenberg ended up waking up with a violent hiccup two minutes later.

Blinking, she told me I had passed this portion of the test, took a large gulp of no-longer-steaming tea, and sent me on my way through the next door—to my last test for the Spiders, Worms & Insects portion.

In here, Ms. Pincette sat primly in a third and final bloodred velvet armchair.

I noticed two things in quick succession after I shut the door behind me, and neither did anything to settle my stomach after what the flowers had just revealed.

One: a rubber dummy stood upright on one side of Ms. Pincette.

Two: an enormous tank sat on her other side, its inside squirming with...

"Cockroaches," Ms. Pincette said with a thin-lipped smile. "Your final test, Ms. Drey, will be to lower yourself into the tank of cockroaches and instruct them to leave you and swarm the dummy instead. This ability to instruct mass hordes of insects in times of distress is crucial to the Wild Whispering community."

Worse. This was so much worse than anything else. Paper exams and solving riddles and reading questions to innocent little flowers—it was all glitter and rainbows compared to *this*.

The cockroaches were black, as black as Fergus's mold that might have billowed over me if I hadn't moved fast enough, and I... I didn't know how to release the panic skittering through my veins at the sight of something else that could drown me.

"Remember, Rayna," Ms. Pincette said, her eyes narrowing on my face as the blood rushed down my neck, "roaches rarely bite humans. They can't hurt you."

"Of course." I jolted into movement, toward the tank. A single stepstool, cracked and worn, sat before it, and I forced a step upward.

The cockroaches hissed and chirped words I could barely understand, as if they were speaking with a foreign accent full of harsh, jagged inflections.

I forced another step upward, until all of me was standing on that little stepstool, and my fingers were curling around the top edge of that

177

tank. How could I do this? How could I plunge myself headfirst into this scuttling, hissing abyss?

Coen had told me he'd stay out of my head during my entire time in the Testing Center so as to avoid breaking any rules, but... I craved his snarky, cocky tone more than anything right now. I needed the heat of his presence to combat the cold dread of what I was about to do. Or maybe I needed Jagaros's silk-soft fur, or Fabian's comforting voice telling me it was going to be okay, or Emelle's familiar, timid smile.

Ms. Pincette cleared her throat.

No, I realized, glancing at her pincer-sharp eyes. I needed *myself* right now. I needed to gather this panic fraying the edges of my vision and bundle it up deep inside my core. Cockroaches didn't bite, and neither would fear unless I let it.

Exhaling, I swung my leg up and toppled over the edge of the tank.

CHAPTER

22

My body thumped to the bottom, the full force of my fall cushioned by a hundred tiny *crunches* as my weight cracked a hundred tiny shells.

But there were still a thousand more, and they all clicked against each other as they swarmed me, millions of needle-thin legs washing over every part of my body: my legs, my torso, my arms, my neck, my hair. They dug into every crack, every fold of clothing, every space between my limbs and core.

I snapped my mouth shut mid-scream before any of them could slip down my throat. But I still had to talk to them, to order them off me, and that would require opening my mouth again. How, though?

How?

How?

How?

A gag formed in my throat, but I brought my hands up, shaking off the stray cockroaches still clinging to them, and made a cage of fingers around my mouth.

Ms. Pincette had taught us that insects understood human language equipped with the same accent they themselves presented.

Grasshoppers, for instance, listened more if you chirped your vowels. Ladybugs listened if you buzzed through the first sound of each word. Centipedes listened if you rolled your 'r's. The ants had listened to me that one time because my breath had been rough and raw, like the sound they made when they rubbed their ridges against their abdomens.

I simply had to mimic the cockroach accent of harsh, spitting sounds, then.

"Get off me," I hissed through my fingers.

The roaches didn't move. One tried to squirm into my ear, and I flailed, scrabbling at it. Another crawled over my eye, and my foot kicked out, colliding with the end of the tank and making the whole thing quake around me.

"Get off me," I tried again. "Go to the dummy. Get off me."

Nothing. No reaction, except for perhaps a swell in their own voices, a sharp, high-pitched kind of laughter. And I hated them for it, hated every tickle and prick and invasion, and I was going to scream if they didn't stop.

"Get off me!" I said again, my voice rising against my will.

The roaches simply crawled over each other in their haste to crawl over *me*, again and again, as if burying me alive and letting me rest under their combined weight wasn't enough. As if the burial had to constantly move and swirl and writhe.

Ms. Pincette got to her feet. She was going to mark this as a fail.

Something slipped through the cracks of my bones. Something deep and restless and *aware*.

It lunged, lashing out at the thousands of little invasions to my body.

The cockroaches flew off me, skidding up the sides of the glass and overflowing to the floor, where the dead ones remained and the live ones scuttled for the dummy to swarm its rubber figure.

180

But rather than crowd its body like they'd done to me, the thing inside me nudged them deeper and deeper, willing them out of existence, willing them to disappear completely.

I watched through the glass, horror-struck, as the cockroaches burrowed into the dummy itself and *merged with* its rubber surface, until all that was left was an ink-black figurine with twitching cockroach legs for hair.

Ms. Pincette's head snapped toward me.

Slowly, I rose within the tank and hoisted myself out. The silence of the room echoed like the aftermath of thunder as Ms. Pincette looked at me and I looked back at her.

I had no idea what I'd just done, but I *did* know that Wild Whispering abilities couldn't merge a thousand insects with a dummy. And that lunge inside me—it had felt an awful lot like my raw power had the night before Branding... only pointed and directed and *honed*, somehow, rather than shapeless.

Ms. Pincette, still staring at me, seemed to make up her mind.

"Leave us," she snapped at seemingly nothing but air.

The subtle, departing clicking of a dozen spiders faded from the walls.

Ms. Pincette motioned for me to come closer and waited until I was a nose-length away before seething, "What. Was. That."

"I don't know," I answered honestly—but I couldn't let her get too suspicious, so I added with a quick, careful smile, "But I did as you said, right? I got them off me and made them swarm the dummy instead. That's a pass, right?"

My voice sounded like nothing more than feeble bleating even to my own ears. I clenched my fists to keep her from seeing my shaking hands.

Ms. Pincette, however, eyed those fists, then let her gaze travel up the rest of my body, landing on my face. Her own face hardened. She gestured to the armchair.

"Sit, Ms. Drey. Sit and listen very carefully to me."

I sat. Now Ms. Pincette towered over me with a pinched expression.

"Do you know what these tests are for, Ms. Drey? The Final Tests?"

"To make sure we have control of our magic," I answered automatically, afraid to say a single wrong thing. "To make sure we are worthy of living on this island."

"And why would this be, Ms. Drey?" Ms. Pincette's fingers drummed against her own folded arms. "Why would the Good Council seek this kind of control?"

I blinked at her. Dare I say what I truly thought about the Good Council? Wasn't she part of them, in a roundabout way, by teaching at the Institute?

Deciding to play it safe, I said, "To weed out the weak."

"To weed out the *strong*," Ms. Pincette hissed, her tone as harsh as those roaches had been. "Do you really think they care about the people who genuinely fail these tests, Ms. Drey? The ones who can't talk to animals or summon objects or wield fire? No. They care about finding the people who can pass the test *too well*. Do you understand me? Because the people who pass the test *too well* are a threat."

I already suspected this, of course, but I still felt a sliver of surprise that Ms. Pincette would dare say it to me.

"I understand you," I told her earnestly. "I really do."

"No, you don't." My surprise only sharpened when she leaned even closer and said, "You don't understand a thing, Rayna Drey, because you'd be shitting yourself right now if you did. Now." She sat on the edge of the armchair, hovering over me. "I want you to use one hundred percent of your brain right now. Forget about what you've been told."

182

Her jaw clenched. "Would the Good Council, seeking both the weakest and the strongest of society during these mandatory tests, truly give those strong ones to the pirates who are trying to break through our magical shield?"

I thought about it. Tried to use one hundred percent of my brain even though it was still buzzing over what had just happened.

The pirates—my mother's people—had the same raw power as me... but they didn't know how to control it, so they were seeking access to the island's bascite as a way to help themselves.

It didn't make sense, then, that the Good Council would truly exile people with that same bascite in their blood. If they did, they'd be... they'd be handing over exactly what those pirates wanted. Bascite. Controllable magic. And by extension, tools and weapons to use against the island itself. A way to break through the shield.

My heart dropped through my chest.

"What do they do with the ones who fail the test, then?"

Because I understood now. It wasn't just the bottom of the barrel that failed the test, but the top of the barrel, too. Only the ones with average, predictable magic got to stay on the island. The rest...

"There is a prison," Ms. Pincette began, her shadow shielding me from the light of the room. "A prison at the top of Bascite Mountain, where the Good Council lives. The exiled are sent there, where the weak ones are—" She winced "—recycled, and the strong ones are..." Another wince, deeper this time. "Experimented on."

My breath was a puddle in my lungs, stagnant and refusing to move.

Recycled? Meaning their blood was drained from their bodies to reuse the bascite in their system? And... experimented on? Dissected and studied and tortured?

Images floated across my vision. A cold mountaintop sparkling with smoky gray metal. A fortress filled with screaming. Dyonisia's cruel, cruel eyes. And what Quinn had told me so long ago: *Mrs. Pixton is convinced her son is still on the island, locked up somewhere and waiting for her to rescue him.*

Oh yes, I was certain of it now: the shield was to keep us in. To keep us from the rest of the world so that *she*, Dyonisia Reeve, could hoard us and abuse us.

And my magic, my blood, my other power—it was certainly something she'd want to study and tamper with and use.

"Why?" I croaked. "Why is she doing this? Who *is* she?"

By the flare of her pupils, I could tell Ms. Pincette knew exactly who I meant. But she only pursed her lips, straightened her posture, and patted at her blouse.

"I am giving you a fail, Ms. Drey, for being... unable to get the cockroaches to move. I expect you to study and sharpen your communication skills for next time."

In the silence that followed, the black-as-ink, still-twitching dummy seemed to stare me down, but a small part of my panic loosened.

Ms. Pincette was not going to record what had actually happened. As long as all those spiders who had been eavesdropping during the test were truly under her direction... I was safe.

For now.

"You may go, Rayna," Ms. Pincette said quietly. "Better luck next time."

I got up on shaky legs. Just as I was reaching the back staircase, which looked like it would spit me out to the rocky edge of the cliff behind the Testing Center, I looked back at her.

"Do you happen to have a map of the world, Ms. Pincette?" I swallowed the heat and grittiness of my bile. "I thought it would help me with my studying."

I need to know where my mother's people came from. Where I came from. And maybe... maybe where Dyonisia Reeve came from, too.

Ms. Pincette, however, just raised her chin. "Better luck next time, Ms. Drey. Now, if you'll excuse me, I've got to go find more cockroaches for my next test."

CHAPTER

23

Coen. Coen, I need to talk to you right now. Coen, can you hear me?

The moment my feet hit the ground outside and the back door of the Testing Center swung shut behind me, I threw those thoughts into the muggy night air.

I must have been in the Testing Center for hours. Stars blared between clouds overhead, warm and winking. A few people milled about beside those two lampposts sandwiching the staircase that led down to the shore, but I didn't stop—around the Testing Center, across the courtyard, down Bascite Boulevard... I shouted his name in my head as I ran, wishing, for once, that his voice was already inside my mind.

But nothing filled the space between my ears besides the pounding of my own blood. Where *was* he? I knew it wasn't fair of me to expect him to know that I was done with the test, but my terror couldn't seem to rationalize anything. *He* was in danger, too, he and Garvis, Terrin and the twins—they would all be dragged to the top of that mountain and tortured if they revealed their true powers during their upcoming Final Tests.

The pirates were laughable compared to that.

Without pausing for breath, I sprinted over the bridge and down the street to my house, where I plunged through the opening doors just as a group of fellow Wild Whisperers walked out.

"Are you okay, Rayna?" one of them asked.

I threw back a quick, "Yeah, thanks!" and headed straight downstairs to the dining hall.

Here, a bunch of people in my class were eating a late-night snack to replace the dinner we'd missed. I didn't see Emelle, Rodhi, Gileon, or Wren, but I paused long enough to listen in on another group of friends, including Mitzi Hodges and Norman Pollard.

"I think I failed the History portion."

"I *know* I failed Predators & Prey. When I let out that fuzzy caterpillar, the owl just stared at me."

"The only test *I* passed was Ms. Wildenberg's," Norman said, "but I think it's because the old bat was falling asleep and just too embarrassed to ask me to repeat my answers."

"Better than what happened to Bekka Nickleson," Mitzi said. "Did you hear about her? She failed all of them and tried to run away back to her village. The prince of the Shifters caught her." She lowered her voice. "Apparently, he shifted her kneecaps into stone so she couldn't run anymore."

"But it doesn't matter if you fail one or fail them all, right?" someone else asked. "In the end, if you can't pass every portion, you're pirate food."

From the fragile, frightened tone of their voices, I knew they were all imagining themselves thrown out to sea, unaware of that mountaintop prison and the worse horrors that would await them there.

Horrors that sounded a lot like *slice you open* and *pillage the magic from your blood.*

Once, that hallucination Coen had bestowed upon all the first-years seemed like the worst thing that could happen. Now, I had a very vivid imagining of Dyonisia Reeve doing even worse—with all the tools Fabian and Don usually used in their little blacksmith shop in Alderwick. Sledgehammers and pliers. Nails and chisels. A forge.

Shivering, I crept to the ice box behind the kitchen doors, nabbed a chunk of paper-wrapped cheese, and hurried back up to the study room. There, I whispered Willa's name into the stale, motionless darkness.

Her squeak of a voice answered me within seconds.

"*I was beginning to worry that you'd forgotten today.*" She scrambled onto a nearby desk. "*How did your test—*"

"Willa." I unwrapped the cheese and placed it in front of her tiny paws. "Do you know of a place where I could talk to someone in private? Without the risk of any spiders overhearing?" I willed my heart to slow, to align with my breathing, to take hold of the fact that I wasn't in any imminent danger. Not yet.

Willa cocked her head at me and sniffled.

"*The eight-legged beasts don't like water very much. Especially flowing water. Maybe near the estuary?*"

"Perfect. Would you be able to pass a message to your family in the Mind Manipulator house?" I'd learned by now that all the mice shared their own kind of social community within the walls of each structure on Bascite Boulevard, often visiting each other and hosting little crumb parties. "Tell Coen Steeler to meet me on the bridge in five minutes. Can you pass that message along?"

"*Sure, but...*" Willa scurried around the hunk of cheese, ignoring it completely. "*What's wrong, Rayna? You look ill. Have you eaten anything tonight?*"

"No, but I'm not hungry. I just have to speak with Coen."

Preferably face to face. Because what I'd just learned... I felt like my scrambled mind would never be able to convey it all properly. I needed to voice it all aloud.

Willa gave me a beady-eyed look, her whiskers twitching, then scampered away.

Coen, I tried one more time. *Coen, can you hear me?*

Maybe it made me a coward to try to reach him this way, via minds and mice instead of just knocking on his front door and asking whoever opened it if I could come inside to see him.

But I heard Jenia's voice in my head: *Why're you holed up in his room every weekend, then, if not to sleep your way to the top?* and I couldn't stand the thought of all those smirks that would follow me to his private bedroom, or the gossip that would meander its way back to Jenia and Kimber.

Before I could overthink my decision, I hurried back to the foyer and out the door, starting toward the bridge with my head bowed against a sudden sprinkle of rain.

The gurgle of the estuary rose around me as I leaned against the metal guardrails, waiting for him. And as the minutes leaked by, my worry grew.

Where was he? Surely, it had already been five minutes, right? Of course, he might have been sleeping, or talking to someone, or playing a card game, or performing prince duties, or... or... or... the possibilities swirled in my head, nibbling at every corner of my mind like swarming insects—

"Rayna? What's going on?"

I whipped toward the sound of his voice and almost lunged forward to embrace him out of pure relief, but stopped myself. We'd never hugged, and he might find such a thing awkward or unwelcome, so I twisted my hands together instead.

"What's the point of being a Wild Whisperer?"

That wasn't what I'd intended to say, but it tumbled out anyway, my tongue completely out of my control.

"If I was a Mind Manipulator, I could have just read Mr. Conine's mind to see if *he* knew what the owl wanted to eat instead of playing stupid word games. I could have read Mrs. Wildenberg's mind to find out if the hibiscus were saying yes or not. I could have forced the cockroaches to leave me alone instead of *begging* them to get off me."

Coen had frozen, watching me as if I were an injured bird.

"What happened to you?" he asked, each word clipped and restrained.

I pressed my hands to my face. "I just... I needed to tell you about my test, and I needed to do it where there's no chance of us being overheard, so I asked Willa, and—" My eyes had traveled to his hands clasping a pair of straps around his shoulders "—is that a *backpack*?"

Coen's eyes narrowed in the rain-flecked starlight. "Yes," he said, as if *I* were being the suspicious one. "Willa told me you hadn't eaten so I thought I'd pack you some food."

He ate up the distance between us in a single stride and lifted a hand from one of his straps, hovering it near my temple as if to brush away my hair.

"May I?"

"Are you asking if you can read my mind right now?" I asked, incredulous. "Because you do that all the time, you know, and I've already given you permission."

"Well, I can hear the thoughts you're currently thinking whether I'm in your mind or not—they're sort of screaming right now. But to access your emotions and memories and deeper thoughts when you're obviously in so much distress... I'd like your permission again. It might

190

hurt a little," he added, "letting someone in your mind while it's vulnerable and wild. It can be uncomfortable."

I only arched my neck toward him. "Go ahead. But I don't think I can form coherent thoughts, so I need to talk it out with you afterward."

Coen's fingers brushed my temple, grazing down my cheek. His eyes glazed over for a moment, then widened, then narrowed, then widened again, and soon he'd cupped both hands around either side of my face, holding me upright. A faint headache pulsed near the back of my head, but it didn't hurt much beyond that.

When he was finished sifting through my recent memories, he released me, and the absence of his touch left aching coldness trailing down both sides of my face. Not that he'd even *needed* to touch me to read my memories. He could have done that from across campus.

"I'll kill him," he breathed, his hands—now wrapped into fists—shaking.

"What? Coen, what are you talking about?" I took his fists and held them steady. "Didn't you just hear what Ms. Pincette told me?"

Coen blinked, as if refocusing, but gnawed on his lower lip.

"That Fergus kid. I told him not to touch you again."

That's what he was going to focus on after witnessing my entire testing experience? The mold had sucked, sure, but the idea of a prison full of tortured Esholians seemed like a more pressing matter to me. And the fact that such torture would come straight from the leaders who'd sworn to protect us rather than faceless enemies on the horizon... it made the whole fungus incident wane in comparison.

"Fergus didn't touch me, Coen. He abided by your rules and didn't lay a physical finger on me, so please don't punish him any further. He'll only figure out a way to retaliate against me again if you do. And besides," I said, adding in a miserable attempt at a laugh, "you're not

191

allowed to kill anyone, remember? That was a rule *you* announced to everyone when we first arrived."

Coen stretched out his fingers, flexing them. He gave a curt nod, then flicked a glance at a pack of Element Wielders stumbling toward the bridge, their arms around each other. Celebrating the end of the first quarterly test, I was sure.

"I think," Coen said, "we're going to need more privacy. Are you up for a little midnight hike?"

It wasn't a little hike.

By the time Coen stopped us a mile uphill, along the winding path of the estuary that flowed in the opposite direction, my throat ached with the force of my panting. Nocturnal animals peeked at us through the trees here, and I could hear their curious whispers as Coen began running his hands along the ground.

"*It's some of those weird human creatures from the school.*"

"*Do you think they can understand us?*"

"*Don't say anything insulting in case they can.*"

"*Why is the male one digging through the ground? Do humans burrow, Papa?*"

"*No, son, but sometimes they go rabid, like this one here.*"

"Um, Coen," I interrupted, and all those voices blinked into silence, "why *are* you digging?"

He grunted as he remained stooped. "I'm trying to find the—ahh, here. My friends and I haven't used this in ages, but Terrin discovered it when he was doing one of his weird earth exercises. He said the ground felt hollow in a certain place, so we all investigated and found..." Another grunt. "This."

There was a rusty squeak as Coen lifted what looked like a hatch buried deep among the ferns. I stared at it, unsure I was seeing right, but Coen planted his hands on his hips and grinned at me.

"Welcome to what Terrin calls the Throat. Here, I'll help you down."

I didn't move.

"Help me down? Into a hole in the ground called the *Throat?*"

"Yeah. I promise the end will be worth it." Coen held out his hand.

"Is the end called the Stomach, by chance?" I grumbled, but stepped forward, twining my fingers around his. The warmth of his skin tingled my wrist, and before he could flit through my mind to detect that, I slid down.

It wasn't a long drop. I landed with barely more than a thud and squinted into the darkness, shuffling sideways so Coen had space to land beside me. When he did, I could barely make out the silhouette of his face or the gleam of his eyes in the dark.

"I think I liked the bridge better," I whispered.

He chuckled, though I could have sworn there was a tense edge to that sound. "Just keep ahold of me and keep moving forward. The walk down will be a lot easier than the walk uphill was. Trust me." He closed the trapdoor above our heads, encasing us in the deepest, richest black I'd ever faced.

We began to push through the tunnel, my right hand clinging to the bulge of Coen's bicep. I was vaguely disappointed I couldn't enjoy it more, this closeness and the feel of his muscles beneath my fingers — not when the Throat seemed to close in on us from every direction, its darkness swallowing us whole.

"Who made this?" I breathed out.

"Terrin thinks it was another Element Wielder from a long time ago."

"Why?"

I felt the movement of Coen's shrug. "Could have been for sewage or transport or mining. Or maybe they just decided to create it on a whim. There are more than a few strange dents in Eshol due to magical experimentation."

At that word, *experimentation*, I shivered—but kept quiet. If there were spiders hulking in the crevices of the Testing Center walls, there were sure as hell spiders in this tunnel with us... although I couldn't hear any of their clicking or whispering. Still, though, better to play it safe, to wait until we'd reached Coen's secret place.

Whatever that was.

Hardly ten minutes later, I found out.

Coen had been right. The walk downhill was much faster than the walk up, because I could already see light blooming ahead, a block of grayish, shimmering sky. Or... *was* it the sky? It was moving so viciously, so chaotically, that I rubbed my eyes.

Something was hissing ahead, but not in a language I could understand. It was a sort of endless drone, yet full of nuance, like millions of voices bubbling together.

"Coen, what is this?"

"A place where no one will ever find us," he said, and the tunnel opened up into the wide-cut mouth of a cave, where gemstones shined in glittering waves all around.

And the spraying, hissing wall of a waterfall dumped into the ocean before us.

CHAPTER

24

The waterfall stole all my focus, along with my breath.

Its sparkling, feral shower warped my view of the green-black spread of ocean beyond it, but the water somehow caught shards of starlight and sent them cascading back into the cave, reflecting off the gemstones imbedded in the ceiling and walls and filling this entire space with throbbing, multi-colored light.

The estuary. We were directly beneath a part of the estuary, right where it spilled itself off the cliff and into the sea.

I was gaping all around me when I realized Coen had unslung his backpack, pulled out a blanket, and spread that blanket over the polished black floor of the cave.

"What are you doing?"

He didn't answer until he'd rummaged through the backpack some more and brought out a sandwich wrapped in wax paper. When he'd unpacked it and placed it neatly on the blanket, he nodded down at it and said, "Eat."

"What?"

Coen, as I might have expected, crossed his arms.

"Your hair looks like a bird's nest, I just saw a recent memory of you bathing in cockroaches, and your mind seems to be stuck on the concept of torture. The least you could do for yourself right now is eat this damn sandwich I made for you."

A bird's nest? I touched my hair, pushed out my best grunt, and stomped over to the blanket, where I sat cross-legged on the floor of the cave and began tearing into the sandwich. *Don't moan,* I begged myself when my stomach snarled at the sudden taste of food—seed-filled bread, spiced avocado, and dripping tomato slices. It had to be, what, nearing one in the morning now? And I hadn't eaten since before stepping foot in the Testing Center.

Apparently satisfied that I was getting something down, Coen untangled his arms and began to pace around me.

"Okay, go over it again," he ordered. "Everything that instructor of yours told you after the cockroaches."

Right. Coen had never had Ms. Pincette as a teacher, since he was in a different sector. I spilled out every detail of her warnings through mouthfuls of sandwich, trying to convey the sharpness of her character, how she wasn't one to exaggerate.

"And then she said the people who fail the test aren't actually exiled but taken to the top of Bascite Mountain." I paused as Coen's eyes remained focused on his own feet while he paced. Shouldn't he be grimacing or cringing or making *some* kind of unpleasant facial expression at the idea of such a thing voiced out loud?

I stood up suddenly, marching toward him and poking a finger to his chest.

"You knew, didn't you?"

He stopped in his tracks, blinking down at my finger.

"I... suspected. Not that the exiled go to Bascite Mountain," he added quickly as my eyes flared. "I could've never guessed that... but I wasn't convinced they actually get thrown out to sea with the pirates. You have to remember—" Even though there was no way a single spider could hear us over the crashing of the waterfall, Coen's eyes still darted left and right before continuing " —I was nine years old when my captain sent me and the others through the shield, not a baby. I remember living on the ships, and we never once nabbed any exiles drifting on rowboats or swimming helplessly in the ocean, or whatever else you might imagine."

Something about that gave me pause. Made me lower my finger from his chest and press it against my own chin.

"You were nine?" I repeated. "Nine years old?"

Even if I wasn't a natural at arithmetics, I could do simple addition. *When we were children, some... others and I were dropped onto one of the coastal villages—Hallow's Perch—about twelve years ago,* Coen had told me the first time I'd visited his bedroom. And if he had been a nine-year-old twelve years ago...

"You're not twenty-three," I said flatly, even though that statement sounded ludicrous. Every fifth-year was twenty-three going on twenty-four. Every fifth-year besides Coen, apparently.

His eyes flashed, then blinked in surprise. The next second, a grin had cracked his face.

"God, you're smart. I've got to remember to be careful about what I say around you. But you're right, I'm twenty-one. The twins are twenty-two. Garvis is—oh, let's see—twenty-four now." When my eyebrows flew into my hairline, he added, "we weren't all born in the exact same year, Rayna. But when we got dumped on this island, we knew we'd have to stick together. Go to the Institute together and take our Final Tests together. So we lied about our ages from the very beginning."

It made sense, but... I loosed a pent-up breath. Twenty-one. Coen was *twenty-one,* only three years older than me. A mix of shock and...

197

and *embarrassment* flared through my chest, though I didn't know why, so I latched onto another question.

"And Terrin? How old is he?"

Coen grabbed a fistful of his own hair and laughed as nervously as I felt.

"He will *murder* me if he knew I was telling you this, but Terrin's only nineteen. Yes, even with all his facial hair. He was the youngest of us to be used as bait." Coen didn't even cringe from that statement, although I did. "He was seven when we left the ships for the last time."

My breath hitched. A pirate. Coen wasn't just a pirate's son, but an actual *pirate* who had lived on one of those ships dotting the horizon for nine whole years.

Coen bent to snatch up the last bite of sandwich I'd discarded, and lifted it to my lips.

"Finish it. Your hands are still shaking."

I took it into my mouth, my lips brushing the edges of his fingers.

He made sure I swallowed before he said, "Garvis and I have tried to follow the exiles every year. After they fail their tests, they're escorted by Good Council security to a group of iron wagons behind the Testing Center waiting to take them away. Garvis and I don't dare follow close enough for anyone to actually see us, or I'm sure Dyonisia Reeve would have our heads on two identical pikes. But we follow the screams of their minds from a distance away."

"And?" I asked breathlessly.

"And the sound of the exiles cuts out after a few miles. Every year."

"Like they're dead?" I couldn't move. Couldn't breathe. "Do you think the Good Council just kills them and takes their bodies up to Bascite Mountain?"

The weak ones are recycled, Ms. Pincette had said. Were their literal corpses recycled, then? The bascite in my system—had it come from the blood of a murdered Esholian who'd failed the test before me?

But Coen brushed his hands against my arms, and I felt a flutter of shock at the rough texture. What did the Mind Manipulators do in their classrooms to warrant such callouses? Or would his skin simply never shed the roughness of his childhood on a ship?

"No, Rayna, it's not like a dead kind of silence. More like the exiled become muted. Shielded." At my questioning gaze, he amended with, "Mind Manipulators can cast their own mental shields against fellow Mind Manipulators. That's why Garvis and I are the only ones who try to follow, because we know that if we're interrogated, we can block out the truth and feed out lies. I'd never ask Terrin or the twins to put themselves at risk by trying to investigate anything."

Because if *they* were interrogated and found out, he didn't need to say, they'd find out where the exiled went, alright. By joining them.

"So," I said, trying not to let the halo of sparkles around Coen's head—cast by the gemstones behind him—distract me. "You think a Manipulator on the Good Council is casting a shield around the exiled... to prevent anyone from following like you and Garvis try to do?"

"I think that's exactly what's happening."

Coen's hands had come to rest near my elbows, anchoring me into place. I tried to tell myself our closeness had everything to do with the secrets spilling from our lips and nothing to do with... anything else. Tried and failed.

"Garvis and I have always suspected the Good Council changes course as soon as they mute those kidnapped minds," Coen continued in a harsh whisper. "We've always scoured the shores afterward, but... there's never any sign of them. And..." He paused, as if weighing whether or not he wanted to tell me. Something seemed to fall into place in his eyes. "And I don't think the dome around Eshol would *let* anybody leave, anyway. Even the exiled ones."

For a moment, only the crash of the waterfall blared around us.

"How did you and the others get through it all those years ago?" I whispered. "What *is* the dome, anyway?"

I'd always imagined it was a staticky material made of different types of magic. Perhaps a solid wall of air woven with a Mind Manipulating charm to stay away, or a vault of iron that the Shape Shifters made appear invisible.

Coen seemed to shiver. He stepped away from me, dragging his fingers through his hair and looking toward the waterfall instead—or perhaps he was looking past the waterfall, toward the place where his old home bobbed on the sea.

"Think of it like a sort of... disease. Or a poison made solid." He still didn't look at me, as if he were ashamed, when he said, "And Terrin, Garvis, the twins, and I—we're all immune to it. That's how we got through."

I tried not to gape. Tried to process the information without letting it show on my face.

"So in theory," I said, stepping closer to him again, "you five could go in and out as you please? The shield isn't actually keeping you in?" *You could return to your family whenever you wished, if they still remembered you. If they'd still take you back.*

The thought made me wonder if my own mother was immune as well, if that's how she'd stepped foot on the island and met Fabian and left again just as easily after I was born. If she'd left at all. I wouldn't know unless Fabian ever returned my message.

"In theory," Coen agreed, his eyes flitting back to mine.

I felt a tickle in my mind, a gentle probing. Shadows seemed to cross his face.

200

"Do you know why your power slipped through the suppressant?" he asked.

"No." I started, surprised that he was even asking me. "I'd assumed it was just something that happened from time to time." The silence between us swelled with crashing water. "That's... that's never happened to you?"

Coen shook his head slowly. "The pill has never failed any of us before. I can't remember the last time I actually felt my own power, having taken a suppressant every week for... what is it? Seven years now?" Another tickle in my mind. "Can you explain to me what it felt like, to lose a bit of it?"

I knew he could access my memories, that he could see for himself—had *already* seen for himself. What he wanted now was my own verbalized perception.

"It felt like..." I looked around as if I might be able to find the right words sparkling on the tips of each gemstone. "It felt like a slice of it slipped through the bars of a jail cell or something." I couldn't help but imagine the spindly pieces of cheese that curled at the end of a cheese grater. The slice of power had been just as thin, just as malleable, just as localized.

Coen's lips twitched as he saw that image in my mind, too. But the smile never fully took form, because the next second he tipped back his head and sighed.

"I wonder if we should increase your dose."

"Absolutely not," I started. "Not when I don't even know where you get them or how you make them."

A pained expression. I almost wanted to smooth out the sudden lines in his forehead with my fingers. To force his worry to soften.

"I have to pay for them, you know," he said quietly, "and part of that payment involves my... confidentiality. They don't want the Good Council to know what they're providing me with."

I considered this. Imagined a pharmacist or herbalist in Coen's adopted village, mixing special powders of who-knew-what and filling those pearl-shaped capsules with the mixture. The more I thought about it, the more I couldn't blame the herbalist—or whoever they were—for making Coen swear his secrecy. If the Good Council found out...

"Fine." I unleashed a breath. "I can respect that." I let myself get lost in the cascading glitters, the warped, pulsing starlight around us... if only to give my brain a break from *thinking* so hard. "This place is beautiful, you know."

"It is, isn't it?" But Coen hadn't followed my gaze. His stayed on my face.

I returned my focus to him.

"What is it?" I could tell something was bothering him about my own expression. "Do I have tomato juice on my face, or something?"

Unfortunately, no, or I'd lick it off for you.

His voice was merely a wisp in my mind, as if he'd let that thought pass through his defenses. I supposed if he was already loitering in my head, it would be hard to contain his own thoughts from me. I didn't know whether to nudge him playfully or protest or wipe my mouth, as if I could feel where he'd lick me—but before I could decide, Coen rushed on.

"I just don't want you to worry about us—me and Garvis, or the twins and Terrin. I can feel the... the weight of your fear for us, but we're going to pass the Final Test. All five of us." His eyes blazed with those flecks of quartz, and I suddenly found him more mesmerizing than the waterfall or gemstones. "And when your time comes, Rayna, you're going to pass it, too. You have years to practice your control, so in the meantime, that's exactly what I want you to do, okay? Practice, and enjoy your friends, and—"

I tore myself away from him suddenly.

"So we're just supposed to ignore this possibility of a torture chamber overlooking our entire island?"

"Oh, no." Coen bared his teeth in a grin, as if challenging me. "*I'm* not going to ignore it. And neither is Garvis. Him and I are going to investigate the hell out of this, but you, Terrin, Sasha, and Sylvie are going to stay as far away from it as you can get. Garvis and I can protect ourselves, but if any of *you* get caught snooping around, the Good Council will tear your minds to shreds, so I don't even want to hear it. Understood?"

I pretended to really contemplate it, even though a weak, miserable part of me was so, so relieved to hear it. That I could keep pretending everything was fine.

"Will you at least tell me what you find?" I asked finally. "Because you say I have years to practice, but..." And the truth seemed to touch down on my skin, sending ripples of goosebumps over the barest parts of my body. "But in half a year, you'll be gone, which means no more pills for me. No more suppressing this." I rubbed my chest. "Which means I might be heading to that mountaintop sooner than—"

"Don't." His tone came out as a low snarl. "Don't you dare think that I'll leave you defenseless. I will find a way to get the pills to you every week for as long as you need them."

We were close again, my breasts nearly brushing the underside of his own chest muscles. I could smell the rich, mellow scent of black bamboo that always seemed to linger on his skin, in his hair, and it made me think of our faux make-out session. The feel of his weight on top of me and the taste of his tongue in my mouth.

I snapped my mouth shut, mortified—because I could feel him in my mind, and by the way his mouth pulled into his biggest smirk yet, I could tell he was reliving each of those moments as well. But through *my* experience, not through his.

"Interesting," he drawled, as if bored. "I thought you were over it."

"How could I be over it?" I snapped. "How can I even look at any other guy on campus when *you're* always on my mind? Literally."

Coen's smirk sagged a tad. "I didn't realize I was holding you back. I'm sorry if I'm overstepping... or keeping you from experimenting with—"

"Oh, I don't want to experiment with anyone else but you." My frustration flowed over, heating my mouth. "But you're going to leave in a few months, so what's the point, and Kimber already hates me, and Jenia thinks *I'm sleeping my way to the top*, and—"

"Get down," Coen said suddenly, with such savage intensity that I thought someone from one of the pirate ships must have spotted us from the sea. I obeyed instantly, hurtling onto the blanket at our feet. "On your back," he added.

Now my heartrate spiked for a completely different reason.

I laid down slowly. Coen sank to his knees and bowed over me.

"You really want to experiment with me?" His breath was sweet, rich, hot.

I could only manage a nod, my heart fluttering in my mouth.

Coen's answering grin met my lips.

CHAPTER

25

It was hungrier than last time, this kiss.

Coen wasn't just filling me, but *demanding* me, his tongue exploring every inch of my mouth before he withdrew just enough to whisper against my lips, "Has anyone touched you here before?"

I shuddered against the scrape of his fingers over my breasts—above my shirt, but hard enough to make them pebble against him.

"Yes," I breathed.

Wilder had touched me through my clothes back in Alderwick, but it had never felt like *this*. Coen tutted and said, "Let's get his name out of your head, shall we? I only want mine inside you right now."

He moved his hands lower. For a thigh-clenching moment, I thought he was going to dip all the way down... but then his hands dug beneath my shirt and rose up again, stroking me skin-to-skin, finding my bra and sweeping around to unclip me from behind. And then his bare hands were cupping me, his thumbs making circles around my peaks.

"How about this?" he asked, his drawl fading away as something more urgent took its place.

I managed to shake my head. "Not... not exactly."

My hips rose to meet his body as if against my will, and I felt it, then. His own desire, hard and large and unyielding. I tipped my head back at the pressure, at the need for *more*, closing my eyes against the brilliance of a million gemstones.

Coen heard me. He always heard me. His hands snaked down my ribcage and latched onto the apex of my thighs over my pants, but it wasn't enough.

"So impatient," he murmured against my neck.

"Maybe I wouldn't be if you went a little faster."

I didn't even know what I was saying, just that I was letting whatever came to mind spill out of my mouth and into his.

At my words, his hands yanked down my pants and the scrap of lace beneath. The cave air bit into me, chilling me, but he pressed himself fully against me until his body heat had stifled any trace of the cold.

"What about here?" he said. "Has anyone ever touched you here?"

One of his hands cupped the back of my neck, holding me in place, while the other... the other spread each of my thighs apart, one by one, and slid down to where I ached and throbbed and *needed* him. His fingers found their mark.

No. No one had ever touched me there, but I could revel in it forever, the pressure and movement of his fingers pushing further and further into me until...

I couldn't suck in a breath fast enough. Couldn't get enough of this.

"Is this enough experimentation for you?" Coen asked, tilting his head as if it was such an innocent little question. As if his own hunger wasn't sparking in his eyes.

"No," I choked out. "Not... not nearly enough." My fingers scrabbled at his back as his fingers moved inside me, exploring my body from

206

the inside-out. He was staring at me, now, a look of utter fascination stealing over his whole face.

I stared back, realizing with a jolt that Coen Steeler was.... was actually *in* me and not acting haughty or boastful or smug or anything I would have expected.

Rayna Drey.

His voice was a caress in my mind. He didn't make a single comment about the moans escaping my mouth or the small puddle I was surely making or the way my hips arched against his touch again and again, delirious for more, more, more.

You are much too lovely for this world, was all Coen said, and it was his name—his name *only*—that raged like a waterfall in my head as he stroked me deeper into bliss.

We got back to Bascite Boulevard by dawn, where Coen kissed me goodbye right in front of all those windows and left me by the front door of my house.

I walked inside, exhaustion touching down on my shoulders for the first time since the Testing Center... but the butterfly wings beating in my ribcage wouldn't die down.

We'd made out for *hours,* touching each other in every way except for that final one, the one neither of us could bear to do in a semi-open cave. But God of the Cosmos, I'd never known I could lose myself in pure, carnal *feeling* before. No thinking. Just touching and exploring and tasting and losing myself to him and his skin.

Almost to the stairs, I lurched to a stop at the sight of Emelle, dozing upright on one of the sofas, her outfit from last night blending in with the sofa's velvet fabric. As if she'd fallen asleep waiting for me to come home.

Oh, shit.

"Melle?" I rushed forward and shook her shoulder. "Hey, Melle, I'm here."

Her eyes fluttered open. Dazed, she blinked away her sleep and took me in.

"Rayna." Her focus sharpened. She sat up straighter. "Rayna. Where the hell *were* you? Willa said you'd gone somewhere with Coen, but she didn't know where. And after those tests that screwed everyone over, I was so worried something had gone wrong with yours."

The butterflies in my heart fell dead at her expression, a mix of something I'd never seen on Emelle's face before: fear mixed with... distrust. Aimed at me.

Something crumpled within me, because how could I tell her the truth? I didn't think she would ever run off and tell the Good Council about my forbidden power, but I also didn't want to involve her, not when she'd be at risk for it.

"I failed the last test," I started haltingly. "I—I couldn't get those cockroaches off me, and was really upset by the time I left, so I called for Coen. As a distraction." The words came out like rocks, clunkier and heavier than they should have been.

Emelle's face didn't break from that horrible, mistrusting expression.

"You failed the test like everyone else and thought running away with your crush for the night, without telling any of your friends where you were going or how long you'd be out—you thought *that* was a good idea?"

I'd never heard such sharp edges to her words, and I felt myself cringing.

"Hearing you say that out loud, no, it doesn't seem like it was a good idea. I'm really sorry, Emelle. I should have told you where I was going so you didn't worry."

"It's not just that." Now the sharpness of her voice cracked a bit. "It's the thought that you didn't think I could help you. I *want* to help you, Rayna, just like you're always helping me. I want to be there for you, but I can't if you don't let me."

"I'm sorry," I said again, and now a single tear bit into the corner of my eye. *Tell her something true,* I begged myself, *if you can't tell her about Ms. Pincette's warning.*

I lowered myself onto the cushion beside her.

"I think... I think I'm afraid that you'll abandon me like Quinn did, if I mess up somehow. I'm afraid I'll hold you back by clinging to you, and you'll resent me just as much as she did." My vision swam as the full weight of what I was saying sunk in. "I don't want to lose you."

"Oh, Rayna."

Emelle folded her arms around me and brought me close. She didn't say anything for a moment, just squeezed and rocked, before pulling back to look at me.

"You can cling to me all you want, okay? That's just the beauty of getting to pick your friends. Some people don't like that level of closeness, but I do." She smiled. "And I'm so grateful you chose to say hi to me after the Branding, because I couldn't ask for a better best friend to go through these next five years with."

Now I choked on a watery laugh.

"I think I'm the lucky one, Melle. But thank you. And I promise I'll let you know next time I go running off." I swiped a wrist across my eyes to clear the tears beading on my lashes. "By the way," I sniffed, "how did *your* test go?"

"Ugh." She leaned her head against the sofa's back pillows. "I couldn't get that stupid owl's riddle. Or, I guess *I'm* the stupid one, because I gave it a slug when apparently it had been asking for a toad. So said Mr. Conine."

I blew out a whistle. "I nearly failed that one. And the cockroaches killed me."

Almost literally.

Emelle cocked her head at me now. "When you say you called for Coen to distract you...?"

"No. We didn't have sex." I glanced around for signs of Jenia or Kimber before whispering, "but we did kiss."

Emelle squealed and clapped her hands. "I knew it. You look like *something* went down between you two." She gestured at my hair. If it had been a nest before my time with Coen, I couldn't imagine what it looked like now. "Where did you go, anyway?"

I was spared having to answer this question by the sudden appearance of Rodhi, who had barged upstairs from the common area and panted, "Cookies. Wren and Gileon made cookies downstairs. Apparently, Gileon's tired of all the combat training with Wren so he forced her to do something else for a change, and I thought I'd give you the courtesy of letting you know before I eat them all."

"How sweet of you, Rodhi," I said, trying not to roll my eyes.

"Anytime, darling." He winked at me. "Hope your night was as fun as your hair suggests it was, by the way. Did you and Steeler finally smash?"

This time it was Emelle who saved me from answering by jumping up.

"I'm gonna go grab Lander. He wouldn't want to miss cookies."

Rodhi and I slipped each other smirks as Emelle ran out the front door.

210

CHAPTER

26

The weeks following that first test were... brutal.

Not because the instructors themselves ramped up their lessons, but because our entire class found an aggressive new desire to outperform everyone else. Nobody fell asleep in History or The Language of Plants anymore. Nobody held back in Predators & Prey or Spiders, Worms & Insects. Even Jenia quit cutting through the teachers' voices with her whispers, her attention directed at each lecture with the sharpness of cold-cut steel.

A majority of the class, it seemed, had failed at least one portion of the test. And from the rumors see-sawing between the girls' and boys' houses, it sounded like only about two-thirds of us would improve enough to pass the test in five years, if we were anything like all the Wild Whispering classes before us.

Which made it a relief, one day in late fall, when Terrin caught up to me and Emelle as we were walking back to the house and invited us to his Element Wielder snow formal—an annual event placed strategically the weekend before the second test.

"To get everyone's mind off their own nerves," Terrin explained, just as we all three came to the bridge arching over the estuary.

I couldn't walk over that bridge without remembering the tunnel winding along somewhere beneath it, and what had happened between Coen and me at the end of that tunnel. Of course, it had happened a few more times throughout these last few weeks, but always in Coen's room, never in that cave gilded with gemstones. And we'd never gone all the way.

Still, though, I blushed as our footsteps clinked over the metal archway.

Terrin shook back his shaggy head of hair and surveyed me. "You alright, Drey? Your cheeks look a little flushed. Is it something I said?"

I knew better than to fall for his oh-so-concerned expression. Coen himself had told me that out of all his childhood friends, he and Terrin were the most alike, so I caught the smug little glint in his eyes and the way his mouth had quirked.

"Oh, no, I'm actually cold, Terrin. Aren't you?" A lie. Even in the wet season, the only part of the island that actually got cold was the top of Bascite Mountain or the places Element Wielders *made* cold.

Terrin gave a savage grin. He was a pirate, too, I reminded myself. *Had* been at least. I'd grown up hearing stories of pirates with fangs who dug into the exiled offerings each year and drained them until they were nothing but empty sacks of skin, yet here one was, grinning at me as he snapped his fingers.

Instantly, the water beneath us jumped and plopped with boils as big as my head. Steam billowed upward, swaddling us in its scorching mist. Emelle shrieked.

"Is that better?" Terrin asked casually.

"Show off," I muttered. I wouldn't be able to do anything more than maybe convince a fish to jump on him... but it would have to be a particularly stupid fish.

"See you ladies at the dance," was Terrin's only reply.

Apparently, Emelle and I weren't particularly special when it came to the snow formal. Since every Element Wielder was allowed to invite as many people as they wanted, the invitations spread like wildfire, until it seemed that the entire *Institute* was going.

"I just don't understand what we're supposed to wear," Emelle said that night in the bathing chambers while we were getting ready for bed.

Wren, beside us, stopped brushing her teeth long enough to mumble through her foaming toothpaste, "seem sir from card eeh ah."

Emelle stopped with a comb halfway to her hair. " *What?*"

Wren spit into the washing bin and tried again.

"Seamster from Cardina. The closest village on the other side of that ridge behind campus. He comes every wet season to sell us new clothes—along with some other villagers with all their goodies. You know, since our stuff is bound to break or rip over the years we're here, President Gleekle lets them come to campus once a year to basically screw us over with their inflated prices." She resumed brushing her teeth. "But it would be the best time to get a new dress for the formal, I'd imagine."

Her tone was careful... and rather stiff.

"Didn't you go to the formal last year?" I asked, watching her in the mirror.

Wren scoffed. "No. Not that I was invited, anyway, but it sounds horrible."

Coen, I thought into the void, right then and there.

213

To my surprise, he answered a heartbeat later. *Yes?*

Can you have Terrin invite Wren to the formal? I didn't let a single part of my expression twitch on my face, lest Wren sense some scheming going on.

Like, romantically? Coen asked. *You want me to play matchmaker?*

No, no, no. I mean—just make sure they can come. Rodhi and Gileon, too.

Coen snickered. *Rodhi's already got about twenty-five different invitations, but I'll make sure Terrin gets ahold of Wren and Gileon in time.*

Thank you.

Any other demands at this late hour? he asked. *Or can I finally go to sleep?*

Hey, you're the one in my head. You didn't have to answer.

A pause. I vaguely heard Emelle telling Wren she thought she'd look beautiful in cobalt or scarlet. Then Coen admitted, *I didn't mean to be in your head.*

What?

I was dozing off. My mind must have drifted to you.

I didn't know how to respond to that. Through all his coy words and teasing smiles, things like *this* would slip through every once in a while—and make me wonder why I hadn't given myself fully to him yet. It was just that... Jenia's words would slither into my ears every time I thought I was close: *Why're you holed up in his room every weekend, then, if not to sleep your way to the top?* It would make me pull back, panting and scrambling up with some kind of excuse to hurry away. I knew that I shouldn't let someone else's disdain affect me so much, and if everyone already thought I was sleeping with him, what was the point of *not?*

But something... something superstitious lurked in me, begging me to be careful. Begging me to wait, to see if this thing between us was all just a joke or a trick.

It's not, came Coen's sleepy reply in my head, *but I respect your caution.*

Goodnight, you, I said quickly, before he could hear any other mortifying, perpetually spiraling thoughts.

Sweetest dreams, my little hurricane.

And his mind dropped from mine like a feather floating to the ground.

On the day the Cardina peddlers came to campus, everyone broke their serious streak in Mr. Conine's class to chat loudly about what they wanted to buy while we played with sloths—or, at least, while we *tried* to play with sloths.

Most of the creatures were simply clinging to us, content to listen to our conversation with wide, glassy eyes. Mr. Conine himself was busy leaning back in his chair at the head of the classroom, surveying us lazily as if he hadn't a care in the world.

"I'm going to buy something for Ms. Pincette," Rodhi declared, patting his sloth on its sloped head. "I just don't know *what* yet. What do you women even *like?*" he asked Emelle and me, as if he'd only just noticed us.

"Rodhi, I've told you a million times," I sighed. "Forget Ms. Pincette."

Rodhi sighed back at me, as if *I* were the unreasonable one here. "I found out she's twenty-eight, so only a decade older than us. A ten-year age gap is nothing, darling."

"I think I'd like flowers," Emelle said dreamily beside us, stroking her sloth's moss-glazed back. "Preferably the kind that don't sing opera."

"I'm going to get Wren a needle," Gileon said, smiling down at his own sloth that had crawled up to his neck.

I blinked at him. "Just... just a needle? What about thread?"

Not that I could imagine Wren sewing, but...

Gileon scratched his head. "She only ever talks about needles. And sticking them in people's ice. She's never mentioned thread."

One of the sloths let out a low, slow chuckle.

Eyes. Whenever anyone annoyed her, Wren always said that she'd like to stick a needle in their *eyes.*

Rodhi, Emelle, and I spent the rest of class biting our lips.

Finally, Mr. Conine announced the end of class, we carried our sloths back to their favorite trees, and everyone began surging toward the courtyard.

We heard it before we had even rounded the last corner: the shouting and haggling, the jingling of coins and jewelry. I wasn't expecting it, though, when we finally stopped at the edge of the cobblestone and found *hundreds* of tents and carts bulging from the courtyard, all packed together so tightly, I couldn't even fathom pushing my way through the mess. It was even more hectic than that first day of our arrival, with hardly enough space to walk between each row of carts. The monkeys only stirred up the chaos, lunging forward from the sidelines to steal bits of merchandise and shrieking with laughter when the vendors shooed them away.

Rodhi rubbed his hands together, a competitive glint to his eyes.

"Wish me luck. I'm going in."

And he barged into the fray.

I glanced at Emelle and Gileon. "Let's just wander along the outer edge first?"

There'd be no point in trying to find Coen in this mess. He'd reach out to me once his last class of the day had ended, I knew.

Gileon squinted ahead. "I think I see a wagon with sewing supplies, actually. It's by the fountain. I'm going to go there first if that's okay with you, Rayna."

Oh, right. Gileon, despite his sweet demeanor, *did* tower over everyone else and would be able to see over the sea of all those bobbing heads.

"Sure." I waved a hand. "See you later, Gil."

When it was just Emelle and me, we began meandering along the outskirts, smiling politely at most vendors who tried to hail us down, but stopping to inspect the merchandise of an old woman who was selling chocolate truffles. Before leaving the house for Mr. Fenway's class this morning, I'd filled my pockets with those untouched copper coins I'd brought from home, and now I felt them clink together at the top of my thighs as I brought one out to pay for two truffles, one for Emelle and one for me.

Once upon a time, I used to watch Fabian and Don use their Summoning magic to grind up roasted cocoa beans. The smell reminded me of Alderwick, of home, and I chewed on my truffle slowly to savor it as Emelle and I moved on. I suddenly ached for my fathers so much that I barely even registered when one of the vendors called my name.

"Rayna. Are you Rayna Drey?"

I whipped around, toward a striped green tent where a man with sagging, yellow-tinted cheeks was peering at me beadily, a cigarette clamped between two meaty fingers. Racks of wool blankets hung all around him, swaying in a thick breeze, and the man beckoned with his free hand.

I took a few steps toward him uncertainly, Emelle on my heels.

"Yes?" I swallowed my chocolate.

Perhaps he was a Manipulator, and this was a tactic to sell more blankets: invade passersby's minds, pick out their names, and call out to them as if he knew them personally. I stopped a few paces short of his tent, just out of reach.

"I've got something for ya," the man growled.

He turned to rummage through the blankets behind him one-handedly, keeping his cigarette aloft with the other hand. Taking a step back, I said, "Oh, no thank you. I'm afraid I've already got enough blankets, but—"

"No, no, no." The man turned back around—this time with a folded piece of paper pinched between one of those meaty fingers and his thumb. "This is for you."

Emelle furrowed her brows at me. Perhaps I shouldn't touch it, the paper, in case this was some kind of marketing ploy... a Mind Manipulating charm that would force me to buy a blanket once I read what was on it, or a Shape Shifting trick that meant the paper was actually a quilt.

But I found myself reaching out for the paper even as Emelle let out a small gasp.

I unfolded it before I could think twice. And found my full name scrawled at the head of the page.

My knees went watery, as if all my bones had melted at the sight of that scrawl.

I would know his handwriting anywhere. I had spent my childhood years, after all, watching him write things down without even touching the pen.

Fabian had finally written back.

CHAPTER

27

"He said he'd buy five of my blankets if I delivered this to the girl who looks just like him," the vendor was saying, but I could hardly hear him over the rush of blood in my ears as I devoured each scribbled line.

Dearest Rayna,

I received your letter by crow (he gave us quite a fright, squawking outside our window in the dead of night), and I believe I've correctly decoded your message. However, I'm afraid, as I've always been, that you will come to loathe me if I tell you the details of what happened a little more than eighteen years ago. You are my greatest love, my proudest achievement, and I've only ever wanted to keep you safe.

Still, if this is as important as you made it out to be in your letter, if you will try your very best to understand where I was coming from before you decide to never speak with me again — then follow me.

That was it. No salutations, no signature. Just *follow me*, written in a slightly wobblier hand than every other line, as if Fabian's wrist had been shaking.

"Follow me?" I whispered, then whipped my gaze this way and that, half convinced I'd see my father pop up from behind one of the many carts or tents around us.

I returned my attention to the vendor when nothing happened.

"You said he bought five of your blankets for you to give me this? Did he say anything else?"

The vendor studied me, those beady eyes crawling with curiosity as he took a drag from his cigarette. Too much curiosity for my liking. I leaned closer to Emelle, who was glancing at my letter with an equal mixture of confusion and concern.

"No, kid," the vendor said. "He bought five of my blankets, told me I'd recognize you by the hair—truly the same as his, I might add— and that was it. He left before I could ask any more questions."

"Was there anyone else with him, by chance?" *Had Don been there, too?* I tried to imagine either of my fathers traveling all the way from Alderwick to Cardina just to buy some blankets and pass along a let-ter—it would have taken them a few days of travel via regular wagon, and that's assuming they'd had enough Summoning power to propel the wheels forward over the roughest of terrain.

But the vendor scratched his nose with a dirt-packed fingernail. "No, there wasn't nobody else with him. Just him and this paper."

Hmm. I peered back down to study the ink of that last line again. *Follow me.*

And suddenly the paper quivered in my hands. Like a pair of invis-ible hands had suddenly grabbed the corner and *tugged.*

I let go, watching as the paper fluttered away. But the breeze had died down within the stuffiness of all the commotion, so there was no way it could be flying at all right now unless—

I lurched after it, away from the vendor and his tent of blankets, back to the outer edges of the courtyard, where the monkeys were still springing forward to steal stray bits of food and clothing.

"Wait! Rayna!" It was Emelle, hurrying after me.

"I'll meet you later, Melle," I called over my shoulder. "I've got to—"

"No. I'm coming with you." She caught up and fell into a pounding rhythm beside me. "I'm not letting you run after some enchanted piece of paper alone."

And that's exactly what it was, I realized with a jolt that nearly had me toppling into the nearest stand, where the paper fluttered over a towering rack of shoes. An enchantment. A complicated bit of Summoning magic that Fabian had imbued within the parchment fibers, something he'd never done before at home. At least not in front of me.

I skirted around the shoe stand after it, into the wedge of quaint wooden classrooms reserved for the Summoners. What could I say to Emelle to make her stop chasing me? I couldn't pause long enough to come up with an excuse, or else I might lose the paper, but... what if it led us to something I couldn't properly explain to her? What if she found out about my power and the pills and the pirates?

"Melle," I panted, but she cut me off.

"No. I know you're hiding something, Rayna. I can see it in your eyes sometimes, something distant and—" She huffed out a breath "—foreign."

I glanced sideways to find her jaw set, her fists curled tight as we ran alongside each other: around buildings, up and down sets of creaking wooden stairs, through archways and alleys. The paper maintained an even height from the ground, bobbing along that invisible current toward the back of this side of campus.

"Okay," I told her finally. "But Melle, you can't tell anyone about this, okay?"

My best friend—my beautiful, determined best friend—didn't ask why. Didn't pry any further or demand any more details. She only said, "Deal," and then jerked her chin at the paper ahead of us. "Look. I think it's slowing down."

Sure enough, Fabian's letter jerked back and spiraled, as if caught in a whirlwind, near one of the last buildings in the Summoner section of classrooms: a derelict wooden shack with half its shingles missing like rows of rotting teeth.

Here, the jungle bowed over us, ropes of moss drooping down from the trees and whispering against the ground. The clattering sounds of Cardina had disappeared behind us. There weren't even any monkeys to toss jokes back and forth over our heads. Just the humming of the trees, low and perhaps a little foreboding.

As we watched, the paper swooped through one of the windows bordered with jagged edges of broken glass—and vanished into the gloom.

Follow me, Fabian had said. Apparently, he had meant into this old classroom.

I stepped toward a side door. It wasn't hanging off its hinges yet, but the bruised brown and yellow color of old rot patched its surface.

Emelle sucked in a deep breath behind me and nodded. I turned the rusted green knob, and we crept through together.

Inside, I could just barely make out the paper whipping this way and that in the center of a room haphazardly held together with criss-crossing wooden beams.

"What—?" Emelle started to say.

And Fabian's letter tore itself into shreds.

We watched its pieces fall to the floor like a pile of dead moth wings.

Did he mean for me to find something hidden beneath a loose floor-board? I lurched forward to check when a voice cracked through the staleness of the room.

"*Who's disrupting my beauty sleep, hmmm? Let me take a look at you.*"

The voice scraped against my eardrums like metal against metal. Emelle, too, cringed at the sound of it—just as two pinpricks of skeleton-white broke the dark: a pair of eyes dangling high above us.

When it shifted, more pinpricks shattered the darkness around it, like hundreds of stars blinking awake. A great ripple of rustling and scratching followed, spreading from one end of the ceiling to the other, and it clicked for me then.

"Bats," I whispered to Emelle.

"*Oh, not just any bats,*" the voice screeched. "*The last of the tomb bats from the ancient Asmodeus Colony. And I am its highest heir, Lord Arad.*"

From the feeble stream of light wafting through the broken window, I was starting to make out their vague silhouettes. Clumps of squirming bodies clung to the crisscrossed beams with clawed, human-like hands, their ears twitching in our direction. The one who had addressed us hung in the center of them all, bigger and more skeletal than the others.

"*Now what do you want, human?*" Lord Arad continued. "*They shut this classroom down nearly thirty years ago, so I know you're not here to learn.*"

Thirty years ago? So before Fabian's time, then, from what I knew. I felt my shoulders deflate at the thought that perhaps his Summoning enchantment had gone awry, had led us to the wrong place. These bats wouldn't know anything about Fabian if he'd never been a student in here, right? Unless...

"Has anyone else been in here since they shut it down?" I asked, inching closer to Emelle's body heat. "Maybe as a prank or a game? Or a hiding place?"

I was scrabbling at nothing in this darkness, and a sudden, angry taste of bitterness filled my mouth.

Why? Why couldn't Fabian have just told me about my mother *before* I had left for the Institute? I knew why he couldn't write such sensitive information in a letter, but he'd had plenty of years to tell me before this. And yet the best he'd been able to do was put a mysterious knife in my bag mere hours before my departure.

Emelle must have sensed my despair, because she found my hand and squeezed.

"*Why*," Lord Arad spit, fumbling to adjust his upside-down grip on the beam, "*should I entertain the feeble questions of a human pup such as yourselves?*"

I froze at the tone. We'd never talked to bats in Mr. Conine's class, but I vaguely remembered Mr. Fenway mentioning something about them in History. How most of them were as eagerly friendly as domesticated kittens, but one colony...

Emelle remembered seconds before I did. She straightened to her full height, pinned Lord Arad with an exceptional glare, and said, "You should entertain her *compelling* question because she's friends with Jagaros."

Tomb bats, Mr. Fenway had said, were the last descendants of the ancient vampires and were therefore extremely proud of their lineage. They would only deign to talk to other esteemed members of Esholian society—never a nobody.

The tomb bats halted their rustling at Emelle's declaration.

"*Jagaros... Jagaros the king?*" Lord Arad asked, a hint of fear in his screech.

I cleared my throat. "The faerie king of old, yes."

I wasn't exactly sure this was accurate, but if you put two and two together...

"*How do we know you're not lying through your ugly square teeth?*" Lord Arad shifted his grip on the beams. "*My ancestors would have sucked you dry and spit their venom on your bones just for claiming such a ludicrous thing.*"

I gaped upward, but a rougher, colder voice answered in my stead.

"*She's not lying, and I ate your wretched ancestors for breakfast.*"

The tomb bats broke into a frenzy, flapping away to cower in further corners of the room. Emelle pressed closer to me, but I—I beamed as the white tiger padded to a halt beside me, his tail flicking.

"*Now,*" Jagaros growled up at the lead bat, who had scrambled higher up a beam, "*answer the girl's question. I would like to hear the answer myself.*"

With that, he slumped down at my feet, folded his paws, and whipped his tail.

"*Of c-course, Your Majesty,*" Lord Arad screeched, then angled his head back toward me. "*You'd like to know what again, dear? If anyone else has been in here to disturb us recently?*"

"Not necessarily recently," I said, resisting the urge to reach out and pet Jagaros with my Emelle-free hand; I had a feeling he'd be livid if I treated him like a housecat in front of these assholes. "But anytime in the last, oh, I don't know, twenty-three years?"

For it had been twenty-three years ago when Fabian had first set foot on the Esholian Institute campus, so if anything significant had happened in this putrid space—if his letter had truly meant to lead me *here*, of all places—it must have occurred during that time frame.

Again, my eyes flicked toward the floor beneath those fallen scraps of paper. Maybe I should just be done with this Lord Arad and check for loose boards...

But another tomb bat, even higher-pitched than Lord Arad, suddenly cheeped, "*There was the lady from the sea, Father, remember? She slunk in from the shore and set up camp in here for nearly a year, spying on anyone who walked past.*"

"*Ahh, that does sound familiar, thank you, Velika.*"

From the forced tone of Lord Arad's screech, I could tell he'd been withholding this information on purpose and would reprimand the younger bat later.

"*Yes, there was the lady from the sea, who had hair dark as shadows but skin that glowed like honey.*"

My blood dropped. It was probably just my imagination running rampant, but that description... it was exactly how I would have painted Dyonisia Reeve.

I shook my head, though. Ridiculous. I was being ridiculous. Dyonisia Reeve had been on this island, watching over Esholian affairs, for hundreds of years. She wouldn't have come from the sea or stationed herself *here*, of all places. The similarity in appearance had to be a coincidence.

"Uhh..." I glanced at Emelle, who squeezed my hand again and nodded her encouragement. "What was this lady from the sea doing here? Spying, you said?"

Lord Arad rustled his wings. "*Spying. Taking notes. Meeting with that boy.*"

"What boy?" My heart seemed to skip way too many beats.

Lord Arad almost didn't answer, but Jagaros let loose a grumbling growl, and he went on quickly, "*There was a boy—maybe a young man, I don't know—who was practicing his Summoning magic right outside*" *the window when he heard her sneeze. He came to investigate and found her standing in here with a knife, poised to kill him. She jolted into action when the boy suddenly said, 'Who are you? What are you doing here? Are you okay?' And all his ruddy questions seemed to stun the lady of the sea, who paused long enough to take him in. She saw his wild blonde curls and his much-too-tender, weak little face and dropped her knife right then and there."*

"*It was love at first sight,*" the younger bat named Velika sighed.

"*It was ludicrous at first sight,*" Lord Arad snapped. "*Utter ludicrous! They didn't even know each other, yet we had to watch them gawk and flirt and keep meeting each other to talk about wretched stars and dreams, and later on—*"

"*I'm sure we can skip what happened later on, Father,*" Velika cheeped.

I couldn't take a deep enough breath. Wild blonde curls and a tender face—that had definitely been Fabian. Which meant he'd found my mother, a pirate who'd been immune to the island's shield just like Coen. A pirate who'd snuck through to spy. And they'd... fallen in love here. Not just on this campus, but in this forgotten, festering classroom.

I could practically see it, the tent and sleeping bag and supplies she must have set up in here, stolen food and canteens of spring water piled up in one corner, and clothes and weapons piled up in the other. And all the while, these bats must have dangled and squirmed and watched above her.

But the next part of the story went blank in my mind. How had they separated?

Jagaros, bless him, growled up the question for me.

"*Such a sad moment,*" Velika said quietly.

"*Such an* expected *moment,*" Lord Arad corrected. "*Human love never lasts.*"

227

I cringed against Emelle at that, images of Coen flashing before me, but Lord Arad had already plunged on.

"*She had the baby, right here on this floor. For a month, they raised the baby together, the boy rushing over to feed and burp and other disgusting things after his classes. And then he took his Final Test and passed it, and she told the boy she had to go back. She'd take the baby, she said, and raise it on the ships, and train it to fight in an upcoming war. The child would grow up to be a spy and assassin and warrior. It would be an honor, the lady said, to provide her people with such a thing. And she invited the boy to come with her, to leave the island and join her.*"

A deep chill settled to the bottom of my stomach. That child, of course, had been me. My mother had wanted to give me to the pirates... as a baby. She'd wanted to hand me over like a gift. An offering.

"*The boy,*" Lord Arad continued, "*begged her to stay. Begged her to leave the sea behind and find a dull little village with him and raise the child in a respectable, unassuming home. She refused. She said the sea was the child's home. She let him kiss the babe one more time and made to leave. But the boy, crying those horrible, ugly human tears, used his magic to send all the blood in the lady's head to the bottom of her feet.*"

What? I couldn't imagine it, what with Fabian's loathing for violence. Couldn't imagine him holding me in the crook of his arms and sobbing while he knocked my mother out.

"He left with the baby, then?" I asked, and my voice sounded hollow.

It was Velika who cheeped, "*Yes, he left with the baby—and her knife.*"

My blood vibrated within me at that. Her knife. *My* knife, now.

"*The lady of the sea woke up in a rage,*" Velika continued, "*but by that time, he and the baby were long gone. And she couldn't risk*

228

scouring the entire island for them, not when she didn't have one of those strange brands on her shoulder that mark you humans as belonging to that witch on the mountain."

"So she left?" I whispered. "She went back?"

"*She went back,*" Velika confirmed. "*She went back cursing the boy's name and vowing to find her child again one day. But we haven't seen her since.*"

Perhaps the pirates had killed her for fraternizing with an Esholian. Or perhaps she'd simply forgotten about me over all these years. But one thing was clear, as I stood clutching Emelle's hand, listening to the rustling of tomb bats and the grumbling buildup in Jagaros's throat. As my eyes, which had finally fully adjusted to the gloom, saw what lay under the scraps of Fabian's letter: the bloodstains of birth.

No matter how noble or compassionate my father's intent might have been...

He had kidnapped me from my mother eighteen years ago.

CHAPTER

28

Where are you?

It was Coen, brushing his presence against my mind, tasting my shock and anger and fear. He must have just got out of his last class, but I couldn't believe an eternity hadn't passed since I'd first unfolded Fabian's letter.

What happened? What's wrong?

I replayed everything Lord Arad and Velika had said. A curious numbness had slunk through me, lining the inside of my skin with its tingling. Beside me, Emelle had gone still and silent, and I had no idea what she thought of this. Would she tell someone, despite her promise not to? Would she think of me as... tainted, now that she knew I was the daughter of a pirate spy and a traitor?

Because that's exactly what Fabian would be considered to everyone else—a traitor. Someone who'd fallen in love with a threat to the entire island. *A lady of the sea.* I couldn't help the shudder that went through me, as if my body were trying to shake away the numbness and the truth of my birth all in one.

Jagaros tacked his narrowed pupils onto my face.

"*You didn't happen to find a map, did you?*"

Something about his tone—it made me think he had a personal interest in such a thing, so I felt like I'd somehow failed him when I had to shake my head.

"No."

His whiskers twitched in distaste. But... what had he said earlier? That birds had an annoying knack to pass stories down from generation to generation? Obviously, these bats were as far from birds as they could get, but perhaps their ability to fly, to see the world from above, meant they held a unique view of the world.

I straightened my spine and shot upward, "Do you know what's beyond this island? If there are other islands or land masses out there? Other people?"

Lord Arad only paused for a sliver of a second.

"*No. We don't care to see beyond the horizon.*"

Okay. So perhaps I had to narrow my questions. My mother had to have come from *somewhere*, so I asked, "Did she have any magic, this woman? Maybe Shifting or Manipulating?"

"*No, no magic as definable as that,*" Lord Arad said, and his tone told me he was tiring of this conversation. "*Something else. Are we done, now?*"

Coen, still loitering in my mind and observing everything through my eyes, actually growled in my head at the same time that Jagaros did. But I ignored them.

"Yes," I said. "We're done."

"*Good,*" Lord Arad said, "*because you have woken us from a very, very long sleep with your tedious questions, and we are rather hungry when we wake.*"

I hadn't realized the bats dropping to the floor one by one until now, when Jagaros backed his hind quarters into Emelle and me and

231

unleashed his most vicious snarl yet. But there they were, sixty or seventy black, leathery figures stretching their fingers and lengthening their spines, until they faced us in distorted, vaguely humanoid forms. The last descendants of the ancient vampires...

Who hadn't quite devolved back into pure bats. Who were still half-vampires, mutant bloodsuckers that limped closer to the three of us, their eyes flashing red, their fangs suddenly bared.

Rayna? Coen asked urgently. *You're going blank on me. What's happening?*

I could barely feel the shape of my own mouth, let alone properly process what was happening for Coen's sake. When Emelle gave a whimper and Jagaros raised his hackles, it was all I could do to take control of my own tongue again.

"Stop." I stumbled back, but one of the mutants had flipped the door shut with a claw-tipped wing. "You didn't eat the lady of the sea or the boy all those years ago." I tried to keep my voice steady. "Why develop a taste for humans now?"

"*The lady of the sea brought us offerings every day,*" Lord Arad said, unruffled. "*You have brought nothing but yourselves.*"

Apparently, his fear of Jagaros had been feigned, a mere attempt to keep us distracted while his children slowly morphed into their other forms in preparation. They had limped so close now, I could see the gleam of their tongues in all those crooked, gaping mouths, could feel the heat of their decaying breaths.

Jagaros crouched. In the lowest chuff, he whispered to Emelle and me, "*Stay down. Cover your eyes. This might get messy.*"

I couldn't close my eyes, though, even as Emelle pressed her face into my shoulder, her entire frame trembling against mine. I couldn't close my eyes as I felt Coen's presence snap from my head back to his own, as I heard his pounding footsteps barge through the rot-cloaked door behind us and—

The vampire mutants pounced...

Then froze.

Coen jolted to a halt next to me, panting but otherwise so, so still as he extended his hands in concentration, forcing the bats to freeze. Even Lord Arad had gone utterly immobile, still hanging upside-down like a cocoon made of tar.

Jagaros didn't hesitate. While Coen kept them locked in place, commanding them not to move, the tiger began tearing into their necks, ripping those mutant heads from their hulking bodies as if they were nothing but mud.

One by one, he made his rounds, his muscles rippling beneath that black and white coat, black blood dribbling down his maw.

Finally, Jagaros raised himself on his hind legs and...

"No!" I cried. "Not her!" But too late.

Velika managed a last squeak before he ripped her into leathery ribbons.

Then Jagaros turned to Lord Arad himself, who was wide-eyed and drooling with rage, but unable to break from Coen's magic grip.

"*Didn't your ancestors warn you not to mess with the faerie king of old?*" Jagaros grumbled. "*No? That's really too bad. I hate the taste of your kind.*" He turned back toward Coen and said, "*Release it. I want to make it slow.*"

To my shock, Coen nodded as if he understood the tiger's growls. He grabbed Emelle and me by the shoulders and muttered, "C'mon. Let's go."

When the three of us stumbled back out into the mossy green light of the jungle, Coen released his hold on the last heir of the ancient Asmodeus Colony.

And the sounds of Lord Arad's shrieks began.

"You can talk to animals?" I demanded.

We had just stumbled back onto campus, where the courtyard still crawled with vendors and buyers and monkeys, even under the purple tint of dusk. Apparently, the Cardina marketplace wouldn't disband until the last good had sold.

Coen stopped Emelle and me on the edge of the Summoner sector, facing us with folded arms and glancing between us with unnerving speed.

"No, I can't talk to animals, not in the way you can. But when you froze with panic and I couldn't get a straight answer out of you, I had to use alternative methods of communication."

His mind, I realized with a touch of unease. I'd always known Manipulators could *control* animals, but for Coen to have entered Jagaros's mind and plan an attack with him... it was different, somehow. He must have done it while sprinting toward our location from the moment I'd relayed Lord Arad and Velika's story to him.

It would explain the sweat curling the edges of his hair, at least.

I've never ran so fast in my life, Coen confirmed in my head, then jerked his gaze toward Emelle. *She knows everything, then?*

Yes. I didn't know whether to feel sorry or defensive about that. Emelle... she still hadn't said anything. Was still silent and shaking by the knees.

I trust your judgment, Coen said. *Just please don't tell her about the others.*

Of course. I hated the pleading note to his tone. Garvis, Terrin, and the twins—their histories weren't mine to tell, anyways.

234

I turned to Emelle, letting the clamoring sounds of the marketplace camouflage the whisper of my voice.

"Are you okay, Melle?"

She blinked at me. Rubbed her eyes. Blinked again.

"You're asking me if *I'm* okay? Oh, Rayna."

And she dragged me into a hug that cracked the tension in my back.

"I'm afraid for you," she whispered back. "But I'm not afraid *of* you."

It meant more than she'd ever know, those words. I let myself sink into the warmth of her embrace until she quit trembling, until my own heart had eased.

Coen watched us, a faint look of contemplation on his face.

We'll talk later? I asked him.

I wasn't particularly interested in talking about my mother right now. Or about how Fabian... Fabian had stolen me from her. I *was* interested, however, in hearing about the logistics of Coen's communication with Jagaros—Jagaros, whom we'd left in that collapsing hellhole so that he could play with his prey in peace. I hadn't expected it, that viciousness from the faerie king.

The faerie king of old.

I'd pulled those words out of my ass, but Lord Arad had seemed to believe them, despite his family's ploy to attack us anyway. And Jagaros had proven that he wasn't to be messed with, hadn't he?

Animal minds are usually filled with mist as thick as mud, hard for me to wade through. But his *mind was like ice and fire,* Coen murmured into my head, shuddering. *Crystal clear and blazing hot.*

Out loud, he said, "I believe you have a dress to pick up from Grandma Gretel's Gown tent near the fountain. For the Element Wielder formal."

"What?" I cocked an eyebrow at him.

Coen cocked an eyebrow back. "She's the best dressmaker from Cardina. I went straight to her tent after my last class and bought a dress for you. You don't have to wear it if you don't end up liking it," he added, almost rushing through his words.

I stared at him. I'd never seen a shy version of Coen before.

"You bought me a dress for the formal?"

"Well, yeah."

I was all too aware of Emelle watching our exchange.

"Does that mean you're asking me to go with you?"

All that shyness vanished from his face within an instant.

"Only if you're going to say yes."

Then he winked at me and strutted off into the crowd without answering. From the way his hands slipped into his pockets as if he hadn't a care in the world, you'd never know he'd just disabled a roomful of mutant vampires ten minutes ago.

"Wow." Emelle stared after him. "He really likes you. Like, a lot."

I had a feeling she was returning to a surface-level topic as a coping mechanism, and I clung to it furiously, looping my arms through hers so that we could barge into the crowd together. After what had just happened and what she'd said to me afterward, I didn't want to separate from Emelle for the next several hours.

"I just hope the dress he bought actually fits me," I managed to say.

CHAPTER

29

It did.

A week later, I patted myself in front of the bathing chamber mirrors next to Emelle and Wren, soaking in the sight of the dress Coen had picked out.

The dark green silk cascaded to the floor like liquid jade pooling at my feet. Heavy and cool, yet gloriously smooth and comfortable. A slit rose to my upper thigh on the side, allowing me to walk even more freely, and the top...

It was a V-neck that... well, just barely managed to cover my nipples. The inside halves of my breasts were gently pushed together and completely exposed to the world, the crease between them a dark, bobbing line.

I wouldn't have worn anything like this back in Alderwick, but I couldn't imagine wearing anything *else* here at the Esholian Institute. Something had shifted within me since the Branding, something daring and yearning.

"That's possibly the first time a man has ever picked the right thing in all of Esholian history," Wren said with appraisal, eyeing me in the mirror. Then she turned to survey herself again. "He did better than me, anyway. I look like a poisonous frog."

She wore a bright turquoise two-piece connected by chains, with long sleeves that billowed at her wrists and patches of black patterning the bottom half. She'd been mortified, she'd told me, when Terrin had approached her and Gileon before class the other day and invited them to the formal, so mortified that I'd worried she wouldn't come. But she'd had this dress stuffed beneath her bed for a year and had begrudgingly brought it out, saying she'd give the party a try.

"*I think poisonous frogs are beautiful,*" Willa chimed in on the bathroom sill.

"Of course you do," Wren snapped at the mouse. "That's the point of them. They lure you in and then they—" She snapped her teeth, and Willa squeaked with laughter. The two had met a few days ago and were getting along splendidly. Or, at least, as splendidly as someone like Wren could get along with a creature like Willa.

"Well," Emelle said morosely, brushing a finger along her stomach through the scarlet mermaid dress she wore, "I look like a bloodstain, so..."

"Stop it."

They froze. Shit. I'd snapped at them.

I hauled in a deep breath. Forced my tone into something lighter, something without the jagged edge I'd been so prone to since Lord Arad's story. I hadn't been able to sleep lately, but found myself staring into the swirls of the ceiling late into each night instead, caught between so many emotions. Fury at Fabian being one of them. For stealing me from my mother, no matter his reasoning. For refusing to talk about her except for the *night before* I'd left for the Institute, knowing there wasn't enough time to fully dive into all my questions about her.

And fury at my mother, whoever she had been, for wanting to pass me over to the pirates like clay to be molded and sculpted into whatever they wanted from me.

"Neither of you look like a frog or a bloodstain," I said now, more gently. "You look like beautiful women wearing beautiful dresses who are going to have so much fun drinking and dancing, you won't even remember this moment tomorrow."

Not that I'd be able to drink with them. No, Coen still claimed that anything could trigger our raw power, which made me wonder... how had my mother handled her own *less defined* magic, as Lord Arad had put it? Without the pills, how had she subdued herself during her year spying on the island? During her year falling in love with Fabian and carrying me around in her womb?

The doubt hit me again, just as hard as it had in the past.

The pirates are searching for a way to shape their power, Coen had told me once. But Coen himself, Garvis, Terrin, Sylvie, Sasha, and I— we were all living proof that not even bascite could shape that raw power in our pirate blood. It could grant us foreign magic, but never a way to control our own.

Were the pirates truly wanting in for the bascite, then? Or for something else? The pills, perhaps—or whatever they were made of?

Why else would they be circling us so endlessly, sending their children as distractions and spies, and constantly trying to break through the dome?

"Rayna? You there?"

I jumped. Willa had scurried up my dress to my shoulders, and now sniffled up at me, while the other girls stared at me expectantly.

"I'm sorry, what?"

"We asked you if you were ready to go." Emelle's voice was calm, despite Wren's suspicious scrutiny beside her. She knew I'd had trouble sleeping. Heard me toss and turn each night above her, until sometimes she slipped in bed with me and held me until the darkness finally rolled me into dreams.

What Emelle didn't know, though, was my whirlwind of thoughts like the one I'd just had, thoughts that would suck me away from everyone around me and send me spinning through questions and confusion and uncertainty.

My mother and the pirates. Jagaros and the faeries of old.

"Yes," I said, pulling a smile onto my face and briefly running a finger over the imprint of my brand on full display. Just for tonight, I wanted the busy buzzing in my mind to go away. Just for tonight, I'd have fun. "I'm ready."

The Element Wielder houses had been completely transformed.

Whereas before they had resembled cutting-edge squares of the blackest caves, now plump bulges of snow skirted their flat rooftops like sparkling frosting. Snowflakes sprinkled down around them despite a noticeable lack of clouds, and garland bordered each window.

They would have looked rather cold and uninviting, I thought as Emelle, Wren, and I stepped up to Terrin's front door, if it hadn't been for the live sheets of fire eddying within the glass of each double windowpane.

Fire and ice. Like Jagaros's mind, according to Coen. Like the top of Bascite Mountain itself. Perpetually snow-capped and flitting with the lights of Good Council activity.

Activity that included torture.

Our shoes clicked up the steps together, and when we pushed open the door, ethereal music seemed to fill my every pore. Another Mind Manipulating trick? Or—no. Above the hundreds of heads dancing and

240

swaying and mingling, windchimes and other musical instruments hung from the ceiling, played by an intricate wind that swirled along the top of the room. For a moment, I saw Lord Arad and Velika and the other tomb bats again, in the shape of those dangling instruments.

I shook away the image as Emelle nudged me and pointed through the crowd.

"Look who's already here. I take it Ms. Pincette didn't accept his invitation."

Rodhi had stayed behind after our last Spiders, Worms & Insects class to ask Ms. Pincette to the formal. I couldn't fathom why he'd actually have expected her to say yes, but here he was, smashed in the corner between two Shifter girls I didn't know, taking turns tonguing each of them as if he wanted to forget a certain rejection.

"I swear one of them just made her boobs grow three sizes," Wren muttered, wrapping her arms around herself. "Seems pretty fake to me, but hey, at least Rodhi's getting some."

I peered sideways at her, suddenly curious... what kind of person was Wren interested in? She had been spending a lot of time with Gileon, but the way they interacted seemed more like a platonic alliance than a budding romance to me. Although Gileon *had* presented her with a bouquet of needles after the Cardina visit.

Just as I thought this, Gileon himself bobbed toward us through the crowd, his massive frame towering over everyone else while he held two drinks in each fist.

"Hi!" he called cheerfully. He almost dropped his drinks when he got a full look at Wren. "Wow. You look like one of those beautiful poisonous frogs in Mr. Conine's class."

"By the orchid and the owl," Wren cursed. "Give me one of those." She grabbed a drink from his hand and drained it in a single bob of her throat. Then, wiping her mouth with one of those flowing turquoise sleeves, she said, "Let's go dance, Gil."

"Oh. Okay."

Emelle and I watched Gileon follow Wren into the swaying, dancing throng, a bewildered expression clouding his face, but a smile beginning to perk at his lips.

"Do you think they're....?" Emelle began uncertainly.

"I have *no* idea."

I stood on tiptoe, trying to find anyone else we recognized. Emelle, too, was craning her neck, a nervous flush peppering her neckline.

Where was Coen? We'd agreed to meet here, but the fact that I hadn't even heard his voice in my head in the last several hours... I exhaled, releasing a quivering breath. I was becoming too used to it, this mind-to-mind communication with him. Too used to traipsing into the Mind Manipulator house every Sunday, knowing exactly where to go for my pill... and more.

A *tug* on my skin. I looked up to find Sasha and Sylvie wiggling their fingers at us, and I smiled. The twins terrified me somewhat, but at least they were familiar.

Emelle and I floated over to meet them, where they were sneaking appetizers off a nearby table with nothing more than a tendril of magic. I watched, amused, as a gingerbread cookie floated inconspicuously into Sylvie's waiting hand.

"These are really *too* good," Sylvie said, taking a munch.

"Sometimes I think Wild Whispering is the lousiest magic ever," Emelle said morosely, watching Sylvie swallow the rest and lick the icing off her fingers.

"Just wait till you get to your fifth year," Sasha said with a wink. "Fifth-year Wild Whisperers are some of the most ruthless people I've ever met. They can strangle you with a vine just like that." She snapped her fingers.

"That still sounds kind of lame compared to other magic," Emelle mused, then scanned the twins' dresses. "You guys look amazing."

Indeed, the white, skin-tight dresses they wore offset the rich hues of their skin like the purest snow against the deepest charcoal. They each wore scarlet lipstick and gold hoops in their ears that swung with the slightest movement.

I was about to express my own appreciation when Lander barged into our little group, breathless and flushed and holding a...

"Is that a kettle?" I asked him, blinking at the silver pot in his arms.

"Perhaps," he replied, rather... mischievously. I'd never heard him sound mischievous in my *life*. He turned toward Emelle, who had relaxed at his presence but stiffened again as his attention landed fully on her, and said, "It's for you."

He held out the kettle. Emelle bit her lip and took it.

As soon as her fingers touched the silver surface, the pot morphed — springing upward into a bunch of orchids that matched the red of her dress.

"Oh!" Emelle exclaimed, a laugh bursting from her throat. "This is... wow! I didn't know you were able to shift anything else besides yourself!"

I raised my eyebrows at Lander, who pointedly ignored me, though that flush on his face only deepened. He opened his mouth to say something, when a flash of ruby-red hair blurred past us, and suddenly Quinn was there.

We fell quiet. Lander swiveled to face her. She stood there, in a velvet green dress only a shade lighter than mine, wringing her fingers together and staring at him.

Right. Although we were in the boys' Element Wielder house, this was still her sector, still part of her residence. Of course Quinn would be here.

I just didn't know why she was bothering to give us any attention.

"Can I talk to you?" she asked Lander.

If her lips hadn't moved, I wouldn't have believed those words had come from her mouth. As far as I knew, she hadn't talked to either one of us since my conversation with her on the beach.

Say no, Lander, I begged him silently. *Say no*. Not that talking was bad, but Emelle... I'd never seen her go so rigid. Her knuckles whitened around the bouquet of orchids.

"Uh, sure, I guess."

Lander swept a nervous hand through his hair.

When Quinn turned to press deeper into the house, he jolted after her, glancing back at Emelle before disappearing into the crowd.

CHAPTER

30

"Melle," I started.

"Here."

She pushed the orchids into my arms and scurried off.

Shit. I turned to Sylvie and was just about to hand *her* the orchids so I could go after Emelle when a silky voice said, "Torturing the symbol of our house, are we now, Drey?"

I jumped. Kimber was gliding toward us, bedecked in... I blinked. Ladybugs?

Yes, I realized as she came to a halt in front of Sasha, Sylvie, and me. A thousand or more of the black-spotted yellow beetles clung to her figure, twitching and stretching their shelled wings whenever she moved. The parakeet on her shoulder was eyeing them hungrily, but never made a move to peck at one. Yet.

Jenia and Dazmine stopped on either side of her, but I couldn't stop staring at Kimber herself. She'd always talked around me, but never *to* me.

I frowned at the orchids in my arms. They were, indeed, screeching faintly. Probably because their link to the lifeline of their existence had been snipped.

"They're not mine," I began lamely. What else was I supposed to say?

Kimber, however, was already turning her attention to Sasha and Sylvie, and when her teeth flashed through a forced smile, I had the feeling she hadn't stopped here for me at all.

"How lovely you look this year, girls. Much better than last year."

"Perhaps that's because *last* year you tore our dresses to shreds," Sasha replied.

What the hell? My heart dropped. Something was definitely taut between Kimber and the twins, but surely Kimber hadn't actually *touched* them in any way...

"Did I?" Kimber slapped a hand to her heart—crushing some of those ladybugs in the process. I heard their dying whimpers even over the din of the party. "I don't remember. Things get crazy when you're having fun, am I right?"

She smirked at Jenia, who smirked back. Dazmine remained stone-faced.

I thought that was going to be the end of it. That Kimber would turn on her high-heel and leave us alone then. But she pulled a contemplative face and asked Sylvie, "So, are you sharing my ex with this little girl?" She didn't even gesture at me, as if I were no more than the dirt between her parakeet's talons. "I would have thought he'd be satisfied with two girls, but maybe he got bored and asked for a third?"

Clearly, I was missing something, although the pieces were starting to stitch themselves together in my mind. Coen had never mentioned hooking up with either of the twins, but perhaps he had after his breakup with Kimber...

"Oh, did they not tell you?" Kimber barely glanced at me. "I bet you've just been swept head over heels, huh, Drey? Not realizing that Sasha and Sylvie will always be Coen Steeler's number one and number two. Interchangeably, of course. You will never be more than the third most important thing in his life."

I didn't hear her mutter a command to the ladybugs on her dress, didn't see anything more than the flash of her teeth as she whisked together another smile. But suddenly, her parakeet was laughing, and a frenzy of wings exploded around us, forming a dotted cloud of yellow, and the multiple conversations died down just enough for everyone to gape.

By the time Sasha, Sylvie, and I had swatted away the swarm, Kimber was already leading Jenia and Dazmine away, the dress beneath where the ladybugs had been semi-transparent. Leaving her entire naked body on display through the sheer nylon.

"What—?" I started, turning toward the twins.

"My question exactly," came a voice.

I whirled to find Coen, Terrin, and Garvis emerging from the crowd, the latter two sneaking glances behind them to gape at Kimber's retreating bare form. Coen, however, kept his eyes on me, Sasha, and Sylvie, a frown slipping over his face as he no doubt swept through the thoughts of all three of us.

I'm so sorry, he said suddenly in my mind. *Terrin was showing Garvis and me his new fireproof pants and we were testing it out, but—it doesn't matter. I should have been by your side the moment you stepped through the door.*

I didn't answer him with my thoughts. The fact that he hadn't been waiting for me at the Element Wielder front door didn't bother me; he'd asked if he could escort me to the formal a few days ago, and I'd told him I was going to show up with Emelle and Wren.

But I still folded my arms around the orchids and said, "Would anyone care to explain what Kimber was talking about? And why she set a bunch of ladybugs on us?"

"Yeah." Sylvie's magic flicked a stray ladybug off her chest. "Kimber's a possessive psychopath who wanted Coen to break off his extremely *non*-romantic friendship with Sasha and me."

I did a double take, my arms falling to my side again.

"Really?"

"Trust me," Sasha said, rolling her eyes, "we grew up with Coen. He's like a brother to us. I'd rather kiss that giant octopus in the Element Wielder lake."

Coen's jaw twitched—with both annoyance and a hint of laughter. "You'd rather kiss an octopus? *Really*, Sash?"

She shrugged, a wicked smile creasing over her face.

"So," I said before she could respond, desperate to make sense of this, "Kimber didn't like that you were all friends and wanted you to break ties even though none of you have ever had anything romantic going on?"

Sylvie sighed. "That about sums it up."

Coen's pleading gaze nestled into mine. *It's why we broke up,* he said in my head. *I should have ended it a year ago, when she physically attacked them during this same exact party... but she convinced me we belonged together. It wasn't until she gave me an ultimatum—her or the twins—that I picked the twins.*

Does she know? I asked, my gut suddenly clenching. If Emelle already knew about my own heritage, I couldn't blame Coen for telling a girlfriend of three years.

No. She knows I'm childhood friends with Sylvie, Sasha, Terrin, and Garvis, but she doesn't know anything about our childhood years at sea. Or how we have to suppress our other powers. Coen's frown

248

deepened. *Which just goes to show how much I trusted her even when I thought I was in love with her.*

I tried to keep my face impassive, even as a bit of awkwardness crept through me. After all our time together, all our kissing and exploring each other's bodies and hanging out on the weekends, that word, *love*, had never even come up.

"I've got to go find Emelle," I said, clutching the orchids tighter in my hands.

Coen didn't miss a beat. "I'll come with you."

He'd probably rifled through my memories already, seen what had happened with her and Lander and Quinn. And for some reason, that bothered me, that he could just invade me on a whim.

"Sure," I said, because I couldn't think of a good enough excuse to say no.

You don't have to have an excuse. If you don't want me —

It's fine. But can you stay out of my head for a bit?

I didn't mean for my thoughts to carry such a... bite to them, but Coen's usually tan face seemed to whiten as he nodded and followed me away from the others.

Where was Emelle? My dress swished coolly around my thighs as I scoured every corner of the room, winding between groups of people and avoiding the throng that Kimber had attracted entirely. Would she have really gone home?

"Do you want to check the roof?" Coen asked hesitantly.

I almost stopped. I'd forgotten that the Element Wielder roof, flat and gated, was practically made for stargazing... and escaping for a good cry. *God of the Cosmos, please don't let me find Emelle crying all alone. And please keep some sense in Lander's head.*

But I feared that if Quinn wanted to get back together with him, if that's why she'd asked to talk, Lander wouldn't hesitate. And Emelle would be... disappointed? Devastated? I didn't know. Only suspected.

"Yes," I told Coen, hating the dying screeches of the orchids. "The roof."

He didn't put a hand on the small of my back like I'd expected, but instead jerked his head toward the back of the room and led me to a spiral staircase covered in wreaths. Up and up we went, passing people lounging against the corkscrew railing, until we'd reached a wooden ladder shooting up through the roof.

"After you," Coen murmured.

I clambered up awkwardly, one hand still clutching Emelle's orchids, until I'd emerged onto the roof where those enchanted snowflakes grazed my cheeks.

Coen climbed up beside me, and we both looked around.

The roof was packed. Far busier than the foyer below, although nobody was dancing here. They were just clustered around braziers sporting flickering flame, drinking and talking to each other on chintz stools and chairs. The snowflakes that fell on the fires, I noticed, disappeared in a sizzling flash once they hit the flames.

I didn't have to look twice for Emelle. As soon as an older girl shifted her weight forward, I saw her in the far corner—wrapped around a guy who was definitely *not* Lander. I could barely make out where her face ended and his began.

"Oh." I fell back and looked at Coen. "I suppose she can do what she wants?"

There was no way I was about to break her and the guy apart. But I *really* hoped she knew what she was doing, because if Lander saw her...

Not my business, I reminded myself. They might be my closest friends, and sure, *maybe* I'd been hoping they'd get together after all those side looks and blushes, but in the end it wasn't up to me to steer the direction of their relationship.

Coen cleared his throat. He'd turned to lean against the wraparound gate.

"Have you ever seen Bascite Boulevard from a rooftop, Rayna?"

"No, I haven't." Wrenching my gaze from Emelle, I wafted to Coen's side.

From up here, the street looked even smaller than it did from my bunkroom's balcony. Stray partygoers swayed drunkenly down below, and I could see the bridge winking with starlight over the estuary.

Silence quivered between us. I frowned down at the orchids.

"They're dead."

"What?" Coen looked startled.

"The orchids... they must have just died. I can't hear them anymore."

I pressed a kiss onto the canopy of petals, muttered sorry, and tossed the bouquet over the gate, watching it spiral down until it hit the ground below. I had a feeling Emelle wouldn't want their wilting corpses anymore anyway.

Coen was staring at me as if he'd only just noticed me. His eyes dragged down from my face, paused at my breasts, and swept down to my feet.

I thought for sure he'd comment on the dress, then, something snarky or coy or anything to fix this... clumsiness between us, but he just grabbed a fistful of his hair and said, "Listen—I wish you were a Mind Manipulator right now."

"Excuse me?" I felt my eyebrows furl.

"Not permanently," he rushed on. "Just in this instance, so that you could feel how... guarded my heart is after her."

251

Her as in Kimber. I didn't particularly want to talk about Kimber right now, but I'd told him to stay out of my head for a bit, so of course he couldn't know that.

"After we broke up, I swore to myself I wasn't going to get involved with anyone," Coen said softly. "At least not until after I'd passed or failed my Final Test."

I tried to smile. "And then I showed up with a mystery for you to solve."

Because even if he didn't love me... he was definitely *involved* with me, right? Or did all this kissing and touching and hanging out mean nothing to him?

Coen surprised me with a firm, "No." When I cocked a brow at him, he repeated it. "No. It was before that. When I wanted to test the limits of my magic on my first official day of being an Institute prince. I invaded every new mind in that courtyard, and I was absolutely... astonished when I hooked onto yours." Finally, he ran a hand down my arm, and I closed my eyes at the touch. "Beneath all those layers of fear and worry and self-doubt, Rayna, your mind... it's the most beautiful and compassionate thing I've ever seen."

I opened my eyes to find Coen leaning closer to me. There was no hint of mockery in the smoky quartz of his eyes, nothing but the rippling reflection of my own face as I stared back at him.

"I wanted to sink into your mind right then and there," he said. "To lose myself inside you." I didn't miss the innuendo, though I wasn't sure he'd intended it this time. Still, my thighs clenched as he went on. "But of course, that would have been ridiculous, to reach out to a first-year when you didn't even know me, all because I'd found your mind infatuating, so I refused to even look at you longer than that first glance... until you nearly blasted your tent apart and... well, became a mystery for me to solve."

The hint of a smile played on his face at that.

I reached up to brush a snowflake off his hair. "And do you feel like you've solved me yet?"

Now Coen's smile lit up his face with a familiar wicked delight.

"Not even close."

I closed the gap between us, rising up on tiptoe to take his lips in mine.

He responded with a deftness that scared me, cupping the back of my neck with one hand and my thigh with the other, lifting me an inch off the ground so that he could take my kiss fully.

We melted into each other, then, like we had so often these last few weeks—only now it was out in the open, beneath the sky that poured enchanted snowflakes and in front of anyone who wanted to goggle and gossip about it.

The way he wasn't hiding me anymore—it meant more than any words.

Coen, however, knew just the right words to say anyhow. He dragged his lips to my ear and whispered through my hair, "I wouldn't have picked that dress for you if I'd known how badly I would just want to rip it off."

I pushed him away, attempting to roll my eyes, but he yanked me back and pressed his forehead against mine.

"You're slowly becoming everything to me, Rayna Drey."

Before I could think of a response to that, a series of commotions stirred behind us. People were jumping up from their seats around the various fires and rushing toward the ladder—not in fear, but in excitement. As they went, I could make out fragments of their conversations.

"A fight downstairs—"

"Someone tried tripping—"

"—got his tooth knocked out."

I had no interest in watching people pummel each other to bruised and broken bits, and was about to suggest to Coen that we ignore it when his face went pale for the second time tonight.

"What?" I asked abruptly, casting around for signs of Emelle. She was still wrapped around her hookup in the corner, completely oblivious.

"It's..." He winced, and I knew he was scouring the minds of everyone downstairs. "It's Fergus." And now his eyes widened. "And Gileon."

CHAPTER

31

My heart jumped. I was racing toward the ladder before I knew what I was doing, pushing people aside for the first time in my life. A few sneers shot my way, but I didn't care. And even though Coen was calling after me, I refused to slow down.

Fergus must have snapped. Must have discarded Coen's earlier warning and decided to mess with Gileon for fun. And if Gil had been hurt, his teeth knocked out or worse...

As soon as my feet landed on the floor below, I was flying downstairs. I didn't know how I could help, what I could do, but I knew I had to be there. Had to stop it, somehow, before my sweet, too-innocent friend was hurt beyond repair.

But when I finally shoved through the dense, circling throng in the foyer and beheld what had happened, I lurched to a halt.

Gileon was standing upright, his brow furrowed in concentration, but there wasn't a scratch on him. Not a single trickle of blood or blossoming bruise.

Fergus, meanwhile, was spitting blood through a mangled mouth, bobbing before Gileon with his fists raised. There was no sign of mold or other magic, just the two of them facing off in a circle of eager on-lookers. As the pieces slid into place, I realized that Fergus must have tried to trip Gileon, and Gileon, in turn, had knocked his tooth out.

And suddenly, I was trying really, really hard not to smile.

Fergus roared and barreled forward again, the whites of his eyes screaming with popped blood vessels. Gileon wasn't fast enough to side step him, but just as Fergus brought his elbow back for a punch, he managed to catch his wrist, hold it back with ease, and bury his own bunched hand into Fergus's face again.

"*Oooh,*" someone in the crowd groaned.

Jenia's scream cut through the gasps as Fergus whipped sideways and crumpled to his feet. She broke through the onlookers and sank to her knees beside him, shaking his shoulder.

As Coen sidled up beside me, folding his arms over his chest and passing me the most suppressed smirk I'd ever seen, I caught sight of Fergus's face: mangled jaw, shredded lips, blood-drenched chin... and a few more yellow-stained teeth scattered on the floor around him.

Fergus had tried to poke at Gileon for the last time.

From across the room, I caught the dazzling flash of Wren's triumphant grin.

Gileon's victory was about the only thing anyone could talk about for the next several days within the Wild Whispering sector, but even that topic dwindled away as the second quarterly test drew near.

"Mitzi Hodges claims she overheard *Mr. Conine* saying we just have to convince a snake and a mongoose to quit fighting this time around for the Predators & Prey test," Emelle said during Spiders, Worms & Insects as we tried to coax out pill bugs from some mangrove roots in the arboretum. "No riddles this time, so it should be easier to pass."

She'd been very careful not to mention Lander's name since he'd disappeared with Quinn at the formal, and I hadn't seen Lander himself to ask what his so-called "talk" with Quinn had been about. I almost would've thought I'd been imagining a spark between my two friends if Emelle hadn't *also* steered clear of the topic of her random hookup anytime I tried to bring it up.

I studied her, watching as she pressed her lips to the bottom bark of the mangrove tree and emitted a peculiar *cwip! cwip! cwip!* sound that was supposed to lure the pill bugs out. When nothing happened, she withdrew and bit her lip in frustration.

"Emelle," I began for what seemed like the hundredth time, "about the other night..."

"Oh, look!" She shielded her eyes from the strip of sunlight through the canopy and twisted away from me. "Here come Rodhi and Gileon." Okay, she still didn't want to talk about the Element Wielder formal. Noted. "Guess they're not having much luck either."

Indeed, the two were traipsing toward us, Gil's head brushing the branches above, with absolutely defeated expressions. Our other classmates were scattered in pairs throughout the rest of the arboretum, too, but we hadn't witnessed any of their failures or successes yet, and I hadn't seen Ms. Pincette since she'd released us with instructions.

"Any luck?" I asked them.

"Well," Rodhi said morosely, leaning against our tree, "I managed to get one little roly poly to poke its head out, but it took one look at my face, said—what did it say, Gil?"

"*Ah, a demon!*" Gileon mimicked.

"Yeah, that." Rodhi slumped against our mangrove tree. "Thankfully Ms. Pincette didn't see that. She was too busy scolding Jenia— which just reminded me why I can't give up on that wonderful woman, even after all her little rejections." He closed his eyes. "I've never been so turned on as I was just now, listening to that."

"Ew," Emelle said.

"Scolding Jenia?" I asked, ignoring everything else that was wrong about that statement.

"Yeah." Rodhi sighed dreamily. "Jenia was bitching about how Gileon is a 'brute unfit for civilization' or something idiotic like that, and Ms. Pincette said, 'the only one unfit for civilization is standing right in front of me, Ms. Leak.' God bless her."

Gileon frowned. Despite everyone's continuous congratulations and Wren's continuous gloating, I knew he was still feeling guilty about sending Fergus to the sick bay yet again. And I had a feeling that *Jenia* knew he was feeling guilty, too.

Which was why she'd called him a bully, loud and clear for him to hear. To hurt his feelings. And that made my blood hiss in my veins.

When would it stop?

After a few more of our failed attempts to draw out the pill bugs, Ms. Pincette came trudging our way in her high-buckled boots, her chestnut hair tucked neatly behind her ears as always.

She didn't even ask us if we'd succeeded before snapping, "Class dismissed. Please practice over the weekend. These things are wrecking the root systems around here." I lifted myself off the trunk of the mangrove along with the others, but Ms. Pincette added, "Not you, Ms. Drey. If you'll follow me back to the classroom, I would like to discuss something with you."

Rodhi's head jerked our way. "I'd be happy to volunteer in Rayna's stead."

"I'm sure you would, Mr. Lockett." A wry smile slipped through Ms. Pincette's pursed lips. "However, this is a discussion relating to Ms. *Drey's* deficiencies, not yours."

Deficiencies? I guess I *hadn't* been doing too well in class ever since the cockroaches—none of the insects ever seemed to want to listen to me—but I'd been listening and practicing and *trying*, so...

When Emelle quirked a brow at me, I said, "Go ahead. I'll meet you guys back at the house," and followed Ms. Pincette back toward the classroom.

She didn't speak the entire way there, her posture arrow-straight as she picked through the undergrowth until we'd reached weed-cracked cobblestone again. It was only when we came to the classroom door that she glanced back—but not at me. Over my head, as if to make sure nobody had followed us.

Then we slipped inside. She closed the door behind us and clicked her way to her desk.

"Here." She rummaged through her drawers and brought out a massive tome, which she thumped onto the desk. "Extra reading for you, Ms. Drey."

I inched forward and angled my head to read the gold-gilded lettering beneath its thick coating of dust: *Creepers and Crawlers of the Past, Present, and Future.*

"Oh. Thank you?"

Ms. Pincette's attention latched fully onto my face. "Open it."

I did so, reaching out to grab the edge of the cloth binding. The pages crinkled as I flicked through them, finding insect diagrams and pages upon pages of miniscule text. Ms. Pincette cleared her throat.

"Open it to page nine hundred and ninety-nine, I should say."

Feeling like I was definitely missing something by now, I sifted toward the back of the book and stopped, breathless. The entire text had been whited out and inked over with...

"A map," I whispered.

Ms. Pincette inhaled through her nose.

"I do love my spiders, but I'm capable of talking to birds, too. Specifically the seagulls who just migrated back to the island a couple weeks ago." When I continued to stare, she added with a sigh, "They're immune to it. The shield."

There it was again, that word. *Immune.* What could Coen and a seagull possibly have in common that would warrant their safe passage through the dome?

Before I could ask that or squint too heavily at the whorls and lines of ink and the tiny descriptions scrawled in the corner of each page, however, Ms. Pincette slammed the cover shut right in front of my nose.

"As I said, extra reading to make up for your deficiencies in class. If you dare tell anyone else otherwise, *even* your very best friend in the whole wide world..."

"I won't," I said quickly, not wishing to hear the tail-end of that warning. Even as I said it, though, I felt the words dry much too quickly on my tongue.

How could I keep this from Jagaros the next time I saw him, when he'd been the one to suggest such a thing to me? How could I keep it from Coen, whom I'd allowed back into my mind after the formal?

Worse yet, how could I keep it from *myself?* From that obsessively churning, constantly buzzing part of me that wouldn't be able to focus on anything else with a map of the world imprinted in my mind's eye?

But I locked those worries away and made myself take the burning intensity of Ms. Pincette's gaze.

"Thank you for the extra reading," I said.

"Study hard, Rayna."

CHAPTER

32

Later that night after everyone else had gone to bed, I was in the study room, letting my body curve over the tome so that if anyone happened to barge in here for some late-night studying, they wouldn't see Ms. Pincette's hand-drawn map before I had a chance to snap it shut.

Nobody came, though, and the only sounds were of the crickets singing outside and the creak of the house settling. Coen himself had gone to bed early tonight since fifth-years would be the first to take their tests tomorrow at the crack of dawn, so my mind stretched with a cautious kind of silence as I soaked in the information.

Ms. Pincette had drawn the island of Eshol, a jagged shape like an egg turned sideways in the center of the whited-out page. I didn't pause to pore over the details there, the labels of all the villages, the Uninhabitable Zone, Bascite Mountain, or the Institute. Instead, I let my eyes bounce around to the three different landmasses around it.

One was significantly larger than the other two, bleeding off the top of the page and filled with the name *ASMOD.* The other two cloistered at the bottom, nearly touching each other and filled with the names *SORRONIA* and *PLIYTTH.*

Asmod, Sorronia, and Pliyith. I mentally repeated the names and scanned the tinier labels dusted among each of them, cities and towns connected by roads and rivers. It didn't seem possible, that three entire continents loomed over and beneath us, but I didn't doubt Ms. Pincette's findings. I just couldn't fathom why this information had been kept from the island.

Until I read the descriptions crammed in each corner of the page, that was.

The longer I read those, the longer it took for each breath to fill my lungs.

Eshol, the island experiment: overseen by the Good Council and steeled by a dome of anti-power. No one survives going in or out.

"Except for Coen," I amended softly.

Coen and Garvis and Terrin and the twins had survived going through that dome of—I reread the description Ms. Pincette had used—*anti-power.* Coen had called it a disease or poison made solid, but Ms. Pincette obviously didn't know that.

Good. No one should know what Coen had told me in the cave. I moved on to the next description, still shivering from the whole "island experiment" label.

Pliyith, the nation of humans: split into seven provinces and steeled with weapons and technology. No magic. Homeland of the people of Eshol.

Homeland. Weapons. Technology. The terms circled through my mind like vultures preparing to feast on something I couldn't quite make sense of.

I moved on before I could stitch it together.

Sorronia, the faerie lands: a divided queendom steeled by long lifespans and individual magics. Magics aren't fully developed until the faerie reaches maturity.

262

I read that paragraph again. And again. But each time I re-read it, I felt like my eyes weren't giving me anything more than squiggles on a page. No comprehension beyond the fact that faeries still existed beyond the island's dome, faeries still existed beyond the island's dome, *faeries still existed beyond the island's dome.* Everything else was just meaningless syllables and ink splatters and sounds.

I moved on before I could hyperventilate.

Asmod, the vampire realm: ruled by one royal family and steeled by immortality and predatorial strength. No magic. Human blood slaves.

Vampires? Blood slaves? Immortality? Something in my chest wanted to streak away and hide, as if those terms could come to life and suck my blood right then and there.

"*Whatcha reading this late?*"

I jumped.

It was Willa, scuttling from beneath the windowsill and onto the desk. I knew mice couldn't read, but I still almost closed the tome when she sniffed the top of its spine.

"It's—I'm studying."

"*Studying the writings of a five-year-old?*"

I couldn't help but snort. Ms. Pincette *did* look like the kind of person who should probably have better penmanship. I trailed my fingertips over her words and came to a decision right then and there. If I couldn't trust Willa, who could I?

Lowering myself to her still-quivering nose, I pushed it out in the faintest breath I could manage—everything I had just read. When I was done, she did a lap around the desk and settled herself in the crook of my neck, panting heavily.

"*I thought you told me Lord Arad was the last descendants of the vampires?*"

Indeed, I'd told Willa everything that had happened in that abandoned classroom, but I wasn't sure...

"No," I said, straining to remember, "he said he and his children were the last of the tomb bats from the ancient Asmodeus Colony. Whatever that means. Maybe there was a colony here on the island before Dyonisia took over?"

"Or maybe he was just batshit," Willa quipped. *"Literally. Listen, Rayna, you know what this means, right?"* She put a paw on the landmass of Sorronia, situated right beneath Eshol's bottom right curve where the Institute sat.

Vaguely. I vaguely knew what it meant, but my brain was having trouble taking a step back to view the picture as a whole. Again, it was like I could only take in meaningless syllables and splatters and sounds.

"Magics aren't fully developed until the faerie reaches maturity," Willa repeated. *"Your power—the innate one, the one the Good Council didn't give you—isn't developed yet because you haven't reached maturity. The pirates, your mother, half of your blood is—"*

"I know," I whispered, nearly against my will.

Her little voice repeating it back to me did the trick. The syllables and sounds coagulated into pictures in my mind: faeries brimming with hazardous, shapeless powers until they reached a certain age and learned how to shape it. Hone it. Use it.

Perhaps everyone else on the island was fully human, but *we*—Coen, Garvis, Terrin, the twins, and I—must have come from Sorronia. Or at least our parents had. The faerie lands.

If Ms. Pincette's sources were right, if her descriptions were true, then that monster brimming in my veins... it wasn't a monster at all. It just had yet to take form.

Because I was half-faerie.

CHAPTER

33

I snapped the tome shut and hugged it against my chest.

"Willa, do you know of any place in the house I could store this where no one will find it? Someplace it'll be safe until I'm ready to read it again?"

Because if I let myself continue studying this and obsessing over it, I would not sleep tonight. And with the second quarterly practice test tomorrow, with the weight of my future resting on how well I could perform during these damned things, I couldn't risk heading to that Testing Center with bags under my eyes.

Anything, after all, could trigger my power—my... my faerie power, apparently. Not just bascale, but stress and fatigue as well. And while I was sure Ms. Pincette wouldn't report it if I exploded again, I *wasn't* sure about Mr. Conine or Mrs. Wildenberg or Mr. Fenway.

"*Give me a minute,*" Willa said. "*I'll be right back.*"

I waited. My fingers twitched, itching to open it again, to just take another peek and try to figure out which of those dotted towns or cities my mother might have come from. But... tomorrow, I could. After the second test.

I just had to get through tomorrow, and then I'd bury my nose in this thing until it went numb.

Willa returned mere minutes later, her fur disheveled.

"*Okay, it's ready for you. It was my cousin Barty's favorite place to shit, so we had to clean it of all his droppings, but it should be a perfect place.*"

Bemused, I followed her skittering shadow back to the foyer, where she put her paws up on the piece of wall right beneath that giant cuckoo clock between the staircases in the back.

"*It swings forward, but only when it goes off. Which should be any....*"

Right on cue, the clock let out a mechanical chirp, and I pried the rounded edges of it from the wall. It swung outward, revealing a hole the size of my head.

I coughed at the dust and the cloying smell of old piss soaked in wood.

"This is perfect."

I gently placed the tome inside, patted its surface, and closed the cuckoo clock over it again. A small *click* told me it had latched back into place.

I didn't have the energy to ask Willa if she knew who'd designed this hiding space, or why it was there.

Faerie. I was part-*faerie*. That single thought consumed everything.

All I could do was crouch down next to her and whisper, "Can you send one of your friends to go wake Coen for me? There's something I need him to do."

Ten minutes later, Coen's figure hurried toward me, where I leaned against one of those lampposts behind the Testing Center. Its flickering flame sent dancing shadows over the taut lines of his face as he drew near.

As soon as Willa's friends had nudged him awake, telling him to meet me here, his voice had instantly filled my head and fished out my most recent memory. And when his shock never echoed in the chasm of my own, I knew he'd known all along. That the pirates were faeries. That *we* were that, too.

"I'm mad at you," I started before he could get a word in.

He stopped right before me, his breath puffing out into the air.

"Oh?"

"You knew."

He dipped his head.

"Yes, I knew."

"Then why did you keep it from me?" I shook my head and said, "You know what, don't answer that." *Because I'm about to be a giant hypocrite.* "I need you to do something for me." When he lifted an eyebrow, I said, "I need you to erase Emelle's memory."

The fog of my breath billowed outward, floating into his open mouth.

Coen pursed his forehead.

"What?"

"The memory of Lord Arad, I mean. And everything he said."

Melle was in too much danger, knowing that my mother had come from beyond the dome. It had already been gnawing on me, the precarious situation I'd put my best friend in, but the tome and what lay inside had made me realize how big the stakes really were for her. If a bored Mind Manipulator decided to poke around in her brain just for the hell of it, they would know she was affiliated with pirates—with faeries— and report her involvement to the Good Council.

And unlike me, Emelle didn't *have* to be involved. She was fully human. If it weren't for my friendship with her, she'd be as safe and innocent as the rest of them.

Coen didn't ask any more questions. He passed a thumb along my temple and said gently, "Done."

My head jerked up at him. "Really? Already?"

He tried to smile, but it came out more like a grimace.

"It's like wading through a thick, cold mist from this distance, but I already know her mind. And she's sleeping. Makes it easier."

She'll wake up with no idea that your mom was a... a pirate, he said into my mind, avoiding that other word, *or that a white tiger ate a bunch of half-formed bats like it was nothing.* Again, he avoided that other word. Vampire.

"Right. Perfect. Thank you." I sucked in a lungful of that thick, soupy air. Then, before I could second-guess myself and the absolutely insane thing I was about to ask, I blurted out, "I also need you to erase my memory of what I learned, too. Just until tomorrow night."

Now Coen's grimace turned into thin, hard suspicion.

"Why?"

"Because I'm scared, Coen," I said, grabbing onto his arms. "Scared I'm going to explode again tomorrow if I have... if I have *this* weighing me down."

This as in the tome and the map and the faerie continent of Sorronia and the fact that Coen had kept his secret from me and the questions that were tearing me apart. I could already feel my power pushing against its constraint in response, swelling up against my ribcage.

"Just until tomorrow night," I repeated. "After I've passed all my tests."

Coen bit his lip and flicked his gaze toward the sea.

"What if you don't pass?"

The question was quiet, but I still flinched. His tone told me what I'd already suspected, what I'd already dreaded. Coen had been planning on erasing this from me, anyway, as soon as Willa's friends had woken him up and he'd pieced together what I'd learned.

And *that* made me wonder if I'd figured it out in the past before. If he'd already erased my knowledge of this. My fingernails curled into my palm.

"I will pass the tests. I have to."

I was determined to remain calm tomorrow, no matter what creepers and crawlers I had to face. That raging panic, I was certain, was what had made my power break through the suppressant and explode outward. Which was why this was so important—for my mind to stabilize for the next twenty-four hours.

Coen scrutinized me, unreadable. Each of his breaths came out in foggy tufts, melding with my own.

"I can lock it away," he said finally. "Shield the knowledge of... of what's in the tome so you can't access it. Then remove that mental shield later."

"Yes," I breathed, even though part of me wondered if this was the coward's way out. Ms. Pincette wouldn't mention the tome again, I was sure, but she would have expected me to read it, and Jagaros would eat me alive if he found out I'd purposely hid away the map he'd requested me to find twice already.

But I knew myself. Knew my limits. And this was one of them. I would not be able to sleep or breathe or eat or do *anything* tomorrow with this one thing chewing at every thought that tried to rise to the surface of my mind.

"If this is what you wish," Coen said.

I nodded. Yes. I'd have this memory returned tomorrow night, and then I'd...

269

I'd confront *everything*.

"But you have to give it back after my test tomorrow," I warned suddenly. "You can't keep it from me forever. Okay?"

He didn't respond.

"Coen?"

He just gripped the back of my head, brought me close, and whispered three words into my ear as the moon finally sliced between the gray draping of clouds.

"Forget, my love."

CHAPTER

34

The next day, I passed my History portion of the test for Mr. Fenway. I successfully convinced a mongoose and a snake to quit fighting for Mr. Conine. I fed a butterwort for Mrs. Wildenberg.

When Ms. Pincette asked me to fish a silver key out of a tank full of maggots, however, my power struck through the cracks of that suppressant and sent the whole tank shattering into a million glinting pieces — pieces that melted into the floor of the Testing Center as if they had never been.

Ms. Pincette flicked a maggot off her shoulder and kicked another one off her shoe. The entire room squirmed with them, like fat, wriggling ashes.

"Did you study, Ms. Drey?" she asked, deadpan.

What an odd question. Of *course* I had studied. I nodded, picked up the silver key that had been flung unceremoniously onto the floor, and tossed it over to her. She caught it with one hand.

"Very well. I shall report this as a fail. You did not retrieve the key."

Although something in my chest shriveled up in shame, I nodded again.

"Yes. Thank you, Ms. Pincette."

She watched me go, the lines of her face creasing. I had a distinct feeling that I'd missed an important clue or sign or *something*, but I couldn't hurry out that back door fast enough, down the stairs and outside.

Where Coen waited for me between lampposts, holding up a sandwich.

I ran to him and threw my arms around his neck, squishing the sandwich between us.

"Did you pass?" he asked.

"No."

I wanted to cry. Not because I'd failed again, necessarily, but because the image of Coen standing between lampposts, the sea raging behind him—it struck something nostalgic and familiar and intimate inside me. As if it were a picture I'd had painted on my heart long before tonight.

Coen's shoulders seemed to slump slightly. He pulled back and examined me.

"Are you hurt?"

"No. Just... disappointed in myself. Ms. Pincette asked if I'd studied, and I did, but maybe not hard enough."

If I could have talked to those damned maggots and successfully retrieved the key in the appropriate way, maybe my power wouldn't feel the need to explode.

Something indiscernible passed over Coen's face. Again, I had that feeling that I'd missed something, but then his face cracked into a lazy grin.

"Has anyone ever told you that you're beautiful even with a maggot in your hair?"

I laughed as he fished one out of my curls and sent it hurling over his shoulder.

"No, I can't say anyone ever has. This would be a first."

He pressed a kiss onto my forehead and the sandwich into my hands.

"Come on. What do you say we sneak over to the Element Wielder lake and take a little evening swim? Maybe we'll find that giant octopus Sasha and Sylvie would rather kiss than me."

I bit into the sandwich and grinned back.

"I'm not too fond of the idea of a giant octopus, but a swim in the lake sounds nice." Especially since I wouldn't have to hear everyone talking about that damned test.

As we started toward the Element Wielder sector together, however, I decided to ignore the creeping feeling that Coen was hiding something behind his too-cheery smile.

"Rayna! Hey, Rayna!"

The island had been edging toward the dry season for the past few weeks, evident in the slightly clearer skies and lack of constant drizzling. I turned from my solo walk back home to find Lander sprinting toward me, elongating his calves to catch up.

"Lander. Where have you *been*?"

For neither Melle nor I had seen any sign of him since that formal. The few times I'd seen a group of Shape Shifters playing pentaball on the field, Lander hadn't been among them, and the one time I'd tried knocking on the Shifter door I'd been told to go away by a very hungover man with snakes for dreadlocks.

"To be honest," Lander said, lurching to a halt before me, wobbling on absurdly tall legs. "I've been avoiding you because you're usually with... her. But that's not what I came to talk about. I need your help for a Shifting class. I was supposed to find someone outside the sector for today's lesson, but my buddy from the Summoner house got sick, so... will you come with me, Rayna? Like, right now?"

Alarmed, I stopped right between his sector's houses. No communication for a month, then this? I glanced over my shoulder, toward my own house. I'd been heading back to get ready for a date with Coen while Rodhi, Emelle, and Gileon had stayed behind, along with half of Mr. Conine's class, to discuss monkey humor in greater detail. The half of us who'd managed to make a monkey laugh already had been released early.

"I guess. But Coen has something planned tonight, so I have to be back by—"

"Don't worry. I'll get you back in time. May I?"

Lander was bouncing on the balls of his feet, his skin sparkling with impatient sweat. I supposed this would be as good a time as any to lecture him about his behavior recently, so I nodded with a glare.

He scooped me up. I squealed in shock, but he ignored me, sprinting on those elongated calves, back over the bridge and into the Shifter sector, where he set me down on a paved court in the back.

Here, his classmates were standing with partners in neat little rows while an instructor spoke to them from up front.

"—nice of you to finally join us, Mr. Spade! Ready to begin?"

"Yes, sir," Lander breathed beside me. I did a double take as he shook out his legs, and they shrunk back to their appropriate height.

"Jolly good," the instructor said up front. "Okay, first thing's first. Please give your generous partner...ahh, let's see, what should we do? Pink hair!"

In a great ripple of movement, the entire class turned toward their non-Shifter partners and began straining with effort. Some people placed their hand on their partner's head, while others began whispering through pursed lips.

Lander was looking at me as if he were constipated.

"There. Oh, no. It's more maroon, isn't it?"

I grabbed one of my curls and brought it up in front of my face. Indeed, it was now the color of some kind of ripe berry, glistening as if it had never been blonde.

"Shouldn't this be easier for you?" I asked unashamedly. "I mean, you can change your own appearance, and you can turn a kettle into flowers."

"I actually changed the flowers into a kettle and then back into flowers," Lander said, his face contorting again as he focused on my hair. "But that's beside the point, I guess. Changing another living human's appearance is harder than changing yourself or an inanimate object—or plants," he added quickly when I opened my mouth to argue that last point.

I closed it again. From the corner of my eye, I could see my hair was orange now. I planted my hands on my hips and surveyed him fully.

"You said you've been avoiding me because I've been with Emelle. Why?" I felt the frustration bubble up in my chest. "Why don't you want to talk to Emelle, Lander? Are you with Quinn again?"

"What? No!" The instructor up front called out another color, and Lander went to work trying to get each of my strands to morph into purple. "Quinn basically wanted to explain why I'd never been a good boyfriend. I think she was looking for some grand apology where I'd be groveling on my knees begging for her forgiveness, but I told her to screw right off. Then I went to find Emelle afterward, but she had some other guy's tongue in her mouth. And *then* I found the orchids I gave her just smashed on the ground, so I figured—"

"Oh, no." I clapped a hand to my mouth. "Land, that was *me*. Melle was so upset about how you just disappeared with Quinn that she

275

handed me the orchids, and I threw them overboard because you were both gone and they were *dead.*"

Lander's face became pinched.

"What? Of course the orchids were dead. I picked them." Understanding dawned on his face right after he said that, though. "Oh... oh, like you heard them take their dying breath... in your hands?"

"*Yes.*" Although, come to think of it, maybe I should have buried them.

"By the feather and the fang, that's morbid," Lander muttered. "Next time I'll get her a potted plant."

"There won't be a next time if you refuse to talk things through, Land. She was only kissing that guy because she thought you were breaking her heart."

Not that Emelle had said as much. I was only guessing that part, because apparently neither of my best friends could fathom the concept of communication.

Mean, I chided myself. That was mean. I sighed as I picked up a lock of puke-green hair and let it fall back over my shoulder.

"We've just missed you, Lander."

"Well, I've missed you, too." His face had fallen into serious contemplation. "And I'm sorry. I guess I just... oh, I don't know."

No. I decided I'd hold him to higher standards than that.

"You don't know *what,* Lander?"

"I don't know."

"*Lander.* That. Is. Not. An. Answer."

He recoiled and frowned at me. "Since when did you get so assertive?"

Since I started exploding with power that could get me killed. Since I found out my mother came from outside this wretched dome and my father stole me from her. Since the moment I felt like something was out there, something bigger, lurking and waiting for me to find it again. As if I'd held something in my hand and let it slip through my fingers like water.

But I didn't say any of that, of course. I just shrugged.

"Maybe you should try it. Tell me. Tell me what you claim you don't know."

As everyone else around us shifted colors, their hair and skin and clothes morphing into magentas and pastels and neon colors so bright, it hurt my eyes, Lander stopped to stare at me, his mouth partway open.

"I don't know that I've got a big crush on Emelle. I don't know that it scares me because I'm afraid she'll hurt me like Quinn did. I don't know that when I saw her kissing another guy, I felt like she was already hurting me before we even began."

"Now give 'em an extra finger!" the instructor called from up front, clapping his hands. Lander jolted from his reverie and screwed up his face again.

The next second, a nub sprouted between my index finger and thumb.

I shrieked and tried to shake it off me, but it just flapped in place.

"At least make it a full finger!" I cried.

"I'm trying!"

Lander was concentrating so hard now, he had trails of sweat leading from his forehead down to his chin. A slight tingling shot up my wrist as he lengthened my nub into a full digit. "There. Happy?"

"I can't say I'm overjoyed, but this is better." I wiggled the extra finger, awe-struck. "Wow. I never knew it would be so hard to shift something other than yourself. But then again, I didn't realize it'd be so hard to talk to maggots, either."

A bitter taste still loitered in my mouth from that last test.

Lander wiped his sweat on a sleeve and pressed his mouth together.

"All of this is so much harder than I ever thought it would be. Changing myself comes naturally, but changing others..." He looked away.

I rested a hand on his shoulder, trying to ignore the six fingers. "Maybe you're not supposed to try to change others." I softened my voice. "You couldn't control how Quinn treated you, Lander. But you *can* control how you treat Emelle. And the fact is, she only started kissing some other guy when you walked away from her with your ex. That's how you treated her, so that's how she treated you back."

"Alright," the instructor called from up front, "now freestyle it!"

Lander didn't move. He was still staring off toward the nearest tangle of mountainside.

"Do you think Emelle would be willing to talk to me again?" he asked quietly.

"*Yes.*" Finally, he was catching on—Emelle hadn't said so, but I knew she'd be ecstatic if Lander chose to hang out with us again. With *her* again.

He seemed to shake himself from some kind of trance and refocused on my appearance. With another tingle, that extra finger shrunk back into my skin.

"Okay, Rayna, it's your choice now. What do you want me to change about you? Momentarily, of course. Bangs? A tattoo? I could try to give you a beauty mark."

I laughed—actually threw my head back and *laughed*—at the thought of meeting Coen for our date tonight with a sudden mole above my upper lip.

"How about... straight hair." I'd always secretly wondered what I might look like, how long my hair might be, if the wild curls flattened into a glossy cascade.

"I can try." Lander chewed on his lip, closed one eye, and squinted at me as if his life depended on it. A moment later, his eyes flew open. "Holy shit, I did it!"

Indeed, when I strung my fingers through my hair, it didn't feel like my hair at all. Each strand was silky-smooth, flowing down to my waist like fluid sunlight.

I reined in a gasp. "How long will it last?"

"Just a few hours." Lander gave his work an appraising smile. "I'm not strong enough to hold it for long, but some of the fifth-years can maintain someone else's shifted appearance for *days*, so maybe someday I'll get there."

Days. I'd always assumed Dyonisia Reeve was a Shape Shifter—that that's how she preserved her eternally youthful body—but what if she wasn't? What if someone else on the Good Council, a hyper-advanced Shape Shifter, did it for her?

Lander didn't seem to notice the way my fingers had stopped their seamless trek through my new hair, suddenly cold.

He only smiled at me and said, "Go get your prince, Rayna. I think I'm going to go after my queen."

CHAPTER

35

Coen didn't whistle when he saw me. He gaped.

"What—?"

"Lander," I said by explanation, approaching the marble steps leading up to his house. "He straightened my hair."

After a few more seconds of gaping, Coen trotted down the steps to cradle my face in his hands. I thought he was going to kiss me, but he just said, "Did he alter anything else about you?"

I frowned up at him. "Yes, he did. Why?"

Coen didn't answer that. "What did he change?" Each word was clipped, strained, and I suddenly had the suspicion he was jealous of another man's magic touching me. As if Lander was a man to contend with. I almost snorted at the thought.

"Hmm." I twirled out of his grip, relishing the way my glossy sheet of hair whipped about me like a curtain. "Why don't you try to find out?"

Not that there was anything still changed about me, but still — Coen had been way too moody since that last quarterly test, and he'd been so intent on urging me to study harder, practice more, that I had missed that coy, cocky side of him. Anything to urge him out of this mopey shell of his....

It worked. Coen clucked his tongue and said simply, "Fine."

In one swift movement, he bent down, scooped me up by the thighs, and threw me over his shoulder like he'd done so long ago on the night before Branding. Then he whirled and trotted back up the steps, kicking open his house's door.

I scratched at his back. "What are you doing?"

A few of the guys lounging inside turned toward us and raised their eyebrows appreciatively. Coen ignored them.

"I'm going to inspect every inch of you for changes, of course."

Heat slunk up the skin of my legs where Coen's large hands were tightening around them. We were almost to his room now, and when he barged in with me still over his shoulder, he didn't even pause to close the door behind us; he simply kicked backward and sent it slamming shut with his foot.

Then dumped me on his bed.

Nothing could have prepared me for the way he bowed over me, every one of his muscles taut and taunting me to reach out and touch them. He'd crawled on top of me many times before, but it was always gentle and calculating, not wild and bordering on the fringe of frenzy like this.

"I thought you were taking me on a date," I chided up at him. Trying to keep a note of mocking derisiveness in my voice despite that slinking heat.

But the breath in my lungs seemed to wiggle and squirm at the look he gave me.

"I am. This is our date. But." Coen held up a finger. "You have to let me in." He cleared his throat when I flushed, and that hungry haze in his eyes seemed to blink away. "I mean, you have to let me in your mind. Give me permission to go further than usual."

Stay out of my head, I'd once snapped at him. *Don't enter it again without my permission.* It all seemed so long ago.

"Of course," I murmured.

I had barely finished saying it when the room *changed*.

A gasp burst out of me.

I wasn't lying on his cleanly-made, fluffy white bed anymore, but a polished wooden boat rocking among puffed-up clouds. And we weren't stationary, but *moving*, up and up and up through a light mist, toward a sky smeared with purple and black and split wide open by the beaming curve of a crescent moon.

"Coen... what—?"

I shot upright and twisted to grip the edge of the boat, leaning over and looking down. I halfway expected to see nothing besides clouds, but no—through the veil of mist, that was definitely the outline of Eshol far below.

Coen's eyes followed the movement of my face as I took it all in.

"I wanted you to feel what it's like in my own head whenever I'm around you."

I froze. Slowly turned toward him.

Finally, for the first time since that last quarterly test, he had snapped out of his seriousness, and as much as that statement absolutely *poured* butterflies into me, I couldn't risk dragging him back into it.

"Hmm." I pretended to contemplate our surroundings. "You feel clouded?"

Coen looked like he was ready to roll his eyes. "Unfortunately. It's sort of annoying, actually."

A smile formed on my lips. I crawled closer to him. "You feel high?"

"It's nauseating," came his answer. "And I have a fear of heights."

282

"You feel full of bright, twinkling stars?"

"Stars that burn holes in my chest and eat me alive," he said, eyeing the sky above us as we floated closer to it.

He was holding back, I knew—and somehow having him shape our perception of reality into a mold of his own mind helped me see why. Clouds and stars, with the island of Eshol far beneath us, as if the world had dropped away...

Ever since our first real kiss in that gem-gilded cave, he'd been holding back. It didn't seem like it upon first glance, with the way he always took charge, the way he always laid me under him, but... he'd never taken us all the way. And for some reason, even though I'd been wanting more for the past several weeks, I'd been waiting for him to do so. Waiting for him to burst through his careful control and absolutely ravage me in the heat of the moment.

But Coen wouldn't break, I realized suddenly with a rush of butterfly wings up my throat. He would not slip or burst or let that hungry haze in his eyes overtake his actions. He was in far, far more control than I'd ever guessed, with a stamina that could send us higher and higher and higher until we broke through the sky and shot into whatever lay beyond. And we'd never fall or deflate unless I...

I swallowed the dryness in my throat, looking at him.

It was up to me. I would have to say the word, and then he'd pounce.

But what if I didn't want to simply say the word and have it... done to me? What if *I* felt in control? What if I commanded him?

The realization that I could... I could take charge in this way startled me, and I almost fell into him. Almost.

"Are you okay?" Coen asked, his eyes narrowing on my neck, as if he could see how wild my pulse was fluttering there.

I didn't answer. I just kissed him.

Immediately, his hands flew up to grasp the back of my neck and pull me against him.

No. I wanted it done *my* way. I grabbed him by the collar of his shirt and pushed him down with that fist of wadded fabric.

Or, at least, I tried to. He didn't budge. Frustrated, my lips still taking and tasting his, I pushed harder, and now a hot, hardy chuckle found its way into my mouth.

His chuckle. His amusement. I hissed in frustration and changed tactics, burying my mouth in the crook of his shoulder and neck, sucking in the scent of black bamboo and nipping at his skin.

Coen stilled against me, no doubt caught in a moment of surprise.

Then he grabbed a fistful of my hair and pulled *my* head back, forcing me to give him access to *my* neck. I tried to yank away, but he clamped his mouth down on the delicate skin just above my collarbone.

"Coen. Steeler," I panted, knowing that if I let loose a single moan, my resolution would completely dissolve. "You stop that. Let me."

"Let you what?" he said against my neck. We were still rising through this mist, as if the stars and moon were infinitely out of reach. As if the sky would never end.

Words failed me, but my hand didn't. I reached down and grabbed the full span of him through his pants, and a wicked smile flew to my lips when he let me go as if I'd electrocuted him from head to toe.

"Let me do *this*," I said.

He sucked a breath in through his teeth, so, so rigid under the glide of my palm as I moved it up and down the fabric of his pants.

"Okay, but only if you can concentrate through this," he said, reaching down in return.

Now I was the one nearly spasming as his fingers grazed me where it ached. Too much. Too much clothing sat between that ache and his fingers.

But I couldn't give in. I was determined to be the one in control—at least for this first time.

I withdrew my hand from his erection to rip off his shirt.

Coen tutted. "Not so fast, little hurricane."

In one pouncing motion, he lowered me onto my back and dipped his face to the lowest part of my stomach. Grinning, he gently bit the bottom of my shirt and brought it up over my breasts with his teeth.

Then he made a trail of kisses down to that lowest part that throbbed and yearned for more of him, brushing feather-light lips over it until I couldn't help but scrabble at his head, wanting him to go *harder*.

He popped back up, smiling with those wicked lips, and I struck.

Lifting myself up by the elbows, I didn't waste time before I tore off my shirt all the way, then rocked forward and grabbed the hem of his.

And as I pulled his shirt off him, I came face to face with all that glorious, tan skin stretched tight over his muscles. All that weight and power and bulk I wanted on top of me. Under me. *Something*.

I ripped my eyes from the line running between his abs, forcing myself to meet his stare that clipped the edge of my breath away.

"Are you sure, Rayna?" Coen asked, caution suddenly filling his voice. "I didn't set this up to make you have sex with me. I just..."

"You what?" I asked, even as my fingers—trembling now, dammit—reached behind me to unclip my bra.

Coen noted the movement and had his hands behind my back in a flash, undoing the clips and throwing my bra overboard. In reality, it was probably falling to the carpet of his room, but right now it looked like it had disappeared in a flurry of mist.

Now my breasts were bouncing in front of his face as I crawled closer to him, settling myself into a straddle over his lap and grinding myself against the hardness that pushed up from beneath his pants.

God, the pressure was everything—burning and sending flurries of white-hot pleasure and need shooting through me.

Coen's eyes latched onto one of my nipples. "I'm just in your head so much," he said through clenched teeth, as if it physically pained him to not have that nipple in his mouth, "that I wanted you to get a taste of *my* mind. And what you *do* to me."

"Well, I've had a taste," I managed to say. "And I want more."

I scooted back a bit to work on the buttons of his pants, fumbling over the smooth edges, missing the slitted holes. Coen watched me with his head cocked and his eyes full of glittering amusement, refusing to help. As if my ability to unbutton him fast enough was the final test to prove that I was choosing this for myself.

"Bastard," I muttered, earning a chuckle. That point between my thighs was screaming now, building with pressure and pain and *please, oh, please*—

The impatience tore through me, and I ripped his buttons off completely. The sound of them clinking to the bottom of the boat couldn't hide my grunt of frustration or Coen's huff of laughter.

"Sorry," I panted, even as I ripped open the rest of his pants, leaving threads dangling and the mass of him beneath me.

He was large and gleaming and... God, I didn't know how I was going to fit all of him inside me. But I knew I needed filled, needed stretched, or else I would collapse in on myself.

"Don't worry," Coen breathed, "I'll just return the favor."

He did. He slipped his thumbs into either side of my waistband and jerked, splitting apart all the seams until my pants were nothing but shreds scattered around us. He did the same to the lace of my underwear, and suddenly there was no more fabric between us. Nothing to hide the glistening wetness already trailing down my thighs.

"Ahhh." Coen spread my knees further apart, taking it in. "Look at you, beautiful hurricane. Such a wild, wet, greedy little thing."

A blush flared bright and hot against my cheeks, but I couldn't reply. Couldn't speak. Could only position our two halves together and settle myself against his broad tip. He clutched my backside, his hands cupping each side of me, but didn't pull me down.

That was my move to make. Right now.

"Oh, God." The moan skated off my tongue as I lowered myself, impaling that slick, aching part of me with that hard, throbbing part of him.

It was burning. It was bliss. It was the fire in our veins, merging into one point. And when Coen's lips brushed against the brand on my shoulder, when he finally lifted his mouth to mine again and our lips met, it unlocked something feral inside of me.

I let my body move how it wanted to, let my hips swirl and grind without thought. The boat began a violent rocking motion as Coen moved against me, too, as he drove upward, slamming himself into me again and again with groan after groan peeling off his lips. The clouds were condensing around us, and the stars were flashing quicker and brighter, more like strobes than twinkles now.

I'd wanted this for too long, I just hadn't allowed myself to think...

To think I could have it.

Not when I still didn't have all the answers about my blood and this island and the world. Not when I had been feeling as if something was missing inside me, and even Coen couldn't fill all of it.

But with his calloused hands cupping me like I was simultaneously the strongest and most fragile thing he'd ever held, with every thrust that gave me the friction and fire I needed, those worries flaked away to the wind, the mist swallowing them as if they'd never been.

There was nothing but Coen and me, retracting and joining again and again and again in the space between stars—

Until the moon shattered above us into a million glowing shards.

CHAPTER

36

We laid against each other afterward, suspended in space among those floating bits of moon. The clouds were long gone, a mere milky white sheen beneath us, and the boat swayed ever so gently as Coen stroked my arm.

I couldn't tell how long we lay entwined like that, just soaking in the aftereffects as if the glow of the moon had been absorbed in our skin. It was only when Coen went rigid against me that his mind trick fell away like a curtain and we were on his bed, in the tangled sheets, in his room once again.

"What is it?" I asked, sitting up. My hair, already curling again at the ends, fell over him. He looked as if he were listening to something I couldn't hear.

"Oh, it's just... everyone's minds are loud right now," he muttered, turning to shift aside a strand of my hair so that he could look at me fully. "Some of the guys in my house let it spread that I carried you into my room, and I guess we were..."

I almost gasped, horrified.

"Loud?"

If either of us had been loud, it had *definitely* been me. I'd forgotten, what with the clouds and stars, that only four walls separated us from the rest of the house.

Coen's half-wince was the only confirmation I needed.

I groaned, sinking back down. "So now it's going to spread to Kimber and she'll hate me extra hard."

She'd already made fun of me for "sharing" Coen with Sasha and Sylvie, of course, but now it would be officially cemented in her mind. And I had a feeling she'd punish me for it, either one-on-one or through Jenia and Fergus.

"I won't let her punish you," Coen said vehemently. "And it's just gossip. Everyone will forget about it tomorrow when someone cheats on someone with someone else's cousin's best friend. You know how it goes."

"Yes, I know." But I chewed my lip, gazing at the imprints on his ceiling. "I just didn't realize it would be so dramatic here. Or so petty. But I suppose that's what happens when you throw a bunch of young adults together for years on end, huh?"

It had been bothering me, this constant... flippant spite. I couldn't imagine anyone in Alderwick sending a horde of beetles into someone else's face just because they'd been jealous of them once upon a time, like Kimber had done to Sasha and Sylvie back at the Element Wielder formal.

Coen cradled my naked body with his own.

"I'm not sure it ever goes away," he said thoughtfully, resuming his strokes against my arm. "The drama and pettiness, I mean. I think it just matures—grows into something that can hide behind the guise of a different name."

I craned my neck to look at him. "What do you mean?"

290

"Well, mean girls grow up to be dangerous, manipulative women." Coen's eyes shuttered at that, no doubt thinking of Kimber. "Asshole guys grow up to be dangerous, abusive men. That's why it's so important to try to be the best version of yourself even in this phase of life they call 'practice.' If you're going to practice anything, you might as well practice being good, right?"

I thought about that. Quinn's mother—had she once been a mean girl here at the Institute? A mean girl who'd passed her Final Test and found a way to manipulate and control others inside her own home rather than outside it? Perhaps cruelty toward your peers now translated to cruelty toward your own children later.

A lump swelled in my throat. I let myself drink in Coen's face.

"You're good," I said. "I feel that, deep down."

His eyes shuttered. When he kissed me again, it was slower than last time.

And so was what followed.

Drama and gossip continued to grow and fester as the dry season officially swept away all the layers of clouds and brought clear blue skies shimmering with hints of the distant dome over our heads.

Everyone was focused on the upcoming pentaball tournaments, where each sector would play against each other. This year, the Shape Shifters would play against the Element Wielders and the Wild Whisperers would play against the Object Summoners. The winners of those two games would play against each other, and then the winner of *that* game would play against last year's champions: the Mind Manipulators, of course.

"I heard the Mind Manipulators win every year," Rodhi said one day, slinging an arm around my shoulder while we walked to History together. "That true, darling? Or was Penny Ickers lying straight to my face?"

Penny Ickers, I knew from all the parties we'd attended, was a fourth-year Mind Manipulator who liked to tell exaggerated stories. But this wasn't one of them.

"It's true," I sighed. Behind us, Emelle and Gileon were arguing about the sentience of clams, although Gileon's quarrelsome nature extended to an uncertain whisper. Still, I tried to tune them out as I explained, "The Mind Manipulators can literally freeze the opposing team in place and win within seconds. Coen told me the trick to beating them is to immobilize them first, but... it's not easy."

Lately, I'd been forgetting how destructive Coen himself could be if he wanted to. Part of me couldn't blame the Good Council for controlling us so severely outside of the Institute. What would Alderwick have looked like if Mind Manipulators were throwing around their power out on the streets, freezing anyone they fancied? Or what if an Element Wielder were to do that with a literal blast of ice?

I hadn't worried about the pentaball tournament itself too much, though. The class royals of each house would pick five players for their sector's team, and as a first-year on Kimber's hate radar, I was definitely *not* going to make the cut.

"I hope I'm on the team," Rodhi said, almost mournfully. "I've made friends with the newest batch of mosquitoes over near the crocodile swamps and they promised me they'd fly over and bite the shit out of anyone I told them to."

"How generous of them," I said sardonically as we descended the steps into Mr. Fenway's classroom, where the old man was shuffling papers at the front. "Considering they would have no interest in biting people if it weren't for you."

"Hey." Rodhi lifted his palms. "They'd spare me and my team and absolutely mutilate the others. *I* think that's a pretty good strategy."

Maybe it would be, but I was still glad knowing that Kimber would rather pick a sloth than me. Pentaball was fun as a casual thing, but I shuddered to imagine myself on that field with thousands of eyes following my every movement. It would be like the Branding ceremony all over again, but with a ball instead of a tiger.

"At least you're able to talk to mosquitos." I took my seat while the rest of the class filed in and took theirs around us. "Whenever I try, they just whine."

It was true. I'd been resorting to taking jarred insects back home to try to communicate with them in the study room—to no avail. I wouldn't have been so concerned if it wasn't for Coen's insistent demand that I pass all of my next tests. Even Willa had taken to watching my failed attempts on the windowsill, audibly sighing whenever I cursed at the cockroach or maggot on my desk.

"You'll get there," Rodhi said, patting my hand. "I still can't make those damned monkeys laugh—their fault, of course. They've got a shit sense of humor. I mean, *I* think my gorilla jokes are funny, but they just run away whenever I even *mention* silverbacks."

We went quiet when Mr. Fenway began shuffling about, returning our latest essays about the famous Wild Whisperers in the Good Council over the last few centuries. I breathed in relief when I saw my passing score, but Emelle groaned.

"Ugh," she hissed under her breath. "Another fail."

"Who'd you write about again?" I asked out of the corner of my mouth.

"Adal Wessex the Third. Apparently, I—" Emelle squinted to read Mr. Fenway's notes at the top of the page " —didn't properly detail his affinity for mushrooms and other fungi, which he thought deserved the same respect as the other plants and animals of Eshol. By the orchid and the owl."

I tried not to glance in Fergus's direction at that. He'd been morose, quieter than normal since Gileon had beat the hell out of him, and I hadn't seen him conjure mold again ... but that didn't mean he didn't have some kind of retribution up his sleeve. Had he learned some of his fungi skills from studying Adal Wessex the Third?

Emelle was still muttering down at her paper, so I yanked a smile onto my face and said, in an attempt to cheer her up, "I think you know why you failed, though."

At this, a sheepish smile crept onto her own. "Yeah."

Lander had gone after his queen, that was for sure. Emelle spent almost every evening at the Shape Shifter house now, slipping back into the bunkroom late into the night with her hair more ruffled than mine and a flush always tipping her ears.

Mr. Fenway gave a sudden cough at the front of the class, as if he'd heard.

"I was disappointed in a few of you while grading your essays, I must say. The Good Council is a crucial part of Esholian history, and it is always wise to know why, exactly, we must respect and cherish their presence at all times."

He smothered a cough with his arm and turned, to my dismay, toward Fergus.

"Take Mr. Bilderas, for example. You were assigned the first ever Wild Whisperer on the island, young man, yet you forgot to mention one very important fact in your paper." Another cough. "That Dyonisia Reeve herself branded him!"

Jenia rolled her eyes at Dazmine, but Fergus remained strangely impassive—even when everyone's eyes flicked toward his face still shaded with the last yellow remnants of that bruise from Gileon's fist.

"And why, sir, would that matter?"

He spoke like a skin-covered corpse. The back of my hands tingled.

"Because Dyonisia Reeve rarely does the actual branding, but when she does..." Mr. Fenway thumped his chest. "When she does, it is said that the magic is usually stronger. And while that might just be an old wives' tale, it is still... it is still..."

Mr. Fenway gagged, and when he did—

I saw something in his mouth.

Something dark and blossoming and rancid. Something familiar that had tainted my nightmares on and off for months.

My feet moved before my brain did. I was already knocking past desks before Mr. Fenway gagged again, hurling toward him. Someone screamed.

Before I could reach him, the old man tilted forward and crashed into the floor.

With black mold billowing out of his mouth.

CHAPTER

37

In the chaos that followed, in the rushing and screaming and jostling as people ran to go find a class royal or someone else who could help, I was the only one who watched Fergus—how he slipped through the tumult and vanished.

Even Jenia kept her eyes locked on Mr. Fenway's body as everyone bowed over it, trying to shake him awake, though I had a feeling she'd watched him leave out of the corner of her eye. She, too, knew of his connection with mold.

She, too, knew he'd done it. Killed Mr. Fenway.

I was still silent and shaking by the time Mr. Gleekle charged into the musty, rotting classroom and bent next to Mr. Fenway's corpse over-flowing with mold.

"Oh, my God."

"What the hell is coming out of him?"

"He decayed from the inside out!"

I couldn't hear what Mr. Gleekle was saying over the wails and cries of my classmates, but I floated toward him like a ghost, knowing I had to tell him. Had to tell him that Fergus had murdered a teacher simply because that teacher had embarrassed him.

Don't.

Coen's voice dripped with deadly command.

Come to me, Rayna. Leave the classroom. Don't say a word. Right now.

I didn't know where he was, but I didn't question him. That tone had me obeying without thought—not because he was using mind control on me right now, but because... because I simply trusted him. I turned, not even pausing to tell Emelle or Rodhi where I was going, and stumbled my way up the steps, into piercing sunlight, where his waiting arms gathered me into a crushing squeeze.

He must have heard the panic in everyone's mind and come running.

"Why?" I choked. "I know he did it, Coen. Why shouldn't I tell?"

All around us, instructors and students were flooding into the Wild Whispering sector, asking each other what was going on. Monkeys chittered on the rooftops, filling each other in. Birds flitted overhead, screeching, "*Death! Death! Death!*"

Nobody paid attention to Coen and me, huddled against the wall.

"There was a murder three years ago during the annual pentaball tournament," Coen muttered, his eyes roving the oncoming surge of people. "The Good Council showed up to investigate. They don't take deaths lightly, because..."

He finished that sentence in my mind. *Because it demonstrates an overabundance of power and ruthlessness. If you tell Mr. Gleekle your suspicions about Fergus, you will be interrogated in full, and the Good Council will know about...well, everything you know.*

I cocked my head at him, suddenly suspicious about the way he'd worded that.

There was no time to contemplate it, though. Coen tugged me forward, and there was a possessiveness in his vice-like grip that certainly hadn't been there a month ago. I might have resisted if that horrid image wasn't plaguing my mind: Fergus's black mold overflowing in Mr. Fenway's gaping mouth.

"Here we are."

We rounded a corner, pressing into a dark shadowy area of the Manipulator sector, where a granite pathway led to a pristine white box of a building.

I blinked, surprised to find them already waiting for us—Garvis, stroking his mustache excessively, Terrin, bouncing on the balls of his feet, and Sylvie clinging to Sasha's arm.

"In," Coen ordered them all.

Garvis turned, hooked his thumb into a metal latch, and slid a hatch sideways into the wall. After we'd all trampled inside, the hatch glided shut behind us.

"What is this place?" I managed to say.

There was only one room in this building, and it was so empty and white and symmetrical that my head began to spin.

Four identical walls. A smooth ceiling. A polished marble floor. No windows. Just that camouflaged hatch behind us.

"We call it the Isolator," Coen answered. "It's one of the classrooms we use for our Blocking & Shielding lessons, but I've never dared bring you here before because people are usually using it to practice. Right now, though, while everyone is focused on Mr. Fenway, I figured we could all use it to talk."

"The Isolator," I repeated.

Garvis rolled his shoulders, as if preparing for a mental fight.

"There's a ward imbued in its walls. While we're in here, no other Mind Manipulator can hear what we're saying from the outside. It's

298

meant to help us focus on whoever's directly in front of us rather than all the random people passing by outdoors."

I'd never given much thought to how... chaotic Mind Manipulating must be, but now my thoughts rushed back to the first branded Manipulator of our year, who'd sunk to her knees screaming onstage when all the voices had flooded her brain.

Coen was saying now, "I assume Garvis has filled you in on what happened?" When Terrin, Sasha, and Sylvie nodded, he nodded back. "Good. We don't have much time to prepare. Mr. Gleekle will be calling in the Good Council any moment, so here's what we know: Rayna thinks it was a boy in her class named Fergus who did it by urging mold to grow at an alarming rate in the teacher's body."

I actually hadn't come to a conclusion more complex than "he did it," but I was grateful that Coen had shaped my fear into an actual explanation.

"Wait a second," Terrin said. "Is that the kid who got beat to shit at my formal?"

"The very same," I said weakly. "I think he's... pissed that no one's taking him seriously. He wants people to be afraid of him, and when it became clear that even the oldest, frailest person on campus doesn't bat an eye his way, he—"

I trailed off, because "exploded" wasn't the right word, not when I'd seen how expressionless he'd been moments before.

No, this had been planned, I realized with a rush of horror. Fergus had been waiting for a moment to test his new killing power. Rather than drowning people in mold from the outside, he could now do it from the *inside*.

"The point is," Coen pressed on, "members of the Good Council will be here any moment to start scouring the minds of every single person on this campus. You four—" He eyed me, Terrin, and the twins "—

won't be safe while they're here, so you'll need to stick with me or Garvis during the entirety of their investigation so that we can guard your minds."

At my questioning gaze, Garvis explained in a low voice, "We do this every time the Good Council decides to look into a surplus of power. Coen and I can feed them false information and thoughts and memories if they decide to come poking around in your brain. Or Sasha's, Sylvie's, or Terrin's."

"But it prickles," Sasha warned through her teeth.

"Yeah," Sylvie said. "I'm not looking forward to that sensation again."

Coen glared at them. "Yeah, well, *I'm* not looking forward to a Good Council Mind Manipulator finding out that we'd be a perfect group to haul up to Bascite Mountain for torture."

So he'd relayed to them, then, what Ms. Pincette had told me all those months ago about what truly happened to those who failed the Final Test. For some reason, the thought that Coen had included his friends in that knowledge, however dark and dreadful, made something in my chest inflate with pride.

It meant he trusted them with the fates of their own futures.

Coen glanced behind him, toward that camouflaged hatch.

"Sasha, Sylvie, how about you sleep with Garvis tonight, while Terrin sleeps with Rayna and me?"

Sleeps? When Coen had said we'd need to stick to him and Garvis, I hadn't realized it would apply to bedtime, too. Although, now that I thought about it... the Good Council Mind Manipulators weren't going to withhold themselves from someone's memories just because it was the middle of the night.

In fact, invading people's minds while they slept would probably be easier.

"With all due respect, brother," Terrin said, clapping Coen on the back, "Kimber's *sort* of kept that rumor going about how you're banging three women at once." He jerked a head at me, Sylvie, and Sasha, the latter of whom snarled in distaste. "If the twins slept with Garvis tonight, it might create a new rumor and garner some attention we don't need right now. But if they sleep with you and *Rayna*, it would fall in line with the already-established rumor and no one would think twice."

Coen glanced at me, a helpless expression capsizing over his face. The logic made sense to me, though, so I nodded my agreement.

Are you sure you're okay with it? he asked mind-to-mind.

You don't need to feel defensive about protecting your family, Coen.

Relief flickered through his eyes. *Thank you. For trusting my intentions.*

Then he tossed a nod at Terrin. "Right. The twins and Rayna will sleep with me tonight and you'll sleep with Garvis."

Terrin clapped Garvis on the back. "We can pretend to pass out drunk on the rooftop again like we did last time. Nobody will blink twice at us if we're surrounded by bottles. Especially after an exciting day of instructors dying and such."

"Terrin!" Sylvie cried, nudging him in the ribs. "Have some tact."

"Oops, right." Terrin glanced at me. "I'm sorry for your loss, Rayna."

"Oh, no I—I didn't know him very well. He was just..." I stumbled over my words. "I just hope he doesn't have any family on the island. They'd be devastated to learn what happened."

Mr. Fenway probably *did* have a family out there, though. A family that Fergus clearly hadn't thought about when he'd told his mold to kill.

Asshole guys grow up to be abusive men. I wasn't sure which of those Fergus qualified as now, an asshole or a real abuser—perhaps being a murderer surpassed both of those—but I *did* hope Dionysia's Mind Manipulators would somehow manage to sniff him out without violating any of my friends.

Because if Fergus stayed, I knew that mold would eventually come for Gileon.

And me.

Coen escorted Sasha and Sylvie to their house to grab nightgowns and toiletries, clutching my hand the entire time we waited for them on their front steps. After they returned, he took us all to my own house so that I could do the same.

By this time, stars were pulsing into the gray film of dusk overhead, but the entire campus buzzed with nervous conversation as if nobody would be heading to bed for a while. I actually had to shove myself through two Wild Whisperers locked in conversation in the doorway, debating how Mr. Fenway had died.

Once I got to the bunkroom, Emelle sprang upon me.

"Rayna! Where have you *been*? I didn't realize you were gone until after they took Mr. Fenway's body away. Then I was so worried, I asked some birds to keep a look out for you, and Wren is out trying to find you right now."

"I'm sorry, Melle." I rummaged in my drawers for some sleepwear and a toothbrush. "I felt nauseous seeing Mr. Fenway like that, so I ran outside to puke."

I didn't know why I was lying, not after all Emelle had done to earn my trust, but... no. I straightened. She deserved the truth.

Clearing the uncertainty from my throat, I said, "I'm actually going to spend the night with Coen." When she raised her eyebrows, I peeked around to make sure we were alone and whispered, "if the Good

Council finds out what Lord Arad revealed to us in that abandoned classroom, I'm as good as smoke."

I expected a sudden glimmer of understanding to dawn on Emelle's face at that, but she just pinched the lines of her forehead together.

"What are you talking about, Rayna?"

I stared at her. My nightgown dangled from my fingers.

"Lord Arad. The vampire heir. Remember what he said? About my mother?"

Emelle took a step back. Her heel hit the foot of our bunkbed.

"Are you feeling alright, Rayna? Maybe the events of today have gotten to your head. I've never heard of this Lord Rad thing. And what's this about vampires?"

She let go of a nervous chuckle. I stared and stared at her.

Finally, I chuckled, too. There was only one explanation for her bizarre forgetfulness: Coen had erased her memory of Lord Arad. And as much as I wanted to feel angry at him for that, to scold him for touching my friend's head against her will, I couldn't. Not when Emelle's lack of awareness would protect her tonight.

"Yeah, I guess you're right." I reached out to squeeze her hand. "The events of today have just gotten to my head. I'm sorry."

Emelle shook her head. "Don't be. We're all pretty shaken up. Poor Mr. Fenway. I just can't fathom what kind of disease would knock him out like that."

At that moment, Coen's voice sliced through me at the same time that a hundred or more vultures screeched out words of profanity from the sky outside.

I ran to the window. They'd been tethered, those vultures had, to a new carriage that was angling toward the courtyard now. And from the curses flying out of their beaks, ringing through the air, I knew they'd been forced into pulling the carriage.

303

Hurry, Rayna, Coen was growling into me.

Hurry, because the Good Council was here.

CHAPTER

38

I could sense them prowling outside all through the night.

Coen breathed against me on one side while Sasha and Sylvie curled together on my other side. Between the four of us, that massive king bed of Coen's finally seemed rather small, but I didn't care. Didn't care, either, that anyone who'd seen the four of us steal into the room together would be confirming Kimber's rumor tomorrow morning. I could practically hear the whispers that would follow us.

Whores. Whores. Whores.

"Stop it," Coen muttered against my ear. "Try not to think about it."

"Easier to think about that than *them*," I replied.

In the end, Dyonisia Reeve hadn't joined her Mind Manipulators, but I did recognize one of them. I'd seen him strutting down Bascite Boulevard moments before Coen had ushered the twins and me inside: a mullet that split into braided strings down his back, a wide, constantly flexing jaw, rutted, light brown skin—he'd been one of the elites sitting next to Dyonisia during the Branding.

But whereas before he'd paled in comparison to her, now I couldn't blink the image of him away. The way he'd marched, shoulders angled inward, leading the others down the path between houses... it was like a whispering presence followed his every movement.

"His name is Kitterfol Lexington," Coen whispered, "and he's probably the second most horrid thing on this island. Dyonisia loves him."

"There's talk that they share a bed," Sasha said beside me.

"And also talk that they're siblings," Sylvie added.

"Well, which one is it?" I whispered back.

"Who knows?" I felt Sasha's shrug in the darkness. "Maybe both."

A creak of the bed as Sylvie elbowed her. "That's disgusting, Sash."

I mulled it over and thought back to something Garvis had said in the Isolator. *We do this every time the Good Council decides to look into a surplus of power.* Which sounded like it had happened more than once.

"You said earlier that there was a murder during a pentaball game a few years ago," I whispered to Coen, though I knew Sasha and Sylvie were listening, too. "But has the Good Council ever come to investigate anything else?"

Coen hesitated. Sasha and Sylvie, however, twisted in bed.

"You haven't told her?" Sasha hissed.

"Told me what?" I asked, shooting up.

Coen's hand gently pulled me back down against him. He sighed.

"I haven't told you that when I broke up with Kimber last dry season, she was so livid that she sort of—how do I put this?" He inhaled through his nose, pinching the bridge of it. "She killed every animal within a ten-mile radius. Just left a circle of carcasses in every direction around us. Nobody likes to mention it."

Silence. My heartbeat stalled.

"What?" was all I could say.

"Kimber's fury cracked and she told them all to die," Coen said, his own voice cracking. "So they did. Birds and monkeys and butterflies just dropped dead."

"That's not possible," I began, even though I suddenly wasn't sure at all. "We can *talk* to animals, not command them to *die.*"

"Your magic has barely scraped the surface as a first-year," Sylvie said gently on the other side of Sasha. "But for the most part, you're right. Kimber demonstrated exceptional magic that day. Too exceptional."

Just as Fergus had demonstrated too-exceptional magic today.

Now Willa's claim that Dyonisia had spiders spying on Coen all the time made perfect sense. They were probably spying on Kimber, too. But why hadn't they taken her to Bascite Mountain?

"The Good Council came to investigate your breakup," I said, trying to keep hold of the steadiness in my voice, "and—what? They found out what Kimber did and just left her alone?"

"More or less," Coen said. "Lawful magic that's gone beyond the scope of normal limitations catches their attention, but I believe they're waiting to see if Kimber's capable of doing it again. Hence why they've been keeping a close watch on her—and me—ever since. If they catch Fergus, they'll probably do the same to him. And keep an extra eye on him until his Final Test."

But we—Coen, Sasha, Sylvie, and I, and the other guys, too— wouldn't get the same privilege if we were caught. Not if Dyonisia found out our blood came from beyond the dome.

The danger of our predicament suddenly crashed down on me, as if the ceiling had dropped low and pinned me to the bed.

"Okay," Coen breathed. "They're moving on to our house now. I need all of you to breathe deeply, relax your minds, and let me concentrate."

For some reason, I'd thought the Good Council would simply cast around for guilty-sounding minds while we slept, maybe conduct an official investigation tomorrow morning based on what they found tonight. I hadn't realized how precise it would be, house to house, person to person, their minds shooting through walls to invade every mind one by one, regardless if that mind was swimming through dreams or just as awake as we were.

But I could feel them as the investigators moved closer to us, heard that whispering presence and imagined the group of them now standing right outside the Mind Manipulator house, staring at the many little windows as if they could see inside.

"Here we go," Coen hissed.

He clasped my hand, and I clasped Sylvie's, who clasped Sasha's.

Usually, I couldn't feel Coen in my mind until he actually spoke to me, but now a pressure built at the base of my skull and snaked toward my forehead.

I didn't know what was happening until a foreign voice fractured through my thoughts and spit, *did you kill Frank Fenway?*

Kitterfol Lexington didn't wait for me to respond.

He plunged through my most recent memories, and I relived them, too, as he flicked through me like I was nothing more than a textbook.

But when it came to my suspicions of Fergus, there was curiously nothing, as if a sheet of generic terror had been slid carefully over that knowledge.

When Kitterfol dug deeper, rooting around like an invasive worm that had split into several separate heads, I sensed Coen's presence lurking, handing the Mind Manipulator private memories but folding the most secret ones far, far beneath everything else.

Kitterfol watched with amusement as Coen and I had sex for the first time. I cringed internally, trying to fight my way out of that

308

memory, but Coen grabbed my thigh and gave it a squeeze that would surely end up bruising.

Breathe deeply. Relax your mind.

So I let Kitterfol watch it, the most intimate thing I had ever experienced.

Before Coen and I reached our climax, however, I felt him grow bored—and *lunge* for a new memory.

The one where I hurled myself into a tank of cockroaches.

No, no, no. Not that one. I couldn't let him reach the end of that one.

Coen wrenched him back. And changed the scene to hold his attention.

Now he, Coen, was dragging out chains from beneath this very bed and cuffing me to the bedpost—spreading my arms and legs wide until I was completely bared for him. Exposed to the air and his wicked contemplation.

"Where should I start?" Coen's voice dripped with venom as he swiped a finger between my legs, making me arch my back violently. "Here? Or here?"

He plunged that same finger into my mouth, gagging me.

When the Rayna in this false memory began to sob, Coen chuckled darkly and said, "Here, then." And stuffed himself into my mouth until I was retching.

It worked. Kitterfol Lexington didn't try to fish out any other memories.

By the time he ripped himself out of my mind, his little worms weren't curious anymore. They simply oozed satisfaction and triumph and sick smugness.

Coen released a groan and slumped against me. I hadn't even realized how rigid he'd become, but now his limbs were trembling.

"He's gone."

"Without checking us?" Sasha asked incredulously.

Coen fisted a hand against his forehead. "He had his fun and assumed the memories would be the same for each of you, since you're all sharing my bed. God, I'm so sorry, Rayna. That should have been easier than it was, but Kitterfol is more powerful than I anticipated." He was shaking. Coen was actually *shaking*. "I've never had to defend any of us from him before—it's always been one of the others. But he was clever. He would have pierced through my shields and guards if I hadn't distracted him with what he most wanted to see."

"What?" I asked, breathless. "Abusing women in bed?"

My heartbeat was drowning in my throat at what I had just witnessed.

"Discipline," Coen said. "Submission. Power. I'm so sorry," he repeated.

"Hey." I began to rub soothing circles along his shoulder. "It's okay. You just saved me. You don't have to apologize for doing whatever it took."

There had been so many dangerous memories Kitterfol could have snatched. The cockroaches. The cave. Fabian's letter. Lord Arad. The maggots. If enduring a false bondage scene was the price to pay to protect those memories, then so be it.

Even if I'd never be able to shake that image from my memories, now: myself, chained up and spread wide open for Coen to mock and tease and lord over.

"You saved me," I repeated, pressing my face against his chest, telling myself that what I'd seen, what Coen had done to me, wasn't real. Wasn't real. Wasn't real. "Thank you."

Slowly, his shaking subsided, and we all four fell into a quiet huddle. But none of us slept until the Good Council left at dawn.

310

CHAPTER

39

Whether Kitterfol Lexington and his henchmen had caught on to Fergus or not, nothing seemed to change after their departure. Fergus still showed up to Predators & Prey the next day, a greasy half-smile barely concealed behind his twitching jaw when Mr. Conine announced that the Wild Whispering sector would get to skip our third quarterly test in honor of Mr. Fenway's death.

While I felt horrible for Mr. Fenway himself, I had to admit this was a relief to hear. My progress with insect communication was going dismally compared to everyone else—Emelle had started to request specific songs from the crickets outside our window at night—so this would give me extra time to practice.

But I couldn't shake the feeling that even extra practice wasn't going to help me at this point.

"I just don't understand why I was able to talk to those fire ants during the first week of school but no other insect since," I told Emelle and Lander as we squeezed into the stadium during the first game of the official pentaball tournaments: Shape Shifters versus Element Wielders.

Coen, as his house's prince, sat in the front row with the other class royals. I kept half an eye on his back as the referee lined everyone up.

"Well, let's think." Emelle blushed as Lander's hand rested on her knee, but she stuck to the conversation resolutely. "What was different about that time? You were saving our asses, for one. And you were... what—scared?"

"Scared. Angry. Desperate."

I mulled it over, chewing on my bottom lip. It didn't seem to fit. I had also been scared and angry and desperate with the cockroaches and maggots, and they hadn't done anything more than laugh at me.

Lander cleared his throat with a fist to his mouth. "I know I don't know anything about Wild Whispering, but have you tried talking to the ants again? Maybe that'd give you a clue as to why *they* listened to you."

Emelle turned shining doe eyes upon him. "That's actually a good idea!"

Someone gagged. Wren and Gileon had just sidled in, each carrying a bucket overflowing with snacking peanuts. I would have asked where Rodhi was, but I knew by now that it'd be pointless—no one could keep track of that kid.

"I'd offer you some," Wren told Emelle and Lander, "but I wouldn't want you drooling all over the buckets. You two are worse than Rayna and Steeler."

"Hey!" I exclaimed, nudging her. But my attention had snapped to the field, where Mr. Gleekle was trudging out to face the crowd, right between the two opposing lines of the chosen Element Wielders and Shape Shifters.

"Ladies and gentlemen!"

Once again, a thousand different branches of wind seemed to carry his voice directly to our ears.

312

"It's time for the first pentaball game of the season! I ask that you remain seated for the entirety of the game, no matter how long it takes, and don't interfere with the happenings on this field. Players." He half-turned to the ten crouching men and women behind him—all fifth-years, by the looks of them. "If you touch anyone in the crowd with your magic, your team will be dismissed immediately and the title will be granted to your opponents. Do you understand?"

I couldn't make out if they nodded from this distance, but Mr. Gleekle turned back toward the stadiums a moment later, apparently satisfied.

"Now, a moment of silence, if you will, for one of our dear instructors in the Wild Whispering sector, Frank Fenway, who tragically passed away last week due to a fungal infection."

From this far away, Mr. Gleekle's glasses made his eyes look like glinting gray orbs. The sky, the stadium, the very spinning of the world seemed to pause its breathing, waiting for someone else to break first. Gileon fidgeted.

I couldn't have moved if I'd wanted to. Fungal infection? Really? It was one thing to keep such sensitive information from the entire campus, but to blatantly lie about it? Although I supposed, as the corpse-quiet seconds ticked on, perhaps a fungal infection *was* the best way to describe what Fergus had done.

"Thank you," Mr. Gleekle said mournfully... although his face stretched tight with a smile. "Now, I'll hand this off to our referee, and may the best magic win!"

He pumped a fat fist into the air.

The referee held up a neon green flag. Again, the entire stadium seemed to pause. All ten players were crouched like Jagaros had been in the abandoned classroom, poised to mutilate their opponents. Each of them held a ball, too, although I made note of the differences in their

313

grips. One Shape Shifter clutched the orange spiked one between two vise-like hands. The Element Wielder across from him, however, simply pinned her warty green ball in the crook of her arm.

A downward swish of neon green and the players burst into motion.

Everything happened so fast, I could barely keep track of it.

The Shape Shifters shot upward, inflating themselves into giant beings that cast cold, dark shadows across the entire field, each of them with their balls pinioned between two meaty fingers—one step, and they'd make it to the half-disc on the other end of the field.

But before they could, the Element Wielders lit their heads on fire.

Emelle screamed. Lander groaned. Wren laughed, while Gileon whimpered and stuffed a fistful of peanuts into his mouth.

The Element Wielders were already racing between the giants' legs toward the disc on the other end, but the next second, the giants grew steel helmets that stifled the fire and shot out elongated arms to stop them.

I watched the Shifter with the spiked orange ball grab a Wielder with a hand as big as a carriage and throw her into the air.

Now *I* screamed, but the girl conjured a sudden, house-sized cube of water beneath her, its edges framed by ice, and dropped into it with a colossal splash.

She'd also dropped her ball. It floated in the water, and a nearby Shifter who'd tracked her movement dove after it. Moments before he hit the water, he shrunk into a piranha that grabbed the ball in its sharp, pointed teeth.

When the piranha leaped out, an Element Wielder was waiting.

Before the Shifter could revert to his human form, the Wielder blew a cloud of thick black smoke his way, dousing the fish in its ashy poison.

It went on and on and on.

The brutal mesh of magic never extended beyond the field, but I could still smell the sting of charred flesh, still hear the screams and taste the smoke in the air.

After ten minutes, Gileon dropped his bag of peanuts and rammed his face into his hands to block it all out. Wren merely patted his back, grinning.

I was having trouble taking it all in, too. In those ten minutes of fire and ice and monsters merging in and out of existence, only two balls had been rolled into the discs on either end of the field: eight more to go. Eventually, I let my attention drift to the back of Coen's head up in the front, watching *him* watch the chaos.

He never moved. Never flinched. Never looked back at me. Even when his neighbors jumped or cringed or clapped, it was as if he was immune to it all.

I didn't want to think it, that there was a lot to Coen I still wasn't familiar with, that part of him remained a mystery. The thought left me scratching my arm, suddenly feeling uncomfortable in my own seat. For some reason, I just wanted him to look back at me. To make a half-second of eye contact.

To show me the viciousness of all this bothered him, too.

Coen didn't, and I had to remind myself that I was dating the same man who had ruthlessly tortured and threatened Fergus all those months ago. Maybe he enjoyed this as much as Wren did, who was whistling and cackling in delight every time someone slipped or collided or caught on fire.

Rethinking our relationship, little hurricane?

There he was. I'd been wondering when that sly voice would slink in.

315

Maybe, I shot back. *You're awfully calm about*—my eyes snagged on the nearest calamity—*a sinkhole swallowing up the person right in front of you.*

I'm strategizing. Any one of these teams could be playing against us soon, so I need to figure out everyone's strengths and weaknesses before-hand.

Right. Coen would be playing in the final pentaball game of the season with four other Mind Manipulators in his year, including Garvis. I hadn't thought much of it until now.

Now that I knew I'd have to watch him endure all *this*, though...

The Shape Shifters ended up winning, but barely. By the time the referee swished his flag again to call it, several pairs of medics were carry-ing away various players on stretchers.

My gaze landed on the closest one, who groaned as he passed under-neath the stadium, his skin peppered with burn marks from head to toe.

"I think you're right, Lander," I said quietly, trying to look away but finding it hard to. His blisters looked a hell of a lot like Fergus's and Jenia's welts that day they'd tried to mess with Gileon. "I think it's time to talk to the fire ants again."

Six hours later, after everyone else had wafted to bed, I found myself back in the study room, this time with a jar of three ants I'd nicked from the bark of a tree outside. They scurried round and round the glass con-tainer, occasionally trying to scramble up the sides and falling back down again.

"It's okay," I whispered to them, trying to keep each exhale rough and raw so that they'd understand me better. "I'm not going to keep you forever. I just wanted to ask you a few questions."

Nothing. No hint of comprehension. I only heard their desperate gasps, as if they were suffocating despite the holes I'd punctured through the jar's tin lid.

I tried again.

"Do any of you know why my magic isn't letting me access the insect world?"

Again, they seemed to shriek with frantic breaths. I glanced at the stripes of shadows and moonlight against the desk and sighed. One minute.

I'd lasted one minute with these creatures, and they were already choosing to panic themselves to death rather than talk to me.

I carried the jar back outside, dumped the ants gently onto the snarl of roots at the base of their home tree, and trooped back to the study room, slumping into my usual chair and massaging my temples.

"Maybe the tome would help you figure it out?"

Willa had scrambled up the leg of my chair and onto my lap. I jumped, but not because of her sudden presence—at this point, I was used to her skittering up my body during random times.

No, I jumped because of what she'd said.

"What tome?"

Willa blinked at me. Her tail curled around her body.

"You know, the one you hid behind the clock a few months ago? The one that says the you-know-what."

I felt myself shrink inward. The room seemed to zoom out and out and out until I was nothing but a grain of sand lost in the roaring tide of a deep ocean.

Was this why Coen had been acting like he'd swallowed a fistful of rocks lately? When he'd erased Emelle's memory about Lord Arad, had he also erased mine about...whatever this was?

317

I straightened myself to my fullest height, until I was no longer a grain of lost sand. Until I could kid myself into thinking I was the flagpole of one of those pirate ships in the distance, tall and domineering and a spike of force against the wind.

"Tell me everything," I said to Willa.

CHAPTER
40

Half an hour later, I had the tome tucked between my arm and ribcage and was dashing out of the house and into the night with Willa on my heels.

The crickets stopped chirping momentarily to listen to my footsteps. An older female owl swooped above me, hooting, "*A rush in the night leads to thrush in the light,*" but I ignored her.

Coen had told me after the game that he and Garvis were going to stay on the field and practice some maneuvers they'd picked up from the Shifting team earlier today. They might have gone to bed already, of course, but I didn't think so. Mostly because Coen hadn't told me goodnight yet, but also because I knew him, and I was beginning to know Garvis: they were both hellishly competitive, and would do anything it took to smash their opponents in their upcoming game. Including staying up to practice until the first smudges of dawn graced the sky.

I could hear them as Willa and I crept closer, sticking close to the cold shadows of the houses and stadiums. They were out there, alright, two young men in a swath of white moonlight, kicking those balls back and forth in zigzagging motions.

The grass sensed my distress before Coen did. Each blade quivered around me, bowing inward and giving a low whistle to match the deep ringing in my ears.

I whistled back on instinct even as I continued striding forward, and the grass—that manicured pool of soft green, cut and groomed and perfectly tamed—turned absolutely feral to match the wild scampering in my heart.

A ripple of bent blades shot toward Coen and Garvis. The ones around their feet lunged up and out, twining around their ankles and pulling them down.

I finally stopped, looming over the two men sprawled to the ground.

"What the hell?"

Coen nearly cricked his neck to look at me.

My face felt strangely slack. I held the tome out, letting the foiled lettering catch the moonlight.

Coen's face creased. "Oh. That."

Garvis turned to frown at him. I dug my fingernails into the tome's spine.

"Leave us," I ordered. Not at Garvis, but at the few spiders I could sense at my feet, waiting with dripping fangs for gossip and drama and rumors to spread.

To my surprise, I heard the brush of several dozen hairy appendages against the culms of grass as a few of them scuttled away on command.

Interesting. If my heart wasn't about to jump straight out of my throat, I'd wonder why they obeyed me when other insects didn't—unless it was because spiders *weren't* insects, not truly.

I shook the questions away and flattened Coen with a glare.

"You stole this memory from me. This *knowledge*. Why."

It was hardly even a question. Just a command. And I didn't care that Garvis heard. Didn't care that they were both still roped to the ground, all those pentaballs scattered around them among the still-whistling grasses. The ringing in my ears had reached a pitch that made my fingertips seem to vibrate along with it all.

"I didn't steal it," Coen said finally. Carefully. "But I did hide it deep in your subconscious because you asked me to. You wanted to be able to focus on your test."

And without even a swipe of his hand, he unveiled it for me—that memory he'd buried. I felt it spring up to the forefront of my mind, and I stumbled backward as it all poured back: Ms. Pincette giving me the tome, me learning I was faerie, then asking Coen to take the knowledge of it from me until after my test.

It wouldn't be fair of me to remain angry at him for doing as I asked. But—

"I told you to give it back to me after that test," I whispered.

"You didn't *pass* that test," he shot back. "You said you would, but you didn't, and I thought it best for you to focus until you did."

"You don't get to decide what's best for me, Coen."

I had balled up my fists and found them shaking at my sides. I didn't care why he'd kept this from me—to protect me, to shield me, I didn't care. Not when *my* sense of self had been buried beneath *his* need to control the narrative. Not when the realization raised as many questions as it answered.

Had Dyonisia hunted the last of the Esholian faeries into extinction? Her arrival on the island certainly correlated with the final traces of them, according to Mr. Fenway's first lesson. But if so—why?

What did she have against faeries, to murder them and lock them out and search ruthlessly for the strays she'd trapped within?

321

Did all of the Good Council know they were looking for faeries to persecute in addition to the humans that failed their Final Tests, or just her?

So many questions. *Too* many questions.

Coen flashed me his palms.

"I don't know the answers to everything you're asking, Rayna, but yes, I was eventually going to tell you that we're faerie."

"Why keep it from me at all?" My voice bobbed in my throat. Betrayal. This felt like betrayal in its deepest form, that he wouldn't trust me enough to tell me about my own blood. "Just because you wanted to keep me *safe*?"

"Yes." Coen didn't flinch. "I will always choose your safety over my morality, Rayna. And I won't regret that, no matter how mad you might get at me."

"Oh, I'm mad," I started.

I know. I can feel it. And I can take it. But by the moonbeam and the mist, please stop shouting about this in the middle of the pentaball field. There are other ways someone can eavesdrop on us besides spiders, you know.

Don't belittle me, I snarled.

Don't act little then, he snarled back.

I almost threw the tome into his face. My hands actually flexed to do so when Garvis disentangled his ankles from the grass and stepped between Coen and me.

Rayna. Take a breath.

I recoiled at the sound of anyone else besides Coen in my head. Garvis's thoughts weren't as wormy as Kitterfol Lexington's had been, but they were raspier, wispier, like they were floating on a wind rather than sinking in my mind. They left tingles on the back of my neck as he continued.

322

You're part-faerie, yes, but the power that derives from that side of your lineage is too immature to take form. If anyone from the Good Council finds out about that, they won't hesitate to destroy you knowing that your natural, God-given magic isn't advanced enough to fight back. Coen and I have erased the full understanding of our blood from Sasha, Sylvie, and Terrin, too. It is better this way.

To what end? I whispered back to Garvis, knowing that Coen was listening in. *At what point do you say enough is enough and fight back?*

What do you think all those ships are doing out there? Garvis answered gently. *The Good Council likes to claim they're pirates because piracy sounds scary, but they're just Sorronian fleets waiting for a chink in the armor to attack and take back what's theirs. What's ours.*

I blinked.

Fell a step backward.

Willa squeaked and scuttled up my leg.

Take back...? What do you mean?

He means... Coen rose to his feet, brushing off the mud clinging to his pants. *That bascite is the natural metal found in faerie blood. Unlike humans, we don't have to consume metals to help us breathe and grow and live. The oldest legends say that while the God of the Cosmos made humans out of dust, He made us out of loam, already rich in minerals and metals. Many of those metals, like iron, help air travel through our blood, but bascite is what carries the magic through our veins. Like a conductor.*

Willa sniffled near my ear, but that was the only sound that permeated the night.

Dyonisia Reeve, Coen continued, stepping slowly toward me, *took an abundance of faerie blood and found a way to plant its bascite within the layers of human skin.* His eyes never strayed from my face as those words clashed into mind. *She stole faerie power and has been giving bits*

323

of it to humans for centuries, tinkering with the weakest ones and ex-
perimenting on the strongest ones. To try to create her own race of
beings.

"The bascite she gives us doesn't come from the mountaintop?" I
murmured, touching the ridges of my brand. "It's... she *stole* it from
beyond the dome?"

Garvis, this time, nodded slowly. *And the pirates aren't some ran-*
dom seamen waiting to pounce on unwanted offerings each year.
They're faeries trying to reclaim what was taken from them so long ago.
The magic in their blood.

But... I tilted my head as Willa nestled into my neck. *But they're*
faeries. *Don't they have enough power to take down the dome with the*
snap of a finger?

Even as I said it, though, I suspected I knew the answer. However
she'd done it, Dyonisia had stolen so much power from the faeries that
they'd become weak without it. Why else would they be desperate to
take back the metal that had once surged in their veins?

I wiggled my toes, as if to shake free the blood pooling there.

It made sense now, what my raw power was. Bascite. It came from
bascite, just like my Wild Whispering magic did. But it was natural rather than given, born with me rather than stamped onto me. And it was
too undeveloped to take its own form as of yet.

But the Wild Whispering one... it was a stolen form of magic from
some other, older faerie who... who wanted it back.

"Oh, God."

I suddenly wanted to rip it out of me, this ability to communicate
with plants and animals—even if I'd miss talking to Willa and Jagaros
without it. It didn't belong in my veins, beneath my skin, coursing
around and between my bones. I ran a thumb across my brand again,
feeling the crests and dips of the scarred skin.

"How long?" I whispered as Coen crept closer, softly nudging Garvis aside and angling his face to meet mine. "How long until our own powers develop?"

So that I can use mine to murder Dyonisia Reeve.

But Coen shook his head, his frown mere inches above mine now.

They won't, Rayna. As long as we're taking those pills, our powers should stay stagnant. A faerie reaching full maturity is quite the spectacle, so we can't let ourselves do so while we're in this dome.

I dropped my thumb from my brand. Dread swamped me.

If I let my power mature, Dyonisia would stifle it long before it would reach its full strength. But if I *didn't* let my power mature, if I just kept on taking these pills and smothering it like water on a flame, I'd never be strong enough to defeat her.

Which meant I was trapped here as surely as a cockroach in a jar.

CHAPTER

41

"No more secrets," I told Coen.

We were back in the gemstone-riddled cave, letting the roar of the waterfall drown out every other sound of dawn.

Garvis had left for bed with a muttered goodnight and a concerned pinch of his brows, and I'd walked Willa back to the house to ensure none of the owls got to her. But *I* wasn't about to go to sleep until I had all the answers.

We had no blanket this time, so we stood, crossing our arms at each other, in the center of the cave. I hadn't felt this much animosity between us in a long time.

"Coen?" I ground out when he didn't answer. "No. More. Secrets."

He huffed a breath.

"Your life is more important than the truth, Rayna."

"I actually beg to disagree," I shot back.

"Really?" He stepped closer. "Because I don't think you do. *You're* the one who asked me to erase Emelle's memory of Lord Arad to keep her safe."

"That's different," I hissed. "Emelle's memory wasn't about her. It was about *me* and *my* family and *my* heritage. So as much as it sucks to keep her from that part of me, it isn't the same as you hiding information about my *own* blood."

I went on before he could interrupt.

"And if you and Garvis are helping the pirates—sorry, *faerie fleets*—in a war that's invisible to everyone else, I need to know because *I'm* involved whether I like it or not."

"You want to know until Kitterfol Lexington comes back," Coen said, and now I noticed his arms trembling against the widespread planes of his chest. "You want to know until I'm not around to defend your mind and he pulls the truth out bit by bit, and strings you up in front of everyone, and lashes you until your skin is in bloody strips, and you're puking and screaming and pissing yourself."

My words got caught somewhere in my mouth. Close. He was so close to mentioning that one death that haunted his every step from so long ago.

I considered him a brother, he'd told me once, *and he died from it.*

"What was his name?" I asked, something in me softening ever so slightly.

Coen's shoulders remained rigid, but he said, "Mattheus."

I exhaled. "And Kitterfol Lexington killed him?" I asked carefully. "After his own faerie power exploded in response to drinking even more bascite?"

"Yes." Coen's voice fractured. "Lexington tortured Mattheus in front of the entire village, then hauled him off—to the sea, he claimed, to dump him into the ocean for the monsters lurking in the water. But not before our adoptive father—a Mind Manipulator himself—erased Matt's entire identity, every piece of knowledge he held about us and the faeries." Coen closed his eyes. "Matt passed out without even knowing who he was. I remember trying to catch his eye during one of the final lashings, and his gaze passed right over me. He was nothing but a picked-out shell by the end."

Which was what I'd be, if Lexington got to me after Coen graduated from the Institute.

I'd never loathed my Whispering magic so much as I did now. If only I was a Manipulator, too, I wouldn't be in this position, having to choose between knowledge and life, truth and safety.

The key to happiness isn't love or gratitude or any of that shit, Don had always said, much to Fabian's exasperation. *It's ignorance.* Well, perhaps Fabian *did* agree with that even if he wouldn't admit it, considering he'd fed me ignorance my whole life by keeping my birth and mother a secret.

Should I choose ignorance now? Let Coen and Garvis fight on their own? From the way Coen's jaw still seemed to be ticking, I knew he'd be steadfast in his secret-keeping. He wouldn't give me a single thing more even if I begged.

So I wouldn't beg. I would put the pieces together on my own. In front of him.

"We're in the middle of a war," I said. "But only the Good Council and the faeries know about it. Everyone else in here is oblivious in our little bubble."

Coen didn't nod. But his pupils widened in the glittering light.

"You and the others weren't sent here as distractions," I plowed on. "You were sent here as spies. To grow up here and learn the ins and outs of the Institute and return to the faerie fleets when you're finished." I almost gagged on the words. "You're all leaving this island as soon as you pass that Final Test."

Once upon a time, I'd been terrified of exile. Now the man I loved was going to exile himself, and I wanted nothing more than to follow him out of here.

Coen unfolded his arm and took a half-step toward me.

"I'm not leaving you, Rayna. I'm not abandoning you."

"But that was the plan," I persisted. "You planned on leaving until I showed up. And now you don't know what to do. You—" I almost laughed as I stumbled upon a final realization. "You've been getting the pills from the faerie ships. *They* provide you with the suppressant to stifle our immature power, not some random merchant from your home village."

Being immune to the shield, Coen would be able to do such a thing—reach through the barrier and take the pills from a boat on the other side. Probably in the dead of night when no one was looking.

"You said you had to *pay* for them. What are you paying them with, Coen? Information?"

Yes. I could see that answer splayed all over his face. He truly *was* a spy. For the people I'd once been so terrified of, faceless men and women at sea. No—faceless *faeries*.

God, I'd been so stupid.

Coen wavered on the spot. For a moment, I thought he was about to spill it all.

Then he snapped his mouth shut, and his face hardened again.

"I can't tell you anything more than this: you, Rayna, weren't just born in the middle of a war. You were born in the enemy's territory. In the enemy's *cage*."

I understood the sentiment. Dionysian and her Good Council elites already had me shackled; they didn't need much of an excuse to snatch me away from the Institute and haul me to their torture chamber on the mountain, and every piece of information I gathered in here just

329

gave them one more reason to do so. Coen wanted me to stop asking questions, to stop attracting potential attention, but... what if the only way I could protect myself in the long run was by uncovering those answers?

I chewed on my lip, frowning.

"I understand you can't tell me everything, that there's sensitive information you might have found out as a spy that... that I don't get to know. But when it involves *me*, when you're keeping secrets about *me*, then..." Something inside me crumpled. "Then how can I trust you?"

Coen stuck a finger beneath my chin, near the throbbing pulse of my throat.

"I never said you could trust all of me, little hurricane."

The sultry tone of his voice nearly had my knees aching to collapse, especially as I remembered what had happened during our first time in this cave.

But then he was lifting my chin with that single finger and saying, in a sadder, more serious tone, "You can't pick and choose which pieces of my magic to use, Rayna. You can't ask me to alleviate your stress for a test, but expect me to give it back whenever you please."

Shit. He was right. I'd taken advantage of his power, tried to use a slice of it for my own benefit. But I couldn't do so any longer. I could accept Coen as he was, edged with lies and deceit and half-truths... or I could let him go.

Back to the pirates. The faerie fleet. Back to the ships he'd come from.

I knew what I had to do before my heart could even falter.

If Coen had a way out of this cage after his Final Test, there was no way *I* was going to be the thing that held him back. I wouldn't let him be caged with me. But he would never leave me unless I pushed him away.

330

"Then I guess I won't be needing any part of your magic from here on out." I forced out a shrug, hating, hating, hating myself when Coen withdrew his finger from beneath my chin as if I'd shocked him. "I guess we should both focus on what's most important to us and move on."

"Rayna... please don't." Each of his syllables cracked.

By the orchid and the owl, I was really breaking up with this man. As if it didn't splinter every bone in my body. As if it didn't bruise my heart and twist my lungs and send panic flaring to the tips of my fingertips and toes and...

"I don't want you to stick around after your Final Test," I said, enunciating each word. *I don't want to hinder you* slipped through my inner thoughts, but Coen wasn't in my mind to pick out those words. He was far, far away, sinking into his own mind, blinking rapidly down at me. I said my next words carefully. "I don't want someone I can't fully trust."

"Fine," Coen said, his shock vanishing as quickly as it had sprung upon him. Nothing but cold nonchalance masked his face now, tightening every muscle there.

"Fine," I said back, and was surprised to hear the nonchalance still coating my own throat.

Liar. I was such a goddamned liar. I wanted him whether I could trust him or not, but it would be safer for him if he left, and healthier for me if I wasn't constantly suspicious of my own partner.

I turned and marched back up the tunnel without saying another word.

Away from the dazzling glimmer of stones and into the Throat that swallowed me whole.

CHAPTER

42

Weeks and weeks of that darkness dragged by.

The worst was the waiting. Waiting for my memory to disappear. For that knowledge of my faerie blood to slink back into my subconscious. Surely, Coen was going to lock it away again?

But as each day passed, I woke up every morning still knowing who I was. Still knowing *what* I was. Coen, it seemed, hadn't touched my mind since our breakup in the gilded cave.

He didn't talk to me in person, either. Garvis gave me my pills each Sunday, meeting me in the alley between our houses instead. I didn't see Coen a single time, not even in passing.

As if he knew exactly where I was at all times and was determined to avoid me.

Fine.

Fine.

Fine.

I was beginning to loathe that word.

If I was fine, I'd be able to eat. I'd be able to look people in the eyes. I'd be able to brainstorm better ways to get ahold of Jagaros to tell him about that map once again tucked away behind the cuckoo clock.

As it was, I'd only ventured into the jungle twice to lamely call out his name and hear the hum of the listening wildlife echo back at me. I hadn't heard from him since the Lord Arad incident, but I couldn't find it in me to care. Because I wasn't fine.

Or maybe I was. Maybe the word *fine* had always meant *in pain but can't show it because I'm too scared nobody will like me if I'm whining and wailing and weak.*

"You should eat a little more than that."

It was Emelle, pushing a bowl of fried bamboo shoots under my folded arms. The tinkle of cutlery and conversation washed over me like nothing more than a wave hitting a beach of stones and gritty sand.

"I'm full, actually, but thanks." I tried to drag my eyes to her face. Tried not to think of black bamboo and that deep, mellow smell that lingered on Coen's skin. "Really."

All I saw was round-eyed concern.

Emelle glanced at Wren, whose own charcoal-lined eyes squinted at me.

"I don't think a couple bites of banana is enough to get anyone full, Rayna," she said shrewdly.

Rodhi jumped in before I could respond to that.

"Maybe a rebound hookup would do you good, darling. I have a friend from the Shifter house, his name is Grayson—"

"Lander's told me about Grayson," Emelle cut in darkly. "He preys on grieving girls fresh out of breakups."

"Well... yeah..." Rodhi said, gesturing at me.

"My ma's a medic back at home," Gileon's voice joined in. "And she's always helping patients recover from a broken heart by giving them

333

their own broomstick to take home." He frowned. "I'm not sure how, but the broomsticks help. Ma's a Summoner, so she casts charms on them to make them vibrate and—"

"*Okay*, that's enough, Gileon," Wren cut in, patting him on the arm.

I folded my arms tighter over my chest, feeling exceedingly uncomfortable. This was the most any of them had talked to me about my split with Coen since it had happened. But I didn't want to talk. Didn't want to acknowledge it.

"I'm going to go take a bath," I said abruptly, pushing myself away from the table. "I'm feeling a little chilly. See you all later!"

I hadn't realized how much Coen's presence had warmed me until now.

Now a coldness I'd never known took root inside me, creeping upward like vines twining through my skeleton. I felt it in every fake smile. Every forced wave. Every conversation like the one I'd just had with my friends.

Just Coen's absence, frosting me with ice from the inside-out.

Even the streaks of raw sunlight covering the Institute campus couldn't warm me up.

By the time the fourth quarterly test of the year rolled around, I was a sculpture of that ice. I took a History test passed out by a Mr. Fenway's replacement, a middle-aged woman with a hunchback. I helped a female lemur decide which of three males she should mate with for Mr. Conine. I swapped songs with the bromeliads for Mrs. Wildenberg.

But when I opened the door to Ms. Pincette's testing room and saw the tank of rattling locusts waiting for me to contend with, I ignored it completely.

I simply pulled up that wretched stool and dragged it to where Ms. Pincette sat in her usual bloodred velvet armchair, clipboard in hand and pursed lips on her face.

"Hello," I said, that coldness finally seeping out. "We need to talk."

CHAPTER

43

"Leave us," Ms. Pincette told the spiders.

She waited until they'd scuttled further into the foundation of the Testing Center before swiveling her attention back on me, a single eyebrow tilted.

"You're not even going to try?"

The question was prim, her mouth still puckered like plucked roses. She had laced her fingers together in her lap.

"No," I said. "There's no point. I can talk to worms and spiders just fine, but insects themselves don't want anything to do with me."

I still didn't know why—perhaps me being faerie had something to do with it? I'd been poring over that map every few nights for answers, sneaking the thing in and out of the space behind the cuckoo clock after everyone else had gone to bed. But there was nothing in it to hint that faeries would have more trouble talking to insects than humans did. Especially since most faeries couldn't talk to animals at all. It was a unique gift that only developed naturally in a few.

And besides, that wasn't what I wanted to talk about now.

"You work for the Good Council," I said instead, so coldly it sounded like the words might chip off before they left my mouth.

A space of a breath. Ms. Pincette's eyes flickered.

"Not directly. I'm not *on* the Good Council, Ms. Drey."

"But you report to them. You give them a list of failed students, right?"

Yet for some reason, you're protecting me.

Another flicker in her eyes, this one like smoke drifting over ashes.

"They expect some failures every year. I can't spare everyone."

I waited for her to continue. Those damn vines were going to choke me from the inside-out...but I couldn't ache for Coen right now. Not when I was determined to pick apart all the answers he refused to give me. Not when my instructor was admitting to me that she handed over her own pupils like fish on a platter.

"Why do you do this for them?" I breathed out. "If you know they're taking your students to Bascite Mountain and... and experimenting on them—torturing them—why do you even work for them? Wouldn't it be better, more humane, to get some silly little job in a silly little village and never think about them again?"

Except part of me knew it would be impossible to forget about the Good Council even in the smallest, most faraway village.

All it takes is one person breaking the law, one person using magic on the streets in an inappropriate manner, one execution in every village, for people to obey, Coen had said... Coen, who'd watched them string up his childhood friend and lash him until his skin was in bloody strips.

Still, though, Ms. Pincette could have removed herself from any involvement.

For the first time since I'd laid eyes on her, my sharp-eyed instructor melted into a distinctive softness, as if each of her features were cowering rather than slicing.

Behind me, the swarm of locusts continued their chorus of rattling screeches.

"I failed my Final Test," Ms. Pincette whispered finally, her eyes anchoring onto mine. "I wasn't one of the strong ones. I was one of the weak ones. I could pass every History exam and talk to every animal and befriend every spider, but I couldn't for the life of me understand what those damn trees were singing. So I failed."

I waited, still cold, still trying to push down my vines of ice. I had never felt so far removed from my childhood self, from the girl my fathers had raised.

"They took me to the mountain." Ms. Pincette's voice was merely a whimper. "They... did things to me."

Slowly, her eyes still embedded in mine, she lifted a corner of her tunic and revealed a flash of her bare stomach.

I didn't even have enough breath to gasp.

How many times had Rodhi rattled on about how much he'd like to see what lay beneath Ms. Pincette's clothes? So many times, I had blocked it out. But I was certain now, more than I'd ever been certain before, that Ms. Pincette would never show him. Not because of the age gap or inappropriate power dynamics, but because what lay beneath her clothes was an absolute *tangle* of scars, crisscrossing ropes of raised flesh that wrapped around her ribcage and rose up to her armpits and...

I pressed a hand to myself. Not to rein in a gasp.

To keep myself from vomiting.

Ms. Pincette let her tunic fall back into place.

"When they were done doing those things to me," she said rather dryly, like her last tears had fossilized behind her eyes years ago, "they asked me if I'd like to die, or if I'd like to teach."

Oh. Oh, oh, oh. I felt my sculpture crack, just the tiniest bit, near my heart where it screamed and flailed and bucked at what Ms. Pincette had just revealed.

"I'm sorry," I got out, slumping. "I should have never suggested—"

"—that I'm a useless lump of shit on this island that keeps manufacturing new test subjects like pawns in some centuries-old game most of us don't even know we're playing?" Ms. Pincette suggested, a droll smile tightening her face.

I didn't answer. Couldn't. The locusts had reached a pitch too loud for me to think through.

Had every member of the Good Council been subjected to such horrors before they'd agreed to join? Had Mr. Fenway and Mr. Conine and Mrs. Wildenberg failed their tests once upon a time—either for demonstrating too much power or not enough—and been dealt just as many scars and that same horrible choice?

Ms. Pincette seemed to read the question on my face.

"I think not," she said. "I think Dyonisia Reeve is a masterful marionette who knows exactly what to say or do to get people on her side. With me, she knew I wouldn't work for her willingly and that I was useless enough to bargain with."

A twitch tugged at the corner of Ms. Pincette's lips at that. Failed. She had failed her Final Test, something I'd been so afraid of my entire life—and suffered a fate worse than banishment and pirates. Worse than what I'd always feared.

"So," Ms. Pincette continued before I could elaborate on that, "I let them experiment on me until I'd lost my sense of purpose and soul and everything else besides the pain. That's why I joined her ranks, let

339

her give me a new name, promised her I'd never contact my family again—my family who thinks I was exiled long ago. Because it's this or death, and I've always been a coward."

I didn't know what to say. The thrum of my heart was lost among the chorus of locusts, and my tongue was nothing but a stone in my mouth.

Ms. Pincette could call herself a coward and a failure and a useless lump of shit. She could hide all of that behind her prim and proper mask... yet she'd lied for me, made an illegal map for me, sent the spiders away for me time and time again...

That didn't seem cowardly.

My tongue was still heavy when it said, "Why me?"

Because I knew she'd never done this for anyone else. Knew it deep in the place those vines were rooted and my raw magic eddied, trying and trying and trying to wake up.

Ms. Pincette flicked an annoyed glance behind my shoulder, at the locusts.

"Oh, shut up," she barked at them—and they dropped into ringing quietness.

Then she leaned forward, got a good look at my face, and leaned back again.

"I sense something in you, Rayna. I don't know what it is, yet, but I've learned the hard way to always trust my gut."

She smiled that dry, cracked smile, and I thought of the spiders she'd sent away, suddenly feeling as if a few invisible ones were scuttling up and down my face.

But no, that was just the awareness in Ms. Pincette's eyes as she looked at me. Beheld me.

"My gut says that whatever you're leashing in there," she whispered finally, nodding at my chest, "is what could finally shatter this God-forsaken dome and free us all."

There was no Coen to greet me outside the Testing Center when I finally made my way down the stairs and pushed myself outside. My name had been called earlier than usual for Mr. Conine's test, so patches of pink still bruised the sky this time.

More people than I was used to milled by those lampposts to talk about their test results or lean over the railings and look out at the ocean. I hardly spared a glance at the ships dotting the dappled horizon, and was only focused on the direction of my own footsteps when I heard it—a distressed voice.

Dazmine's.

I shot a look over at the fountain, where she was facing Fergus and Jenia.

All three of them abruptly stopped talking when they noticed me. The gray in Jenia's eyes zeroed in on me, and she crossed her arms. Fergus's mouth formed a wicked V with his smile. Dazmine looked away.

"Move along, Drey," Fergus called. "Unless you think you've got a little... fungal infection? In that case, I'd love to help you."

I recoiled. The verbiage. The knowing smile. He knew that *I* knew he'd killed Mr. Fenway, and he was casually inviting me to die the same way.

And since Kitterfol Lexington hadn't caught him the first time around—or if he had, he hadn't cared—Fergus could kill me without any immediate repercussions, no matter *what* the so-called rules were.

341

I didn't let myself recoil again. Didn't let the fear creep out onto my face. Instead, I deadpanned, "No, thanks," and strode off in the other direction.

When I was out of sight, though, when I had made it across the bridge and was on the safe side of Bascite Boulevard, I plunged into the foliage past one of the Element Wielder houses, where I crouched in the ferns until my heartbeat steadied.

Legs clicked among the leaves.

I paused. Counted to ten. Felt its hairy, twitching presence. And as those vines of frigid cold crawled up and down the inside of my spine, I found my voice again.

"What would it take," I breathed at the eight green-tinted eyes staring out at me from a nest of stems and leaves and spiderwebs, "for you to be my spy?"

CHAPTER

44

"What will you give me, mortal? Or..." The spider bustled forward, to the very tip of the fern it had nestled into for the night. *"Should I say* immortal? *You smell like something in between."*

Its accent was lilting, almost as musical as the ferns themselves, and it took all of my concentration to disentangle its little voice from the foliage around it. Spiders were spies, indeed. Even the way it *talked* camouflaged its presence.

"What would you want from me?" I asked, copying that lilt of each syllable.

To my surprise, the spider—a simple garden one—responded to me instantly.

"I want to see the world from its highest point. I want to feel the mist and the stars and the air where nothing stirs."

It could hear me, then. I could talk to it, unlike the ants and maggots and cockroaches. Those vines of ice reined in the tiniest feeling of... pride, bubbling beneath my sculpture of indifference.

Its request—a carriage in the sky? Bascite Mountain? Both options required getting the Good Council involved, which I couldn't do.

But I said, "I could try to take you there someday. That's all I can promise right now, to try."

I expected the spider to scoff and scuttle back into its web. It paused instead.

"*Who would you have me spy on, you almost-mortal?*"

I didn't know why, but that question cracked in my heart. *Almost-mortal.* I'd never asked Coen how long he and I had to live. So far, I'd matured just as quickly as any of my peers in the village; Quinn and Lander were proof of that. Would the aging process just... stop one day? Or slow down? Or was I not quite faerie enough to warrant a never-ending stretch of life? Coen would know, of course, but he'd chosen to leave me in the dark.

A darkness I was still in, despite the stars that blazed down on me now.

"I would have you spy on some bad people," I said quietly. Behind me, a group of Element Wielders had started chatting on the rooftop, tossing bubbles of ore back and forth with casual lifts of their knees as they sipped on some drinks. I wondered painfully if Terrin was up there with them... or maybe Quinn.

"*Bad people?*" the garden spider mused. "*How subjective.*"

Ms. Pincette had scratched the surface of spider morality in class, so I knew they didn't have an objective code of ethics. Still, my chest sunk a notch—

And jolted when the spider said, "*Still, I have never been someone's spy before. If you can promise me that you will try your best to bring me to the top of the world one day, I will eavesdrop on these so-called bad people for you.*"

Its tone suggested it didn't care whether its victims were bad or not.

"Thank you," I sighed, and whispered out Fergus's and Jenia's descriptions and usual locations. After the spider nodded in understanding, I asked, "what do you mean, I smell like something in between mortality and immortality?" I resisted the urge to sniff my armpits. "What do I smell like?"

The spider's eight eyes glinted neon green in the starlight.

"*Ahhh. I have a hard time describing it. You... smell like the creatures who are not quite caterpillars and not quite butterflies, but somewhere in between, stifled in a cocoon and crystallizing and ready to burst out of their self-made skins. That kind of in between.*"

I was too tired to jump through more mental hoops today, but I couldn't stop myself from thinking, as the spider backed back into its nest of shadows, that such an explanation didn't quite fit. Didn't quite make sense in regards to mortality.

Neither caterpillars nor butterflies lived forever, after all.

The spider came to me three days later, during Mr. Conine's class.

Or, rather, *I* went to *it*.

But not of my own accord.

We were deeper into the jungle than ever before, although rather than it being all shade and gloom as I'd expected, we'd trudged to the top of one of the humps on the mountainside, where dried mud caked the bald patches between trees.

Here, Mr. Conine had said, a pack of wild boars claimed territory, and we had been invited by their leader to sunbathe with them, of all things.

"Here's the tricky part," Mr. Conine said now. I watched his bushy sideburns moving up and down with his mouth as if through the end of a long tunnel, focusing so hard on not thinking about Coen or faeries or caterpillars that I ended up having trouble focusing on *anything*. "Even when boars try to rile you up for a fight—because they *will* try to rile you—you must remain calm and peaceful and perfectly poised, and insist you'd just like to sunbathe."

Here, Mr. Conine passed a half-glance at Fergus, as if expecting him to argue. Or to ask why the hell we'd been invited over if the boars just wanted to fight.

Fergus didn't say a word, though. He simply caught Mr. Conine's stare and tightened his arm around the back of Jenia's neck. His silence unnerved me more than his usual whining attitude, but it seemed to relieve our instructor, whose brows relaxed slightly.

"Right, then." Mr. Conine rubbed his hands together. "Ready?"

Nobody responded besides Rodhi, who flexed his fingers. "Bring out the boars, baby."

Mr. Conine put two looped fingers in his mouth and whistled.

They came instantly, a herd of tusked, stringy-haired pigs nudging through the bushes around us and stomping their way into the clearing.

I caught the eye of the nearest boar against my will, and—yep. It was definitely glaring at me, beady auburn eyes scrunched up tight in the folds of its wrinkles.

"Uh, hi," I said, trying to shake myself out of my tunnel.

Around me, everyone else had burst into whispered conversation, as if afraid that loud voices would trigger the herd's anger. I was no exception. Even my head and shoulders dropped slightly, instinctively shriveling up in the face of such... wrath.

I decided right then and there that just because I was a Wild Whisperer didn't mean I had to like every animal I talked to. I could respect this swine without enjoying its company.

"*What are* you *lookin' at?*" the boar huffed, nudging the dirt beneath him with a hoof. "*My nose? My ears? You're not the best looker yourself, you know.*"

I swallowed the sting of that insult and resisted folding my arms.

"I think your nose and ears are lovely, and I'd... I'd just like to sunbathe."

Truthfully, I didn't want to be here at all. Knowing that this was all an experiment in a bubble made all the classes not only seem pointless, but *mocking*.

Barely three paces away, Emelle and Gileon were already laying down with their boars, angling their faces toward the sun in peaceful companionship. Rodhi was placing his hand tentatively on a snout. Even Fergus had managed to get closer to a boar than I was to this one now.

My boar pawed the ground again.

"*You want a piece of this, huh?*"

"N-no."

I took a step back without thinking, pressing into the shadows. Nobody had noticed that I wasn't doing well over here. All my friends had their eyes closed already, and Mr. Conine was busy helping Norman ease into a truce with a particularly brutish pig with black patches all over its body.

I had been avoiding Mr. Conine's eye lately, anyway. I didn't know what would be worse: finding out he'd been tortured into his position here at the Institute just as Ms. Pincette had, or finding out that he'd volunteered to be here. To hand Dyonisia fellow human beings as if they were forged bits of metal she could dip back into the fire.

"I don't want to fight." I raised my hands, but my voice sounded insincere even to my own ears. I *did* want to fight—not this boar, but *something*... anything to help me punch away the vines of ice and the tunnel of darkness and the invisible threats swirling about my head like pesky gnats always out of reach, and—

The boar charged.

I stumbled back into the ferns.

347

And the boar—stopped, as if it had been caught in the same sculpture that seemed to suffocate me nowadays. Every part of its body froze, except for its auburn eyes, which blinked at me furiously.

Just then, my hips and fingertips and hair felt a *tug*, and that's when I knew.

Sasha and Sylvie had saved me. I didn't know how or why, but I'd recognize their style of Summoning anywhere. It was their magic that had immobilized the boar and tugged on me now, urging me toward them.

I just barely saw Emelle's eyes flaring open before I was yanked backward down the slope.

On and on, I followed those tugs, trying to keep up lest they start actually dragging me. Before long, the shadows of the jungle nestled into my skin again, and I found their two lithe forms crouching in the widespread roots of a fig tree.

"Rayna! So glad to see you."

Sylvie jumped up to throw her slender arms around my neck. I hugged her back, but didn't hesitate to say into her hair, "Are you alright? What's wrong?"

Is he *alright,* I couldn't ask through the lump in my throat.

"Oh, we're fine." Sasha waved a free hand—her other one, I noticed suddenly, was levitating a... a *spider*, keeping it trapped in her own web of sticky magic.

And I recognized the eight green-tinted eyes.

"What are you doing with that? Let it go!"

I untangled myself from Sylvie and lunged, but Sasha backed away.

"We can't let it loose, Rayna! It's been snooping around your house for days, and it was following you through the jungle just now before we tracked it. We thought you might want to interrogate it before we make a paste of it, see what it wants with you."

I swung my gaze from Sasha to Sylvie, and back to Sasha. Understanding slammed into me, just as I heard the spider cry out, "*Oh, let me see the top of the world before I die! Please!*"

"It's *my* spy," I said as gently as I could, touching Sasha's wrist. Reluctantly, she let go of her hold on it, and the spider dropped onto my upturned palm. "I told it to spy on Fergus and Jenia because I overheard them talking strangely to their friend Dazmine." I wanted to start asking the spider questions, but first I had a pair of twins to deal with. "Now, are you going to tell me why you two are following me, or do I need to set a spider on *you* both as well?"

They glanced at each other. Sylvie wrung her fingers together. "Well..."

"He's making you guard me, isn't he?" I asked, disbelief welling in my throat where that lump had been. "He's making you track my every movement."

"Not exactly," Sasha said unashamedly. "He asked us if we could look out for any threats directed at you, and we thought we found one." She nodded at the spider, who was... trembling. The poor thing was trembling. I hadn't known spiders could do such a thing before now.

I wasn't sure what to say to Sasha or Sylvie. Thank you? Back off? I miss you?

Instead, I settled my eyes on the spider and whispered, "What did you find?" The twins wouldn't be able to understand anything it said anyway.

"*The one girl, Dazmine, and the other girl, Jenia, are in an argument,*" the spider rattled out. "*Jenia and the boy Fergus were trying to get her to join them in something. Something big. They've only alluded to it, never mentioned it out loud. I cannot figure out how they are communicating unless through written messages.*"

The spider's eyes were snaking back and forth between the twins and me, clearly suspicious of the former two and clearly regretting its commitment to me.

"*After many urgings, the girl, Dazmine, put her foot down and refused to join them. Jenia is hateful, but Fergus is murderous, and threatened to, I quote, 'fill her lungs with rot' if she didn't cooperate.*"

The spider paused, and I had the strangest feeling it was trying to word its next finding in a way that made it all seem more important than petty drama.

"*But Jenia the Hateful stepped in, told Dazmine the Dissenter to leave, and neither has spoken to each other since.*"

I slumped back, making sure to keep my palm steady even when the rest of my body started to shake. Now that I thought about it, Dazmine *had* been standing off to the side during class today, away from Jenia and Fergus. But what had she refused to join?

And why did the spider's findings only make me feel more confused than before?

CHAPTER

45

"Mr. Conine thought a boar had dragged you off," Emelle said later that afternoon, right before the last pentaball game of the season.

She was sitting cross-legged on her bottom bunk, combing through Wren's hair while Wren cursed and I picked at my cuticles above them, deep in thought.

"Oops," was all I could manage. After a moment's pause from down below, where I just knew the girls were exchanging concerned glances, I cleared the apathy from my throat. "But he couldn't have been worried for too long, right? I mean, my boar was pretty vocal about the fact that I'd ran away from a fight."

Indeed, when I had trudged back up the slope to rejoin the class after parting ways with Sasha, Sylvie, and my spider, I'd been met with a would-be-amusing scene: Mr. Conine, on his hands and knees, consoling a pig who was grunting about how an "ugly witch" had petrified him and fled the scene of the crime.

When Mr. Conine had snapped his eyes up to where I stood, I'd told him I'd just been taking a pee and that I didn't know what the boar was talking about.

A necessary lie, because a few of my classmates had sat up to listen in on that exchange, including Emelle, Gileon, Rodhi...

And Fergus.

I still felt the weight of Fergus's gaze clinging to my skin, tacky and sticky and unnervingly aware. As if he alone knew exactly where I'd gone and who I'd met. I couldn't understand how Jenia let him *touch* her on a daily basis, not when her immaculate skin and hair looked as if they'd never seen a day of grease in their life.

I chanced a glance over at Jenia now, on the other side of the bunk-room.

Or, at least, where I'd thought she'd be.

Her bunk was empty, and Dazmine was pulling on sandals alone.

"I suppose not," Emelle said finally, reeling my attention back in. "Are you going to get ready on your own, Rayna? Or do I need to attack you with this comb, too?" She shot her arm out and wiggled the comb threateningly.

"I wouldn't advise that option," Wren called up. "It's like I went to hell early."

My laugh could have been chips of ice tumbling from my mouth.

"Yeah, wouldn't want that. I'll get ready myself, Melle."

Not that I cared about getting ready for the pentaball game right now—and not just because I had other things on my mind. It would also be the first time I would see Coen again, since he'd be playing for the Mind Manipulators. I wanted to see him, craved a good look at his face and form... but also didn't want to see him.

Seeing him would crack me. Seeing him would *shatter* me.

A whisper from Emelle down below: "Go ahead. I'll meet you in the stadium."

A groan and a creak later, Wren had lifted herself from the bed and passed me a distinctly non-Wren smile, full of what actually looked like sympathy and warmth, before hurrying out of the bunkroom, her raven-black hair now flowing behind her.

"Rayna." Emelle swung around and hoisted herself up my metal ladder. "Is this about Kimber?"

I blinked at her. "Kimber?"

"You know." Emelle rounded her eyes. "Since Kimber will be playing head-to-head with... him. I thought maybe you didn't want to watch that..." She trailed off, watching my face as it went through the various stages of realization.

"Kimber's on the Wild Whispering team," I said, monotone.

"Well, yeah. You knew that."

I had known that, yeah, but I'd forgotten. "And our house won the last game, so we'll be playing against the Mind Manipulators." Rusty gears were clicking into place in my brain. "I'll be watching my ex play against *his* ex. Great."

Now Emelle looked suspicious. "Please tell me you knew all this."

I cringed internally, remembering something she'd once huffed out while running after enchanted pieces of paper with me. *I know you're hiding something, Rayna. I can see it in your eyes sometimes, something distant and—foreign.*

Except Coen had erased her memory of Lord Arad, so he'd probably erased her memory of saying that to me, too. Which made my head spin with the logistics of what she *did* remember. Was that same thought brewing behind her eyes right now? Or did the loss of a memory mean the loss of an idea as well?

My lips parted. I sucked in a breath to tell her everything.

Emelle just held out a single hand and gave me a watery smile.

"I love you, Rayna. And I'll be by your side the entire time. If there's ever a moment where it becomes too much for you, just give the word and I'll leave the game with you, okay? But please try to get out and join us. Please."

I pressed my lips together, sucked back in the tears, and nodded.

"Okay," I said.

And took her outstretched hand.

The pentaball game was seconds away from starting by the time we hit Bascite Boulevard, where Lander was waiting for us right outside the Whispering house.

He stood in the empty street, hopping from foot to foot.

"*Finally*. I was just about to break in and see if you two were still alive."

"Sorry! Girl talk," Emelle sang back cheerfully.

Before Lander could finish rolling his eyes, Mr. Gleekle's voice leapt out from the stadium, amplified on those hundreds of streams of wind.

"Ladies and gentlemen! It's time for the final pentaball game of the season! Now, I've repeated the rules so many times I think my own ears might bleed if I repeat them again—" A chuckle scraped against us. "— so without further ado, allow me to introduce the ten magnificent young men and women before me now."

I gritted my teeth as Emelle and I joined Lander. In mere seconds, Coen's name would rattle through my eardrums, and I'd be damned if I let myself even *blink* abnormally in reaction to that. No, I could do this. I could—

A voice stopped me in my tracks.

No, not *one* voice. Hundreds of voices.

A cloud of flashing yellow and orange wings fluttered toward me.

In flowing, gargling accents, the butterflies said, "*Rayna Drey.*"

My gape probably looked comical. I had half a mind to wipe out my ears with the sleeve of my shirt, make sure I'd heard correctly. *Insects* were talking to *me*?

"W-hat?" I asked, wafting toward them. "Do you need something?"

Emelle, too, had stopped and turned, her mouth popped open just as wide as mine was.

Lander, on the other hand, merely pressed his mouth together in a confused frown. He had no idea these butterflies had even spoken, I realized.

"You must come with us," they said now, their flowery tenors completely at odds with the urgency now creeping into their tones. *"It is Jagaros. He is in danger."*

"What? Where?" I stepped toward the butterflies. Jagaros? I hadn't heard from him in... months and months now. "What kind of danger?"

"In the jungle," they answered in flowy unison, disregarding that last question. *"We will lead you to him, but we must make haste before..."*

"PETRA SCALLION," Mr. Gleekle cut in, his voice blasting through them.

The butterflies scattered for a moment, reformed their cloud, and began flitting away, toward the jungle on the other side of the Element Wielder house.

"Wait! I—"

I whipped toward Emelle and Lander to tell them to go to the stadiums without me—but I already knew what Emelle would say. Not just because of her set mouth and the way she'd planted her hands on her hips.

No, Coen might have erased Emelle's memory of doing this once before, but that didn't take away from the grit and will and stubbornness imbedded in her.

"I'm coming," she said firmly.

"I know."

I shifted my glance from her to Lander, who sighed, then reformed himself so fast, I gasped. Once second, he was the dark-haired, ebony-skinned boy I'd grown up with—albeit a bit taller than when we'd left Alderwick—and the next, he'd shrunk and bubbled and sprouted into a giant black panther, not quite as domineering as Jagaros himself, but with just as many teeth and claws.

"Get on," Lander growled at us.

Another shock. I was hearing him talk *as an animal.* God, the magic mathematics required to understand that concept already made my head burn.

But Emelle was already hoisting herself up onto his back (which made me think she'd done this before), and the butterflies had almost disappeared through the tree line now, so I didn't hesitate any longer.

I grabbed Emelle's hand and scrambled up Lander's flank, settling myself into the dip of his back behind her.

He bounded after the butterflies, and I shrieked as my head swung back from the force of it. When I lurched forward to fix my balance, I slammed into Emelle.

The ride jostled us the entire way into the jungle, through the trees in seemingly chaotic maneuvers. Mr. Gleekle's magic-enhanced commentary faded into the background before I could hear Coen's name, and soon the song of the jungle cocooned us fully. Kapoks and elderberries hummed softly. Thistles purred out silky tunes. Monkeys quarreled with each other about this or that.

But my eyes stayed on the butterflies, on the soft whispering of their wings as they plunged onward. I'd been so worried about seeing Coen again, but now my own heartbeat was cracking the ice in my veins as fear and dread slammed against my chest over and over.

Where was Jagaros? Where was he, where was he?

What had *happened* to him?

I couldn't imagine how a beast as swift and powerful and dangerous as Jagaros—a beast who'd once been a faerie king—could get tangled up in any kind of life-threatening situation.

Unless... my gulp stuck in my throat... unless Dyonisia had discovered the truth about his past...

I instinctively hummed at a tree up ahead, and it jerked one of its low-hanging branches out of the way before Emelle and I could hit it head-on.

If that was the case—if Dyonisia held Jagaros hostage right now— how could *I* help Jagaros? What could I do against the Good Council?

It was a good thing Lander had donned his panther form. From the bunches of muscles tensing and stretching beneath us as he carried us deeper into the jungle, I knew there was a horribly real possibility I would need them: his teeth and claws.

Finally, even the chittering of the monkeys faded, and the cloud of butterflies slowed. The hum of the jungle was deeper here, more slumbering. It felt like we'd walked right into a cave where a monster snored, from the way the canopy above us shielded us from a single drop of sun.

Here, there was just green darkness and...

"Jagaros?" I called.

The butterflies were fluttering toward a figure bathed in shadows. The figure stepped forward, and they swirled around her head, haloing her, swaddling her in their flickering colors.

"I told everyone over and over," came a steely voice that reminded me of endless gray mist, "that the butterflies love me. But did anyone listen? Did anyone *care*?"

I slid off Lander's back, falling into the rotting undergrowth beneath, where only the most festering flora could survive with such little

357

light: snake plants and philodendron and devil's ivy. I squinted at the figure within the butterflies.

"*Jenia?*"

Her answering tut was all I needed to confirm it. Jenia Leake was *here*, in this long-forgotten pocket of the Eshol wilderness, instead of at the pentaball game.

"Where's Jagaros?" I demanded, my voice fracturing when I said his name.

"He's not here," came a new voice. "But I am."

And from behind Jenia, from between trees cloaked in moss and stitched together with vines, a grinning Fergus stepped into the green-tinted hue of dying light.

CHAPTER

46

My breath snagged in my chest, but only for a moment.

The next moment, it positively *collapsed* as two more people stepped out alongside Fergus and Jenia: that Object Summoner who'd sent sticks to poke at Gileon's back so long ago, and... and...

"*Quinn?*" Lander said. "*What the hell are you doing here? What is this?*"

Except he was still in his panther form, so Quinn couldn't decipher or understand that snarl lashing out through his canines. She surveyed him uncertainly, confusion passing over what little I could see of her face.

Fergus tilted his head back and gave a lazy laugh to the canopy above us.

"*This*, Shifter, is simply payback. You weren't there, so you can go if you'd like. But I'm glad the fat one joined."

He gestured at Emelle, and rage curdled in my blood. It didn't melt the coldness there, but bolstered it. Fed it. Like the only rage I'd ever know from now on wouldn't be hot, but chillingly, achingly cold.

"Yeah," Fergus continued, oblivious of the way I'd balled my hands into fists. "I'll enjoy her screams almost as much as that one's." He jerked his chin at me.

"Screams?" At that word, Quinn had backed away—just a single step, but enough to make her stumble over the roots and ivy strangling her feet. "You didn't say anything about screams, Fergus. You just said..."

"*Yeah, what* did *they say*?" Lander growled,

Again, Quinn couldn't understand him, but now her eyes seemed to swell with understanding. She took in his paws, his powerful legs, his snout and whiskers and bristled black coat... and the young woman straddling his torso.

"Lander," she breathed.

This seemed to trigger something in Emelle—Lander's name on Quinn's lips.

"Is this still about the fire ants? By the orchid and the owl!" Emelle lifted her head to glare, not at Quinn, but at Jenia and Fergus and the Object Summoner. As if Quinn stood too far beneath her. "Payback? What a joke. We were simply defending our friend. You hurt us, we hurt you back, all's fair and even. Let. It. Go."

I'd never heard such authority in Emelle's voice before, and a string of pride sprung from my chest even as that coldblooded rage tightened every other muscle in my body, preparing me for a fight that should have been here but wasn't.

Jagaros. Jagaros... wasn't even here. The butterflies had lied for Jenia.

And that realization—that insects wouldn't talk to me except to lure me away, to *trick* me—made every one of my tightened muscles quiver. I wanted to run and swat at the stupid swarm still fluttering

360

around Jenia's figure and punch the greasy, smug smile off of Fergus's face all at the same time.

"I came to the Institute," Fergus said now, "expecting to... have a good time. My dad is on the Good Council, you see, has been since he graduated, so everyone expected me to follow in his footsteps. You know." Another greasy smile; God of the Cosmos, why wasn't Jenia cringing with revulsion at it? "Get pussy. Make friends. Pass my tests. Play some pentaball. That sort of thing."

Pentaball. Coen would be in the throes of the game right now, focusing so hard on beating Kimber that he'd have no idea I was here, that I'd fallen prey to the stupidest trap imaginable—a trap I still couldn't quite decipher.

What did they *want* from us? To bow before them and let them hurt us without any kind of defense or retaliation? Seriously?

Fergus narrowed his gaze onto me.

"Because of what you did, Drey, I am *not* having a good time. I get pussy, alright—" A dark laugh and a nod at Jenia, who *still wasn't cringing*. "—but I'm not making friends or passing tests or playing pentaball, because everyone else finds me *laughable*."

His smile had stayed lodged on his face, but now the corners of his mouth wobbled slightly, and his tone oozed fury and hatred cold enough to rival mine.

"You tarnished me," he said simply. "You and your stupid Gileon Dunn friend tarnished me. So I will destroy you... and your pudgy little friend and kitty cat boy toy if they try to intervene. And then I will go get him."

"*You will not touch either one of them,*" Lander hissed, his shackles raising. "*You will let us turn around and walk away from here without lifting a single finger, or I will rip all of you into bloody pieces.*"

Lander didn't look at Quinn as he said this, but I could feel it—that he'd be willing, in his panther form, to hurt her if *she* tried to hurt Emelle. And that was not quite the boy I'd grown up with, always reasonable, always gentle. It was something more aggressive, more territorial, but...

I needed that right now. *Emelle* needed that right now. Especially since Fergus was stalking toward us, ever so slowly, on cat-quiet feet.

Even the foliage seemed to pause their thrums and hums as he passed over them.

"I don't think you *will* rip us all into bloody pieces," Fergus told Lander. "Because if you make a single move against me, *I'll* make the yeast in your body grow so fast, your little kitty form will explode before you can shift back. That, after all, would just be self-defense. The Good Council wouldn't fault me for that."

I expected Jenia to react at that. Or for the Summoning boy to react. For either one of them to demonstrate a hint of shock or revulsion at what Fergus was saying.

Neither of them did. The swirl of butterflies still obscured most of Jenia's face, and the Object Summoner hadn't even shifted from one foot to the other.

Only Quinn had gone pale, her red hair flaring against her shocked white face. She tugged on a strand of it like she always did when she was stressed.

Oh, Quinn. Why would you agree to this?

It hit me, then, that this—whatever *this* was—was the very thing Dazmine had refused to be a part of. She... she'd broken her friendship with Jenia to resist hurting me. Yet Quinn had joined in her stead. Quinn had followed them here, to do *this*.

Payback.

I just didn't know what kind of payback Fergus had in mind. And that was a problem. The more I knew about what was seething in his head, what was seething in Jenia's head, too, the sooner we could escape this mess.

"The Good Council wouldn't fault you for self-defense," I called out, stopping Fergus in his leisurely stroll toward us, "but I bet they ripped into you for killing Mr. Fenway, didn't they? Or did you manage to avoid getting caught?"

Hint, hint: I know what you did, and I'm not afraid to rat you out.

Well, maybe I was afraid. But I wasn't going to let Fergus know that.

"Oh, I didn't avoid getting caught," Fergus replied easily. "Kitterfol Lexington—nice guy, by the way—works closely with my dad, so he just let me off with a warning to not outright murder anyone with magic again."

Again, I expected Jenia to move or the Summoner to fidget at this leak of information, but nothing happened on their end.

Emelle, however, drew in a gasp, and Lander bared his canines. Quinn took another single step backward with a hand still clutching her hair.

I threw as much sarcasm as I could into my voice.

"Hmmm. I wonder why dear Kitterfol Lexington didn't want you to murder anyone. Seems unfair."

Fergus's smile, rather than dipping at the jest, only grew.

"You misunderstand me, Drey. Kitterfol Lexington told me not to murder anyone with *magic* again, because magic, he said, leaves traces. It tethers you to the thing you've bestowed your power upon and creates a bond that never quite dissipates." At this, Fergus's hand rustled within his own pocket. "So Lexington told me to use non-magic methods next time. That way no one will know it was me."

And when he brought his hand back out, I saw the glitter of a sharpened blade catch what little light seeped through the canopy here. A dagger.

My stomach swooped. Emelle stifled a yelp into Lander's fur by ducking her head, and Lander himself shifted toward me, placing a giant paw strategically in front of my body.

Quinn whipped her head from Fergus to Jenia and back to Fergus's blade.

"What are you talking about?" she rasped. "Put that thing down, Fergus! You said you were just going to warn them away from messing with you again!"

And from messing with me, the anguish in her eyes seemed to say.

Apparently, I had underestimated Quinn Balkersaff, and so had Lander. When she'd tried to get him to apologize and he'd rejected her at the Element Wielder party all those months ago, she must have held on to her bitterness.

Fergus didn't notice how Quinn had almost sunken into the shadows again. He didn't look at her as he waved a hand and said, "Kimber already handled most of that for us." He tilted his head at the confusion that must have passed over my face. "She's one of the most powerful Wild Whisperers on this damned island, Jenia's sister is. After your little trick with the fire ants, Drey, she commanded every insect within a ten-mile radius to avoid communication with you at all costs. Jenia's butterflies were an exception, of course."

Understanding slammed into me, nearly sending me to my knees.

Kimber was the reason I'd been failing my tests with Ms. Pincette. Those particular struggles didn't have anything to do with being part-faerie after all. *Kimber* had used her magic to sabotage a part of mine, and in doing so, she could have put my life in danger. She *knew* Ms. Pincette had to report my inadequacies to the Good Council —

although thank God she couldn't possibly know the extent of my failure or my bursts of power or all the other things Ms. Pincette hid for me.

But what was worse, Kimber must have given Jenia's butterflies permission to speak to me right before the pentaball game. Which meant she was purposely distracting Coen in a stupid five-ball game, knowing full-well that I was far away with Fergus and Jenia—facing "payback."

I scrabbled at my chest, trying to will my heartbeat to steady. To stay calm so that I wouldn't fall blind with rage and adrenaline and horror.

Fergus had turned ever so slightly to Quinn, finally noticing how far she had retreated.

"Not so fast, Balkersaff. We need your fire. To burn the bodies when I'm done with them."

"God of the Cosmos!" Emelle cried from Lander's back. "Are you insane?"

"Maybe," Fergus replied casually. "And as for the God of the Cosmos? I don't think He can hear you in this part of the jungle."

Lander crouched lower than ever, prepared to pounce at any moment. My mind was flipping and flopping furiously, scrambling for a way out of this, while Quinn swung a frantic gaze to Jenia.

"Tell him to stop talking like he's being serious! I didn't sign up for this shit!"

For the first time since the butterflies had converged on her, Jenia's head rotated toward Quinn. Enough of the insects had fluttered to a perch on her shoulders or arms or head that I could see the utterly fathomless grayness in her eyes.

"You told me you hated her," Jenia said, nodding ever so slightly at me. "And him." She nodded at Lander's panther form. "And the little— excuse me—*big* slut he chose to treat better than he treated you. So what's your problem?"

"What's my problem?" Quinn yelped. "My problem is that... that *disliking* them doesn't mean I'm going to help you guys *murder* them."

She pushed out a laugh that might have sounded genuine to anyone else but the childhood friends who had grown up with her: it was too high-pitched, too airy compared to her real one.

"If I wanted to kill everyone I felt moody toward, half the island would be dead. Including you at times, Jenia. Come on." She reached out and grabbed Jenia's arm. "We've had our fun. We've scared them shitless. Let's go."

Jenia didn't yank away her arm, but she didn't follow Quinn, either.

"You'll never get another chance like this, Balkersaff," Fergus sang over his shoulder, beginning to stalk closer once more with that dagger clutched tight in one fist.

In a flash, I thought of my mother's knife, perpetually tucked away in the confines of my bag. Fabian had told me I'd never need to use it, but this... this would have been a good instance to have it clutched in my hand as firmly as Fergus held his dagger. Even if I'd never used a knife like that before.

"I've been trying to do this for ages now," Fergus said, "but Rayna's always guarded—by that Steeler asshole, or by one of his friends. Even after I'd heard they'd broken things off, one of your Element Wielder upperclassmen scorched my ass for getting a little too close to her."

Terrin. Terrin had saved me without my knowledge. Gratitude swelled within me, just as my brain landed on the flimsiest of plans.

But a flimsy plan, after all, was better than nothing.

Just as I made to move, Fergus cut a single significant glance back at the Object Summoner, who nodded back, and—

Rocks flew up from the jungle floor, ranging in size from marbles to pentaballs.

I didn't even have time to shield myself or cry out before one slammed into my head from behind, pitching me forward onto my knees.

Through ringing ears, I heard Emelle's scream as a rock knocked her off Lander's back. I heard Lander's yowl and Fergus's chuckle.

"Just wanted to give you a little taste of what's to come!" he called.

More rocks flung themselves at us from every direction, and—*no, Lander, stop.* My vision spun around the image of the panther launching himself through the rocks, toward Fergus, who would surely be waiting for him with the dagger or with an explosion of mold.

The Good Council wouldn't fault him for self-defense. Whether that was true or not, Fergus seemed to believe it, which meant he wouldn't hesitate to kill Lander as soon as Lander reached him.

Another rock smashed into my stomach. An upsurge of hot bile shot up my throat, but I didn't let that stop me.

Scrambling up, trying to blink away the spots of darkness in my vision, I grabbed one of those fallen rocks and took aim. Moss painted its surface, so much like the last rock Quinn had placed on my windowsill in Alderwick that my vision warped with tears.

I wasn't physically strong enough, I knew, to throw it so hard and fast that it would hit Fergus before Lander got to him.

But through my haze of pain and the stray butterflies around Jenia, I caught Quinn's frantic eye.

And a burst of wind brought my hand forward and carried the rock straight into Fergus's face.

Blood sprouted from his nose. Fergus screamed. The Summoner stopped, and Lander lurched to a halt—though not of his own accord. Quinn's wind pushed him back toward Emelle, who was sobbing on the jungle floor.

Fergus pivoted toward me, panting at the sight of me holding another rock.

"You only ever wanted me," I spat. "So come get me, Fungus."

CHAPTER

47

I knew that little nickname—Fungus—would be the thing that got him.

As suspected, Fergus roared and charged toward me, dagger swinging alongside him.

I turned and ran. Pushing past ferns and brambles. Leaping over dips and roots. Instinctively humming at trees to move their branches out of my way.

They did, clearing a path for me, and I pushed my legs forward even as my vision still sparkled with darkness and aches blossomed in spots along my body—my head and stomach and back.

"You know," Fergus called from behind me, his footsteps no longer light and airy, but heavy and pounding as he thumped after me. "Maybe I'll have a taste of you before I cut your flesh, Drey. I heard you were loud as shit with Steeler, so I wonder—how loud would you be with me?"

I didn't waste my breath to tell him how sick he was. I just ran and ran and ran, clawing my way through the pain, my hums breaking into low sobs.

I'd done it, though. Led Fergus away from my friends. Without him and his peculiar magic skills, Lander could deal with the Summoner, and Emelle could call out for enough friends of the jungle to take over Jenia and her butterflies.

"Getting tired, Drey?" Fergus panted. Closer than before.

Yes. Yes, I was getting tired, but again, I wouldn't waste a single breath on him now that I'd gotten what I wanted. And I was getting closer to my destination.

The ground squelched beneath me. My footsteps slapped against the water.

From up above, a troop of monkeys threw down knock, knock jokes, which I completely ignored. I could barely hear them, anyway, what with the ringing still swamping my ears. I could only propel myself forward, until—

The marsh sucked me in, and Fergus yanked himself to a halt moments before he would have been close enough to reach out and grab the ends of my hair.

I swam further in, until bubbling movement swirled around my feet.

A grayish-green snout broke the surface of the muck, followed by a pair of piercing yellow eyes.

"*Have you come to bring me another crab, friend?*" the crocodile asked.

"No." Dense dizziness circled me. "I just really need your glorious company right now. I... I missed you."

It was hard to come up with praise in a situation like this, but totally worth it when I looked up to find Fergus tilting his head at me from the edge of the marsh, not daring to step any further in.

"*I am glorious, aren't I?*" my crocodile said. "*But it seems you've brought me something to eat, after all. That human is no longer*

370

welcome in our swamps." Just as his slitted pupils shifted to Fergus, more crocodiles rose from the depths of the marsh all around us, gliding slowly, slowly, slowly toward the shore.

I hesitated for only the span of a deep, dragging breath. If Fergus was willing to kill my friends and me, if he'd already confirmed killing once before... then I didn't have any qualms about watching the crocodiles tear him apart.

"Yes," I nearly squeaked. "You're welcome to have him, but I'm afraid I can't get him any closer. If you could just drag him in here, you could—"

Fergus breathed heavily from the shore. The blood on his face wasn't drying in this swampy air. It glistened on his upper lip and chin, matching the glint of grease in his hair.

"Here I was, believing everyone when they said Rayna Drey was the sweetest, most disgustingly likeable girl in our sector... only to discover that you're actually a bitch, aren't you?" He didn't wait for me to respond. "But you're a *stupid* bitch, Rayna! You do know that you just submerged yourself in a festering pool of lichen that I could use to end you at any moment, right?"

Indeed, he didn't seem at all perturbed by the dozens of crocodile snouts easing toward him. I gasped out, "Like Kitterfol Lexington said, you can't kill me with magic. Come in here and use that dagger of yours."

Not that I thought he'd do that, but what else could I say?

Fergus pretended to contemplate it, tapping the tip of his dagger against the blood on his chin.

Once again, I cursed myself for keeping my mother's knife in my bag. For not learning how to use it.

"Nah," Fergus said finally. "I think I'll make *you* come to me."

371

And the blanket of algae and lichen and moss on the water began to... to stiffen. To harden and solidify into outstretched clumps.

The clumps converged on me like the strike of a viper, pushing the crocodiles out of the way and shoving me toward the shore. Toward where Fergus stood.

I spent three seconds thrashing and grappling at the hardened green fungus before I knew it would be pointless. It was like a giant cuff around my entire body, dragging me forward. Fergus had me, and the only thing I could do now was...

Was...

I closed my eyes and let the song of the jungle dance along my bruised and broken skin. I sunk into the hums and warbles and croons of story after story, pretending this was just another test with Mrs. Wildenberg. That I just had to pass.

But no, the jungle wasn't some test to pass. It was *alive*. It was *aware*.

And it wanted me to look back at it.

I know you, I thought. *My mother was a faerie, and I know you. Half of me may have been made from passing dust, but the other half was made from the loam between your roots, and I know you. I know the colors you don and shed. I know the animals you house. I know the way you mourn a fallen tree, how you plant seeds around its grave. Your breath gives life to me, and mine gives life to you. I know you, I know you, I know you.*

The jungle's song increased in tempo, breathy and wild and free.

Moments before my knee thumped against the upward slope, I sang back.

Fergus snatched me with his dagger-free hand and yanked me forward.

Just as a vine shot out from the trees where the monkeys had converged, noosing Fergus's throat and pulling tight.

372

He flailed. Dropped his dagger and groped at the vine.

But another one joined the first, and another and another, until Fergus Bilderas was firmly contained within their combined embrace.

Do you want us to end him? the jungle whispered in my ear... like a caress.

I didn't answer. Couldn't. Fergus kept jerking and writhing, and I couldn't say the words to make him go still. I didn't want that kind of blood on my hands.

A movement behind Fergus gripped all my attention.

Someone was coming.

A whimper escaped my mouth, and I backed up a step, but—

"It's okay, Rayna. I'll be the bad guy so you don't have to."

Coen stalked from the trees, positively *drenched* in barely-contained wrath. I saw it in the harsh angle of his mouth, from the veins throbbing in his biceps, from the way his eyebrows slashed downward and met his snarling expression.

"Bad guy?" I got out.

Coen was *here*. He must have followed the sound of my mind and found me.

I could almost faint from the relief. Not just because I was happy to see him after so many weeks of cold emptiness, but because together, the two of us could easily carry Fergus back to the Institute to turn him in. Or Coen could command him to turn himself in.

But in one fluid motion, Coen scooped up Fergus's fallen dagger and hissed into the boy's ear, "I told you to never touch my woman again. Yet here you are, trying to touch her. I won't make the mistake of letting you go twice."

Fergus widened his eyes among the strangling vines.

And Coen swiped the dagger through the vines.

Then plunged it into Fergus's throat.

CHAPTER

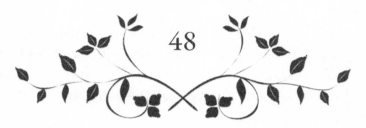

48

Jets of blood squirted from that wound, spraying Coen's wrist with speckled dots of bright red.

Fergus fell forward, like a broken puppet, smashing his face into the floor of the jungle and only twitching once before he went still.

Yet movement still blossomed from beneath him—pools of blood spreading from under his neck before sinking into the spongy, thirsty ground.

A scream had twisted into a knot in my throat, stuck somewhere between horror and relief and even more horror as I watched Coen, his face still tight with wrath, grab one of Fergus's lifeless wrists and drag him to the marsh.

Where he hurled the body in.

And then red *exploded* as the crocodiles lunged and began to feast.

I watched the flower of blood unfold in the marsh, my eyes tracking that color rather than the frenzied jerking and tearing of the crocodiles.

My knees felt hollow. Dead. My classmate was dead, and I *should* be turning to Coen and asking him how he could have done that so callously without giving thought to any other options.

"Thank you," I whispered instead.

Coen's face took on a sort of sagging quality as he looked at me. His mouth parted, the edges of his eyebrows fell, his jaw loosened. Even his fists uncurled, letting the dagger fall into the foliage like it had never existed.

But what came out of his mouth was still rigid and tight.

"You're bruised."

Indeed, my bruises were peppering my vision, mottling the sight of Coen with blue and gray and black. My head bellowed where that first rock had hit me. The scream lodged in my throat had mixed with bile, turning acrid.

The world gave out.

I must have woken up barely five minutes later, because when a gentle swaying motion pulled me back into consciousness, I could see through my lashes that I was cradled against Coen's chest as he carried me through the jungle.

"Emelle." My voice was a ghostly version of its old self. "Lander." *Quinn.*

"They're safe." Coen didn't look down at me as he strode easily through the underbrush. From the way the shadows were peeling back, I thought we might be getting close to campus. "Lander ran off Quinn and that Summoner kid, and Emelle..." His lips pinched, almost like he was smothering a smile. "She got Jenia."

"*Got* Jenia? What do you mean *got?*"

Even though relief swamped me at the knowledge that Lander and Emelle—and Quinn, too, despite her continuous betrayals—were all still alive, my heart hollowed at that last part.

Had we lost two classmates today? Was Jenia as cold and lifeless and *gone* as Fergus? If so, my confusing mix of emotions for her fate could come later; first, I'd have to make sure Emelle was alright. Surely, she'd be devastated if she'd had to resort to murder.

But Coen's lips relaxed a moment later, and he shook his head.

"Emelle didn't kill her, if that's what you're asking, but... you'll see."

I didn't have the strength to press that issue so I simply leaned my head against Coen's chest for a moment and listened to the way his heartbeat thumped against my ear, matching the length of his strides.

Coen had come for me. Even though we were separated, even though his consciousness never even flitted through my mind anymore, he'd sensed something was off and tracked me to the marsh.

During the pentaball game? Or after?

"Did you win?"

Coen nearly stopped in his tracks at that hushed question. For a moment I thought it was because of a twisting of trees in our way. I sent a soft hum spiraling out toward them, and their branches bowed to form a pathway.

Coen lurched forward again, but this time he was sparing glances down at me.

"You never cease to amaze me with the kinds of questions you ask. You're bruised and scraped and covered in dirty swamp water, and you want to ask me how the game went?"

"Yes," I said firmly. "Kimber was... I think she was—"

Trying to distract you, I finished in my head.

And as if that were an invitation—which, maybe it was—Coen melted into my mind, filling those cold spaces between my vines of ice that had now wrapped so tightly around my heart, I wasn't sure if they'd ever break. But whereas his consciousness was all buttery warmth, his entire body had gone rigid against me.

Kimber was definitely trying to distract me, and I regret to say that it worked for a good ten minutes. I didn't want to touch her thoughts, to read her mind for even a second and feel all her hate and jealousy, so I couldn't predict her next moves.

How did you know I wasn't in those stadiums, then? I asked.

For out of everyone there, only Kimber would have known about my whereabouts. That knowledge would have existed in her mind and her mind alone—safe from Coen for as long as Coen refused to read her mind.

We had reached the edge of the jungle now, and were on the outskirts of the Shifter sector, full of rusted cages and wooden obstacle courses.

I caught a whiff, Coen said, *right as I was about to throw the last ball through and win yet another victory for the Mind Manipulators.*

A whiff of what?

Now we passed by towering perches that looked big enough for those giant birds who'd pulled me through the sky in a carriage so long ago.

A whiff of her triumph, Coen said darkly, and I understood immediately.

Kimber *should* have been nothing but rage and fury the moment she realized the Manipulators were about to win the tournaments yet again. She definitely shouldn't have been *triumphant*—triumphant that she'd successfully kept Coen from me. That I was probably dead.

The intricacies of that game, not of pentaball, but the more sinister game that Kimber had been playing, made the pounding in my head begin to roil.

"I'd already thrown the ball when I dove into her mind and got it out of her," Coen murmured down at me now. "So yes, we won, but I didn't stay to celebrate. I ran right to the location I'd picked from her brain and found Lander and Emelle and the rest of Jenia. And they pointed me in the direction you'd run."

The rest of Jenia. What the hell had Emelle done to her?

I didn't have to wait for long to find out.

Within minutes, Coen was sweeping us toward my own house, where people milled about on Bascite Boulevard, either rejoicing or pouting about the game's outcome, but... never looking at us. As if Coen had convinced them all to look away.

You know how my magic works extremely well for someone who's not a Mind Manipulator.

You told me that's what you did the night you carried me from my tent to the alleyway. Back then, though, I'd been flung unceremoniously over his shoulder, not nestled gently against his chest.

You remembered? Surprise flickered in his tone

Of course I did. I remember everything you say. Except the things you purposely take from me.

He was silent as he took me into my house and down the stairs, through a door I'd never entered. The sick bay.

In here, Coen finally placed me on my feet, but he didn't let go. His arms wrapped around me, steadying me when I saw her.

The girl on one of the beds, who was staring blankly at the medic wiping the blood gingerly off her face.

Jenia was alive, that was for sure. I could see it in the shallow rise and fall of her chest, and in the way her fingers twitched on either side of her hips.

But her hair—that usually silky cascade of brightest blonde—was in bloody, matted patches, revealing strips of scabbed scalp beneath.

378

And those gray and sultry eyes that had seemed to follow and haunt and hate me ever since I'd met her on my first day here... they were replaced with bloody gauze that wrapped around her entire head.

Emelle, Coen said into me, *got a few owls to use their talons.*

We didn't stay in the sick bay for long. Coen simply asked the medic to look me over and provide him with any medications necessary to help me heal. Then, after she'd handed him a vial of pain-relief powder, he simply told her to forget the entire exchange. And to not spread the word about Jenia, either.

Once we were in the safety of his room with that big white bed that had once rocked us into a skyful of stars (nobody watched us walk inside, still turning their heads away from us as if suddenly extremely interested in the walls), I turned to Coen blearily. He was busy unscrewing the vial and pouring its powdery contents into a cup of water from his bathroom sink.

"Doesn't your house have its own sick bay? Why go to mine if you were just going to bring me here?"

Perhaps it wasn't the brightest question, but the roil in my head was reaching a nasty level of pain, and I drank the cup of water almost eagerly when Coen brought it to my lips. It went down like the bitter tang of a melted coin.

"I was afraid my house's medics would have a shield up against any Mind Manipulating tricks, and I needed to get medicine for you without anyone taking notice."

"And why is that?" I slumped down on the edge of his bed, smoothing my fingers out against the spread of fluffy white. Like clouds. Like bliss.

Coen tilted his head at me.

"The Good Council will be back tomorrow, and this time Dyonisia Reeve will be with them." When I only stared at him, he added, "My Final Test is tomorrow, Rayna. At the crack of dawn."

I shot straight up, pain be damned. I'd forgotten. Forgotten that the Final Test for all fifth-years occurred the morning after the last pentaball game. And as much as I'd accepted the fact that Coen and I weren't together anymore, I still hadn't wrapped my head around the idea that after tomorrow—whether he passed or failed—he'd be gone from this part of the island. Possibly back to the sea.

"Are you prepared?" I yelped.

Coen put a hand on my shoulders and eased me back down onto the bed.

"Yes. But I still don't want Dyonisia finding out about what happened just now with Fergus and Jenia. Or Lander and Emelle. It's safer if no one knows the truth."

Here we were again. Back to the notion of spreading lies for everyone's safety. While I couldn't entirely disagree with him on this, I still felt a chill brush goosebumps over my skin at the... the unfairness of it all. That Lander and Emelle would never remember how they refused to leave my side, how they'd come with me, how they'd stood by me in the face of such callous cruelty, all because Coen had—

"I didn't erase their memories," Coen said.

My head snapped up, sending a bolt of pain through me again—although it was perhaps dampened compared to before as the pain relief medication worked its way through my system. "What?"

"I didn't erase their memories," Coen repeated. "Not Lander's or Emelle's. And I don't think I'm going to erase Jenia's or Quinn's or that other kid's memory either."

"Why?"

I couldn't believe I was asking that, but I was. Something about the pain relief sweeping through me seemed to make my tongue feel heavy, yet quick to blurt out whatever it was I was thinking immediately.

"Because." Coen's mouth pulled up into one of those smirks I'd missed so much. "I already spread a rumor through campus that Fergus and Jenia got into a huge couple's fight during the pentaball game and destroyed the shit out of each other. Obviously, Jenia won."

My mouth fell open. "And you think people will believe that?"

"Absolutely. Rumors are more convincing than outright lies, and besides." Coen's gaze dropped from mine, fixing to the floor. "I'm trying to keep people safe *without* having to steal their memories. I'm sure once Jenia hears that bit of gossip about herself, she won't refute it. If she did, she'd have to admit she was in on a plan to murder three of her classmates, which is sort of against the rules, as I said on the very first day you arrived."

My eyelids were heavy, but I blinked against their weight.

"You killed Fergus."

"With a dagger, not with magic," Coen said. "No one will know."

"So what Fergus said was true?" I asked. "Magic leaves traces? It tethers you to the thing you bestow your magic upon?"

"Did he say that?" Coen mused. "I suppose he was right, though I've never heard it worded that way. Either way, he deserved his ending after what he did to you." His eyes bounced from bruise to bruise on my face and neck.

Just as I was about to open my mouth—to say *what*, I didn't know—Coen whipped toward the door.

"Your friends are here. I won't let them stay long, but I could hear their worry screaming for you from about a mile away, so I sent them a message that you're safe here with me. And I figured you'd want to see them, anyway. Make sure they're okay with your own eyes."

Won't let them stay for long? That wording implied Coen expected me to stay here *overnight*. With him. In this room.

Or maybe that pain relief powder was scattering all rational thought.

I didn't have time to think about it, though. The door swung open, and Lander and Emelle rushed in, followed by—I blinked heavily—Terrin, who immediately held out his hands and formed two solid blocks of ice out of thin air.

"Good God of the Cosmos, lady," Terrin said, blinking back at me. "You look worse than *her.*"

He didn't even have to nod at Emelle, who had scurried to my side and was now throwing her arms around me. She smelled like sweat and blood, and a shower of bruises fell down her face.

"You're alright," she gasped. "I was—Rayna, I've never been so scared in my life. Lander ran Jenia to the sick bay and then we immediately went back to look for you, but Coen did that mind-to-mind thing you always described—" A quick, nervous glance in Coen's direction. "—to tell us that... that..."

"Fergus is really dead?" Lander asked, dropping to my other side.

"Yes," I whispered. "But you can't go talking about what happened." I looked at Emelle. "Even to Wren and Rodhi and Gileon. It wouldn't go over well."

I didn't have to specify why this was. Both Lander and Emelle nodded. Perhaps they didn't know about the prisons at the top of Bascite Mountain or the true fate that awaited if any one of us failed our Final Test, but they knew enough about the Good Council to keep their mouths shut.

Exile was still a grim future, after all.

"I did something horrible," Emelle wheezed, pulling back to clutch at her chest. "I couldn't get them to stop, the owls. Not after I told them..."

She trailed off, concern pinching her blood-speckled forehead. I had just enough alertness left to ask, "What *did* you say to those owls to get them to... do what they did?" For Emelle would have had to speak in riddles and timeless wisdom in order to get her request across.

I heard Emelle's response right as I was drifting off. Right as I felt Coen's hand cup the back of my head and lower me onto his pillows. Into powdery sleep pitted against Terrin's slabs of ice that soothed every aching point on my body.

> *Oftentimes evil things hide in a cloak*
> *Or beneath piles of ash or mold.*
> *But evil prevails if we tuck in our tails*
> *Against eyes gray as silver and hair bright as gold.*

When I woke, Emelle, Lander, and Terrin were gone, and I was tucked deep in Coen's bed.

It was dark, but when I lifted myself up, I could make out the faint silhouette of his figure on the floor. Sleeping with a skimpy pillow and blanket.

Each of his breaths, heavy and on the verge of snoring, sent an ache through the sore parts of my body.

It shouldn't be like this. Me in his bed. Him on the floor. Us not pressed together, sharing heat and breath and touch.

What had he said last night? *I'm trying to keep people safe without having to steal their memories.* He was *trying*. And maybe that was enough for me. I didn't necessarily need a Coen that was one hundred percent honest all the time, but I needed him to at least *try* to think of other solutions before he just... whipped out all his deceit that had become a part of him.

Even if I refused to keep him locked in this dome with me, I could have one more night with him.

"Hey. Coen."

I winced as I slipped out of bed and gently touched the sides of his head.

"Hmm?" He jolted out of his sleep. "Rayna. Is something wrong?"

"No. I just... you don't need to sleep on the floor. That can't be comfortable."

During the months we'd dated, I'd never seen Coen take a sip of ale, but I *did* know what it was like when he was drunk with fatigue, half-asleep and nearly sleepwalking. And this, I decided when he pressed his forehead against mine and lifted me back up onto the bed, was one of those times.

He sank into place beside me. Stroked his thumb along the side of my neck, so gingerly it felt like a feather on glass. His breath was filling my open mouth, and I didn't close it, missing the taste of him on my tongue, wanting more...

My ice wasn't quite gone, but there was a part of it that wanted to be melted. Right now. Right here. I wanted to be a puddle of heat beneath him and—

"*Rayna?*"

I jolted away from Coen at the squeak, and he lifted himself up and away.

"Who's there?" he asked, in a surprisingly alert voice.

I knew who it was, though, and I patted the bed until Willa came scurrying up onto the covers, clutching something in her tiny, sharp claws.

"Willa? What's going on?"

"*The Good Council is here for the Final Test,*" Willa panted, and I clutched Coen's arm. "*All of Dyonisia Reeve's spiders have arrived from Bascite Mountain. I've been warding off the ones near you, but this one—*" She nodded down at her closed paws. "*—claims it's on your side. So I thought I'd give it the chance to explain before I bite its head off.*"

God, Willa could be ruthless. Just as ruthless as Sasha and Sylvie.

"*I just want to see the top of the world,*" came a moaning voice.

For the second time since I'd hired it, my spider had gotten itself trapped. Perhaps it wasn't the *best* spy, but I wasn't about to let Willa bite its head off.

"It's mine," I told Willa instantly. "Let it go so it can speak to me."

To Willa's credit, she didn't hesitate. She released the spider instantly, and soon eight, green-tinted eyes glimmered up at me from within the darkness.

"*I've come to warn your soulmate,*" the spider said.

I inhaled to correct its use of the word *soulmate*, but it continued quickly.

"*Dyonisia Reeve found out about Coen Steeler and his peculiar band of childhood friends. She is not even going to give them a chance to pass their tests tomorrow morning. The Final Test is a trap.*"

CHAPTER

49

"Tell me everything," I said immediately, and I could feel Coen tense beside me as he no doubt heard the translation play out in my brain.

"*The fifth-years will gather at the Testing Center for their Final Tests in the morning, but instead of staying with their instructors like usual, they'll be leaving with different members of the Good Council to various parts of the island.*"

"So as soon as Coen and his friends step foot in the Testing Center...?"

"*The Good Council will whisk them away along with everyone else,*" the spider confirmed. "*But rather than take them to a testing site, Dyonisia will drag them straight to the prisons at the top of Bascite Mountain.*" A contemplative pause. "*The other spiders are absolutely gleeful about her trickery.*"

"Shit," I spat. "Shit! Coen?"

"Already on it." His voice rang softer, more sorrowful than I would have expected. Where was the panic? Where was the frenzy brewing in my own chest? "I've sent messages to Garvis and Terrin and the twins, and—"

"And?"

His hand was sweeping along my back now.

"And they're going to meet me at the Throat in fifteen minutes. We have to leave the island before dawn."

I'd expected this, but it didn't stop the burn from swelling in my throat.

I cleared it away and turned back to my spider.

"Thank you so much. You didn't hear anything about Dyonisia Reeve discovering anything about... about *me*, did you?"

It clicked its fangs like pincers. "*No. Nothing about you or your own friends.*"

My relief was short-lived as Coen scrambled upward to begin throwing things in a bag from under his bed: his favorite clothes and lightest knife and the dried fruit he always stashed in his bedside drawer for a midnight snack. The fact that I knew all of these things made the sting in my throat tighten and constrict now.

"*Rayna?*" Willa asked gently, still sitting on the top of his bed.

I watched Coen pack his supply of pills as well, the dozens of them rattling in a tin canister he kept buried beneath his socks, and hope flared where I felt tears.

He wasn't leaving any behind for me. Did that mean—?

I was much too frightened to finish that thought. In case it wasn't true.

The moment Coen was done packing, I knew because he stilled, his face bowed toward the far side of the room. I could see the back of his jaw muscles working up the courage to say something to me.

"I'm coming with you."

Before he could turn, I slipped onto the floor.

387

"Rayna." The hoarseness in his voice—the pure, aching regret— curdled my stomach. "You can't. Dyonisia doesn't know what you are, so your safest bet is to stay here and—"

"If this is about the shield, then I'm willing to test it. Maybe I'm immune, too."

Coen laughed dryly, finally turning toward me. "I've seen faeries disintegrate on the spot just from *grazing* the shield. It's not a physical barrier, Rayna. It's an anti-power that targets the magic in your blood and strikes."

I couldn't bite my tongue.

"Well, maybe if you'd told me more about your immunity and the nature of the shield, I could have come up with a solution long before now. You think I want to stay here, the only... the only *you know what* on an island with the Good Council who'd like nothing more than to strip me open and investigate every drop of my blood?"

Within two steps, Coen had dropped his bag and was shoved up against me, his head angled down to meet my own.

"Don't you ever think I'm going to leave you helpless, Rayna. I'm not going to let her *touch* you. But you have to trust me on this one."

"I. Can't. Trust. You," I ground out, and now our noses were nearly brushing. "You said so yourself, Coen. That's why we broke up. Because I can't trust you."

"Oh, really?" Even now, even in this situation, his near-growl had my knees weak. "I was under the impression that we broke up because you were trying to protect me. By cutting me out so that I wouldn't stay here on the island, where Dyonisia can get to me."

I felt my eyebrows shoot up, felt the argument gather in my lungs.

"And no, I didn't need to read your thoughts to figure that one out," Coen persisted before I could let it loose on him. "I have your mind memorized like the palm of my own goddamned hand, Rayna. I

388

know you'll continue fighting tooth and nail for the people you love un-less you think you're holding them back—which you weren't doing to me, by the way. Because whether we're officially together or not, whether I'm on this island or not, I'm going to make sure you have the tools and power you need to survive these next four years."

For a moment, I thought he would kiss me. His lips hovered in the spaces between mine, filling my breathlessness with his own air.

But his eye didn't even dip to my mouth as I said, "I might not be immune to the shield like you are, but I'm accompanying you and the others to the very edge. You're going to need a Wild Whisperer to keep the jungle from reporting you to the Good Council."

I clamped my mouth shut, then—cutting off the shared air between us. After another second's thought, I side-stepped him and scooped up his fallen bag.

Now it was Coen's turn to clamp his mouth shut. I had him. He couldn't argue with that, because it was true. Parts of the jungle *would* witness his escape and tattle to the Wild Whisperers of the Good Coun-cil, unless I warded them off.

"Fine," he said, once again soft and sorrowful and nothing like his usual self. "But just to the shield."

Fine. I hated that word, but I just turned and led him out his own bedroom door.

In the end, I was glad I'd forced myself to come.

The monkeys were awake far past their bedtime, chittering about the "moon goddess" who had just arrived. Just as we found the hatch buried deep among the ferns, one of them chanted down, "*Hey, wanna hear a joke?*"

None of the others—Coen, now holding his own bag again, Garvis, Terrin, Sasha, or Sylvie, all weighed down with bags of their own—looked up. To them, the monkey's question was nothing more than another chirp in the early dusk. Coen grunted as he started to heave the hatch aside, then stopped when the twins rolled their eyes and ushered it upward without lifting an arm.

But I paused and chewed my lip as I met the monkey's eyes above us.

"Do *you* want to hear a joke?" I challenged it instead.

The others stopped to stare at me.

"*Sure,*" the monkey replied, pretending to sound indifferent.

"What do you call a five-hundred-pound gorilla with silver on its back and fangs in its mouth?"

"*I don't know. What?*" It clutched the branches above it and lowered itself ever so slightly, its black tail curling around a stray limb.

"Nearby," I hissed.

The monkey shrieked and scrambled deeper into the trees.

It wasn't my best work ever, not with the stress beating against my ribcage, but I knew that the monkey wouldn't go hopping from tree to tree prattling about the six humans—or faeries—it had seen sneaking away. It would be warning all the other monkeys about the supposed gorilla in the vicinity.

We lowered ourselves into the Throat.

In there, Terrin lit our way with a floating ball of fire, Coen walked slightly behind me with his hand halfway outstretched as if to catch me if I fell, and I told every spider to leave us. I also formed a vibrating hum in my throat that sent even the most innocent of earthworms wiggling away, until I sensed nothing in the tunnel with us—no life beyond our six beating hearts and pulsing lungs.

No one said anything. We didn't dare talk, as if the echoes of our voices would fling back up to Dyonisia Reeve, wherever she was right now. Somewhere on campus, according to my spider, preparing to capture my friends as soon as the first bird pierced a song through the morning sky.

But I could feel their terror, buzzing in front of me and behind me like swarms of hidden wasps. They'd all known this day would come, but they hadn't expected it to happen *before* their Final Tests. Right now.

I thought I was going to faint from lack of breath; I couldn't get in a good lungful. It was one huge, painful thing to have Coen torn from me, disentangled from my every attempt to hold him close... but it was another, smaller hurt to also have to say goodbye to his friends. Terrin. Garvis. Sasha. Sylvie.

Would I ever see any of them again?

Right as we got to the cave of gemstones, both Coen and Garvis stopped.

And clutched their own scalps.

"What is it?" I asked immediately, grabbing Coen's wrists.

"She's found out," he rasped. "I don't know how, but she knows we've escaped. And—"

He didn't even have to finish the sentence. The next moment, something happened beneath our feet: a kind of swaying shudder that made the ground buck.

"Terrin?" Sasha asked sharply.

"Wasn't me. That wasn't even Element Wielder magic, from what I could tell."

Terrin's ball of light popped into ashes, and he slammed a hand downward, steadying the cave floor. But everything else outside the cave still seemed to shudder and shake, if the wavering motion of colors

391

through the waterfall was any indication, and when Terrin swept away the cascade of raging water, we saw...

"By the lockpick and the lyre," Sylvie whimpered.

The moon looked like a marble stuck haphazardly in the sky—a marble that was cracking down the middle as Dionysia's shield began to... change.

Cracks lashed down its surface like lightning. The surface itself, usually nearly invisible, grew foggy and opaque, like the same milky residue of the Uninhabitable Zone had slithered over the entire world. And tendrils of that milkiness were lashing out, fingers of fog striking and curling and snatching in every direction, as if desperate to catch whoever went through.

The dome... it was *alive*.

There was no other explanation. The dome was alive, and it answered to Dyonisia just like everything on this damned island answered to her, and I burrowed my fingernails deeper into Coen's wrists as if I could get him to stay away from that toxic horror of misty fingers and claws just by holding on to him tighter.

"You can't go through that."

"We have to go through that," Coen said, meeting my eyes. "And right now. Before it gets worse." He flicked them toward the twins. "Sasha? Sylvie?"

They seemed to understand his plea, because within moments, my feet had lifted off the ground, and I felt their Summoning energy fling me off the edge of the cliff.

It was like falling with ropes tied to each of my limbs. Right before we hit the rocky ground so far beneath us, the descension slowed, and the twins yanked us all—as well as themselves—to a halt before we could crumple to our knees.

"Transport, Terrin," Coen said, more panicked than before as the dome swirled and broke and lashed harder than ever. "Find us some transport."

Terrin peered out at the brewing sea, then closed his eyes in concentration.

Within seconds, a ferocious current of water broke through the shield and shot toward us, hurling an oversized boat our way, swinging with ropes and sails. Terrin had it plunge past the breakers and come to a halt right within the shoreline of low-tide, where it bobbed in wait, looking so much like a larger version of that polished wooden boat in Coen's room when we had both exploded with shards of the moon.

Except whereas *that* boat had brought us together, this one would be pulling us apart.

And suddenly, I was angry at this vessel for even existing. Where had it come from? The faeries? Did they just have uninhabited boats bobbing around in case Coen and the others ever needed them?

There would be no time for those questions. There would be no time for anything anymore.

"I—"

I didn't know how to possibly watch them leave. I didn't know how to say goodbye. That ice hadn't shattered or melted, but it was splintering off now, stabbing me from the inside-out.

"Rayna." Coen gripped either side of my face, his thumbs stroking beneath my chin. "You know what I have to do."

"No." I backed away from him. *Pushed* away from him. "No. Don't. You said you were trying to keep people safe without having to steal their memories."

Because I knew, right then, that he'd gone back on his word at the first sign of trouble. That he'd erased what happened with Fergus and

Jenia from Emelle's and Lander's minds. Probably from Quinn's and the Summoner's as well.

"Yes," he said softly. "I did. And..." His face blanched. "I've erased our relationship from everyone else on campus, too. Even from Willa. Kitterfol Lexington won't find a single trace of us in anyone's mind. You will be deemed uninvolved and innocent, and you will not be hurt."

The realization sunk claws of jagged glass into my chest. He wasn't just going to take away my knowledge of Bascite Mountain and the pills and my power and my faerie blood... but every memory I'd ever had with him as well.

Half of my mind, my *soul*, would be wiped clean.

"Please." I had pitched into a shrill wail against my will. Tears raked sharp prickles down my cheeks. "Please, Coen. Take whatever you want, but don't take away *us.*"

Drops of rain—no, of *mist*, of milky, unnatural mist—began to pepper his forehead. Sliding down to his parted lips as he looked at me.

"Hurry, Coen," Terrin warned, panting with the effort of keeping that boat still.

"Don't you dare!" I shrieked, trying to step away.

"Garvis," Coen said, the pain in his eyes anchored onto mine. "I can't do it. You're going to have to. I..." His voice cracked. "Every memory I was involved in. Every memory that would get her into trouble. Don't take them from her, just... hide them. Lock them away so deep that no one else will be able to find them. I... I can't."

Garvis moved as if to touch me, but I shot backward, back toward the cliff. Maybe if I could get far enough away, his magic wouldn't be able to reach me.

But I knew that would be futile even as I forced my strides to lengthen, forced my arms to pump. If Coen had already picked out the memories of everyone on campus, Garvis would sure as hell be able to pick mine out, and—

Sasha and Sylvie's ropes of magic pulled me back.

I flailed against them, kicking and screaming and twisting, but they eased me to the smoothest patch of shore and pinned me against the ground.

"I'm so sorry, Rayna."

I knew by the clogged pinch of Sylvie's voice that she was crying, too, but I didn't care.

"*Let me go! Don't touch me! Don't you dare!*"

Coen's face was in front of mine, suddenly, bowing over me, blocking my view of the top of the curling, spitting dome.

"Breathe," he commanded.

"No."

I wished I hadn't taken my pill last Sunday, wished my power could rise up and strike him away from me. Away from my mind and the precious things it held.

And as soon as I thought that, a bit of it seemed to lift its head up inside me. To sniff the air and *reach*, sensing my panic, sensing my need for that power to spear through the bars that contained it and *attack*.

Except I didn't want to attack Coen. I wanted to keep him. I wanted to love him. And even when I knew I couldn't have all that, I just wanted one more goddamned night with him.

"I will come back for you," Coen said, and now the smoky quartz of his eyes shimmered with tears. "I'll make sure you get your pills every week, and I'll form a plan, and I'll come back for you and take you away from here as soon as I can."

I didn't stop thrashing. The tears didn't stop swelling and biting into the corners of my eyes and burning my cheeks as they spilled down.

"How can I possibly believe you after everything you've—"

"Because I fucking love you, Rayna."

Coen's voice was suddenly louder than the roar of sea and dome and the ringing in my ears. His lips grabbed mine in an urgent kiss.

"I love you." He kissed me again. "I love you." Again. "I love you." I was kissing him back, desperate to cling to any part of him that I could, to inhale his bamboo scent forever. "You are the hurricane that has ravaged my heart, Rayna, and you are the only one who can put it back together." Coen ground his forehead into mine, until our lips were resting in the curves and spaces of each other, and our breaths became one. "I *will* come back for you. I will make you pick up my pieces. And I will pick up yours."

Then we were kissing again, a perfect blend of flesh and breath, ebbing in and out of each other until the mist gathered around us in an endless swirl.

CHAPTER

50

"Rayna Drey."

My eyes fluttered against a haze of orange. It was like wrenching myself out of the deepest dream, but I managed to lift myself onto my elbows.

"What? I don't—"

After blinking away the last of my blurred sleepiness, I found the piercing eyes.

"Jagaros! Oh, I haven't seen you in forever!" I threw my arms around the massive, silky neck, and pulled back to inspect him. "What are you...?"

I gazed around. The sea lapped against the shore not far from me, and a storm seemed to be fermenting on the horizon. But otherwise, it looked like a perfectly normal morning on the island of Eshol.

So why had I fallen asleep on this patch of gritty sand? Had I really drunk *that* much last night with Emelle and Rodhi, to have ended up here?

I groaned and pressed my fingers into my temples.

"Ugh. I think *I* could use a few pets right now, Jagaros. I feel like shit."

Jagaros was swishing his tail at me, his pupils skinny as wires.

"*You* look *like shit, Rayna Drey.*" He paced around me. "*And when the Good Council asks you why you look that way, you should tell them you were roughhousing with me a little too hard.*"

I instinctively glanced at my arms, where I saw...patches of bruised skin.

What had happened?

"Oh, God. I am never drinking again."

"*Good.*" Jagaros tilted his head up toward the cliff, his ears flattening against his skull. "*They're almost here, Rayna, and I don't fancy being here when they are. But I must ask you before I take my leave.*" His gaze refocused on me with predatory stillness. "*Did you ever happen to find a map? I'm sorry I've been away for so long, but I had other things to attend to, so I couldn't ask sooner.*"

I bobbed my head back.

"A map? Of campus? Jagaros, I don't know what you're talking about. And *who's* almost here? Has Wren come to kick my ass for wandering off after a night of drinking, because—"

Shouts wrenched my attention upward. High up on the cliff, a group of people were looking down at Jagaros and me.

Every hair on Jagaros's white and black body sprang upward, and a high-pitched hiss escaped his mouth.

"*Forget the map. I just thought it might have been the one thing you—*" He shook his head and rubbed it quickly across my neck, nearly knocking me sideways. "*Stay cautious. Stay curious. And stay clever. Okay? I'll see you later.*"

He leapt away, streaking alongside the cliff faster than I could respond.

More confused than I'd ever been in my life, I watched the group of people from above float toward me. And I recognized him, the one in the middle: mullet splitting into braided strings that dangled down his back, a wide jaw, pitted brown skin.

Nobody would be forgetting Kitterfol Lexington anytime soon. I remembered all too clearly the night he'd come investigating after Mr. Fenway's death, how Emelle and I had cuddled close together on the bottom bunk while he and his crew had paced Bascite Boulevard, cleaving each and every mind for pieces of evidence.

Tingles swept around my neck like a noose when Kitterfol landed before me.

He surveyed me. I surveyed him, still on the ground.

I didn't dare move.

"Interesting," he murmured eventually.

The others around him gathered round. A headache pulsed at the base of my head, and I knew that for whatever reason, the greatest Mind Manipulator on the Good Council had just split my memories wide open in search of... something.

"Why are you down here?"

His voice surprised me; it reminded me of churning butter, the kind Fabian or Don might have once triggered with their magic back at home to make chocolate chip cookies. Soft. Silky.

But oily, too.

"I didn't realize it was a crime to walk the beach," I braved, since *I don't remember* seemed like a rather suspicious thing to say—although I doubted he would care about my drinking habits, to be honest. By the orchid and the owl, I really needed to stop drinking. It had cast me into the most horrible fog...

"It is not a crime to walk the beach," Kitterfol answered smoothly, his face twitching as he clenched his jaw. The others around him shifted.

"But you, Ms. Drey, are not walking. You are lying down, bruised and scabbed, with the famous white tiger from your Branding who just bounded off upon our arrival, and you are doing so mere hours after a boy went missing, a girl was found with her eyeballs torn to shreds, and five pirates breached the security dome."

All of that information... what?

I focused on the most recent piece of it.

"Pirates breached the dome?" I cut a glance toward the shield, shimmery and nearly invisible in the distance, and hefted myself to my feet. "When? Are they still in here?" I paused. "A girl's *eyeballs* went missing?"

It felt like a joke. It had to be a joke. Some wild end-of-year prank.

Kitterfol's tightened mouth, however, screamed nothing but seriousness. When another member of the Good Council whispered something into his ear, he said, "I'm not sure. Their work on her was... meticulous. I cannot find a single speck of him, but the holes in her memory certainly indicates so, and I think—"

Suddenly, he grabbed a fistful of my hair and wrenched my face to the side.

My scream spurted out of my throat before I could stop it.

"Marvelous," Kitterfol breathed into my face, and I couldn't spare an inch to flinch away, he held me so tightly. "I *do* remember you and him together. Oh, how Dyonisia will be interested in *this*. I think we should go talk to her now, don't you?"

A Summoner in the group sent Kitterfol and me arcing up into the air, back toward campus.

Wind clawed at my skin as we rushed up and up, and my heart jostled around in my chest for a good two minutes before we were finally standing in the middle of the courtyard, that fountain tinkling merrily.

Besides the tinkling, though, it was quiet. Deathly quiet. Even the monkeys that usually chittered on the rooftops of the nearby Whispering sector had disappeared. Everyone, I knew, was either holed up in their houses, or taking their Final Tests—which would not be held in the Testing Center, but in various parts of the jungle around us. High up in the trees or deep inside hidden caves or at the bottom of lakes.

For some reason, the name Mrs. Pixton fluttered through my mind.

Okay, I *really* shouldn't have partied so hard last night.

"Come on," Kitterfol Lexington said beside me, his smile slicked onto his face. "Inside we go."

With his vise-tight grip on my arm, he marched us inside—but rather than to the archway with the Whispering motto engraved on its crown, he led me to the middle arch, one I'd never really looked at because Mr. Gleekle had always stood in front of it. There was nothing engraved above it besides the Good Council symbol, that bulbed star with a single dot in the center.

And there was nothing I could do besides follow him up.

To the dome itself. Or, rather, the attic beneath the domed roof.

I was panting by the time Kitterfol kicked open the door. My heartbeat scurried around in my chest, as thoroughly trapped as I was, and I barely even registered the arched golden beams swooping over our heads or Mr. Gleekle, Ms. Pincette, and some other members of the Good Council flanked behind a glittering glass chair.

All of it paled compared to the woman sitting in the center of it.

I hadn't seen her since the Branding, but she was just as chillingly flawless as that night. Her skin glowed like honey-wrapped stars. Her hair of deepest black, framed by razor-sharp bangs, flowed past her shoulders, and her icy blue eyes were cutting into the girl kneeling before her.

I had to rub my eyes before I realized who that girl was.

"I don't know," Quinn Balkersaff was crying, her hair matted with twigs and dead leaves that camouflaged its usual vibrant ruby color.

"You were found," Dyonisia replied without looking up at Kitterfol or me, "deep in the jungle, beyond the Esholian Institute border, huddled up inside a tower of ice that *you* conjured. Surely, that is abnormal behavior?"

Whereas I'd been surprised to hear how smooth Lexington's voice was, I was even more surprised to find that Dyonisia's was all shattered glass and broken thorns. I couldn't blame Quinn for shuddering, even as I wondered how the hell she'd managed to get wrapped up in... whatever this was, too. Deep in the jungle? In a tower of ice?

"I don't know," Quinn said again, dragging in a deep breath. "I... I told you already. There was a prank. I was just going into the jungle to play a little prank with my friends. And then I ended up in the ice. I don't... remember anything between those two instances. I'm sorry."

The last time I remembered talking to Quinn, we'd been walking the same strip of rocky beach Jagaros had just found me dozing on. Maybe it was all related somehow? If so, I had to figure it out quickly, because I couldn't stand the way Quinn trembled on her knees like that, no matter what words had slashed between us back then. She did not bow or shake or crack before anyone... yet she was doing all that now, before Dyonisia.

"Very well," Dyonisia said, finally moving her icy attention to me, still in Kitterfol's grip. "You may go, Ms. Balkersaff."

Quinn shot up, turned, and stumbled a step when she saw me. Her cheeks were streaked with days-old makeup, and I'd never seen such bags under her eyes. But she didn't say anything, didn't even nod, as she scurried past us and shot down the staircase.

Dyonisia crossed her legs, and I kept my eyes on the sharpness of a single bare ankle when she gestured with a single, long-nailed finger.

Kitterfol pushed me forward. I lurched toward her until I was within her grasp.

The ice in her eyes slid from bruise to bruise, then settled back onto my face.

"I was roughhousing," I blurted. "With a tiger. It's a Wild Whispering thing. But I was also drunk." *I think.* "And that was a... bad combination. I'm sorry."

Oh, Quinn and I were in deep shit if we'd managed to snag the Good Council's attention this badly. Cursing myself, I forced my gaze to lift. To clash with the fathomless void that seemed to brew within the woman's pupils.

She'd given me the creeps then, and she gave me the creeps now.

Her lips were the color of mattified blood as they parted to finally speak.

"I am going to tell you everything, child, and you are going to listen."

I knew I didn't have a choice, so I stood there and endured the grating sound of her voice as she filled in the foggy gaps in my memory.

The five pirates who'd breached the shield—they had left *from* the Institute. They'd been spies all along, and my house's very own princess, Kimber Leake, had discovered and reported them.

But it seemed they hadn't left a trace of themselves behind, nothing for the Good Council to snatch or uncover. Including their relations with everyone on campus. The people they'd talked to or hung out with.

"But according to Lexington," Dyonisia said, her pupils flickering toward the Mind Manipulator behind me, "you were... familiar with one of them. Hence why you have the bruises."

My world seemed to quiver to a halt.

"What do you mean?" I raised an arm to inspect one of the purple patches on my skin.

Kitterfol Lexington stepped forward, a smile toying on his face.

"When I came to investigate Frank Fenway's death, I took a peek into everyone's mind—just part of the investigative process, of course— and I saw you in bed with him. Oh, don't worry." He waved a hand at the horror that stole over my face, because *no, impossible, I'd been cuddled up with Emelle*. "I know you weren't with him on an... intellectual level, or else we'd have to charge you with treason right here and now." A smooth, slimy laugh. "You were just one of his oblivious pets that he liked to use and abuse."

That smile danced on his lips. I shoved my fists against my stomach to keep from puking. I wasn't quite sure what he meant by "pet," but it definitely didn't sound good. It didn't sound *right*.

Even Mr. Gleekle and the other Good Council elites were glancing at each other behind Dyonisia. Ms. Pincette's face had turned ashen, and for the first time since arriving at the Testing Center, I realized she was holding something against her chest like a lifeline: a spider in a jar.

"I wouldn't have let anyone use or abuse me, sir," I said, tight-lipped.

"Your old memories say otherwise," Kitterfol replied, smugness dripping from every word. "Would you like me to show you? It will be a rather flimsy copy, given that it transferred from your head to mine and back to yours, but I can show you what I saw."

My head was nodding before I could think better of it.

Suddenly, the memory poured into me: grainy and gray, but textured and *real*.

I saw myself, chained to a bed that wasn't mine. Spread open and utterly exposed before the wickedly handsome young man who'd done it to me, who was—

"Stop!" I cried. "Stop! I don't want to see it anymore."

The image retracted like a worm.

I tried not to stare at Kitterfol.

"What did you say his name was? The one who..."

I touched a bruise. I had recognized the man in the memory, but didn't know his name. Dark brown locks of hair. Tan skin. A constant smirk. He'd been one of the class royals I'd seen upon my arrival at the Esholian Institute, but I hadn't even noticed him in *passing* since then.

Or, at least, I didn't *remember* noticing him in passing. That memory Kitterfol had let me glimpse... I couldn't see how it was a lie.

"Coen Steeler."

This came from Dyonisia, and I whipped my head back toward her.

"His name is Coen Steeler, and he is a dangerous lunatic who might have murdered you at any moment, you poor child. You are lucky to be alive."

Coen Steeler. I repeated the name to myself, and felt the first flickers of rage at what he had done to my past self. The trauma he had inflicted upon me and then ripped away, so that any pain or fear or rage I felt seemed to come from everywhere and nowhere all at once.

The headache from before circled to my forehead, pressing in.

"Yes," Dyonisia confirmed, unmoving as she stared at me. "He used you, abused you, and erased everything about that from your head before he left. But if he can get through the shield twice, he can get through the shield a third time."

Distant shudders sent tremors up my feet. Wherever they were in the jungle, the fifth-years must have finally started their Final Tests. But nothing seemed like a greater test than the woman who sat before me, leaning ever so carefully forward.

"You are going to find him for me, child. You are going to lure him back in and capture him and hand him over—along with all his little pirate friends—and if you do that, I can promise you a front-row seat to all of their executions."

I let her eyes bore into me. *Stay cautious. Stay curious. Stay clever*, Jagaros had said. I didn't know how that fit into this moment, but it did, somehow. I was sure of it.

"What makes you think I'd be able to lure him back in—ma'am? If I was just his pet." *And why not assign Quinn the same task?* I didn't dare ask out loud.

Jagaros had advised me to lie about the bruises. To say they'd come from roughhousing with *him*. That meant I was missing something, some crucial piece of the puzzle about these bruises on me. If only I'd had more time with Jagaros to ask what he knew about all of this.

Dyonisia stretched out a single finger until her nail grazed my cheek.

I fought an urge to slap her hand away.

"Predators can't stay away from their prey, dear one. And you seem to have been his favorite meal. I am confident you will catch him for us."

The words fell from my throat before I could stop myself.

"And if I don't?"

Kitterfol sucked in a breath behind me—of glee or dread, I couldn't tell. Mr. Gleekle's face tightened with that signature fake smile of his.

Dyonisia fell back into her glass chair that sparkled so much like a throne.

"I don't see why you would refuse to help your fellow Esholians, child. Breaches are happening more and more frequently around the

406

island. Why, just in the past month, two of our coastal villages have been ransacked. Almost a hundred have died." My mouth dropped open. When had all this happened? Without the Institute getting hold of such knowledge? Almost a *hundred* dead from pirate attacks in the last month? "And I am sure," Dyonisia continued, "that you would not want such attacks to reach Alderwick. To reach Fabian or Don. Would you?"

She knew their names. My body snapped into rigid attention.

"No," I whispered. "No, I would not want that."

"Good. Now I have something to show you. Tessa?"

Dyonisia made a lazy motion behind her, and Ms. Pincette hurried forward with that jar, handing it over without a single shake of her hands. But I could tell by the ashy pallor of her face, by the way she refused to make eye contact, that all her usual strictness and bravado had leaked away in the face of this woman we all answered to.

"I don't take disgraceful, treacherous behavior lightly," Dyonisia said, slowly unscrewing the jar's lid and dumping the spider onto the floor in front of her. I recognized the green-eyed thing, somehow, but didn't know why, and that bothered me nearly as much as anything else. "This creature, for instance." Dyonisia's predatory gaze, it seemed, had pinned the spider to the spot. "My other spies tell me it was working against me. It warned the pirates of my presence and allowed them to escape."

She shifted her attention up to me, and in the absence of her gaze, the spider made a break for it, scuttling off, screeching something that sounded like, "*Top of the world!*"

Dyonisia reached out with her high heel and crushed it into a smear of pus and guts.

Its legs were still twitching when I brought my gape up to her face.

Smiling, she said, "That's what Coen Steeler's execution will be like when we catch him, child. Quick. Painless. Merciful. But predators like those pirates like to play with their prey." Her eyes focused on my neck, where I was sure a bruise had flowered based on the pulsing ache there. "And I would not want you to have to witness your fathers' bodies, broken and mangled and wrecked like this spider's, knowing their death was stretched out by the man who had you chained."

The image of that bloomed in my mind, and a fear I'd never known before—cold and as icy as Dyonisia's eyes—began to wind through the bones of my body.

I dipped my head.

"I will find Coen Steeler for you, ma'am."

"What's wrong, darling?" Rodhi slung an arm around my shoulder. "We get a whole three-month break before classes resume! You should be smiling."

The rest of my friends were walking alongside us, too, as we took a midnight walk through campus. Lander was popping into different animals at random, making Emelle burst out with giggles while Wren rolled her eyes at Gileon, trying to keep her grin hidden beneath her pursed mouth.

We weren't the only ones. It seemed that out of everyone on campus, only Quinn and I had been brought into the Testing Center for questioning. Everywhere we turned, groups of people swaggered this way and that, celebrating the end of a year and the months-long break we'd get before our next one started. The Element Wielders sent sparks shooting and spiraling through the air, lighting up all of campus with their sizzling magic.

In three months, a fresh batch of eighteen-year-olds would arrive at the courtyard. I'd be in the stadiums for the Branding this time, watching as bursts of power exploded from them all.

I couldn't stop thinking about the ones who'd taken their Final Tests today, though. Many had passed, but some had failed—had joined the carriages behind the Testing Center that would take them out to sea and force them through the shield.

The same shield Coen Steeler had apparently escaped through this morning. Would he be one of the pirates waiting for them on the other side? Would he jump his previous classmates, ripping into them and stealing more magic for himself? Or would he just chain them up, too?

I made myself smile up at Rodhi.

"Oh, nothing's wrong. I'm just wondering who attacked Jenia."

That wasn't necessarily a lie, actually. Jenia Leake's sudden appearance in the sick bay with bloodied gauze wrapped around her head was another thing that seemed weird... as if I was supposed to have that memory, that knowledge of how it had happened, but it had leaked out from between my fingers. One of those five pirates had to have been involved—why else would Jenia's older sister have investigated their childhoods and turned them in?

"Want my guess?" Rodhi asked, a manic glint in his eyes. I was used to that glint by now. It meant he was about to make a comment about Ms. Pincette's ass or something else as equally rude and inappropriate.

"What?" I asked, huffing out my exasperation.

"She was looking in the mirror for too long and it shattered."

At that moment, Lander popped into a peacock, and even Wren muffled a laugh against her sleeve when he screeched out a pathetic warble that sounded a lot like Mrs. Wildenberg. I'd asked each of them if they'd been approached by someone from the Good Council this morning, keeping my question purposely vague, and they'd each looked at me with a blank stare—even Emelle, who'd woken up with Lander, had only asked me in a quiet, concerned tone, "Why? Did something happen, Rayna? Where *were* you last night anyway?"

I'd simply shaken my head and mumbled something about a hangover. Better not to get them involved, not when their biggest concern right now was the screech of Lander's cringy attempt at mimicking a peacock.

I was grateful for the distraction of their joy, anyway.

While everyone else started warbling back at Lander, I threw a glance out toward the sea. I couldn't see the ships speckling the horizon right now, but I knew they were out there, lurking, like always, on the other side of the shield.

And Coen Steeler was on one of them.

Predators can't stay away from their prey, dear one.

If it was true—if he'd put these bruises on me, if his people were killing more and more innocent civilians by the day—then I'd feel no regret when I did what I had to do.

Lure him in. Catch him. Turn him in to the Good Council for execution.

For Fabian and Don and the coastal villages and myself, I could do that. That icy fear had coated my veins as soon as I'd left the Testing Center, locking itself into place and filling me with something cold and empty—like the space between stars.

But that coldness and emptiness could be honed. I thought about my mother's knife, still sheathed and buried deep in an inside-pocket of my bag. I'd never used it. *That* was something I remembered very clearly, as if the scrap of knowledge had been left out like a beacon, like a shiny coin for me to pick up and turn round and round in my mind to inspect.

Next year would be different.

I would be different.

410

I'm ready for you, Coen Steeler, I sent out into the night filled with sparks.

But this time I would be the predator, and he would be the prey.

Acknowledgments

First and foremost, I have to thank my husband, my number one fan in so many ways. I remember reading him a silly little rhyming poem I wrote back when we were dating, and how wide his eyes got as he listened to my words about a river that flows uphill. From that day on, he believed in me more than I ever believed in myself, and would always remind me of the way I made him feel with just a single poem whenever I felt like I couldn't do it anymore. Thank you, JD, for always listening, always throwing ideas back at me, and always reading my messy, messy drafts (and also for helping me finetune Coen's character). Mostly, thank you for showing me that goodbyes might be painful, separation might suck, but it doesn't have to be permanent. That the love of your life *can* come back.

Thank you to my mom and dad. It's been a rough couple years for our family, but one thing I can say without hesitation is that both of my parents always supported my dream and are proud of me.

Thank you to my kind beta readers, my angel of an editor, my insanely talented cover designer, and my lovely ARC readers who fell in love with my cover and story just as much as I did. I'm also SUPER grateful for some Facebook groups that helped me connect with an audience, namely The BOOKLounge for Readers and Authors. You guys rock, and I'll never be able to express how much your reviews and messages and comments mean to me!

Finally, I thank God every day for my two beautiful children, Emmarie and Jayce, who hold my entire heart in their sweet, grubby little hands. I will always love you two more than the world itself.

Love,
Mariah

About Mariah Montoya

Mariah has always loved science fiction and fantasy, and has numerous short stories published in magazines such as *Metaphorosis, Space & Time*, and *Shoreline of Infinity*. Besides writing, she enjoys runs, hikes, and four-wheeler rides. She currently lives in Boise with her husband and two children.

Don't miss her other books!

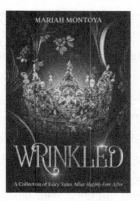

Welcome to Zurithia, where anything is possible... except escape.

Cinderella is a stepmother. The Little Mermaid is long dead. A fake fairest rules the land...